TRADER'S HONOUR

RETURN OF THE AGHYRIANS BOOK 2

PATTY JANSEN

CAPRICORNICA PUBLICATIONS

GET FREE EBOOKS

DID YOU KNOW?

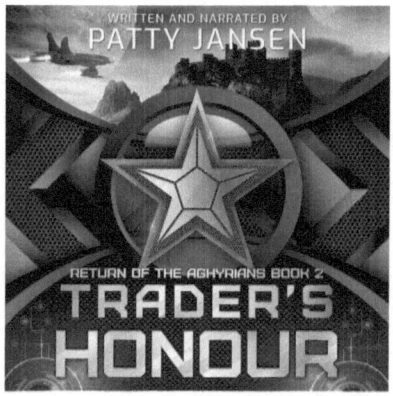

Trader's Honour is also available in audio. Click the image or visit https://pattyjansen.com to find out more.

1

THE ENVELOPE LAY in the middle of the table, between the silver tableware and the gold-rimmed plates. A bowl with rolls of fish bread stood on one side, and a steaming terrine of bean soup on the other. Father, dressed in his Lawkeepers tunic, sat at his usual place at the head of the table, Mother on the other end and little Liseyo with her silken hair on Father's right hand side. Old Rosep stood at Mother's elbow while ladling soup into her plate and talking to her in a low voice.

All of them were looking at that envelope.

Mikandra hesitated in the doorway. Her face still glowed from having run from the hospital against the biting wind to be home in time for dinner. Father cast a Meaningful Glance at the envelope, and then met her eyes in that severe way of his that said *Young lady, I demand an explanation.*

Mother stopped talking to Rosep, and Rosep scurried out the room as fast as his sore knees and bow legs allowed, shutting the door behind him with a soft snick. The fire popped.

"Good evening, Mother and Father." Mikandra sat down at her regular spot at the table, facing Liseyo, who looked at her with large eyes.

Into the heavy silence, Mother said, importantly, "A Trader Guild courier brought this for you this morning."

Totally unnecessary. The envelope could have been anything if it wasn't so unforgivingly carmine red, and that colour meant only one thing: Trader Guild. And the Guild only ever used couriers to deliver these types of messages.

Mikandra licked her lips and, avoiding her father's penetrating gaze, picked the offending object off the table. The paper was heavy and smooth in her hands. It exuded a faint smell of ink, which was old-fashioned and classy all at once. A white label affixed to the front held her name, written by hand by the Guild's calligraphers in Coldi and Mirani script. Mikandra Bisumar. As if there was any doubt.

She clutched it on her knees, out of the reach of her parents' penetrating gazes, and met Liseyo's eyes, whose expression said, *Well, aren't you going to open it?*

Mikandra didn't want to, not here where her parents were watching her, not now, before she'd sorted out this part of her future, because certainly, the Trader Guild wouldn't use a courier if her application to the academy had been rejected, would they?

The thought filled her with panic. She hadn't expected a reply so quickly; she had expected a rejection, because almost everyone who didn't come from a Trading family got rejected, right? Because at night in bed, she'd been telling herself that she was full of stupid dreams to even have applied and that she should prepare herself to bandage frostbitten fingers in the hospital for the rest of her life. And if her dreams ever came true . . . well, didn't the older people say that dreams looked good when you were young, but seemed silly in a yeah-like-that-is-going-to-happen way when you were older?

Going to the academy had been such a silly dream, something she'd never seriously thought would happen, but now she had this letter and all of a sudden, the dream that had been her childhood wish became frighteningly *real*.

She didn't want to open the letter at the table while her family was watching.

But Father would never let her leave the room. He'd stop her before she could reach the door, grab her by the arm and lift her up so that her shoulder would be jammed up against her ear and that his fingers would dig into the soft flesh under her arm and demand that she show him the contents. She still had the bruises on her arm from last time he'd done that. That time it had been about her not wanting to audition for the boring classic theatre. This was worse. Much worse.

He said, in his hard and unforgiving voice, "Open it, daughter." In that unemotional tone that masked his worst kind of anger.

No choice then.

Mikandra turned the envelope over and prised her fingers under the seal. The waxy paper ripped. Her hands trembled and made sweat marks on the red paper.

Folded inside the envelope she found a cream-coloured sheet and some printed papers, all in the antiquated dialect of Coldi which was the official language of the Trader Guild.

She spotted the words *Registration details* at the top of one of the sheets.

Her heart thudded like crazy. The field of her vision narrowed while black spots danced in the edges. It was as she'd hoped, dreamed and feared.

The very large, looming, huge problem of course was that this response came before she'd worked up the nerve to tell her parents that she'd applied.

Slowly, her hands trembling, she unfolded the cream-coloured sheet. In the same, neat calligrapher's hand, it said, *We are pleased to inform you that you have been accepted in next year's Academy intake. You are to return your acceptance within three local days of receiving this notice, and then report to our Kedras headquarters at the beginning of the Academy year . . .*

The rest of the letter detailed accommodation and course material.

The words blurred before her eyes. She knew those details; she had seen similar letters sent to some of her friends and their older brothers. Those boys from the established Trading families, not the *daughters* of mere bureaucratic Lawkeepers.

Liseyo and her mother stared at her.

Her father's voice came from far off, as if through a thick sheet of glass. "And?"

Mikandra looked up and met his hard expression that

seemed to never change whether he presided at the court or berated his daughters. Surely he *had* to know what this meant, but then again, Father was the type of person who refused to acknowledge that he could read cues and demanded that the obvious be stated to his face in words, because that was the only way you could *be honest about yourself.*

She said, as determined as she could make it, "I'm going to the Trader Guild Academy next year."

There was a moment of intense silence before Father brought his flat palm down on the table in a thud that made Liseyo wince and all the plates rattle. "You what?"

"I'm going to the Trader Guild Academy."

His lips were pressed together in a thin line, making his face look even more narrow than normal. His nostrils flared.

Mother started to say, "But Mikandra, why didn't you tell us that you—"

Father cut her off. "How is it that my eldest daughter continues to be an embarrassment to me—"

"I get into the place where young people most want to go to study, and it's an embarrassment?" She was bad at fights, but she'd prepared that line over and over, by saying it to the ceiling when she lay in bed at night. Even so, she was sweaty and trembling all over. This had been a dream for her since she was a little girl. She didn't mind fighting over auditioning for the theatre, because she didn't *care* about the theatre. She cared about this.

Silence. Father glared at her across the table. By the way his hands gripped the edge of the table, he was not far from exploding.

"Why didn't you tell us that you applied?" Mother asked again, in a more timid voice, glancing at Father. Her eyes had that *Do not swear at your children* expression.

"You would have stopped me," Mikandra said.

Her father snorted. "With good reason. It's that sister of mine—"

"Aunt Amandra had nothing to do with it."

Another silence. He raised his eyebrows. "Didn't she have to sign the application? Doesn't it have to be signed by a licenced Trader?"

"I'm not going to apprentice with her."

He frowned. "Give me that letter." He held out his hand.

Mikandra hesitated, wondering if when he threw it in the fire it would make any difference to her acceptance. She didn't think it did. It was just a piece of paper. Despite the antiquated appearance of its official correspondence, the Trader Guild would have everything recorded, saved and backed up many times on the network. They would have this letter flagged as *awaiting reply* at the Trader Guild office in the city.

She held out the letter. Father snatched it from her hand and looked at it in stifling silence. His face did not betray any emotion. Did he read any Coldi at all?

Because schools and tutors in Miran would rather die than teach the language of the enemy people from Asto, she had spent many nights curled up in the armchair by the fire in her room, poring over books to teach herself, while listening intently for footsteps on the stairs that might belong to someone unexpectedly entering her room and discovering her secret.

Father's mouth twitched. "So, who signed? Ilendar? Didn't we tell you that it was not appropriate to associate yourself with that boy anymore?" No, he did not read any Coldi. The name of her sponsor was written clearly on the page facing him. It gave her a small spot of satisfaction.

"Lihan Ilendar is not a boy. He got his licence two years ago." Why did he always ridicule her friends? "And I didn't sign with him." The moment she was old enough, she'd wanted to run to his house and tell him that she'd apply as she'd promised him, but she had seen so little of him recently, and wasn't even sure where they stood in their relationship anymore.

He lowered the letter. "Then who did you get to sign your application?"

"Iztho Andrahar."

"Under the *Andrahar* licence?" He made it sound like a clap of thunder.

"Yes." She met his gaze squarely.

He spread his hands and rolled his eyes at the ceiling.

"If you really wanted to be part of that deplorable profession of greedy money-grabbers, why didn't you ask my sister?"

"I did."

She remembered Aunt Amandra's serious face as they sat in her office. *Trading is no life for a nice young woman,* she had said, and her voice exuded a tone of sadness.

And Mikandra had wanted to shout, *But what about you?* But she knew how Aunt Amandra had obtained her licence— through a childless uncle—and how much it had cost her, like never being able to marry either within Miran or bring home her longtime, not-so-secret Coldi lover. Now that she was High Councillor, she did mostly Mirani politics anyway. Likely she had no time for an apprentice.

Father had gone red in the face. "So, let me recap. Because my sister wouldn't let you apply for apprenticeship under her licence—for very sensible reasons—you went to the Andrahar Traders and asked if they would let you apply under theirs?"

"Yes." Simple as that. And to be honest, she'd been astonished that her scheme had been successful.

"The Andrahar brothers! What were you thinking? They've been trying to hold the council to ransom for more than a year. Ever since Iztho decided to pull out of a deal with them, single-handedly causing the eviction of the army from Barresh and the resulting two-day war. Singlehandedly causing the boycott of Miran by all the entities of *gamra.* Singlehandedly causing us so much hardship. As if that wasn't enough, the Andrahars want to flood Miran with foreign produce. I've been talking about it at the dinner table many nights. But no, you don't listen to any of that, and ignore the fact that the Trader Guild is trying its very best to bring down the council whose laws I uphold. Excuse me if I don't jump up and down with enthusiasm."

Mikandra wanted to ask him, *Is there anyone in Miran you don't disapprove of?* but that was just like Father, and he'd always been that way. By the same token, he would visit the Andrahar Trading office and have long talks with the brothers as if they were his best friends. "Why, Mikandra? We made sure that you had a comfortable path for your future. Why fly in the face of everything your family has done for you?"

"Because . . ." Mikandra wanted to say, *Because I'm different* and *Because I want to do more for Miran,* but that would require

222

talking about the Healer Eydrina Lasko's visit and how she had put her hand up Mikandra's private parts and declared that she carried the family's curse of infertility. And as consolation had offered her a job as apprentice healer, which, in Father's words, qualified as *a comfortable path for the future*, which translated into *keep this useless woman off the streets.*

Mother said, "I saw Eydrina a few days ago, and she said some lovely things about your progress at the hospital. I don't understand why you would want to leave. You've been extremely privileged to get the opportunity to work with her. So many girls would love to take your place."

Mikandra screamed inside, *Then let them!*

She hated the hospital and its cold and clammy corridors filled with never-ending tides of misery. She hated how the majority of health problems of those poor people would go away if only the council got its act together and installed windows and heating in the city's housing apartments. Or gave the homeless a place to shelter at night so they wouldn't be attacked by mara-marang in the streets.

But saying those things aloud was Not a Proper Thing to do for a girl. Because Mother was right: many girls *would* love the opportunity. Because girls were supposed to like caring for sick people and not question the causes of their sickness, because simply caring and being compassionate was in their gentle natures or some thing like that. And failing to Care, without question, for the Unfortunate meant that you were a heartless and mean person.

If Father insisted on hearing the obvious stated to his face so that he could get Officially Angry, Mother loved to make her feel guilty.

And both of them were still waiting for her reply, her all-pervasive reason that justified the diversion from the path that they had set for her. The reason was too big to be explained in a few words, especially if those few words were *Because I hate everything I'm allowed to be.* The only thing she could think of saying was, "Because I want to see more than just this city and I don't just want to travel for the sake of travel. I want to do some-thing useful for Miran." As soon as the words left her mouth, she knew they sounded dumb and what was more, had nothing to do with the real reason. And that real reason was much deeper than anything she could put into words.

Sitting at the table in the Ilendar house—where Father didn't like her to be, because having boys as friends was inappropriate and because he had some unspoken feud with the Ilendar Trading family.

Listening to Lihan's father talk about his experiences at the academy.

Hearing the stories of how his father signed huge and important deals. Because of Aithno Ilendar, the council could afford to build new schools. Because he sold staple foods to Asto—yes, gasp, the home of the Coldi people—and quarried Mirani marble to the master builders of Damarq. The turnover was massive. Real money, which, when he paid his council levies, enabled the council to do real things.

The reason that she applied was also because, while she sat there at the Ilendar's table, she could feel the implied assumption that Lihan would follow in his father's footsteps. Because he was a boy, because that was the easy path for him, because he'd been conditioned from birth for the fact that he'd have a successful business and live comfortably.

And she felt like shouting *What about me?* Because assumptions about her future involved the theatre or the hospital.

Father snorted. "See, that is why young girls are not fit to make decisions like this. You do things for frivolous reasons. Trading is not a frivolous occupation."

"I know that."

"No, you don't. Young daughter, you have no idea. You will be slaughtered at the Trader Guild headquarters. Kicked, quartered, sliced to tiny emotional pieces and packed up in a box. They'll bully and pester you until you run home in tears. You do not half understand the profession. Go and talk to my sister and hear her stories. Listen to what she says about the infighting, the bullying, the backstabbing, the politics, the murders . . ." His voice had risen with each item he'd listed and he needed to pause for breath. "There are a lot of Traders who become so disheartened that they just vanish and are never seen again, leaving their families and their countries nothing except a trail of debt. *Because you wanted to travel* indeed." He blew out a forceful breath through his nose. "How come they even selected you?"

He picked up his spoon and stirred his soup.

Mikandra clutched the envelope under the table. She felt very small and very stupid. *How come they selected you?* She wondered that herself. Surely there were many candidates who were traditionally more worthy. To get selected, she would have had to have been approved by the majority of Mirani Traders. Beyond the Andrahar brothers, who would have voted for her?

Mother said, her eyes pleading, "I thought you had a good chance of becoming someone important at the hospital. Eydrina was going to recommend you for surgeon training."

Mikandra shrugged, feeling closer to tears than she dared admit. She'd wanted this since she was a little girl, damn it. Since seeing Aunt Amandra come to the house in her uniform, since hearing her stories about travel and other worlds. Since Aunt Amandra had spoken so eloquently about the *opportunities* that existed in Trading for women, since they were better at maintaining networks similar to the Coldi social networks. And if you understood the Coldi, and they respected you, many doors opened for you that were normally closed.

"I am stunned by your audacity," Father said into the heavy silence. "I will be talking to Iztho Andrahar."

Mikandra looked up sharply. He was going to do what? "Why? It's his decision to sign me on." And why should Iztho Andrahar care about what some self-important Lawkeeper thought?

"Because I want him to understand that you're not going, and I can't believe for one moment that he signed the application with full knowledge of what he was doing."

What? "Why wouldn't he?"

"The Andrahar family is very traditional, and would assign their succession in the line of the oldest son of the oldest son. So, if it is true that Iztho signed for your training—"

"—why won't you believe me?—"

He raised his voice. "—If it is true, then their intention is to use you for a bridging period until he has a son only to cast you out later, or . . . some other reason."

"Lots of Traders use bridging employees. There's nothing wrong with that."

He glared at her. "Whatever his reason, you are not going."

"But why? It's my life and my decision. It's not as if I'm going to get married and—"

"How would you buy your own business? How would you pay for an office, for an aircraft, for Exchange fees, even before you've started earning anything? If you think that we are going to pay for that—"

"Asitho, please."

Father glared at Mother. His face had gone red and now slowly resumed its normal colour. He put the letter down and pushed his plate onto one of the corners. "I'll deal with this after dinner."

He started eating. The only sound in the room was the clinking of the spoon on his plate. Mikandra looked at her mother without raising her head. She met Mikandra's eyes, her spoon half-raised to her mouth. Her expression said, *Did you really need to do that?* Mikandra felt like shouting *Why do you let him do this to you?*

Mikandra then looked at Liseyo. She had also started eating, meek and pale. She had barely moved during the discussion and had her gaze firmly fixed on her plate. Her cheeks were so pale and poking from the sleeves of her severe dark red dress, her wrists were so thin that Mikandra often wondered if she was healthy, and wondered if Eydrina Lasko had already put her hand up her private parts or if she was still too young for that. And maybe Father had realised that he would never have a male heir and he was disappointed with Mother for not giving him any sons and angry with his eldest daughter who refused to behave like a good girl should.

Embarrassing indeed.

Mother deserved better than this. Liseyo deserved better than this.

She started eating as well, although her stomach felt like a big knot. However, that only lasted for the first couple of bites. She never had any time to eat in the hospital, and she was hungry. Eydrina was always saying that she was much too thin.

Most of dinner went past in the company of only the popping of the fire in the hearth and the soft clink of spoons on plates.

When Rosep decided it was safe, he came to clear the plates and brought bread and eggs. He met Mikandra's eyes briefly and glanced at the letter under Father's plate. He collected all empty soup plates, except that one. Questions hovered in his expression. Even if he hadn't heard what had been said—and he wasn't the type who listened at doors—he'd been with the family since she was a small girl, and knew how arguments went. Father won, even if he lost.

Mother filled the uneasy silence with small talk about the theatre. The company was taking on the classic play of *The Invasion*, and now it was time to think about the new costumes. She cast a few pointed looks at Mikandra, and suggested that the girl who played the role of the legendary Tinandra Elendar wasn't very good, and *oh did you know that are some vacancies in the choir and we could really use a contralto to back up the old woman who has trouble keeping time?*

Also *Your sister plays in it as well and it would be so nice if we could make it a family production.*

And *We got Genny Manudrin to do the costumes and the dresses will be gorgeous.*

Mikandra grew more and more annoyed with the chatter. As usual, Mother was glossing over the big issue that hung over their heads, or rather, that was written on a letter underneath Father's plate. Ignoring it and hoping it would go away.

When dinner was finished, Father rose, and Mikandra rose after him, as custom dictated. He went over to the door and took his cloak off the hanger. He looked like he was going to go back to his office.

"Father, wait please."

He stopped with his cloak halfway to his shoulders.

"Can I have my letter back?"

Father looked at her and didn't move.

Her heart thudding, she continued, "I need the number that's on the letter for the reply."

"Didn't you hear what I said earlier? I said you're not going."

"I still don't understand why."

"Because if I thought it was appropriate for a young lady to go to a place such as the Trader Academy—which I do not—you would be working with my sister. Her refusal to sign you should have been a sign for you."

"She is busy with her council work."

"Look me in the eye and tell me that was the reason she gave you."

Mikandra met his eyes. No, it hadn't been the reason and she wasn't going to be untruthful about it. She hated it when Father did this.

"You are thankless and ungrateful for everything I, your mother and Eydrina Lasko have gone out of our way to do for you. I and your aunt are working very hard to protect our ways and our nation. The Andrahar brothers would open the flood-gates for foreign Traders and businesses and destroy Miran. They'd pillage us. They'd dig up our mountains and raid them for minerals. They'd build huge factories and fill them with guest workers. What do you think *my colleagues* and your aunt's colleagues, notably Nemedor Satarin, would have to say about your joining the very people who are trying to bring us down? That is the embarrassment, if I have to spell it out to your face. You are not going."

"I still need the letter." She bent over the table, snatched the letter from under her father's plate and ran for the door.

"Wait a moment, young lady!" The floor vibrated with his steps. His hand closed on her upper arm.

From close up, he was terrifying. His typical narrow face, his ice-cold light-blue eyes. His long straight nose, his long straight hair, platinum white. All prime characteristics of the Endri. She could see the veins in his eyes, the pores in his skin. Pearls of sweat glistened on his upper lip. The nails of his carefully mani-cured hands dug into the soft flesh underneath her upper arm.

"Asitho," said her mother, quietly in a soft pleading tone.

Father sniffed, and continued as if Mother hadn't spoken. "Clearly, I failed to make myself clear to you. Being of the Endri is about being grateful and giving back to our city and those less fortunate than us. It is not about running off to some foreign place and spending lots of money there, and taking all the money out of our city and wasting it on frivolous pursuits. If, despite my strong advice, you decide to go, expect *no* financial help from me or your mother, or my sister. You will also be stricken off the list of owners of the family estate and you are no longer welcome in this house. You understand?"

She glared at him, and he glared back.

"Asitho, leave it," Mother said. "Let's talk it over later."

"No, we will not, because she will not listen. Not now and not later. I have no idea how I've ended up with such a brat for a daughter. Everyone has been far too accommodating with her all this time. She should have been married last year and taught manners."

"I thought we covered the marriage issue," Mother said.

Liseyo was looking on from her seat, her eyes wide like those of a scared animal.

Father glanced aside. "Did we? I don't remember that. I must get back to it." His nostrils flared. Oh yes, he remembered when they'd last broached the marriage issue, when Geonan Takumar had visited, looking for a young girl. *To amuse me* he'd said, while undressing Mikandra with his eyes. And later, Mother had pleaded Mikandra to take up the position in the hospital *Because he will marry you off to that old creep if you don't take it.*

"Can I go? You're hurting me." Mikandra looked pointedly at her arm in Father's grip. She would have another nasty bruise next to the one from last week. "I'm not a toddler."

"Then don't behave like one." But he let her go because hurting your wife and daughters was also not part of the honour code.

Mikandra rubbed her arm. While still meeting Father's eyes, she stuffed the letter between her breasts in the bodice of her dress.

Then she ran up the stairs taking two steps at a time, through the hall, scrambled into her room and slammed the door behind her.

2

I T TOOK A WHILE before Mikandra's heart stopped racing and her breathing calmed. She listened for Father's footsteps on the stairs, but only heard his and Mother's voices in the living room and the clangs and clinks made by Rosep in the kitchen while cleaning the dishes.

Phew.

She pulled the letter out of her dress, unfolded it onto her desk and smoothed out the wrinkles. It was printed on heavy and smooth paper that she had heard people in the oases of Kedras made from the fibres of a plant. It was an old-fashioned and lengthy process, and the paper was expensive. If she held it up to the light, she could just read the Trader Guild pledge in Coldi script which served as watermark. She knew the words by heart.

I dedicate my life to the Trader Guild.

I will recognise the Guild's authority above all others.

I will respect and obey the Trader Laws at all times, and report on those who break them.

I will honour and respect my fellow Traders, regardless of their race or origin.

I will accept them and their families as my kinsfolk.

I pledge unswerving loyalty to the Trader Guild and in return, expect unswerving loyalty of the Guild to me.

The words came to her like those of a childhood song.

She had practiced them with Lihan when he was about to be admitted to the academy, and they'd made silly pacts to go to the academy together. But of course he'd gone first, being two years older and of a proper Trading family, and of course he couldn't possibly marry an infertile girl, no matter how much the steamy-breathed kisses in the little alley behind his house had suggested that he wanted to. That was a happy time. He was to leave for Kedras the next day. He had never shown anything except friendship to her, except on that day. *I didn't want to ruin our friendship,* he had said when she asked him why.

Then he left and the next time she saw him, he was in uniform, with a group of apprentice friends, talking and laughing. She'd gone up to greet him, but his manner had been cool and distant, and although she very much wanted to remind him of the fact that he'd kissed her and she wanted him to do it again, she couldn't, because of his friends. She had never spoken personally to him since. Neither had she worked out what had changed and why he had acted so cool. Maybe kissing *did* ruin the friendship.

He'd completed the academy, got his licence and travelled a lot, as Traders did.

Right now, she wanted to tell him her news, wanted to see the smile on his face and the dancing light in his eyes. Wanted to hear *Yes, now we can be together.* Wanted *someone* to be happy about the news that she'd been accepted.

But it was not going to be like that, and she'd known this since first setting eyes on him in school. He was an only son. Regardless of his wishes, his family's succession was his main concern. She did not enter that picture. She would have to do this alone.

The sheets that followed the official acceptance letter detailed course materials she would get—navigation, politics, government, piloting. That thought was exciting and scary. She'd flown in Aunt Amandra's private craft a few times, but had been too scared to ask if her aunt would teach her, because of what father might say. But she knew all the theory. There was a box over there in her wardrobe that held a stack of pictures of aircraft. She could tell all the models, despite the fact that few foreign craft ever came to Miran. She could tell their operation, knew their engine type, propulsion system, safety procedures, pretty much anything about each model.

She knew everything about flying save the feel of her hands on the controls. And that was going to be a real problem. Her family was as far removed from flying as the city of Miran was from the sea. Father called travel *a waste of time and money*.

How would she even get an aircraft—oh, it said *For students who do not bring their family aircraft or who otherwise have no access to a craft, vehicles can be provided at an extra charge.* How much? She had no money. Father had just told her that he wouldn't pay.

The next sheet contained information on room allocation in the Trader Guild complex and advice on how and when to get there. Mikandra did a double take when she saw how much the flight to Kedras would cost. She had some savings, mainly from money given to her by her grandmother, but the cost of a flight would make a substantial hole in her finances.

Money, money, it was all about money.

Presumably she would be taught and funded by the Andrahar brothers, because there was no way she could afford it otherwise. But how much would be paid by them, and how much would she remain indebted to them? There were so many questions she had never thought to ask.

The package also included a booklet on required pre-knowledge. She'd done the test and had obviously satisfied the selectors, but it was nothing like this. She had, perhaps innocently, assumed that students would be taught the basics of navigation from the ground up, but the brochure used a lot of technical words she didn't know and had never heard. Her knowledge of Coldi deserted her.

She'd thought getting into the academy was the hardest part. She was wrong. This was way out of her league. It was scary.

Maybe Father was right. Maybe she was too innocent, too provincial and too stupid to do something like this. Maybe she only applied because of Lihan. She let the letter fall on her desk.

The only light in the room was provided by the flapping oil

lamp on the wall, which Rosep would have lit while she was at dinner. The pool of light cast by the lamp faded out before hitting the opposite wall, so her cupboard and the end of the bed vanished into darkness.

Her room was on that side of the house where sunlight only shone for a few weeks in high-winter, and the rest of the year the icy wind crept in through the cracks. The fitful fire in the hearth did little to dispel the cold and she went to put a couple of fire bricks on, which smothered the flames and made them smoke.

Rosep had pulled her blankets tidily over the bed. In the light from the fire, it looked very peaceful, like a girl's room with all the frills and dresses. She hated it.

There, on the outside of the cupboard door, was the hideous dress Mother wanted her to wear to the theatre. On the table by her bed lay the text of the play. Why had she ever agreed to do that stupid audition? Because Mother made her feel guilty, that's why.

Because she was weak and couldn't say no. Because her stupid tendency to please people made her do the things she was expected to do.

Why was she like this? Why did she always crawl in a hole when Father got angry? Why did she always give in to Mother's demands? Why didn't she dare tell Father that she didn't think it was a bad thing if foreign Traders could come to Miran?

She was such a wimp.

Mikandra strode to the wardrobe and flung the dress onto the floor. She slammed the wardrobe door. She took the wad of paper with the text of the play—a stupid old-fashioned drama about some ancient event in Miran's history—off the night stand and flung it on the bed. Papers flew like butterflies.

Stupid play with its pompous, self-righteous language. Stupid events in the past which still caused people to have hangups about participating in *gamra* society. The boycott had not started because the other *gamra* entities had cut off Miran, but because Miran was continuously obstructing foreign investment within its borders with arcane rules.

Because the council was stubborn and inflexible and old-fashioned. And then they were surprised that other worlds and nations of *gamra* got angry.

The Invasion indeed.

She spread the papers out over the bed.

Stupid traditions.

Stupid Endri arrogance.

Stupid notion of being all nice and pretty and utterly *useless*.

So, she was *not good marriage material*, huh? Only to be passed to old creepy men who wanted a plaything. So, when she tried to be useful regardless, they treated her like this, huh?

Shut up and learn your lines, huh? Live the rest of your life in some sort of stupid fantasy oblivious to the burning of Miran's society around it. Pretend Miran was still at the top of its glory. Pretend everything was like before *The Invasion*. Like the Coldi cared, like the Trader Guild cared. Those people were just laughing at Miran.

Clothes, plays, music, arts.

Stupid-fucking-make-up.

While in the poor parts of the city people froze to death and homeless were left to be eaten by wild animals. And then the Endri nobles sent their girls into the hospitals to put bandages on their wounds?

And *that* was Miran's culture?

She went to the mirror, picked up the eye paint brush and dipped it in the paint. She wrote on the wall *If you want to shine, be like a star.*

There, that was better already, a much better use of eye paint than putting it on her eyelids where it irritated her eyes and made her look as if she'd been crying.

Bah, crying was for helpless damsels.

But that still didn't make the decision any easier. She let her shoulders sag. It was easy to be angry in this room. Being angry when facing Father was a whole different matter. Or saying that she didn't want to be in that play when Mother was crying.

There was a knock on the door. Mikandra looked from the door to the wall. If that was her father again, he'd be even more angry with her for painting on the wall. If that was her mother, she would say how disappointed she was in her eldest daughter. If it was Rosep, he would complain about having to repaint the wall and tell her father.

There was another knock.

"Sis, it's me," a small voice said. "Open up, please."

Mikandra sighed and went to open the door. Her sister slipped inside. In the low light, her face was a pale oval. She glanced from the dress on the floor to the papers scattered over the bed to the text scrawled on the wall. Her eyes were wide. Scared.

Mikandra sometimes forgot how young Liseyo was, and how much what Mother and Father said was still law to her.

"Why is it so cold in here? Hasn't Rosep lit the fire?"

Mikandra gazed at the dark hearth. The fire was producing lots of smoke but no flames.

Annoyed, she poked the smouldering fire bricks aside and fanned the tiny glow in the coals underneath. Flames licked the corner of the fire bricks.

Liseyo sat down on the bed amongst the scattered papers. She picked one up, and then a couple more, shuffling the sheets in order.

"Mother borrowed this text off Gisandra Tussamar. It's very old and precious." There was a tone of accusation in her voice, a tone that said that the noble lady would not appreciate it if her precious play got flung over the bed out of order. She was right of course, and that was the annoying part.

"Don't you start, too, Liseyo."

"This is my favourite retelling of *The Invasion*. I'm going to play Dinandra."

"Isn't that a role for someone older?"

"They'll make me look older, with white paint in my hair and lines drawn on my face. I get to wear a really nice old-fashioned dress. I think you should join, too. It'd be great fun."

Mikandra sighed. "It's a hideously skewed view of history. There are plenty of documents in the library which say that there was no invasion at all. That the Coldi who came were weak and hungry. They say that the Mirani defenders killed a lot of them before the Coldi could make it clear what they wanted. It's not as if they spoke our language. *Flaming creatures came down from the sky* indeed. Where is the truth in that? They came in battered aircraft. They didn't shoot and weren't aggressive. The truth is that Miran had the watchtower, and the watchtower keeper used telescopes. Asto is by far the clearest point of light in the sky, and the Mirani council back then *knew* that people lived there. So why were they still surprised when these people came?" She spread her hands in frustration.

Liseyo's mouth twitched. "Does it matter if it's accurate? It's just a story."

"None of the historical plays is ever *just a story*. There are children in the audience, and this stuff is being taught to them as fact. They hear that Miran was glorious, yet the evidence is that it was not. We are far heathier, better clothed and better fed than the people back then. The children learn that Miran was attacked, but the evidence is that these people came for help, not to conquer."

"Baaah, you're no fun."

"This has nothing to do with fun. It's about the way we learn to see people from outside Miran, and those views start when children are taught this sort of crap."

She let an angry silence lapse.

Liseyo's eyes were big. "I just wish you wouldn't talk like this. It makes me scared. I don't like it when Mother cries. Father is really angry this time, a lot more angry than he was when you refused to go to the theatre. Why do you do this?"

Mikandra sat next to her sister and closed her in her arms. Her shoulders were so thin. "Oh, Liseyo, I'd tell you, but you're not old enough to understand."

"That's what everyone in this house says, and I'm sick of it. Try me. Why do you hate everyone so much?"

Was that what they thought? "I don't hate everyone. I just want to make a difference and do something that helps."

"Being in the hospital makes a difference. There are a lot of sick people who need you."

"It's all fake, Liseyo. Everything we're allowed to do as girls is fake. The theatre, art, music, healing, nothing makes serious money or is anywhere near places where real decisions are made. Nothing is really important. While we're in the theatre rehearsing the plays of centuries ago or in the wards covering up the problems of the city, they make decisions on our behalf, and nothing gets solved. Being in the hospital is just putting dressings on infected wounds that people wouldn't have if they had houses so they weren't sleeping in the street and attacked by maramarang, or if they had heating and didn't get frostbite. I want people to stop the glorifying of Miran. I love Miran, but there are things wrong that we need to make better. I don't think we can do that alone by shutting ourselves off from other people and other worlds."

"So, does that mean you're going?"

Mikandra shrugged. For a moment she wished she'd never received that offer. Everything else she'd done in her life in the way of protest was gentle and reversible. She'd cut off her hair when Mother complained about her wearing it in a ponytail, but it had grown back. She'd walked around in hunting clothes in the city when she'd hidden that stupid dress Mother wanted her to wear so well that no one in the house could find it.

But she had never done anything or said anything that challenged her life with her parents and sister in a way this did.

If she went to Trader Academy, there would be no way back to this house or this room. She would have to be fully independent, and, since she would not find a husband to share her living costs, she would have to earn enough to support herself.

Money frightened her and the thought of not having any frightened her even more.

In the semidarkness of the room, Liseyo was like a pale ghost with her soft cream-coloured hair and huge eyes.

"When you were gone, Father said again that he'll disown you. He really means it."

Mikandra shrugged again. If his anger when he got wind of her infatuation for Lihan Ilendar was anything to go by, he would, too.

Apparently, when Father first took up his position as Lawkeeper he had been wronged by Mariandra Ilendar, Lihan's mother and the Ilendar Traders' account keeper. Mikandra never quite understood what the problem was, except that Father chose to remember it whenever a situation came up where an Ilendar family member would benefit from something he did, or something he approved, allowed or paid for.

"Why does he hate us so, Liseyo?"

"He doesn't hate us. He just doesn't want us to be left alone when we're old." Liseyo's eyes glittered.

Mikandra's heart jumped. *No, please.* "Did Eydrina come to see you, too, and put her hand up . . . there?"

Liseyo nodded. She looked at her hands clasped in her lap. A tear leaked out of her eye and ran down her cheek.

The horror. Two infertile girls in the family. No heirs, no respectable marriages, no future matrons of noble houses, no grandchildren.

"Eydrina says it's especially bad in our generation." Liseyo's voice sounded hoarse. She wiped her eyes with the back of her hand. "I can see that it's true, with girls who can't have children and so many others suffering madness. It gets worse all the time." She looked up and met Mikandra's eyes. "You know what it said in the Foundation Declaration, that us Endri have the obligation to look after the city and the laws and all the Nikala workers? We can't do that if we can't even keep our own families alive. Our people are dying." Her lip trembled.

Mikandra nodded. The lack of children born in the Endri nobility had been discussed by many, and no one had come up with a solution. New blood, some said, but when someone married into the Nikala merchants or worker class, the chance that there were children was even less. There were also no records of Mirani Endri fathering children with any of the people from other worlds.

The increasing number of Nikala in the council, like high councillor Nemedor Satarin, already proved that no one needed the Endri, not even to maintain services in Miran. Except those new people had never been taught about responsibility and duty. They wanted money for everything, even for healing, and a lot of the Nikala workers didn't have any, so they went hungry and were sick all the time, and that meant more trouble for the Endri class to fix up, and *they* had to do so with fewer and fewer people. It was a constant downward spiral.

She stared into the hearth. The fire had expanded to cover the new fire bricks she had thrown in.

Mikandra got up to poke the half-burnt bricks from this morning into a better position.

"What are you going to do about that letter?" Liseyo asked.

"I don't know." Panic crept up in her. She had three days to decide the rest of her life. "I dreamed of this for a long time."

"If you accept, you'll have to leave." Her sister's eyes were wide with fear.

"Yes."

"Then where will you live?"

"At the Guild headquarters, I presume."

"At Kedras?" The world whose major function was to provide a home for the Traders from all over the settled worlds.

Mikandra nodded. She took Liseyo's hands, which felt small and fragile, in hers. "I haven't made a decision yet." Liseyo's eyes were big, and glittered with tears.

A bit later Mikandra added, "I'll think of something." Although what she wanted was clear in her mind, how she was going to do it was not. "Just take care, Liseyo. Whatever I do, I do for you, you understand that? Even if it makes Father angry."

Liseyo said, softly, "I don't want you to go. Mother and Father will pick on me doubly hard. They'll tell me that I don't appreciate what I have, and they'll keep telling me that they gave you the opportunity but you wasted it." Her lip trembled. "They'll tell me to go to the hospital in your place, because you embarrassed them. I want to stay in the theatre. I know you hate it, but I like the theatre."

Who would look after Liseyo if she left? Who would make sure that she didn't blindly follow whatever Father said and set her own wishes aside? Who would make sure that when she did stand up for herself, Father wouldn't hurt her? Who would stop her being married off to a much older man if she became troublesome?

"Will you please promise me to stay here?"

Mikandra looked down. "I can't do that."

"Please?" Her sister's voice was no more than a whisper.

Mikandra's eyes misted over. She didn't want to leave Liseyo, but if she stayed here, neither of their lives would ever improve. "Be strong, Liseyo. For me. I'll sort something out." Eventually. But things were likely to get worse before they got better.

3

I N THE DARKNESS of the night, Mikandra lay awake for a long time, trying to decide the path of her future. She could, of course, do nothing and let the offer lapse as Father wanted. That way, she could stay with Liseyo and protect her against Father's anger.

But even then, she could never be home all the time, and if Father decided to marry her sister off to some old man, there was nothing she could do to stop him. Liseyo would have to learn to fight for herself. If an old man came to her wanting marriage, she would have to make him decide that she wasn't a good option.

She lit the lamp on her nightstand and read the letter over and over again. It mentioned the costs, but didn't say where she could go to meet those costs. They just assumed that the Trader Guild students were from rich families and brought their own money. Could she safely assume that *sponsorship* by Iztho Andrahar meant that he would be paying for her?

She was embarrassed that this thought had not crossed her mind at the time when she had applied and was even more embarrassed that accepting would mean being indebted to a family she had not realised Father hated so much.

She knew there'd been some trouble that concerned Iztho

Andrahar's dealing in Barresh, but was it really as bad as Father said?

The fuss about the two-day war in Barresh seemed longer than a year ago. It was the first time in living memory that the Mirani army had been defeated. Granted, Miran was by far the biggest nation on Ceren and most of the other nations were no more than loose groups of primitive tribes living on the coastal fringe of the Mirani continent. Barresh was a coastal enclave on the far western coast, and had been a thorn in Miran's side for hundreds of years.

As far as she understood the Barresh war, there had been an uprising of the locals against the Mirani troops stationed there as part of Barresh's status as protectorate of Miran, and she failed to see how a single man could have enough influence to start a war. And cause defeat of the Mirani army? One single man?

At the time of the war, she'd just started at the hospital and the deluge of injured soldiers that came in had caused major problems. Those men spoke of bands of natives fighting unfairly with blue fire. Some said new weapons. The more superstitious would talk of dark magic. Whatever it was, the "fire" was real and dangerous. Many soldiers died under her hands because too much of their skin had been burnt.

None of the survivors—and she treated many in their agonising recovery—spoke of the involvement of any Mirani Traders in the conflict.

In contrast, they mentioned that the influence of Asto was everywhere in Barresh, and that was the real reason the war had been fought: because Asto had been trying for hundreds of years to get a foothold on the continent that provided its population with so much of its food. So, likely Asto had supported the rebels in Barresh with blue-fire-spewing weapons, and the Mirani army had been unpleasantly surprised.

What did Iztho Andrahar have to do with it?

That made her think that she should go and find out what the issues were, and the thought annoyed her. She wanted to accept the offer and wanted all this other stuff to just go away.

Who cared what Iztho had done or hadn't done? He was a Trader and that meant by default that he was honourable. If he had been involved, it would have been because he acted according to the Traders' moral code. Call her naïve, but she believed that.

She'd never get a chance like this again.

She wanted to go, but she was just so . . . afraid of the future. Afraid to leave her family and travel, afraid to go to this huge place that was the Trader Guild headquarters, full of strangers. She, a daughter of a lowly administrator who had never travelled offworld. She'd get no help from the Mirani Trader apprentices. They were all boys and Mikandra wasn't sure whether they'd shun her because she was a girl, or because she wasn't from the right family. Both, probably. Making friends from elsewhere seemed like a scary thing to do. If she did, the boys would report back to Miran and she'd be shunned anyway for "loving foreigners". She'd seen that happen to Aunt Amandra.

Was that only a small price to pay for the opportunity, or would it forever harm her chance to do well and would she end up worn out and bitter, like Aunt Amandra? Worn out and bitter, with no money and no home to return to and no inheritance?

So what? Go and leave her mother and Liseyo? Or stay and protect them?

She had only three days to decide.

She finally fell asleep and woke up with a shock to see that no one had come into her room overnight to remove the letter from the Trader Guild. It still lay on her bedspread, mocking her with its three-day response ultimatum.

Mikandra got up, dressed in the warm clothes she wore under her hospital gown. First her underthings. Then a thick woollen dress because that's what girls had to wear. The corset went over that. And a jacket with long sleeves. Then stockings that were always itchy. Then she folded up the letter and tucked it in the pocket of her dress.

She decided that she'd go to the hospital and pretend she wasn't going to accept the offer. If she didn't feel any sadness over it, or if she felt good about being in the hospital, she wouldn't go. If she did feel that she should leave—although the prospect scared her—she would do something about it later today. Both the office of the Andrahar Traders and the Trader

Guild offices were close to the hospital and she would walk past them on the way home.

She pushed aside the curtains, letting a cold draft into the room. The night had brought a thin layer of snow, the first for the season, just enough to cover the street. A trail of footsteps in the neighbours' yard marked where the kitchen hand had gone out the gate to pick up the grocery deliveries. If it got any colder, the footsteps would remain white. For now, they had turned black wherever the kitchenhand's boots had touched the ground.

She turned back to the room, walked past her desk and stuck her ID pass in her pocket, just to be sure. If she went to the Guild, they'd probably ask for that.

Mikandra went down into the kitchen, where Rosep slaved over the hot stove already, preparing the evening meal while Father, Mother and Liseyo had their breakfast.

Liseyo looked even smaller than usual. Her eyes were puffy and Mikandra thought that she'd been crying. She ached for her sister, the girl who should have been a boy. The oldest son of the oldest son, discounting the fact that his oldest child was a daughter. Father loved those traditions. He'd taken over the Lawkeeper's business from his father and now he had no son to continue his business, and passing it to her or Liseyo didn't even cross his mind. Mikandra often wondered what went on behind the closed door of her parents' bedroom.

This morning, Father was in his official Lawkeeper robe, which he loved to wear outside the court although he didn't have to. He quizzed Liseyo on her schoolwork.

Who were the Foundation families?

Ilendar, Andrahar, Takumar, Tussamar and Zithunar.

What is the first principle of the Foundation law?

That Miran is not complete without both Endri and Nikala people.

And the second?

That each part of the population does the tasks assigned in the bylaws.

How many seats are in the council?

One hundred and thirty-one.

Who sits in the council?

One seat from each family, and a seat can be allocated to others if the family relinquishes it.

Mikandra knew all the answers, but Liseyo faltered through and grew more timid with every question.

How is the High Council elected?

Liseyo shrugged and looked down at her plate.

Father sighed and rolled his eyes. "We just had the election and your aunt won a place in the High Council. We went through the entire process. Where is your sense of observation?"

Liseyo said nothing. She wiped her eyes with the back of her hand.

"It's happening right in front of you. We discussed it then. Try to remember."

There was a heavy silence.

Eventually, Liseyo blurted out, "I don't know. I forgot."

"Then I shall take steps so that you won't forget."

Mikandra itched to shout out *Can't you see that she's upset?* But there was no time for an argument. She had to go to the hospital or be late.

She collected her cloak from the hall and left the stifling atmosphere in the house for the crisp morning air.

Snowflakes still descended from the sky, adding to the slippery slurry in the streets. The clouds hung low over the city and occasionally blanketed the roofs of the Endri family houses, each in its own walled yard. Some houses, like the neighbours', were painted white, but those made from natural stone had turned dark grey with the humidity. Patches of lichen bloomed in weather like this, with orange ooze leaking from the little plantlets. By mid-morning, the groundsmen would be out scrubbing the stuff off the walls.

They were about to go into low-winter, that season when life in Miran seemed to come to a halt as everyone hid indoors from the cold and blizzards. It was the season of long dinners where grandmothers would tell old tales about how every year the suns got jittery and debated jumping out of the sky.

It was a good story that frightened young children, but of course these days, people knew that Ceren's orbit was elliptical and the sun-cycle—the twenty-day rotation of both suns around each other—only seemed to speed up during that time because the planet's comparative speed was less when it was further away. There was no annual judgement and no curses by irate ancestors, but those things all made for good frightening tales.

True to the stories which said that at low-winter the ancestors sent clouds to eat the city, buildings vanished in and out of the mist while Mikandra walked down the hill. One moment, the watchtower was gone, next only the top would be visible and the next only the bottom. She'd been up there once on a clear day, and seen the entire city underneath her, and the mountain valley that was the city's home, a patchwork of bean crops and oil seed fields. She'd seen the mountain slopes that rose to the southern end of the city, with meadows that were fragile green with tiny flowers and burbling brooks when the snow melted, plains of waving dead grass when the suns passed overhead and the wind was merciless and dry, and fields of snow in both high and low winter. The day she climbed up had been one of the rare occasions that the view to the east was clear, and she had seen all the way down the mountain pass into the blue haziness of the eastern plain.

The view from the Mirani watchtower was famous in all the settled worlds, so incredible that people claimed you could see the curve of the horizon, although Aunt Amandra said it was nonsense, because you couldn't see the curve until you were much higher.

Mikandra remembered that when she was young, she would occasionally see some foreigners climbing the many steps that wound around the outside wall and remembered her grand-mother complaining about *tourists* as if they were some scan-dalous thing.

The watchtower had been built in the old days, when the city was young, and people feared attacks from outside. Yet the only time that it might have helped its citizens, it had failed. Like the city walls, like so much in Miran, it was a relic of the past. The city guard made a show of putting men on tower duty, but it was a symbolic role. The air and land around the city was these days monitored by the Exchange. Technology had moved on.

Mikandra entered the hospital grounds, and climbed the steps into the building.

With the first snow came the first cases of frostbite and an increase in the number of people visiting the hospital. Scores of patients waited in the cavernous foyer, which echoed with the voices and shufflings of the sick. Coughing and moans. Sorry heaps of people sat on the hard chairs, huddled in filthy matted cloaks. Mikandra knew a lot of the faces. She'd seen them with frozen fingers or weeping sores or skin infections, hacking coughs and other ailments caused by the cold. They were Nikala, all of them.

A few harassed-looking nurses walked around, taking records of each patient and their ailments. One greeted Mikandra with a weary smile. Calintho, youngest daughter of a branch of the Takumar family. She couldn't help thinking *another girl shunted into a thankless job*. Bet Calintho was infertile, too.

But she clamped down on those thoughts. She was going to be positive today. Cheerful and dutiful. The perfect self-sacrificing healer. But the letter in her pocket still reminded itself of its presence by poking a sharp corner through the fabric of her dress.

Mikandra hung her cloak in the cloak room and paused in the doorway to the emergency ward where patients were taken for first treatment. Her mentor Eydrina Lasko stood by the bed of an elderly man who had been brought in yesterday with a hacking cough and for whom the regular ward had obviously not yet provided a place. Eydrina was a middle-aged woman—married to an upper city administrator, but with no children. She wore her bushy curly hair—an indicator that she was of the Nikala class—in a loose plait over her back and had tied the springy curls that escaped the tail with a headband.

She hadn't seen Mikandra come in, and continued to examine the patient with competent hands.

The bed next to him had held a new mother with a fever yesterday, but today there was a young man with his leg propped up on pillows. He looked asleep. The bed on the other side held an elderly woman—a homeless grandmother who came here often, usually with feeble excuses that barely justified keeping her in the hospital. She usually cried when she was told she had to make way for patients in greater need.

Then there were people with bandaged heads from attacks of the flying maramarang that scavenged on rubbish after dark, someone with a broken leg, others with sores. Most patients were old. Most were men. Most were homeless.

Looking at her tutor, surrounded by a sea of misery, Mikandra felt a dread creeping up in her. This was only the start of low-winter. Things would get worse when the real cold hit.

Eydrina looked up.

Mikandra forced her face into a smile and entered the room. "A good morning to you, Eydrina."

Her tutor returned a weary smile. "You seem pretty cheerful for the fact that winter has started. It's not a very good morning, not by anyone's standard."

"Oh. Anything happened?"

"Just the usual, made ten times worse by the weather."

"What do you want me to do?"

Eydrina gave her a long list of patients to be looked at, to wash, change bandages and clean wounds, to prepare for operations—most of them involving old men having part of their legs removed. A woman with a dreadful cough needed a massage and hot compresses on her back to help her clear her lungs. Some patients needed to be moved to other sections of the hospital. The maramarang victims needed to have their wounds cleaned out with a solution that stung badly. Mikandra dealt with a cantankerous old man and a slightly younger man who had claw marks all through his hair. She had to shave it, very carefully, before she could wash his skin. The hair was disgusting and so full of filth that she couldn't see where his head started and his hair stopped. She nicked him twice, because he was involved with an argument with the man in the next bed —with scratch marks all over his face—and wouldn't sit still. Apparently, a fight about a sleeping spot had put both of them in the path of a horde of maramarang. The scavengers were about the size of a baby and had big fur-covered wings with huge claws that they used to rip their prey but that served just as well for opening rubbish bins. They were hotbeds for disease.

Mikandra washed, massaged, cleaned, rebandaged.

Kitchen staff brought breakfast, which some patients needed help to eat. Some didn't eat at all. New patients were seen by the emergency healers, of which Eydrina was the leader, and brought into the ward unless they needed a surgeon's immediate attention.

It was busy. It was cold. It was tiring and depressing.

Mikandra couldn't help thinking that as Trader she could bring so many things that would make these people's lives better. She would bring in money for Miran so that hospitals could buy the best medicines and equipment. The best people even.

That was if *gamra* would lift the boycott that had been in place since the Barresh two-day war.

Of course she could also make things better while staying here, if she really cared. She could lobby the rich Endri families for money to have windows put into the ward—

—except glass was imported from Barresh and none was coming in because of the boycott—

She could find another supplier. Surely someone on the east coast could make glass.

And she could ask for donations for further medical supplies—

—whichever ones didn't fall under the boycott, which weren't many.

It all came back to that boycott.

That problem was much bigger than her and she couldn't fix it.

So what about something she could fix, like the lives of patients?

What if she asked Liseyo to put on a theatre performance to cheer up the patients? That would be a nice thing to do. She could see Liseyo in her role, playing the ladies of the past, her little face smiling. Wasn't life about making the people you loved happy?

Was running away really the best solution?

∾

Somewhere around midday, the emergency nurses brought into the ward an old man whom Mikandra had seen several times before. He was tall as her father but thin like a skeleton. He usually shaved his head—badly, because his scalp was marked with scabs from where he'd cut himself—but he had no army tattoos or other markings that gave him away as Nikala. On an earlier visit, he had given his name as Leitho. That was a typical Endri name, and he had both the build and the language to be of her class, but she'd checked and there was no Leitho in the Mirani register who was of the right age, and no Endri families admitting to having lost a family member of similar age who was now living on the streets.

This time he'd come in because he had scraped the skin off the top of his nose and cheekbone. A wound on his forehead oozed sticky fluid into his eye. The skin around it was tight and swollen.

In line with her determination to be cheerful, Mikandra forced a smile when she went to his bed. "Here you are again."

"Ye—ye—yeah. 'M a bit clumsy in old age." His lips were cracked with the dry air and flaky from frost exposure.

"It looks like you have a nasty fall on your face."

"I fell down the stairs. You know, between the city office and the guard headquarters."

Mikandra nodded. She knew the stairs. They got very slippery after frost. "Did you hurt anything else?"

"Just my head. On the railing."

Was there a railing? She couldn't remember. "It looks nasty."

The wound above his right eyebrow looked at least several days old.

She got some warm water and disinfectant to wash the wound. Eydrina would have to glue the sides of the cut together.

While she washed his face, he constantly moved some part of his body. His arm shivered, his leg jiggled, he waggled his head from side to side and she had to tell him to keep still. Which he couldn't.

When she had first come to the hospital, Eydrina had warned her about this. *Don't pay any attention to all the old guys constantly waggling and jiggling or it will drive you crazy.* The cause of the jiggling was pretty obvious from the smell of him.

His foul body odour was laced with the distinctive sweetness of menisha brew. The orange tinge of the whites of his eyes confirmed the buildup of poison in his body. His arms had withered to sticks, covered with paper-thin skin with irregular red blotching that would flake in dry frosty weather. Late stage menisha poisoning. He would probably not see the end of low-winter.

She poured water into a glass and added a spoonful of powder that would help his body rid itself of some of the poisons, although a proper detoxification would take days and days of drinking a weak solution every day.

Annoyingly, his addiction also meant that she could not use menisha extract to help kill his infection. It was one of the few medicines still available without restriction; the fungus grew in the gorges region of the Mirani highlands and needed no import permits.

She mixed the powder in the glass. The fluid went milky. "Before I send you to the surgeon, I want you to drink this for me." She held up the glass.

His face showed disgust. "I don't need that. My head needs fixing. I am doing fine everywhere else."

"You have to drink this before the surgeon can fix your head."

He pushed himself sideways on the bed, trying to climb out. "If you're going to be like that, I'm leaving. I don't want that stuff."

"Your wound is infected and needs to be stitched before the infection gets any worse and you get seriously sick or worse."

"Why does everyone tell me I'll die?" His voice rose into a squeak.

"You will, if you don't stop drinking. Your body is breaking down because of the poison. Your eyes are orange. You're smart enough to know what that means."

He did not meet her eyes, but did not protest either. He took the glass in trembling hands, glancing at the tray next to his bed.

"You'll bring the bowl?" The fluid in the glass sloshed around with his jiggling.

"All here."

He brought the cup carefully to his mouth, but experienced a shaking attack halfway and spilled some of the medicine on his disgusting shirt. He took a careful sip and winced. "This stuff makes me see things, you know?"

"That's why we keep you here while you drink it." Yes, she knew. The hallucinations were caused by withdrawal from the menisha poison. Incidentally, Endri suffered much worse with both the drunkenness and withdrawal from menisha poisoning.

She sat with him until he'd finished the concoction, then dragged a screen curtain around his bed and gave him the bowl. By the time she rose from the bed, he had already pissed out a quantity of bright orange fluid.

"It burns," he whispered, his voice hoarse. His eyes were wide and definitely more orange than they had been during his last visit.

"It burns, it burns!"

"I know. You should try to—"

He gasped. "Like evil. We're surrounded by evil. Listen to me. The people running this city are evil. They hold us as prisoners. They know the ancestors' secrets, but they are keeping the secrets from us. You're a girl from one of the Endri. The council will listen to you. You must go to the council and demand that we be freed. Some of us have gone over to the other side."

"Sure, I will do that." She patted his hand.

Always agree with them, Eydrina had instructed her. The men were bound to become violent if caught in an argument while having hallucinations, and there were already enough fights in the wards without deliberately adding to them.

"You must free me. They come at night and take me to the room with the glass vials. They will pour ice over me. They stick things in me. You must help me."

"Yes, I will help you. That's what I'm for."

He grabbed her arm. "Listen to me. Promise me."

"Yes, I promise to help you."

She felt sorry for him and hoped he found the strength to

fight whatever demons inhabited his mind. This vile drink ruined so many lives. Why had no one banned it yet?

Mikandra pushed the curtain aside to leave him alone in his agony and continued with the other patients.

And all the while, her forced cheerfulness couldn't stop her mind churning over the choice she must make soon, and every time she thought about it, she changed her mind. She was selfish to accept, because, awful as this place was, people needed her here.

But she wanted to be useful to Miran, and while being in the hospital looked useful and a good thing to do, all they did in the wards was treat recurring problems that would simply go away if only these people could afford to heat their homes. Heating required money, and money required a job. Traders needed an office and support staff. They provided a lot of employment in the city. They provided goods. They made huge financial contributions to the council. And the Mirani Traders were the top of the Trader Guild. They were the lifeblood of a city like Miran, and had always been. Miran needed Traders. The Trader Guild considered the Miran chapter of its organisation too old-fashioned and quaint. So the Mirani chapter had accepted her, a nontraditional choice, a sign that they were willing to make changes. She should act on the trust that the Guild wanted to put in her.

But Liseyo . . .

And so her mind went around and around in circles.

4

SOME TIME towards the end of the day, Mikandra sat down for a precious moment of rest. She poured tea from Eydrina's red and gold teapot and took it to the tall stool in the corner of the emergency room where a window looked out over the city.

There she sat hunched over, with her frozen hands clamped around the cup, savouring the warmth of the tea seeping through the glass. The wind had died, and grey, fuzzy clouds hung so low that they obscured the watchtower. The many roofs squished together inside the city walls were normally red, but the mist and the impending dusk rendered everything in soft grey-laced colours. In a way, it was pretty.

Where she sat inside the hospital, nothing was pretty. The old man Leitho had collapsed after a bout of vomiting and had been taken into the emergency ward with urgency. Mikandra was afraid to ask about him, because he would probably not come out again. A couple of war veterans had almost become involved in a punch-up. One of them had brought a bottle of menisha brew inside his cloak and nurses had a hard time trying to get it off him while he was drunk.

An old man had been brought in with infections on his leg and feet that were so bad that he had to go into surgery immediately to have the leg removed.

She was so tired. Her legs ached, her back ached, and behind her, a man called for a healer.

Mikandra found herself thinking, *Please, let Eydrina take care of it.* She had barely sat down. Just one moment of rest. Her feet felt like they were about to fall off, both with the bitter cold and fatigue.

"Healer Lasko! Healer Bisumar! Someone! Please come." The voice grew more insistent.

Heaving a sigh, Mikandra put down her tea. So Eydrina was out and wasn't going to take care of it. She retied her apron and walked between crowded rows of beds.

Two soldiers of the street guard waited in the emergency room, which was bare and white with only a treatment table and cupboards of emergency supplies and a few basic monitors that the hospital could afford.

The men carried a stretcher of the type used by soldiers in battle with a bundle of blood-soaked fur that, if Mikandra looked closely enough, might conceal a man.

Not another one. Even without counting Leitho, they had already lost two homeless people this morning.

She gestured at the table and the soldiers heaved their load onto the sterile surface. The body, wrapped in fur, looked small enough to be a child. A chill crept over her back. She hated it when young people were involved.

"Who is this, and what happened?" she asked, pulling on gloves.

The guard glanced over his shoulder. Two emergency room nurses were preparing instruments on the bench against the back wall.

Eydrina Lasko's voice drifted from the next room. "Coming."

Mikandra squirted disinfecting spray over the front of her apron.

The soldier said, "Dunno how he came t' be like this, mistress. Found him in the street this morning. Dunno how long he's been there. Looks like he's been had by the maramarang real bad. Blood everywhere. Din' look too good."

Mikandra repressed a shudder. If no one came to a victim's

defence, the flying scavengers would rip a person to shreds. She'd seen that, too.

"He *is* still alive, right?"

He swallowed. "Think so, lady. Couldn' be sure."

Mikandra looked at the bloodied mess cemented together with ice. Something underneath moved, and there was a sound of short ragged breaths.

Guess that satisfied the definition of "alive". Only just.

She tried pulling away the fur, but it had frozen together, and maybe onto the victim's skin, it was hard to tell. She turned to the cabinet behind her to get a scalpel.

"I covered him up like ye told me t' do." The young man's face had gone pale. Oh right, this was the soldier who was likely to faint at the sight of blood; she'd picked him off the floor before. "Ye said t' keep them warm, lady, so I did."

"You did well. You can go now." Before he fainted and she'd have to deal with that, too. "It's all under control now —Eydrina!"

The men left, and Mikandra tried to figure out where best to cut the fur so she wouldn't slice the patient. She peeled away a corner of the disgusting fur blanket—made from a couple of cloaks stitched together in the way soldiers reused their old clothes. A couple of chunks of ice fell off.

She found the victim's hand, covered in blood. When she wiped it off, the skin underneath was pale blue with teeth marks from maramarang which barely bled despite being open. She fingered the skin of the wrist—very cold—for the artery, which wasn't where she expected it to be, because his muscular tissue was attached in an unusual way.

There was a pulse, but very weak and irregular.

Eydrina came into the room, dressed in her surgical gown, gloves, and her bush of curly hair tucked under a cap.

She took one look at the table. "Heavens. Another one." She folded back the cloth covering from the tray she had brought. Underneath lay an assortment of needles and surgical instruments, as well as bandages. "How bad?"

"Skin is blue, pulse is very low. Severe bleeding somewhere.

We need to get all this stuff off him before we can see, but it's all frozen. You may want to call the surgeon."

"Already did that. Let's have a look."

Eydrina took another scalpel and also started working on the blanket. A lock of the victim's hair fell free. It was course and bright red. What the. . . ? A foreigner?

"Heavens," Eydrina said.

Mikandra met her wide eyes. That fitted with the unusual structure of the wrist.

She freed another section of furs, slowly uncovering the man's head. His breaths were fast and laboured. A dribble of pink fluid ran from his mouth. His lips were blue.

His left cheek and forehead were a tapestry of scratches and bites, messy, but none of them more than skin deep. Blood had run into his shoulder-length hair, most of which had come out of its ponytail. The skin on his temples was covered in large brown splotches of pigment. That and the red hair made him Kedrasi.

Mikandra removed the frozen fur, and cut away a thick jacket splattered with blood and hard with ice. Underneath, she found a blood-soaked red uniform.

"Oh no, it's a Trader Guild courier."

Eydrina lifted his eyelid and shone a light into his eye. The iris, sand-coloured as for a Kedrasi, was a small rim around his pupil and didn't react to the sudden brightness.

"Get his shirt off," Eydrina commanded.

That was easier said than done. The shirt was wet and in places caked with ice that Mikandra didn't dare pull for fear of pulling his skin off with it. She worked with the scalpel. It almost felt like sacrilege to cut the red tunic. The fabric was tough, well made, like everything the Trader Guild provided. Underneath, the man's skin was very pale and clammy.

His lower abdomen was a bloodied mess, with gashes exposing ribs and intestines.

Maramarang attacked a victim's arms and head, and never got to the abdomen unless they'd already ripped the flesh off the limbs.

Eydrina said, "This is not a maramarang attack. He's been stabbed."

Several times, she pointed out, in the chest, back and lower abdomen, with the knife going through the chest wall between the ribs and into his lungs. His chest was moving fast in laboured breaths.

The surgeon came into the room and as she examined the victim, his muscles cramped and stiffened several times. Eydrina had attached the heart rate monitor and the line on the screen jumped wildly in between periods of quiet.

His eyes opened a slit. He tried to cough or speak, but only pink froth came out of his mouth.

Mikandra met her mentor's eyes and read despair in her expression that said *He's too far gone.*

"But he's Trader Guild," Mikandra whispered.

The surgeon said, "I know. I can't help him. Not with what we have, and probably not even with what we don't have."

So she only gave him a dose of a painkiller that would probably be too strong for his heart so that he could go to sleep peacefully.

Not long after Mikandra started at the hospital, Eydrina had given her long lectures about patients and how to assign priority. *Make sure that at first you save who can be saved, and let no one with minor ailments die from neglect.* And, *When there is only so much medication—and however much you have, it won't ever be enough— you have to decide where you are going to spend it. It should be with the patients you are sure you can save.*

Mikandra couldn't stop looking at the man's labouring chest which was already becoming more quiet. Her heart beat in her throat; her eyes pricked with tears. Trader Guild, her heroes, the people who could make a real difference. She had been accepted to become one of them. He was a Guild employee, not a member, but regardless, this was one of the people she'd swear to protect.

He must have unwittingly walked into a trap set for someone else, or tried to break up a fight, something foreigners did for no clear reason.

Then a more disturbing thought: the guard hadn't known how long the victim had been in the alley, but with the ice in his clothes, the man had clearly been exposed to the weather for a quite a while. Would this have been the courier who had brought her the letter that she carried in the pocket of her dress?

He would die for the Guild, and for her, in a hostile place far from his home. And she was worried about what her father thought about her wish to join the Guild?

One thing she clearly remembered from her last meeting with Iztho Andrahar, the one where he had signed her application. She could still see him sitting by the fire in his private room. He'd asked her to come to his house, which was unusual. He seemed relaxed, very reflective and not his usual taciturn self.

He had spoken a bit about the political situation in Miran with the boycotts, and then he said, "There are many things people accuse us Traders of, and especially people in the Mirani council. The Trader Guild, with all its members and its network throughout *gamra* is like a very large family. As you do with family, they always take priority over everything. For many of us, the Guild is a closer family than our non-Trading family. It is closer to us than our origins or place of birth. Because of this, the Guild has the power to break governments, to financially destroy entire nations. It is a power that must be used with caution. It also means that sometimes you will need to stand strong in a current of different opinions. That requires extraordinary courage." His eyes met hers in an intense look. His irises were so light blue as to be almost white, exceptionally light, even for a Mirani Endri. "To be a successful Trader, you will need to maintain the courage that burns in you because people will relentlessly try to cut you down."

He had said *maintain the courage*. He had placed his trust in her because he thought she'd displayed courage by coming up to the most successful Trading family in Miran and bluntly asking them to sponsor someone who was not related and of the wrong family and the wrong gender.

He trusts me and has hopes for me.

It hit her like a blow to the head.

Of course she couldn't refuse the offer, no matter how much her family was against it and no matter how much trouble it would get her into. She might be shy and unwilling to fight with her parents, but she had courage. How was it that she'd allowed herself to forget that?

She owed it to the dying courier and his family to act on the message, to go to Kedras, and *succeed*. Dreams didn't exist for adults to belittle them as silly or childish. They existed for inspiration.

While the nurses packed up and cleaned the floor, Mikandra sat next to the bed and held the courier's hand. It was so cold and clammy. Eydrina came in looking for her, probably to give her a job to do, but took one look and left again.

The man's heart beat for the last time not much later. She placed his hand on the fast-cooling body and arranged his ripped tunic so that, if you ignored the slashed fabric, it looked like he was asleep. It was not the first time that she'd seen someone die, but if it was up to her, it would be the last.

Eydrina said behind her, "Clean him up and you can go home."

Mikandra faced her tutor. She felt like telling her that she would never come back, but this might not be the time for that announcement. It might be wise to pretend nothing had changed for a few days yet.

While Mikandra was washing blood out of the courier's neck, his ID card fell out of the pocket of his tunic onto the bench. She picked up the card and stared at her own face reflected in the black metallic surface. The card would need a reader to divulge the courier's name.

In the inner pocket of the remains of his jacket, she found his message satchel, wet, but otherwise unharmed. It felt empty.

"What do you want me to do with this?" she asked, holding it up.

"It will need to go to the Trader Guild," Eydrina said. "I'm thinking that they'll have a thing or two to say about this."

"I can't imagine they'll be impressed." It was sure to put her aunt in a difficult position as both a member of the council and the Guild.

"They'll be livid." Eydrina took the satchel from Mikandra, opened it and slid the ID pass inside. She put it on the bench next to the door. "I'll ask one of the boys to deliver it."

Mikandra walked past it on her way out of the room. The front of the satchel had a clear pocket, inside which there was a card with names where the courier had to deliver documents. The man's last-ever delivery had indeed included her letter. There were a few young men of her age on the list, as well as other names she recognised. Ilendar, Andrahar, Tussamar and others.

So yes, the Trader Guild would make a big stink about this. They would say that if decent medicine had been used, the man might have survived. They would demand to see treatment records. They would see how Eydrina and the surgeon had decided not to treat the man. They might even demand that the surgeon and Eydrina explain themselves in the Trader Court.

They would say that the attack was motivated by Miran's hatred for foreigners. They would say this was proof that Miran was sliding into anarchy. There would be official Guild protests to the council, and then the local Traders would get up and say that their Guild was right and that the council were idiots and failed in their basic duty to protect citizens.

Then traditionalists in the council would argue that this was proof of the increasing influence of foreign control of Miran, because the Guild's headquarters were at Kedras and their agenda was foreign and that they were therefore trying to control Miran. Mikandra could already hear Nemedor Satarin's words. *Do we let this alien, foreign entity control the way we do things in Miran? Do we grovel at the feet of these organisations that are run by people whose only aim is to cut us down?* She'd heard so many of his speeches, which the Nikala workers lapped up like honey.

But beyond Miran's borders and in the hallways of the *gamra* assembly, people would say that Nemedor Satarin's response to the incident was extremist and dictatorial and justified the boycotts to Miran. They might even strengthen the boycotts.

Whatever the reaction, one thing was certain: it would not improve life in Miran.

5

MIKANDRA TOOK off her apron, found her cloak and left the building through the draughty foyer with its unending stream of patients. The main desk would close at night, except for the worst of emergencies, but some people would wait here until morning. They had nowhere else to go.

Out in the street, she turned up the hill in the direction of the Foundation Square. The air was cold and wet and shards of mist floated low over the city roofs. This morning's snow had melted and the paving stones were cold and wet enough to be slippery. Judging by the way the city's lights reflected in the clouds, there would be more snow tonight.

On each side of the street, shopkeepers were shutting doors and pulling down blinds. The baker's assistant carried a basket with bread outside and put it in the porch of his shop. Within moments, a bundled-up man with his hair in a mess of matted curls had scurried out of an alley. He plunged both arms into the basket and came up with an armful of rolls, which he tucked into a bag under his cloak. As he scurried off, two other men made for the basket, both at least as scruffy and long haired as the first man.

These people were the shame of Miran, proof that the Foundation agreement wasn't working as it should.

She came out into the Foundation Square, a rectangular space flanked by the business district downhill, the markets to the left and the council buildings and library uphill.

The Foundation monument stood in the middle of the square. The five pillars on the ancient pentagonal platform were silhouetted like black fingers against the lit facades of the council building and the library.

Mikandra climbed the three ancient steps up the monument's platform. The weathered stone felt gritty under her feet and a mist-laden breeze whipped all her hair to one side.

The monument was an ancient thing, dating from the time that the first people settled this highland valley.

Before the city was founded, the two peoples had lived somewhere on the upper plateau near the gorges where the menisha fungus grew. The Nikala ancestors, who were hunters and harvesters, lived in the canyons. They made their living harvesting moss, fungi and lichen off the sheer walls, and fishing in the streams. Their descendants still lived that area today. They were people with strong arms and hands with claws on their thumb and little fingers.

By contrast, the Endri cave dwellers had built an entire underground city on the very top of the plateau. They lived mostly indoors and occupied themselves with art and music, while they grew their vegetables in large caves and bought meat and fish off the harvesters in exchange for items of clothing, healing or trinkets. If the tales were to be believed, the two groups were continuously at war.

After the last and most bloody conflict in which the cave dwellers were almost wiped out, a few of the survivors had fled their underground city, carrying all they owned on the backs of twelve tiyuk. They'd walked for days with their pack animals over the freezing passes and icy mountain slopes until they came to a valley with green grass, a burbling creek and a view of endless plains that no one had ever seen before.

They had set up camp on a hillock next to the creek, they built houses from river stones and started to work the fields. They'd divided the land up between the families. The harvest was poor and the crops they'd brought from their cave too soft to do well in the thin and cold air, but they were determined to survive, and they did.

At the end of the growing season, a group of the Nikala whom they used to fight sought refuge in the valley. They were sad and sorry people, diseased walking skeletons who begged their former enemies for help. They had walked all the way from the highlands carrying their sick without any pack animals and resorting to eating maramarang whenever they could catch them. And everyone knew maramarang were terrible eating.

The Endri realised that they needed people to work their fields and build a wall around their sanctuary against further attacks from the large body of hunters still on the highlands. They promised that the Nikala could live inside the walls if they helped build those very walls and helped farm the crops to feed the settlement. And so the classes had been born.

An agreement had been put into law, signed and witnessed by the Foundation families. The Nikala would continue to work the land if the Endri looked after their protection and shelter from the weather. The Foundation agreement had survived the expansion of Miran into most of the continent, it had survived the Coldi invasion and the subsequent hasty development of a Mirani flight and space program, and its connection with other entities of *gamra*. The agreement had worked for so long.

Foundation was the heart of Mirani society.

The Foundation monument stood at the place where the agreement was said to have been signed, and probably dated from a hundred years after Foundation. In its heyday, it would have been a magnificent building, but the roof once upheld by the pillars had long gone, and since no one had thought to extend the lighting to the monument, it stood ghostly and forgotten against the more modern splendour.

Yet people hadn't forgotten it. From the window at the hospital, Mikandra saw people walk across the stone platform every day. School children who learned about the city's history, couples who came to be married under the eye of the ancestors. They were often simple folk, but every now and then, there would be a high-profile wedding and the town square would be full of people.

What would those ancestors think if they saw the city now? Some of the Endri, especially the older women, believed that the ancestors watched their city from the sky. They believed that the ancestors guided the hands of those in power.

Mikandra reached out and touched the rough stone of one of the pillars. "Please," she asked of the ancestors. "Tell me if you approve of what I'm about to do."

This was her point of no return. Here, she could either go uphill, and home, or downhill to the Trader Guild office.

Home and comfortable certainties or the unknown, hardship and distress.

Was it more of the same that had never made a difference to anyone in the last few centuries, or was it something new and frightening?

Courage. She balled her fists against her chest and raised her face to the dark sky. The wind whipped her hair into her face. A couple of snowflakes landed on her forehead and cheeks. It all came down to a simple pledge, spoken by children entering school.

I swear by the blood of my ancestors that has flowed in this place that I will do my best to make things better for my family, for my people and for Miran.

The road best taken would not always be the easiest one.

Mikandra stepped down from the monument and turned downhill.

The Trader Guild office was housed in one of the older buildings surrounding the square. In the huge echoing foyer, merchants came for bidding wars to buy the latest imported goods. There must have been a recent delivery, because the hall was full of men in thick cloaks displaying their family colours. Most of them faced the back wall of the foyer where columns of codes and numbers scrolled over a screen. Each represented a consignment of goods entered by a Trader's staff. The four-digit codes represented the Trader offering the goods. She couldn't see any under 1101, the prestigious Andrahar licence, but there was 1102,

Tussamar Traders, and a few others she recognised. The merchants queued up at the counter underneath the screen to put in their bids. Apparently, or so Aunt Amandra had told her, this was a really primitive way of passing goods to local merchants.

She wrestled through the hall without attracting much attention. A wide stone staircase led up to the second floor, where the high-ceilinged Guild foyer was more quiet.

There were only a few people up here, one of them talking to the desk attendant, a Guild employee in carmine red. Had they heard about the dead courier yet?

The other men in the room were merchants, probably here to pay for the deals they'd sealed downstairs. Mikandra sat in the upholstered chairs to wait her turn, listening to snatches of the merchants' conversations, mostly about goods they had purchased.

The sound of voices drifted up from the hall downstairs. A few more merchants came up into the foyer and settled in the chairs next to Mikandra.

"Can I help you, lady?" the Guild employee said.

There was only one lady in the room, and Mikandra went up to the counter under the gazes of all the men. She tried to ignore them, but felt self-conscious. As Trader, she would have to get used to this. Aunt Amandra said that after all her years as the Mirani chapter of the Guild's only female Trader, people in Miran still watched her every move.

"I came to deliver this." She produced the letter with her notice of acceptance.

The employee looked at it and frowned. Looked at her again. His frown deepened.

Behind his counter was a door which bore a sign *Traders only beyond this point*. One day soon, she would walk into that room, and all the men would look at her.

"That is . . . unusual."

"Sure." She smiled at him.

"I better see if I have been given an acceptance satchel for you." He sounded like he thought the letter was a mistake.

While he rummaged behind the counter, it went quiet in the

foyer. Mikandra turned around and smiled at the merchants who were all staring at her.

As it turned out, and to the employee's obvious surprise, he *had* been sent a satchel, a bundle of books and something that felt soft and would be her apprentice uniform. Once you were a Trader, you rarely wore non-uniform clothes anymore. Goodbye frilly dresses.

She left the building clutching the parcel, feeling more confident about herself than she had been for a long time. The courier would not die in vain. Iztho had not placed trust in her for nothing. The ancient ancestors would see that she was true to her promise to Miran.

The commercial precinct was on the other side of the square, and right on the corner, above Merchant Ranuddin's exclusive clothing store was her destination: the double doors that led up the stairs to the Andrahar office.

She'd been there a few times before she applied, but not since that time.

The light was on in the windows above the shop that overlooked the square, and lights blazed in the stairwell. She wondered who was here and what she would say if Iztho was away. He had signed the application, but she had not seen him since. Also, she had very little interaction with the three other brothers beyond having passed them upstairs in the office. Whenever she had come here, Rehan usually wore a detached and aloof expression and barely noticed her, Braedon would nod politely and carry on with his work, and Taerzo was the only one who would smile.

What would she say to them if Iztho wasn't in?

She pushed the door, and it wouldn't open.

What? Hadn't Iztho said that there was always someone at the office day or night?

She rattled the door, but it was locked. Through the glass, she could see the bar of the lock in place. Her breath steamed in the cold.

Well, this was something she hadn't factored into her plans. How would she let the brothers know of her acceptance if there was no one in the office?

She let her gaze roam the square, from the brightly-lit council buildings to the library and the covered market hall, now with all the doors closed for the night.

Merchant Ranuddin himself was pulling down the blinds over the windows of his business. As was typical for the Nikala merchants, he dressed more elaborately than the Endri. As seller of exclusive clothing, that effect was heightened with his immaculate thick and lush cloak, his high boots with trim of fur and embroidery.

He gave her a strange look that made her feel underdressed and inadequate in her plain hospital clothes. She smiled awkwardly. "I'm after the Andrahar brothers."

"They're not here," he said from within the fur-rimmed hood of his cloak.

She had noticed that. "Do you know where they are?"

"They closed up and sent everyone home. Some big thing going on, apparently, or so the gossip has it. You know how Traders are. The entire world will know what's going on before Miran knows it."

She ignored the underhand stab. "Do you know where they went?" But as she said this, she suspected that it might be about the announcement of a marriage.

Merchant Ranuddin shrugged. "Home, I guess."

"All right, thanks."

"What do you want anyway, girl? A nice lady like you shouldn't be out here at a time like this and in weather like this."

"I'm fine, really." Although she was shivering so much that she could barely speak, whether it was from the cold or nerves she couldn't tell. She cast a glance at the sky, which had indeed grown alarmingly dark.

He gave her a *you don't look fine* glance but fortunately remained quiet.

There was nothing for it. She made her decision, and now she wanted to let Iztho know. She needed to know about practical information, such as money, and where she'd live until she went to Kedras. The Andrahar house wasn't far from here. The scavengers didn't come out until much later, right? All the attacks always happened after midnight, or so she told herself while hurrying through the streets.

She walked close to walls, her hands in her pockets and her ears hidden under the upturned collar of her cloak, doing her best impression of something inedible in the eyes of marama-rang and hoping that whichever street gang had killed the Guild courier would not find her.

The Andrahar house was one of the oldest in the Endri quarter and in the best position. It lay on a slight rise, and over-looked most of the city while it was still comfortably far removed from the city walls. The yard was bigger than those of surrounding houses, covered with pebbles and surrounded by a tall wall that spanned an entire block. Wall and house were painted white. The wall had an elaborate front gate, which she had never seen closed. A path of whitestone pavers led from the gate to the front door, hidden within the darkness of the over-hanging porch. A distant light peeped through the leadlight windows of the door; she guessed it was somewhere at the far end of the hall or beyond, but no other light was on. Not in the room next to the door which was Iztho's, not in the study or in any of the upstairs bedrooms.

What if the brothers were out celebrating?

What else could this be about than Iztho's announcement that he was getting married?

When she visited Iztho in his room, an elaborate maroon dress had been hanging on the outside of the wardrobe door. She'd guessed it was the Andrahar family's official wedding gown—no one had seen that garment since Isandra and Jihan married many years ago—and figured Iztho was about to announce his choice of bride. Rumours of an impending marriage had been around for years.

Iztho mentioned the dress when he noticed her looking at it. Yes, he was getting married, and no, it wasn't locally. She wanted to ask him if that wasn't a problem with the family succession, but that seemed an improper question to ask.

Mikandra walked up to the door. Somewhere inside the house, a male voice shouted. The tone sounded angry.

She knocked. The voice stopped, and in the silence came the

sound of footsteps. A moment later, the door was opened by Taerzo, the youngest brother. Relief flooded her.

She smiled at him, holding up the letter. "I got in. I got the letter of acceptance this afternoon. Father is furious and I wonder—"

He did not return her smile. Then she noticed that he wasn't in uniform.

Traders always wore uniform, even if they didn't work. She didn't think she'd ever seen Aunt Amandra out of uniform.

"Is anything wrong?" Her heart jumped.

"You best come in," Taerzo said.

6

MIKANDRA STEPPED into the hall, which seemed impossibly warm and smelled of freshly-baked fish bread. Taerzo closed the door behind her.

She stomped the snow off her boots on the mat, slipped them off and put them next to the men's boots lined up next to the door. She selected the smallest pair of slippers she could find on the rack under the cloak stand. They enfolded her feet with luxurious warmth, and the fur that lined the inside had not yet flattened with use.

She followed Taerzo—wearing similar footwear—across the hall into the living room, where traditional oil lamps burned in sconces and their flapping flames made grotesque shadows on the walls. With its marble flooring, antique hearth and hand-crafted furniture, the house was the epitome of old-fashioned noble Endri households. Well, except for the hub with its blinking lights in the corner of the hall.

In the living room, Braedon sat at the table behind a huge pile of books. He glanced up when Taerzo came in, looked back at his books and then up again at Mikandra. He raised his eyebrows and raked his hair behind his ear. Apart from Taerzo, who was not that much older than her and was considered to be the joker of the family, she found Braedon least intimidating. He was rather plain, straightforward and quiet. He did not wear lots of jewellery or other display of status like his two older brothers. He came into the hospital quite a bit, and was always courteous and kind to the nurses or surgeons and knew a lot about healing.

He gestured to the seat next to him.

Mikandra sat, still clutching the letter. On the page in the book facing him were long columns of financial data. He had a reader on his other side, which was, apart from the hub in the hall, the only concession to technology in this very traditional house. The screen glared more columns of figures.

She was going to tell them what happened, but Braedon brought his fingers to his lips.

There were voices at the back of the room, in a section partitioned off from the dining area by a sliding door.

Through the glass in the door, she could see the second-oldest brother Rehan in front of the hearth, facing a man who sat on the couch.

"Anyway," Rehan was saying, the words only slightly muffled by the door. "Whatever has caused it, your behaviour has been nothing short of grossly inadequate. You're going to have a lot of explaining to do, and unless I'm satisfied, I will call in the Guild Lawkeepers, and they will get to the bottom of this."

"You're not going to sack me?" The man sounded incredulous.

"You've worked with us for long enough to know that is not our style. Make no mistake, I would very much like to sack you, but it does not solve anything. Sacking you does not put our accounts in order."

"Um . . . I guess."

Mikandra realised the man on the couch was the Andrahar account keeper, Trimon Estredin, the husband of one of her mother's theatre friends.

"You guess?" Rehan continued in his booming voice. "You guess? There is no room for guesses. What I want is your reason for delivering poor work. Why did you approve these books? Why did you sign all these pages that clearly don't balance? Where is the missing money?"

"I'd have to sit down and go through. I honestly don't

remember the details of all those accounts."

There was a heavy thud of some object hitting wood. "Bullshit! That's fucking bullshit and you know it. You know what happened. You were there. This is your work! Get the fuck out of here. Go to the office. Come back when you have something to say. Don't dare run away. Don't think we won't find you."

The man rose and left the room at a run. A moment later, the door shut.

Heaving a big sigh, Rehan opened the partition doors. "Fucking numbskull. Blubbering nitwit." He stopped a few paces into the room, and frowned at Mikandra. Met her eyes. His hair, normally a silk-like curtain over his back, had become entangled in the clasp of his cloak. His cheeks were red. "What's this about? Any more problems?"

Mikandra lifted the letter.

"I got my letter of acceptance," she said, but she no longer felt exuberant. Something was very wrong.

"The fuck you did?"

Braedon said, "Rehan, please mind your—"

"Don't tell me what I can or can't say in my own house. We don't have the time to deal with fucking pambies."

He still looked at Mikandra. His expression was so penetrating that she felt like fleeing. He had the typical narrow Endri face, pronounced cheekbones, strong eyebrows, the hairs bristly and white. His eyes were almost as light as his older brother's, but his lips were much fuller and expressive, a bit like Braedon's.

He was very tall, and held his back straight and proud. At least he wore his Trading uniform, the khaki shirt and trousers with the ornate belt and his high boots. But she couldn't see the medallion with the emblem of the Guild and the licence number.

"All right, you win. No more fucking swearing in the presence of women, eh?" He blew out a breath and turned to the window.

Mikandra looked back at Braedon who at least didn't terrify her as much. "What's wrong?"

"We've had our licence suspended by court order."

What? A big black hole opened in Mikandra's mind. A suspended licence meant no sponsorship. It meant no work, no place for her to go to. It meant—how was that even possible? These were the *Andrahar* Traders, the most influential in all of Miran. "What happened?" Black spots crept into her vision.

"We're trying to sort that out. Someone has officially accused Iztho of smuggling. The documents support the claim."

"Is he here?" Please.

Braedon shook his head. "We haven't heard from him for a few days, ever since this crisis broke. We can't raise him on the network. We put out a missing person call."

"Missing?" The ground fell away underneath her. She heard Father's voice *You know how many Traders disappear and are never heard from again?* Many of those, too, took down their business with them, or vanished because the business was already in trouble.

How was that possible? The Andrahars were the best Traders in Miran. Iztho signed her on, which meant he *had* to see a bright future for the business.

"What . . . what are you going to do?" More importantly, what did it mean for her, but she was too scared to ask that question.

"On a most immediate level, we need to find money to pay a major debt. On top of everything else, we found that our accounts are in a mess, and that our accountant—the one who was just here—has been fudging the books. I don't know how or why it happened, but we need to pay our main creditor, the Hedron Mines." He waved his hand at the books. "That's what I'm doing here. Trying to find two hundred thousand credits to pay that account so that we don't slip further in trouble while we wait for the court case to get the suspension lifted."

That was such a huge amount of money that Mikandra's head reeled. From her father's talk, about half the monthly budget of the Mirani council.

Rehan again gave him a sharp glance. Signalling his brother to tell her to go away and stop divulging business details?

"What . . . do you want me to do?" She had trouble keeping her voice even. She had just *accepted* her place. Officially. The acceptance would have been sent to Kedras immediately. She *wanted* to go. "Can I help?"

"I think you may be better off waiting at home—"

"Please?" No, she couldn't go home; she made her decision.

Braedon's eyes met hers. Not as light as Iztho's but still light blue. His expression said, *This problem is bigger than all of us.* He sighed. "It's really not the best time—"

"Please? Can I help, and I don't mean make the tea, because I'm no good at that."

Rehan said, "She's got to go home. We do not have time for another run-in with Asitho Bisumar on top of all this."

A meaningful look passed between the brothers.

What run-in?

Taerzo said, "Iztho sponsored her."

"She was going to work for *him*," Rehan said, his voice hard.

To Mikandra's ears, everything they said over her head sounded like *What is she even doing here? What was our brother thinking?*

"Honestly, I could use an extra pair of eyes," Braedon said. "Seeing as we can't trust that idiot of an accountant—"

"Oh, he'll be back," Rehan said. "If necessary, I'll lock him in the office until he tells us the full story. He will fix his mistakes, and we'll see how he copes with that before we decide whether or not to keep him."

"He is not here now, and it would still pay to have someone who's completely independent to check the accounts."

"I can do that," Mikandra said. "I do accounts for the emergency ward."

Rehan's icy gaze—annoyed—went to her.

She returned his stare. *Courage.* She straightened her back. Rehan Andrahar was an overbearing, rude, foul-mouthed bully, but he did *not* frighten her. "I can do sums and read long and detailed financial reports and write summaries. I do that every day at the hospital. If you want to check the books I can help." She held up her letter. "I have this."

"Have you sent in your official acceptance?"

She nodded.

Rehan glanced at his brothers and when neither responded, he blew out breath in a sniff. "All right. We have a lot of accounts to go through. Show her the court documents."

A very small victory. But clearly neither Rehan nor Braedon thought that she ought to be there.

Taerzo's eyes met hers. One corner of his mouth lifted. It was through him that she had gotten the idea to apply. He was a friend of Lihan Ilendar's and had been visiting one night she was at Lihan's house. He'd said *Things need to change. Miran needs to change. The Mirani chapter of the Guild needs to change* and *change* meant accepting non-Mirani-born Guild members and allowing them to settle in Miran. It meant appointing different people from the traditional Traders. Women, non-Endri.

Braedon gave Mikandra a letter in a similar red envelope as the one she had received. Another message delivered by the dead courier?

None of the brothers looked at her as she opened it and unfolded the couple of sheets that were inside. The Trader Guild stamp was on all of them—the date in Trader Standard a few days ago—including the Andrahar licence number 1101.

There were a few copies of documents with lists of items, times and values, but she had no idea what they meant. There was a summons to appear in court on 4515-13-25, which was a Trader date and corresponded with . . . um . . . at least more than a Mirani suncycle, perhaps even two. She'd need to sit down and work it out properly. Kedras days were shorter than Ceren's, they had only one sun, so no cycles, and divided their short year into arbitrary months. She thought there were fifteen, but she wasn't sure.

She really needed a timer to work it out.

The main letter was a single page, in Coldi, with the emblem of the Trader Court stamped and signed at the bottom. It was oddly disjointed and curt in tone.

Matter to be dealt with: criminal charge concerning the illegal import of menisha fungus, brought by the Barresh Council. Illegal product found in a consignment of goods shipped from Miran to Barresh under the permit of the Andrahar Traders as per the attached documents.

Mikandra studied the page, which was nothing more than a list of goods and quantities, one of which was underlined. *Dried Menisha fungus.* She used it whole or in powder form in the hospital. When boiled in water, the fungus made a powerful tea. When dissolved in spirits, it made the brew that ruined the lives of so many.

Mikandra frowned. "Since when is the export of menisha illegal?"

Taerzo replied. "Barresh is the only entity that has banned it. Probably to spite us, because it's the only thing they used to import from us in any quantity." His voice trembled with anger.

Mikandra had often hoped that Miran would ban it. If Barresh imported it in quantity, they were likely to have a problem with abuse by citizens. Barresh was not very big, so the abuse would be obvious. She couldn't blame anyone for banning menisha.

She went over the page again, studying the other items listed in the shipment. "It seems a bit odd to have a couple of dried bags of fungus mixed up with a delivery of tiles, marble and— what's quartz for?"

"It's a stone used for carvings, trimmings, ornaments and clear displays. Mostly artificial. With exception of the fungus, these are all specialist construction or industrial materials."

Rehan said, "This claim is rubbish. This whole suspension, the court case, the threats. They're all rubbish. Iztho doesn't deal with the stuff. Braedon does, but he only sells extract, not the whole dried fungus. We don't have this shipment on any of our books, and not on our courier logs. We don't sell anything to Barresh. They don't have the money to buy anything we sell."

"But if you don't have the shipment on your books, it would be easy to prove your innocence."

"It should be," Braedon said, "But unfortunately, evidence given by the Exchange takes precedence over anything we can supply. They're supposed to be always right."

The Exchange *was* right, because they had to be. When they established anpar lines between worlds in different systems, there was no margin for error. It was vital that they knew the weight and content of each craft that they transferred, and collected that data even if the craft remained on the same world and didn't use anpar lines.

She asked, "How would you prove that they're not right then?"

· "Any transport the Exchange logs comes from the nodes involved. Since there was no anpar transfer, the main Exchange hub in Damarq would not have logged anything that wasn't also recorded elsewhere. The first step will be to ask for the logs from all directly involved Exchange nodes, Miran and Barresh to see if it matches up. To get this type of information requires lengthy processes."

"What do you think happened? Is it an error?"

Rehan snorted. "Barresh has made up this charge to punish Iztho for whatever went on there last year. Now he is missing, and we've got the Hedron account due and thanks to the suspension, no fucking money to pay it."

Taerzo said, "I'm betting Barresh has something to do with Iztho's disappearance."

Braedon said, "Hang on, brother, let's not make assumptions we can't prove. Let's worry about the money first."

"It's rubbish!" Rehan said, speaking into the window. "It's fabricated nonsense. We don't sell agricultural produce and we don't smuggle. We don't sell to Barresh. We pay our bills on time, especially to the Hedron Mines."

"*We* do," Braedon said. "We can't be sure about Iztho. Can you be sure that *he* didn't sell to Barresh?"

"Yes, I'm sure!" Rehan whirled at him. "Because he wouldn't do that sort of thing. There is no point for him to do it, even though he's an arsehole who never let us in with what-ever he had planned. Disappearing for days on end, refusing to talk to us. Making decisions without us . . ." He glared at Mikandra and she was sure agreeing to train her was such a decision. He blew out a breath through flaring nostrils. "So what is our response to his arseholery? We all stake out our little corner of work and ignore what else goes on in the rest of the business. As long as we don't have to deal with him. And now there is a problem and we have no idea what the fuck has been going on in our administration. That doesn't look good, huh?"

"It's not your fault, brother," Taerzo said. "I can't see what else we could have done. As you say, it's not like he ever makes it easy for anyone to work with him."

Rehan whirled around and grabbed Taerzo by the collar of his shirt. "We should have kept a closer eye on him. We should have checked his books, asked what he was doing. I know he didn't want to share anything, but we should have forced him. I am at fault. You are at fault. We're all at fault." Rehan had gone red in the face. "When that whole fucking mess blew up in Barresh, we should not have let him sort it out, no matter how much he told us he was on top of things."

Taerzo coolly yanked his shirt out of his brother's grip. They were about the same height, except Taerzo still retained the lankiness of youth. "There is not much point in being aggressive about it. I'm not your enemy."

"Then shut your smartarse mouth. You have no fucking idea what you're talking about."

"Who, exactly are you accusing of being an arsehole?"

"Are you applying for the title? Great. You're an arsehole. Happy now?"

"How is anyone supposed to work with you? You're just as bad as him—"

"Shut the fuck up!" Rehan whirled and slammed both his hands on the table with such force that the pile of books next to Braedon wobbled.

Mikandra sat as if frozen, not daring to move or make a sound. No one at home fought like this.

Braedon said, without looking up from his work, "Hey, man, go be a nuisance somewhere else. I'm working."

Taerzo went to the couch and sat down, his back stiff. Rehan went back to the window and stared into the darkness. He stood with his legs apart and brought his weight onto one leg and then the other and back again in a fluid movement. "Hurry the fuck up, all right? I want this resolved. I have work to do."

Braedon glared at his brother's back. "Nothing is going to happen before the court case."

"Then we get ready for the fucking court case. Prove that even though Iztho's an arsehole, he is the right kind of arsehole. He did not do this."

7

A FTER A LONG and tense silence, Braedon shoved a pile of books across the table to Mikandra. "I want these two accounts checked." He went on to explain in a low voice that they kept one account for each of their large clients, and a running account for business payments. There were always a lot of interaccount transfers. Apparently, the accountant had admitted to the fact that the books didn't balance and that the running account had been bleeding money in undisclosed small payments.

"We need to find this money. Or any money. Iztho has so many accounts set up that it's impossible to trace where the missing amount went. We are looking for any accounts that we didn't already know about, particularly personal ones, because we can still access those and we might be able to scrape enough together for a downpayment to the Hedron Mines that will keep them happy until we solve the issue in court."

"When is the court case?"

He mentioned a date in Trader years that translated into midwinter in Miran. A fair while away, and just before the academy started. For Mikandra, it would either make or break her future, and if she wanted to stay and take up her spot, she desperately had to make herself useful.

"So, when I go through these books, is there anything in

particular that I should be looking for?" Rehan was looking at her in the reflection in the window.

"Anything irregular. I've found small amounts of money disappearing, all of which is starting to add up to quite a bit. The missing money has got to be somewhere. The less time we take finding it, the better. I appreciate your help." He cast a sideways glance at Rehan.

Rehan wheeled on the spot, his boots noisily sliding over the marble floor. He glared at Braedon and marched out the room.

If he was so impatient, why wasn't he helping? Or were accounts beneath him?

Mikandra opened the first book.

Columns of neatly-written figures. Amounts of produce sold, amounts imported. Cost, quarantine levies, council tax.

Braedon explained. "Add up the income. See if it matches the running balance given at the bottom."

"Don't you have all this on the system?" She thought Traders were all modern and advanced.

"Yes, but those figures have had entries left out or deleted so any pages where you find an incorrect balance give them to me and I'll check with the system which record is not entered."

Mikandra started on the first page and did as he said. The balance matched. She turned to the next page. It matched, too.

Rehan's voice drifted in from the hub in the hallway, ". . . Iztho, for fuck's sake, this is not a joke anymore . . . I know we didn't exactly part on good terms last time we saw each other, but please, stop being stupid and come home. This is about everything we have worked for."

This was followed by silence. Then a thud against the wall. Rehan's fist, she guessed.

Mikandra turned page after page. Added up, compared, turned the next page. Braedon worked next to her. He was very quick with sums and turned his pages much faster than she. Trying to keep up with him became a challenge. It got late and later, long past the time she normally went to sleep, yet she didn't feel tired.

Taerzo came to collect one of the books and sat on the couch with it.

She had gone perhaps twenty pages when she discovered the first irregular transfer. A relatively small amount of money that came from an item called *proxy fees*.

She showed Braedon.

"Yes, that's like the others. They are nondescript entries for strange items. I have no idea what proxy fees are or why Iztho should be collecting any fees. Any fees that I know of are expenditure, not income. Likely it doesn't show on the system and there is no account with that name or other information where the money has gone. I don't understand why the accountant let all this slip."

Two options, really, and stories about his work as Lawkeeper that Father had told at the dinner table had attuned her to these things: either the accountant had been a fraud or Iztho had been trying to unobtrusively bleed money away from the business accounts.

"How long has this accountant worked for you?"

"Quite a long time. Before I got my licence."

"Does he have any problems at home?"

Braedon gave her a *how am I supposed to know that?* look.

Mikandra shrugged. "It could be that he has a personal problem, like gambling or . . ." *drinking.* She shuddered. ". . . a severely ill relative and he's used the money to cover his debts."

"Could be." His frown deepened. "Doesn't help us right now, though."

They kept working.

Taerzo fell asleep on the couch with his feet propped up on the armrest. His arm hung off the couch, twitching occasionally. The book lay open on his stomach.

Mikandra stared into the room.

Behind the couch stood an old cabinet. It was an ancient thing with three sides of engraved glass and glass shelves, all meticulously kept free of dust. Inside, on the shelf, stood a box with its lid open.

On a bed of the finest embroidered silk lay a simple river stone such as boys skimmed over the water when the river was calm enough to form quiet pools. It was attached to a gold loop at the narrow end. Its surface had been polished a bit, and circling its widest point was a band of silver. Though she couldn't see them from here, she knew that its surface was engraved with letters so fine that a magnifying glass was needed to read them. Yet she knew the text. Every child in Miran started their education with these words. *We uphold the justice and the peace.* In the ancient language.

This was the Foundation stone, which gave the heir of the five Foundation families the right to veto any decision made by the council. There had been much misuse of this right, which was why the other four stones sat in a cabinet in the main foyer of the library after having been returned to the council, voluntarily or by force. The Andrahar family was the only one of the five families to still have their stone, and she had never dared hope to see it.

Rehan came back into the room and paced around the table, between the cupboard and the couch, around the middle of the room and back again. And again. And agai—

"Stop it, brother," Braedon said.

Rehan whirled around. "What?"

"Stop pacing. It's annoying. Sit down. Go to bed."

"And you think I can sleep?"

"Go and talk to Mother, then." Braedon cast a glance at the closed door on the far end of the living room, which would be the matriarch Isandra's room.

Rehan's expression was furious. "She's asleep. I'll go when we have something to tell her about how we're getting out of this mess. She'll be happy in her room until that time."

"Whatever. I don't care. Just stop pacing around."

"I want to fucking do something. I've got clients waiting for me." He stuck his thumbs in the loops in his belt and drummed his fingers on the leather.

Mikandra stared at those fingers. Heard Eydrina's voice *Just ignore the waggling and jiggling. It will drive you mad.*

Menisha addiction.

She looked up into his face. He met her eyes. There was no sign of discolouration in the whites, but that was a late-stage problem. The inability to concentrate—or add up sums—was not. Her cheeks glowed. She had to look away.

The cupboards against the back wall contained the family's precious tableware and glasses. One of the cabinets held an assortment of bottles. There was bound to be some brew amongst those. Menisha was a popular late-night drink for cold winter nights. Almost every family would have some. The fact that Endri didn't present to the hospital with addiction problems didn't mean that there were none. *Just look at Leitho.*

They were just more adept at hiding their troubles.

Heart thudding, she went back to work.

A recalcitrant brother, violent fights, a wayward accountant and addiction. What had she let herself in for?

She thought of her room and Liseyo. She thought of running back to the Trader Guild to say that she'd changed her mind. But that would just prove to Father the fact that girls were soft. This was stuff that went on in the world of the Traders. She would have to deal with it.

Courage. Maybe Iztho had wanted to involve her in the business because his brothers were on a path to destruction. Maybe he had appointed her because he thought they would be reluctant to misbehave in front of someone who was either a stranger to the family or female, or, as it was, both.

Mikandra worked, turning over pages and pages in the books. She found more irregularities and wrote them all down on a separate sheet of paper. With each amount she found, her feeling that the accountant had hidden the money intensified.

Taerzo was still asleep on the couch, but Rehan had finally sat down to help with the accounts, even though he kept getting up to walk around the room a few times before sitting down again. His restlessness drove her crazy, but she didn't say anything, because he couldn't help it, much less do anything about it. She glanced at his hands, but didn't spot any of the characteristic tremors or clumsiness. Those were the symptoms that usually came before the restlessness, or rather, the restlessness was a result of the tremors. Either he hid the tremors well or he didn't have any.

When he did sit down to work, he was fast. Lightning fast, ripping through pages faster even than Braedon. She secretly checked one or two pages of his work, but found no errors. So much for a reduced concentration. Did he perhaps have access to a medicine that masked the symptoms?

Eventually, Mikandra found herself staring at a page without seeing what was on it. Her eyes felt scratchy. She wondered what the time was, but surely it must be close to dawn.

She sighed and leaned her head in her hands.

"How are you going?" Braedon asked. "Are you tired?"

Exhausted, but she didn't want to admit that.

She spoke into the space under her arms. "It's all very strange. I mean, if the money that's reported here in these transactions actually existed, there would have to be a record of it in these books. Could it be that there is an account book missing?"

"I've taken all I could find."

"Could it be somewhere else? You see these strange entries?" She pointed at the page of errors she had listed. "They're for things like *proxy fees* where we don't have information that tells us where the money came from. They're all income, where you said, Braedon, that a fee should be an expenditure. We have a whole page of them, and they're distributed over a handful of these vague terms, like proxy fees, account correction—"

Rehan said, "Account correction is when the exchange rate is more favourable than expected at the signing of the deal."

"But that amount is usually added up with the entry for the deal," Braedon said.

Rehan nodded. "True."

Mikandra continued, "The amounts are small enough not to attract attention, but there is no evidence that the money exists. I wonder if this is a cover for transfers to or from other accounts. Supposing that *proxy fees* is not an item but a code for an account, there might be a book for it somewhere, especially since none of these amounts can be found on the system."

Rehan looked at the list, frowning deeply. Then he met her eyes. Did she see a glimmer of respect in his expression?

Mikandra said, "For example, I've seen no data from the Trader account in Kedras."

"We don't hold an account in Kedras," Braedon said.

"Don't all Traders have one, regardless of whether they use it?" She read that in her course information.

"Yes, but—" Braedon froze. He looked at her and a disturbed expression crossed his face. "Maybe there are some books left in his room."

"I'll have a look." Rehan strode to the door, stopped and flicked his eyebrows up at her.

"You want me to come?"

"You needed the books." In a *don't-be-so-stupid* kind of tone.

Mikandra scrambled up from the table and left Braedon to his calculations.

Rehan walked ahead of her in the cold hall. The wind buffeted the front door and an icy draft came in through the cracks, making the flames on the oil lamps flicker.

Iztho's room was off the hall to the left of the front door, past the coat stand with a collection of furry cloaks, past the rack with the outdoor shoes. There were still wet puddles on the floor from her boots.

Rehan opened the door into the dark room. The faintest glimmer of light came in through the window, a grey-blue glow that indicated that daylight would not be far away. The glass sported an impressive array of ice flowers. A pitcher of water on a table just inside the window had frozen solid.

The hearth, opposite the door, was dark and empty, the bed neat. Two comfortable chairs stood on either side of a low table in front of the hearth.

Rehan made for the bookshelf on the far wall and started pulling books off and going through them. Mikandra looked at a different part of the bookshelf, reading the titles. She had no idea what she was looking for, and all the books in this section related to history, with titles such as *Miran before the Invasion* and *The Highland Trek* and other titles that related to Foundation and first settlement. There were so many of them. She didn't know Iztho was interested in history. All these books must be worth a fortune. However, she could see nothing that looked like an account book and she felt reluctant to start rummaging through her employer's personal belongings.

So instead, she sat on the couch, clamping her hands between her knees. It was so cold in this room, so empty, so tidy. Almost as if he'd planned to leave.

That thought made her shiver.

She thought back to the last time she'd seen him.

Contrary to her expectations, he had asked her to come to his house. When the Andrahar housekeeper let Mikandra in, she had informed her that Iztho wanted to see her in his private room. The woman had not shown any discomfort over that order, but it would normally be considered highly inappropriate for a young unmarried woman to be alone with a much older unmarried man. The housekeeper's name was Gillay, Mikandra remembered. Where was she now?

Once inside the room, Iztho told her to sit down on the couch near the hearth. He poured her tea from the teapot the house-keeper had brought. On the table stood a plate of cakes, but Mikandra felt too nervous to eat anything until he bade her to have one.

They were traditional Mirani cakes, sweet and sticky.

He had said, "You may find it strange that I've asked you to come here."

Away from the hubbub of the office, it struck her even more how deep his voice was.

"A bit," she said, wiping crumbs off her knees. His blue eyes were so penetrating. At least he wasn't looking at her body, which was very modestly hidden, thank you very much, but his gaze still made her nervous. Why was he interested in her?

A roaring fire burnt in the fireplace and the firebricks the family used must have been excellent, because there was no smell. A beautiful metal-plated and engraved lute hung above the mantelpiece, a magnificent instrument with a well-worn leather strap. The metal strings were shiny in the places where his fingers would touch them. There were whispers that he played and sang extremely well.

A maroon dress hung on the wardrobe door. Elaborate embroidery with beads made her think it was the family's wedding dress.

He said, "I want you to understand, away from the office and the glamour and money of our position, that Trading is a harsh business."

"I know," she said. She'd heard Aunt Amandra talk often enough.

He shook his head. "I don't think you really know. You look at your aunt and you think you know, but she is foremost a politician. Even within the Guild, she has used her licence as a way to work herself into the Trader Court and doesn't do much business. She does not live the Trader life. Never has."

Mikandra had known that, but it still felt painful to hear it voiced so clearly and dismissively.

Iztho continued, "Yes, there are the long days, five Exchange jumps per day, the need to be alert at every place and with every customer. The competition, the battles with regulations and the people who think that you are rich and are trying to screw you, and the people who think you are rich and trying to screw them." He said that without flinching. "The things you hear about as non-Trader. There is also a darker side I want you to know about: the politics."

She nodded. She knew about that, too.

"Again, I don't think you really understand. Yes, the Mirani council is full of anti-Trader rhetoric, and has always been. You will see that if you read the accounts of council meetings hundreds of years ago. You should read them. They're very entertaining and worth reading. And before you say that it was a very different time back then, some of those debates look like exact repeats of the meetings as they were held a year ago."

Before the election, with the old council in place, before her aunt and Nemedor Satarin had replaced two old high councillors and Nemedor Satarin, of the Nikala merchant class, had brought a group of merchants into the council.

"With the new council, something fundamental has changed. On the surface, the same conflicts are at play, but because the council now has a group of protectionists, their laws get passed. Nemedor Satarin doesn't want us to bring in products from outside. According to him and his mates, that would be unfair to local growers. It would corrupt Mirani culture and give foreign elements a foothold in the country. With the protectionists,

Nemedor Satarin holds the majority vote in the council. His people are very loyal. They will try to obstruct any law that is backed by Traders. Your aunt is a single voice of moderation. She ran with Nemedor Satarin because she believed he could get Mirani industry going again. They did get industry going, but when the boycotts came in, no one was buying, because no one in Miran has any money anymore, so the projects are idle and bleeding money. Not so long ago, the head of a factory vanished. His family said he was being blamed for the lack of sales. Some of those in industry are so desperate that they ask us to carry the goods illegally. Miran can't keep going like this. We either relax our import laws or we slide into anarchy. The council is stubborn and sticks to its ideals.

"Your aunt has stopped commenting about it when I meet her. I'm not sure where she stands anymore, or whether she will be in a position to help the Mirani Traders when the time comes and the situation implodes. We don't talk about it for fear that she will be accused of betrayal and risk her safety. Or ours. That's how things are in Miran."

Mikandra looked up, realising that she'd drifted off into daydreams. Looked at the empty hearth and the empty hook on the wall above it. The doors of the wardrobe, also empty.

The lute was gone. And so was the wedding dress.

Was that significant? She turned around, but Rehan was no longer in the room. He'd left a pile of books on the table.

8

MIKANDRA WENT into the semidarkness of the hallway. Rehan stood at the hub, his back to her. He leaned with his head against the wall above the unit and thumped both his white-knuckled fists against the wall.

Mikandra thought he might have heard her, but he didn't react, and continued bumping his fists into the wall.

"Um—excuse me?"

He turned around. His eyes met hers. The wild-eyed stare reminded her even more of Leitho, who also went wild when in withdrawal. She held her breath, waiting to be told that evil people were after her and that the end of Miran was near. He would collapse and she would have to treat him and call Eydrina to the house. At the very least, he would be exhausted. And angry with her for revealing his secret.

She stood frozen, waiting for all that to happen.

He breathed out heavily.

The expression in his eyes cleared.

The madness seeped from him. He shook his head and frowned at her. "Did you want to say something? Sorry I—didn't hear."

Mikandra wanted to say *Look if you have a problem with a certain substance, there is something you can use . . .* but there was no way she could say that to this very powerful and high-strung man. She couldn't believe how he'd just *breathed away* his trance. How did he do that? His body would be full of poisons. There was no way he could just ignore the effects and go on as if nothing had happened. Become *normal* again with a mere snap of his fingers.

Still puzzled, she said, "I think . . . I think I may have discovered something that could be relevant."

"You have?" She sensed the relief. "What?"

"The dress is gone," she said.

"What dress?" In a *what are you wasting my time for* tone.

"The wedding dress."

He gave her a stupid look.

She went to the door of the room and pointed. "When I came in here last, it was hanging over there." The door of the wardrobe that was now empty.

"Iztho doesn't have any use for dresses. You probably mistook some other garment for a dress."

"It was the family wedding dress."

"How do you know what it looks like? The family wedding dress hasn't been out of Mother's wardrobe since she got married."

"It's dark red and has small beads embroidered on in flower patterns. There are lines of rose-coloured beads down the sleeves in a netlike pattern."

He frowned and glanced at the wardrobe again.

Mikandra continued, "Earlier on today, I went to see Iztho in your office in town, but it was closed. I thought—when Merchant Ranuddin said there was some big thing going on— that you'd given everyone a day off because Iztho had announced officially that he was getting married."

"Merchant Ranuddin is a gossiping fuckwit who would do well to keep his mouth shut."

In the uncomfortable silence that followed, he met her eyes in a *dare challenge me for saying that* way. His expression softened. "He knows that we say that about him. It's a standing joke." Another silence. "But it's true. He loves spreading 'news' stories that have no base except in his imagination."

"Iztho *told* me that he was getting married." She wasn't going to back down either.

"Take it from me: Iztho isn't getting married. We all wished he did, but none of the candidates Mother brings up pleases him. He isn't getting any younger, and the family needs to think of succession. He needs to marry so we can all have families as well."

It was customary for Trader men to marry very late, after they had established their business, but Iztho was well past that stage. On top of that, most families had long since done away with the order of marriage—where the elder child had to be married before the younger one could. She didn't even know that some families still adhered to that. What was more, it never ceased to amaze her how the Andrahar family could both acknowledge and ignore Calliandra Azthunar and her twin sons, and the fact that Taerzo spent more time at her house than in his legitimate home. The parentage of those twins had to be Miran's worst-kept secret. And here they were pretending to stick to traditional customs and doing the *we-have-no-heirs* dance?

She bit down on the temptation to say something about it. "Iztho said the lady was someone from outside Miran."

Rehan's frown deepened. He strode to the wardrobe. "Take it from me: if Iztho had any plans whatsoever to get married, we'd know about it."

"Like you know for certain that he didn't smuggle menisha fungus into Barresh."

"Don't try to be smart with me."

"You said yourself that you aren't sure what he is doing half the time."

"I said don't be so fucking smart with me." But his brow remained furrowed. He opened the wardrobe's door. Inside hung a couple of uniforms and a spare cloak. He opened the other door and found shelves with shirts and underwear. "You're dreaming. Our family's wedding dress will be in Mother's wardrobe, where it has been all the time."

"Ask her."

He gave her a vicious glare. "I will, when she's up. And she'll tell you that you're dreaming."

"The lute is also gone." She wasn't going to be intimidated by him.

Rehan opened another door in the wardrobe. Trousers and boots. "He never travels without it. Last we heard from him was on a run to Kedras. He would have it with him. He takes it everywhere."

He rummaged amongst towels and shirts. "Nothing here." His voice sounded almost gleeful.

Then he turned to the desk and opened the top drawer. Shut it again with a too-enthusiastic thunk. Slid open the next drawer. He froze.

Frowning, he took out a rectangular flat box, set it on the table and opened the lid. The bed of satin inside was empty.

Neither of them needed explanation. This type of case was only used for wedding armbands.

"What the fuck . . ." He met Mikandra's eyes. The glow of her triumph was sweet.

The box would have held two armbands made of silverwork. She could almost see them on the satin. They were about as wide as her wrist, and each had an overlaid pattern of flowers and swirls in fine filigreed silver. A fine chain linked the two.

Mikandra had never seen these armbands in their unused state, only on her mother's and father's wrists. On a couple's wedding day, the celebrant would take the armbands and snap one shut around an arm of each of the couple. The lock was designed to never open again. Then the celebrant would detach the chain that still linked the two and hang it around the woman's neck, to be given to the couple's oldest son. Mother still wore hers under her clothes.

Rehan pushed the satin aside looking in the corners for clues. But he found nothing and put the box on the desk. Scratched his head.

Braedon poked his head into the room. "Found anything in here?"

Rehan gestured at the box. Braedon picked it up and frowned.

"She seems to think Iztho told her he was getting married," Rehan said, with emphasis on the *seems to think* part.

"He *told* me. Big difference." She glared at Rehan. What was it with this man that he so casually dismissed her all the time?

Braedon snorted. "Married, to whom?"

"Someone from outside Miran," Mikandra said.

"Rubbish. He needs to provide an heir. No one outside Miran can help him do that."

"I don't know his reasons, but that's what he told me." Mikandra was getting angry. This family was just stupid. Didn't any of them talk to each other? Imagine if she treated Liseyo like these brothers treated each other. "I was sitting here, and he was on the other side of the desk. The wedding dress was hanging on the wardrobe door over there. If you don't believe me, that's fine, but don't keep telling me this 'we need an heir' nonsense, because everyone knows it's nonsense, and no doubt Iztho knows that, too. If he didn't tell you he planned to marry, that's his problem, not mine. This box contained armbands. They're gone. If that is not enough proof, then I don't know what is."

Both Rehan and Braedon gaped at her.

After a short silence, Braedon said, "All right. But who is this person supposed to be?"

"He didn't tell me a name."

Rehan said, his voice annoyed, "We've had no contacts outside Miran for potential candidates. Mother would know."

Taerzo also came into the room. "What are you all doing in here?" He frowned and looked from one to the other. "Whoa, did I interrupt something?"

"Do you know anything about Iztho getting married?" Braedon asked.

His eyes widened. "What?"

"Well, there is this." Braedon gestured to the empty box.

Taerzo's mouth fell open. "You have got to be joking. After all this fuss that came with refusing Liandra Satarin? After all these years of fucking us around? Of making us wait, and making an idiot out of me? Of telling me to wait, wait *because Father would have liked it this way?* Traditions, blah, blah, blah. What the fuck . . . I have no fucking words! The fucking arsehole. Fuck it. If this is true, I hate the fucker if I didn't do so already. Why fuck me around for all this time and—"

Rehan said, "Taerzo. We have no proof that it was actually happening."

Taerzo breathed heavily, his face red.

"Hey, man, calm down," Braedon said.

Taerzo glanced at Mikandra. "Sorry." But he balled his fists against his sides. "But just thinking about it makes me angry. Think of all the shit Calliandra has had to put up with for not being married."

Braedon said, "Could he have made a deal with someone without telling Mother?"

Rehan said, "Why would he do that? I mean—if he really got married, that would be a huge deal and a lot of pressure off his shoulders. He'd be one of the most desirable men in Miran and I'm sure Mother gets proposals almost every day."

"Maybe it's someone he fell in love with?" Mikandra said.

The brothers looked at her as if she was mad.

Taerzo snorted. "No way. Have you *ever* seen him with a woman?"

All three brothers shook their heads.

Braedon said, "He's not interested in women. I always thought of him as . . . you know . . ." He shrugged. His cheeks were red.

Rehan shook his head. "He's plain not interested in anyone. And certainly, he's such an arsehole that I can't imagine any woman ever falling in love with him. Ever."

Mikandra thought of Aunt Amandra, who'd had an on-off relationship with the same Trader for many years. Mikandra had seen Ydana Ezmi a few times. He was Coldi, from Hedron, and the leader of their Trader Guild chapter. When he visited Miran, he wore Mirani clothes and lived like a shadow in her house. Mikandra knew him as a kind man, if very formal and reserved. Aunt Amandra said he'd learned to be quiet in Miran. Not like his normal self, she said.

Father spoke of the relationship as scandalous, and his remarks hinted at his sister having discussed the subject of making their relationship legal. Mikandra wasn't sure whatever had happened there, except she didn't think there had been a wedding. These days, no one mentioned him. Mikandra wasn't even sure if he still came to Miran or if the relationship was still going. Maybe a breakup was behind the reason for aunt Amandra to run in the elections. And maybe the need to remain secretive and the resistance from her family had broken the relationship.

Who was to say that Iztho couldn't have developed a similar relationship? As the one expected to provide the family's heir, it would be doubly devastating.

Then another thought: if Iztho had fallen in love with an "unapproved" woman, what was to say that he hadn't simply left his brothers, taken some money and eloped with her?

There was a small sound in the hall and the family's housekeeper, Gillay, came into the doorway, looking into the room. "This is a very strange time for you all to be standing here." She was middle-aged, with a round face, large bosom and rounded hips straining against the apron she wore over her dress.

When no one reacted to her words, she continued, "Breakfast is ready."

There were nods all around.

Breakfast was a good idea.

9

M IKANDRA FOLLOWED the brothers into the dining room, where Gillay hastily put an extra plate on the table without batting an eyelid or questioning her presence.

She ladled soup from the terrine in the middle of the table and placed plates with rolls of fish bread next to each soup plate.

The soup smelled heavenly. It was thick and rich and creamy. The bread radiated warmth and spread a wonderful aroma through the room. When Mikandra broke a piece off, steam rose from it. Rosep made fish bread, but it was nothing like this.

No one said anything while they ate. Braedon's face was pale. Taerzo's hair was all mussed up from sleeping on the couch. Gillay came back with tea, poured out cups and left again with a tray of soup and a steaming cup of tea. "I'll bring this to the mistress."

She left in the direction of the living room. A moment later came the sound of voices. Then the click of a door.

It was easy to forget that there was another person still in the house. Mikandra didn't know the family matriarch Isandra very well and only remembered the talk about when she had turned her back on a rival Trader when he had come to offer his condolences at her husband's funeral. "You were not his friend in life and you shall not pretend to be his friend in death," she was rumoured to have said.

"So," Rehan said after a while. "There is no money that we can trace easily. I don't think there is any point in keeping going through these accounts."

Taerzo said, "Could we borrow for a short time?"

"I have no idea who could lend us as much as we need."

Braedon nodded, and fell into silence again.

After a bit longer Rehan said, "We have to make a plan. We try to look for money for a few more days, then if we don't find enough, we try scouting for a loan. A couple of loans, if necessary."

"Could we bring forward the court case?" Taerzo asked.

"I don't know that bringing it forward would go in our favour, even if we could. We may need that long to give ourselves the best chance."

Taerzo nodded.

"We could talk to the Hedron Mines," Braedon said. "Ask them to extend their deadline."

"Hmm, they tend to be strict with their payments," Rehan said. "I don't hold out much hope there. Unless you go in person. Would you do that?"

Taerzo shrugged. "I could, but every time I go there, I feel they hate our guts already, and that's without me begging for money." Then he folded his hands under the table and muttered, "Oh, man."

"We need someone to prepare the court case," Rehan continued. "Braedon?"

"Yeah, I'll do that."

"Get all the Exchange records for the days of the supposed crime. Take it to be investigated independently. Find a Lawkeeper who is not going to screw us over. Find someone at the Guild."

Braedon nodded.

"Meanwhile, I'm going to comb everything in the office, and grill the accountant to see if I can find out what has happened to Iztho and the money."

They all nodded.

Mikandra wanted to shout, *What about me?* but at that moment, there was a knock on the front door, and everyone went silent, giving each other *Are you expecting someone?* looks. Gillay went to open the door. Her voice sounded in the hall, and a male voice replied.

Mikandra's heart jumped. That was sure to be her father. He might have said that she was no longer welcome in the house and that he'd cut her off from her inheritance, but nothing her father did was ever simple. He wouldn't want something like this to "ruin his reputation", so no matter what he said, he would try to find an "acceptable" solution.

Gillay poked her head into the dining room. "Sorry, Master Rehan, but there is someone at the door to speak to all of you. Do I let him in?"

Rehan frowned.

Mikandra's heart thudded.

"It's urgent, he says. From the council."

"All right."

Gillay left. Braedon mouthed, *The Council?* pretty much voicing what Mikandra felt. Not her father then?

There were voices in the hallway. A man's voice which didn't sound like her father.

The door opened and into the room came no other than High Councillor Nemedor Satarin, his cheeks red from the cold. "Good morning all." His voice sounded upbeat. "I hope I'm not disturbing you at this early hour."

The brothers returned greetings, all curt and professional. Emotionless. Traders did that game very well in public, but she now knew Rehan well enough to almost hear his voice saying *what the fuck. . . ?*

Nemedor Satarin stopped a few paces inside the door. "Mind if I join you?"

Rehan gestured to the empty chair next to Mikandra.

Nemedor Satarin pulled out the chair and sat down. Nikala were much less tall than Endri, and Nemedor Satarin was not a tall Nikala man. Even when seated, he was shorter than her. Some people would call him a midget, but never to his sharp-nosed face.

He already wore his council uniform at this early hour. Diamond drops of molten snow twinkled in his hair, which was too short-cropped to show that it was curly.

He glanced at Mikandra and raised one eyebrow. His dark blue eyes met hers. Mikandra had never spoken to him or seen him close up, but Father had told her that the man's memory for people was legendary. If he didn't know who she was before coming into this room, he would now.

A silence lingered while Gillay poured tea for him. Rehan's face was blank and emotionless. Braedon's expression was downright suspicious.

"I have come to make a proposition on behalf of the council," Nemedor Satarin said after Gillay had left the room.

"From the council or from you?" Rehan wanted to know.

"The council."

Rehan nodded. Braedon leaned his hands on the table at the wrists, in a position as if he might grab something any moment. Taerzo leaned back in his chair, his arms crossed over his chest.

Nemedor Satarin continued, "I understand that it's hard for you to discuss these matters, but it has come to my attention that you may be in a position of difficulty."

"Are we?" Rehan said, his voice and face unemotional. Oh yes, addicts did that blank look very well.

"Well, the rumour goes that you are, so I thought I'd come to check on you, because the council cares about Mirani businesses."

Rehan said, "Thank you, but we're just fine."

Mikandra's thought was: how did the council know this? Trader communication was meant to be private.

Nemedor Satarin smiled. "Well, that's a relief then, but if, by any chance, there was a problem—"

At the time Braedon said, "We're fine," Taerzo said, "Well, it depends who's offering."

The two brothers glared at each other and were silent again.

Mikandra wanted to shout *He's playing you!*

A small smile crossed Nemedor Satarin's lips.

"We at the council care about our Mirani Trading families, the employers of the city and indeed our entire nation. We don't want any of our businesses to go under."

"Naturally," Rehan said, oh so cool.

"It is also in our interest that employers can keep doing their business, and if there are problems, the council is there to help."

"Certainly," Rehan said again.

After a short silence Taerzo asked, "What form, exactly, would this help take?"

"Assistance. With permits, approvals. Finance." He met Mikandra's eyes briefly, still puzzled, and looked away again. "Would you be interested?"

"Depends," Braedon said.

Mikandra wanted to shout *don't*. Iztho had warned her about him.

Taerzo said, "Just how much money are we talking about?"

"Enough to see you through whatever problem has occurred." He smiled. "Come and see me in my office."

He rose and put a piece of paper on the table. "Well, I must go now. That's all I wanted to say for now. I don't need a reply. I'll leave this here so you can think it over."

He nodded, opened the door and went into the hall where he put on his boots, cloak and left.

As soon as the door closed behind him, Rehan picked up the paper and read it.

"Fuck."

"What is it, brother?"

"Loan for up to two hundred and fifty thousand credits."

Taerzo laughed aloud. "All our problems are solved. The council lends us the money, we pay it back as soon as we can after our accounts are unfrozen."

"I don't know if it's a good idea to accept this loan . . ." Mikandra began.

Taerzo looked at her. "What do you mean?"

"Well." Mikandra licked her lips. "When I came here to sign my application, Iztho warned me about Nemedor Satarin. He said he's undermining the Trader Guild and warned me not to get involved with him."

Rehan said, "Is this another one of your mysterious recollections?"

"I swear he told me!" Mikandra felt the ground slide from under her. Tears pricked in her eyes. Iztho's warning had been very strong.

"Knock off tearing into her, brother," Braedon said.

Rehan glared at him. "If she wants to be one of us, I want her to handle the heat. No kid gloves. If Iztho thought she has what it takes, I want her to show us, and I'm not going to hold back or pander to any of that no fucking swearing in front of women nonsense."

His eyes met her squarely, as if issuing a challenge.

"You can swear in front of me all you like. There is no bullying tactic that my father hasn't already tried on me. None of them worked very well. Iztho warned me. I'm passing his warning on to you. At least you can't blame me for not telling you."

Rehan glared at her.

Leitho had his hallucinations. Rehan wanted word fights. Bring it on.

He blew a forceful breath from his nostrils and crossed his arms over his chest.

"Iztho hates Nemedor Satarin," Braedon said in a milder voice for Mikandra's benefit. "It seems personal more than anything. I don't know exactly why or how they had a run-in in Barresh, but the hatred stems from there. The man is an army general who has gone into politics. Iztho is . . ." He spread his hands. ". . . Iztho. Different. Needing space. He doesn't promise anything. He doesn't tell people where he's going. Nemedor Satarin is hard-line, unforgiving and ambitious. He doesn't suffer fools or people who change their minds. They're not characters that will ever be friends. We don't agree with a lot of things Nemedor Satarin does, but one thing he does do well, and that is to help locals."

Mikandra said, "If Nemedor Satarin had a run-in with Iztho in Barresh, why would he offer the Andrahar Traders a substantial loan?"

"He said it was the council's money," Taerzo said.

"How is council money different from personal money? They both smell of politics."

"The council has an official policy to help locals."

"Then why does he come here in person out of office hours? I don't trust that man. His version of cleaning up Miran's streets involves letting the homeless die and be eaten by maramarang. He won't spend money giving the poor houses, but he'll lend you this much money? What other conclusion can you draw but that he has a hidden motive?"

"Whoa," Taerzo said. "That's putting it a bit strong."

"I happen to agree with her." Rehan didn't meet her eyes. "I also agree that we may not have another option. I'd be a lot happier if we could arrange our own solution." He looked at Taerzo. "Do go and ask if we can defer the payment to the Hedron Mines."

Taerzo's expression was incredulous. "What? This is the best offer we get and you want to turn it down? This is a council offer, not from him personally."

"I don't know yet," Rehan said. "I don't want to offend him. He's a powerful man, but I wish to hell I knew what he wants from us, and until I find that out, I think it pays to stay the fuck away from any deals he wants to offer."

"Then what do you suggest we do?" Taerzo's voice trembled with anger. "I need money. I need to get back to work. I have a family to feed."

"We all do, but none of us will be able to work until the court case anyway." Rehan was definitely annoyed now.

"Oh man." Taerzo put his head in his hands.

A moment of silence passed.

There was a noise elsewhere in the house and soft shuffling footsteps. A thin figure came to the doorway.

It had been a while since Mikandra had last seen the Andrahar family matriarch. She cut an imposing figure even in her old age, with her back straight and her silver hair falling over her shoulders. She wore several layers of fur wrapped tightly about her shoulders.

Her sharp gaze went around the room and rested on Rehan.

"Is there anything going on? I thought I heard Nemedor Satarin's voice."

"You did."

"What by all of the ancestors was *he* doing in here?" Sharp eyes took in her three sons and came to a rest on Mikandra. There was no surprise in her expression.

"Well, um . . ." The change in Rehan was incredible. "There has been a problem."

She raised her eyebrows and he continued, "Apparently someone has reported Iztho for smuggling menisha into Barresh."

"Rubbish," she said.

"Yes, that's what I said, too, but we'll need to prove it, and the court has suspended our licence until that time." He let a small silence lapse. "And the Hedron account is due. Nemedor Satarin offered us a loan."

"You will accept money from that man over my dead body."

"My thought, too, Mother, but we may not have a choice—"

"You don't have a choice? What are you? Pambies? Did Father and I teach you nothing?"

"We don't *have* any money to pay them."

"Then you *make* money."

"We're not allowed to work."

"But you are allowed to sell things, right?"

Taerzo's expression changed to one of horror. "Surely, you don't mean . . ."

"In lean times, tighten your belt. That's what Father and I always did, and if you think we've been this well-off all our lives, think again. Why do I have such spoilt pambies for sons?"

She breathed out through flaring nostrils.

"Where is Iztho?"

"I don't know. I can't raise him on the system," Rehan said. "Either he has turned off his beacon or he's ignoring my calls." He left the third option unspoken.

"Keep trying. He's bound to send some form of communication." She seemed very cool for someone whose son was missing. "As for the money, sell one of the aircraft. Sell two. Sell the office. We do not accept charity from the council, especially not that man. If you want a loan, get it only from someone who you have to go and beg for it, not someone who offers, because that person has other motives. That's all I have to say about it." She turned to go.

"Mother," Braedon said.

She turned around, annoyance on her face.

"Did you know anything about Iztho getting married?"

Her face twitched. Her eyes met Mikandra's, the expression in them sharp. "How many times do I have to tell you that I do not care about gossip? We need to pay our debts and get the court off our backs. Then we can worry about marriage." She looked at Mikandra again, but there was no emotion, or even recognition in her expression. "Ancestors know he's fussy enough. One would be forgiven for thinking that he wasn't interested at all."

She turned and was gone. Her shuffling footsteps disappeared in the hall, into the living room to the other side of the house.

"Sell the aircraft," Taerzo muttered. "I sure as hell am not selling mine. If I need to move the family—"

"You do this victim stuff very well, brother," Rehan said.

"What the fuck is that supposed to mean?"

"I mean who the fuck couldn't keep his dick to himself in the first place? Whose fault is this family of yours?"

"Those boys are our heirs."

"Yes, for the time being. And now stop asking for special considerations because of them. We all suffer equally." Rehan rose. "Mother is right and I don't know why I didn't see it before." He dug in his pocket and threw a bundle of access keys onto the table.

Mikandra looked into his face. The expression of pain she saw there made her eyes prick. He breathed out through flaring nostrils.

Braedon said, softly, "Are you sure?"

"Sure. Someone needs to get us out of this fucking mess."

Neither Braedon nor Taerzo touched the keys on the table.

Rehan continued, "Sell it, because we're getting nowhere. Wherever the money has gone, the trail is covered up well. I suggest that you try to get some sleep. The accounts will still be a mess tomorrow morning."

Braedon said, "But if you sell, you can't work—"

"Just take fucking the keys out of my sight, before I change my mind."

Braedon finally took the keys and slid them in his pocket. "If that's what you want."

"I still think we should accept the council's offer," Taerzo said.

"And I think you're a fucking idiot. Now go to bed before I strangle you. No one will be talking to Nemedor Satarin or the council on our behalf, is that clear?"

A tense silence followed.

Braedon nodded. "I think you might be right. Still, brother, if I think of how hard you worked to be able to afford that thing—"

"It's getting old. I could use a new one." But the pain showed in his face. He met Mikandra's eyes. "If you want to be successful, you have to make sacrifices."

This statement was followed by another pointed silence.

Taerzo rose, his mouth twitching. "I'm going to take the boys to school." He left.

Braedon rose, too, and Mikandra followed him, feeling lost and scared. Rehan went to the hall and took his cloak off the stand.

Braedon said, "Where are you going, brother? The bedrooms are that way."

"I'm going to chase the accountant. I think there is more to his story."

"Go to bed. Do you really think you'll get a reply out of him by waking him up early?"

"The fuck with the time. He's screwed us around and I want to know why. I'm going to go to the office and bring all his books here so he can't get his grubby hands on them. Then I'll go through everything, and I'll wring his neck for every mistake I find. When I come back, I'll make a budget for how much we need and what we'll sell to cover it."

He met Mikandra's eyes, and she asked the question that had

bothered her since Nemedor Satarin came in. "How do you think Nemedor Satarin knew about the suspended licence? Isn't Trader Guild correspondence meant to be private?"

Rehan said, "This is Miran, people talk all the time. In fact, no one in this damn town can keep their fucking mouths shut."

"Who would have told him?"

"Any of his friends in the Guild. Antho Tussamar and his cronies—and *they* are our competitors who would like to see us bound by some sort of deal."

He turned on his heel and strode through the hall. A blast of freezing wind came in when he opened the door and stopped again when he slammed it shut.

Braedon sighed and looked at Mikandra. He looked pale, sad, wrung out. "It's probably best if you go home."

But she couldn't go home. Her father would kill her. "What time do you want me to come back?"

Braedon shrugged. "I don't know. I don't know if there is any point—We'll have to wait until the court case."

Please, no. That was too long. "I can come back and keep checking the books." *Please.*

"I think it's settled. I don't think there is any point in looking for that missing money. It's going to take too much time." His mouth twitched. "I'm sorry about this. But at the moment, we are in so much of a mess that I can't make any promises. I'll try to do my best to honour Iztho's promise to train you, but if it all falls to pieces . . ." He shrugged. "The case may take a long time. Court cases often do. If it drags out and we have to suspend business operations for longer, we might not have money to train you. We may have to spend it on lawyers instead."

Mikandra filled with panic. She wanted to scream *I'm homeless. I defied my father so that I could be here and he's not going to let me back into the house* but that made a poor argument and was her own choice—a poor one as it turned out. She wanted to argue *But Iztho trusted me. He said I had courage,* but that would sound like whingeing, especially in the light of what Rehan had just done. In fact, she was deeply impressed with his action. Never mind the swearing. He took no nonsense and was prepared to go back to basics to solve his problems.

And she should take her inspiration from his actions. She was not a *pamby*. She said, "No matter what has happened, I really want to take up this apprenticeship."

"I understand."

"I don't know that you really understand." She hesitated and then said, "This acceptance is my only way out of misery. Would you marry Geonan Takumar?"

The brief look of horror on his face was worth more than any words. "Look, I promise I'll do my best. That's all I can offer right now." He seemed genuinely sad.

Mikandra nodded. There was nothing more left to be said. There were not going to be any heroic deeds for her.

She left the house and trudged through the snow-covered yard, through the gate and into the street. Small flurries of snow drifted from the uniform grey sky, whipped up by the wind which was cold enough to come straight from the highlands. Passing people hid their faces in the upturned collars of their cloaks.

What now? She was too tired to go to the hospital. She had already given her acceptance to the Guild. She couldn't possibly go home to face Father's anger. If she went to Aunt Amandra's house, her father would be told. Eydrina would be angry with her.

There was no one in the city whom she trusted and who didn't have a connection with her family or the hospital. And the only person who had shown any confidence in her ability to sort things out for herself had gone missing.

She believed Iztho about his marriage and the more she thought about it, the more she became convinced that he had eloped.

With all the pressure on him to get married, he might have snapped. He might have had a lover for quite some time and had been delaying an official wedding with some approved Mirani girl. He might have become complacent about rules and made a mistake about the imports.

So, while the brothers sorted out the business side of things, how about she tried to find him, since none of them seemed to be overly concerned with his wellbeing.

If he had eloped, it would clearly be with this woman, and it might help her to find out who she was and where she was from. If Rehan was willing to sacrifice something he had spent years working for, surely she could spend whatever savings she had in trying to find the man who had offered to be her tutor.

It might not be easy, but she did have an idea for a starting point. And for that, she would use her own connections.

10

T HE ANDRAHAR accountant's wife, Zimana Estredin, was the librarian for the theatrical society, and she happened to be a woman who was widely known as a terrible gossip. Since Rehan had sent the husband to the Andrahar office, the wife would be at home alone. A perfect time to go for an innocent chat.

The Estredin family lived in the merchant quarter above a bakery, in a dark but comfortable apartment on the third floor of a block that was four floors high. These buildings were very old, made from local dark granite, rather than the lighter sandstone brought in from Bendara, with high ceilings and elegantly carved door frames. Mikandra's footsteps echoed in the stairwell with its well-worn tiles. A man dressed in a heavy merchant robe came the other way.

"Good morning, lady."

Mikandra nodded, bending her head and hoping that he wouldn't recognise her. She stood out with her typical Endri cloak, and her silver curtain of long hair—yes, it's loose, Mother, no matter how annoying that was. Being a noble woman was not about comfort.

She reached the apartment, knocked and Zimana opened the door a fraction. Her eyes were wide—frightened about something? Then her expression cleared and she opened the door further. "Mikandra! Not working today?"

She was a middle-aged Nikala woman, short with big hips, wearing an apron over a thick felt dress.

"I'm on my way to the hospital. I'm working a late shift," Mikandra lied, and wondered why the wary face when she opened the door.

"Come inside where it's warm. The snow is so early this year."

Mikandra stepped into the hall. Zimana shut the door behind her. The entire wall on the right-hand side of the hallway was one bookshelf full of folders. When she was little, Mikandra had been mesmerised by all those books, until she found out that they were all texts of plays.

"What can I do for you?"

"Mother asked me to pick up the text of a couple of plays she's been considering for the company when *The Invasion* is done."

Zimana frowned. "Oh? I don't know anything about that." She looked worried. "Did she tell you what these plays were called?" She turned to the shelves.

"No, I'm sorry. She just asked me to drop past before or after work because you'd have it ready for her."

"I must be getting old. It's completely slipped my mind. How stupid of me."

Mikandra cringed inside. She didn't mean to make the woman feel horrible or guilty. "No, forget about it. I think I must have misheard what she said. Sorry to disturb you." Mikandra turned to the door.

"I'm sorry I couldn't help you. Do you have time for tea?"

"I've really got to rush to the hospital. By the way, I saw your husband this morning. He was in an awful hurry. He didn't look very well. Is everything all right?"

Zimana's cheerful demeanour slid from her. She sighed and stared into the distance before meeting Mikandra's eyes. "To be honest with you, no. He had a bad day with his employers yesterday. I'm afraid he's going to lose his job."

"That's terrible. What happened—oh, I'm sorry I probably shouldn't ask. It's none of my business."

Zimana sighed again and shook her head. "It's all right. The theatre people are all friends, right?"

"Please, don't tell me anything you don't want to share."

She sighed. "Everyone will know very soon anyway, if they don't already. You do know that my husband works for the Andrahar Traders?"

Mikandra nodded. "Must be a pretty demanding job. I hear they can be really rude." She smiled inside. *I'll get back at you, Rehan Andrahar.*

"Yeah, it's not a good idea to be around if any of them are angry. You must also have heard the gossip about them."

"I'm not sure that I have." She smiled as innocently as she could. "I've been pretty busy. Unless you're talking about the rumour that Iztho is getting married to a woman from outside Miran?"

"Oh no, that's not gossip. That one is general knowledge."

"Is it? I only heard a vague rumour."

"Oh no, it's definitely true."

"Who is she and where is she from?"

"Barresh. Her name, apparently, is Anmi Kirilen Dinzo."

Yes! Mikandra's heart jumped with the joy of success. This was exactly what she needed to know. Let's see what else she could find out. "That doesn't sound like a Barresh name at all. Don't they usually have double names, personal name, family name, like in Miran?" Their names were usually three syllables each, and their last names ended in -u.

"I honestly don't know any more about it, but it's the truth as sure as I stand here."

"How did you find out?"

"The neighbour is a silversmith. He did the armbands."

The empty box in Iztho's room. That part at least checked out. "Is there a date set?"

"Not that I've heard. But I expect him to announce it soon."

No, Iztho had ordered the armbands made in Miran and had taken them to be married in Barresh, foregoing the huge traditional ceremony that a marriage of that level would attract in Miran. It was exactly as she had thought.

"Anyway, that's not what my husband's trouble is about. Some sort of thing has blown up about their licence, and my husband has been caught up in all of this, because there is money missing from accounts. He was called to their house and Rehan outright threatened him."

That was not how Mikandra remembered the conversation. "That's terrible. Maybe he should look for other work."

"That's what I told him, but no, they won't even sack him until the missing money has been found."

"That sounds fair enough."

"But Trimon had nothing to do with it."

"Does he know what happened? He can just say his bit and be done with it. They can't make him stay."

"It's not that simple at all. You know, the brothers have been fighting for years. It's Iztho and the old lady against the rest of them. Ever since that mess in Barresh, she's been protecting him. He can do no wrong with her, but his heart isn't in the business, a fool can see that. But she adores him, and she vetoes a lot of the other brothers' decisions. Rehan has been trying to get control of the accounts for ages. Now Iztho has gone and hidden money and my husband is getting the blame. He never worked specifically for any of the brothers. He was just trying to steer his way between the conflicts. Hope you'll never find out what happens if you get yourself on the wrong side of a powerful man." Her eyes glittered. "When they start spreading the reputation that my husband is not trustworthy, he'll never find work again. He did not mess up the accounts, honest." She buried her face in her hands and cried. "What will we do to survive?"

"If your husband has done nothing wrong, then he has nothing to fear." She cringed inside as she said that. Having seen the accounts, the husband had every reason to be extremely worried.

Zimana sniffed and wiped her eyes with her apron. "Anyway, I'm sorry to bother you with my troubles. I know you're a nice girl and believe that truth and honesty rule, and I wish I could share your optimism. I fear the brothers will wring him dry and throw him on the street, just for doing his job. Be glad you're with a nice, happy and stable family."

Those words still haunted Mikandra while going down the stairs and into the street.

A *stable family*. Fancy that. Was there any family in the Endri nobility that was stable? Wherever she looked, there was mess behind a thin veneer of civility. Her own family, the Andrahars, Aunt Amandra and her forbidden lover. Antho Tussamar had to resort to training his nephews as heirs because neither of his sons had children. Calliandra Azthunar was an only child and the sole survivor from her branch of the family. She owned the house and she had probably already put the ownership in the name of her sons in case the Andrahar family exploded and Taerzo had nowhere to go. And that wasn't even considering the many families who had members who were crazy and addicted, or crazy because they were addicted. None of them were stable.

And we let these people govern the nation?

A steady drift of powderlike snow blew from the sky. It heaped in mounds on the lee side of walls. It was like a coarse mist and softened outlines of buildings and shrouded the council buildings on the opposite side of the main square in a white haze. The Foundation monument stood deserted, its five fingers pointing up at the sky. The Andrahar office was still closed, and while she walked past, a bored shop attendant in Merchant Ranuddin's empty shop watched her. Eventually, the trouble in the Endri families would hit Merchant Ranuddin, too, when he no longer had customers for his overpriced clothes.

The Miran Exchange, where Mikandra needed to go for the next step of her plan, was to the left of the square, downhill from the Trader Guild headquarters. It was an ugly square building, whose centuries-old halls and stairwells echoed with voices of the past. The draught that descended the stairs smelled of wet stone, from meltwater dripping off people's cloaks. In places, the stone steps were cold enough for the water to freeze over.

The upstairs hall buzzed with many voices. People lined up

for the counter at the far end. A huge display listed available flights out of Miran and their status. Several, including this afternoon's flight to Barresh, had been marked *full*.

Well, drat, that was annoying. Now what was she going to do tonight? She'd hoped to sleep on the flight so that she didn't have to get an expensive room in one of the guesthouses with added risk that her father would find her there. Maybe she could pay for a priority seat and still leave tonight.

But the longer she stood in the shuffling line, the more she realised that the Exchange was unusually busy. People even lined up for the communication booths, where people who had no access to a private hub could send messages or talk to their friends or relatives, or business partners, in other towns or offworld.

The employees at the counter looked flustered and harassed. People argued.

Slowly, the line progressed until it was her turn.

"Lady, can I help you?"

"How much is a priority seat on this afternoon's shuttle to Barresh?"

"The shuttle?" His expression was one of surprise. Endri did not usually travel on the shuttles. "Sorry, all seats for today booked out, even the priority ones. Next available flight is tomorrow morning, but I only have regular seats available on that one."

"I'll take it." She'd just have to hang around somewhere tonight.

While he checked her pass and entered details, she said, "I've never seen it this busy here. Is there anything special going on?"

He gave her a strange look of the are-you-serious kind, and the merchants behind her, who had been talking loudly, fell quiet. In the uneasy silence, the clicking of the machine that issued the ticket sounded loud.

"No, nothing special," the man said. He handed her the ticket chip, which Mikandra put in her pocket.

"Have a nice trip, lady."

Mikandra traversed the hall back to the stairs while feeling the weight of a thousand gazes on her back. All those people in

the hall were Nikala. Merchants mostly, but also other
commoners in administrative positions. People from Miran's
middle class.

Clearly, something had happened that made all these people
want to leave, like an unfavourable law passed by the council.
But no one was going to tell her because she was Endri, and the
High Councillor's niece to boot, and considered to be part of the
problem. Or something like that.

The burst of energy she had felt earlier in the morning was
fading fast. And drat, the snow was getting worse. If this kept
up, all flights would be cancelled and she wouldn't even be able
to leave tomorrow morning. If that happened, with this many
delayed passengers, who knew when she could finally leave?
She had considered waiting overnight in the airport waiting hall,
but didn't want to be stuck there for days.

She stopped under the building's porch staring at the white
drift. Already the council buildings were barely visible. A couple
of people ploughed through a snow mound in front of the Trader
Guild headquarters.

The Trader Guild, of which she was now officially a member.

The Trader pledge went,

I dedicate my life to the Trader Guild.

I will recognise the Guild's authority above all others.

*I will respect and obey the Trader Laws at all times, and report on
those who break them.*

*I will honour and respect my fellow Traders, regardless of their race
or origin.*

I will accept them and their families as my kinsfolk.

*I pledge unswerving loyalty to the Trader Guild and in return,
expect unswerving loyalty of the Guild to me.*

The loyalty of Traders to each other above their loyalty to
their nation of origin was always a sore point with the Mirani
council. But, having accepted her position, she could now draw
on that loyalty. She hated asking for help, but the only thing she
wanted from the Mirani chapter of the Guild was a place to sleep
for the night.

11

THE STEADY STREAM of people coming in and out of the Trader Guild building consisted mostly of Nikala merchant men from well-off families or their employees in uniforms that identified the family they worked for. The ground floor hall was full of talking and yelling merchants, and the poor Guild employees behind the counter were feverishly entering bids into the system, which then made it onto the large screen at the back of the room.

Mikandra went up the stairs to the Guild foyer. This time there was a queue of couriers and other people. Some of them were young men from Trading families, who were probably here to accept their offers. They were chatting and laughing, in that loud and entitled air that Trader's sons did so well. One or two cast strange looks at her. She was the only woman in the line.

The Guild employee who had served her yesterday still worked behind the counter, or more likely he had gone home and was now back. It was hard to tell. The office would adhere to Trader time, which was the same as Kedras time, and Kedras had a much shorter day than Ceren, all of which meant that she had no idea how long the shifts were.

Slowly, the queue grew shorter. A group of Trader sons went to the counter and came back with the same satchel she had been given. They sat on the seats in the hall, occasionally yelling something to other Trader sons behind Mikandra in the queue. The merchant in front of Mikandra went to pay for his purchases. He moved away and it was her turn.

The Guild employee raised his eyebrows. "Weren't you just here yesterday? I've sent your acceptance. You should hear from headquarters soon."

The young men waiting on the seats looked around and frowned at her. Mikandra wished they'd mind their own business.

Her cheeks burned. "I was wondering if you could help me." She spoke as softly as she could. "I had . . . a disagreement with my father. He wants me to refuse the position and I'm not welcome home until I give up my position, but I'm not going to. Now I can't go home. Is there somewhere . . . I can stay for tonight?"

He chuckled. "Not impressed, is he?"

It had gone very quiet in the hall.

Mikandra shook her head and looked down. This was the most embarrassing thing she'd ever done. Asking for help was not the way she liked to live. She saw her father's stern face before her, and heard the words he often repeated. *We Endri provide for the common people. That has been our task as written into the Foundation treaty.* She hadn't earned the privilege of Trader Guild protection. Asking for help one day after acceptance was distasteful.

Someone in the room was muttering something about the Andrahar brothers.

"Isn't it your sponsor's task to look after you?" the man asked.

"He's not here. The family has a lot of problems."

"You can say that again."

Another heavy silence. Maybe he expected her to gossip.

"Please? I've been accepted. The pledge says *all Traders.* Don't people say *your bond with the Guild will be stronger than that with your immediate family?*"

He blew out a breath. "For a little while then."

"Only for one night."

"Sure, but if your family remains unaccommodating, you will

have to call on the other Andrahar brothers to support you. Come."

He opened the door behind him, the one with the sign that said *Traders only beyond this point* and let her into that inner sanctum. This was not how she had expected to enter this place for the first time.

Mikandra had only ever seen pictures of the room beyond: high ceilinged, with arches and elaborate carved stone flowers. Bookshelves lined the outer walls, stacked from top to bottom with heavy tomes. The floor was filled with an assortment of chairs and couches surrounding antique tables. Wooden tables, too. Only the rich could afford to have wooden furniture imported from Bendara. The carpet was soft underfoot. A row of three lead glass windows looked out over the central square, where people battled across the open space against the snow drift in a landscape of whites and greys.

Three Traders sat talking around a table by the blazing fire. They fell quiet, frowning at her.

One of the men was Antho Tussamar, the head of the Mirani chapter of the Guild. He sat with his back to the window, his enormous body jammed in an armchair and spilling over the armrests. As she passed, his watery eyes met hers. He would know what she was doing here. She had no doubt that, as traditionalist, he'd have something to say about it, too.

With him were the identical Bisumar twins who, despite their family name, were only marginally related to her. She remembered the boys being at her school when she first came. Arrogant, bullying boys who confirmed every bad thing people always said about Trading families. They'd left when Mikandra went to her second year and Antho Tussamar was probably their mentor. Which probably pegged them as conservative as well.

Their gazes were questioning. One of them signalled to the employee who had led Mikandra into the room, and the man responded with a hand gesture. Mikandra didn't know the Trader sign language well enough to make out what was being communicated. She didn't like the way one of the twins looked at her.

The employee led her through the room into a corridor with

similar soft carpet and traditional oil lights on elaborate sconces on the wall. They passed a small kitchen where the cook stood at a central table mixing something in a bowl. A mouth-watering smell of fresh bread spread out from the kitchen.

The rest of the corridor had doors at regular intervals, each with a number on a neat sign affixed on the wall next to the door, and underneath a narrow but deep recess in the wall that, at a couple of the rooms, held a message satchel. One of the doors stood open, revealing a small room with a couch and a desk and two chairs. A few bags lay on the floor.

The man opened a door to the left into a similar room, this one neat and unused. "You can stay in here, just until you have something else sorted out."

"Thank you." Mikandra didn't dare to ask about any time limits or cost. She also realised that she might have her apprentice uniform, but if she wanted to go to Barresh inobtrusively, it was probably not a good idea to wear it. Nor would it be a good idea to draw so much attention to herself on the shuttle. She had no spare regular clothes and no money. Those things were all in her room at home.

He continued, "These rooms are for visiting Traders. We don't have a great number of those at the moment." The statement was heavy with meaning. "Visitors use these rooms for overnight stays. They're not really for living in long term."

"I understand."

"The cupboard door folds out into a bed. There are sheets and blankets on the top shelf. The bathroom is at the end of the hall. You'll find towels and soap there. Make sure that you lock the door to the change cubicle. We do not have separate sections for women. You'll have to get used to that. Everything at Kedras is mixed gender."

"I know. Thank you. Could I arrange for a messenger to go and pick up some things for me? It's not far—only in the city."

"Sure, I'll send one of the boys along."

"Can I also order anything to eat?" The smell of cooking made her feel dizzy.

"I'll put your order through to the cook." He took out a

reader and tapped with his index finger. "I'll take your licence number for the courier and the food—"

"I'd like to pay for it, if I can."

"No, sorry, charge only. Everything you use here is charged to your account at the end of each month."

She could do nothing except watch him punch 1101. "Leave your message and the address in the slot outside the door. Someone will come and pick it up. The food will be served in the common room."

Drat. So here was Rehan, giving up his precious aircraft so the family could pay bills and she wasn't even allowed to pay for her food? What sort of impression would that make?

The image of his haunted face as he dropped the keys on the table would not leave her alone. If she was Taerzo, she would now be deeply ashamed of herself.

Mikandra dumped her cloak on the couch in the room. In the drawer of the desk, she found a folder with sheets of thick paper and there were pens in a stand which consisted of a block of polished marble with holes that fitted the pens.

Everything in this place breathed old-fashioned quality.

She sat down and wrote a couple of notes. One for Rosep, instructing him to go into her room and send by return courier her hunting clothes, spare underwear and a few other things, including her account codes of her private savings.

One to her parents, explaining that she held them no ill will, but that she had made her decision.

The one to Liseyo was hardest to write. What could she say to the sister she loved dearly, who she didn't want to leave alone, and who she wanted to protect? Everything sounded horribly trite, including the last sentence *I'll be back to look after you and to take you on adventures.*

Finally, she folded all her notes, put her family name on them and stuck them in the slot next to the door.

Then she made her way back through the corridor. The cook glanced sideways as she passed, and nodded a polite greeting. "Are you ready for your meal now?"

"Yes, thank you."

"I'll bring it out soon."

She entered the common room, where Antho Tussamar still sat with the twins. The men fell silent while she sat down at a table in the corner furthest from the hearth.

After a while of sitting in silence, one of the twins rose. "Anyway, better go back to work for a bit."

His brother muttered agreement and the two left the room one after the other.

They met the cook at the door, coming the other way with a tray which he carried over to Mikandra's table. "Here you are, lady."

"Thank you."

He bowed and left.

Mikandra lifted the lid off the tray. There was a bowl of soup underneath, bread and steamed fish, beans and herb sauce. The smell was heavenly.

The tray's lid was dripping condensed water all over the table so she put it on the ground, leaning against the empty chair next to her.

When she looked up again, Antho Tussamar had twisted in his seat. She met his droopy and watering eyes.

"I heard you'd turned up." He grunted while pushing his enormous body out of his seat.

Mikandra ripped a piece of bread off a roll and put it in her mouth. She was starving.

He shuffled to her table, pulled out the seat opposite her and settled into it while waving his hand at her. "Keep eating, keep eating, you're much too skinny." His voice was breathy as if the action of shifting seats exerted him.

She picked up her spoon and started on the soup. It might have been because she was so hungry, but it was the best soup she had ever tasted. It would have tasted even better had this man not been at the table with her.

"Good, huh?" he said.

She nodded.

"The cook is the best in Miran." He folded his hands over his stomach and watched with a bemused look on his face while she ate. The soup was very hot, and a few times she burned herself, but she was so hungry that it was gone very quickly.

Antho Tussamar launched into a monologue about the food, about the fish which was caught locally, the beans, which came from the fields outside the city, the herbs which he said the cook went to pick himself on the mountain slopes.

Mikandra was glad that she had the food to keep herself busy, because otherwise she would have no idea what to say to this man. He was the head of the Mirani chapter of the Guild, and, according to Rehan, likely to be the one who had leaked the details of the court case to the council.

"Anyway, I'm glad to see a protege of mine entering the Guild."

Of his? "I signed with Iztho Andrahar." And she was pretty sure that the Andrahar family and the Tussamar Traders were on opposite sides of the import disagreement.

"Oh, I know, but I was talking to him perhaps a year back, and I said to him, 'Why don't you take an apprentice who is different from the others?' Since he doesn't have a son, you know."

She knew that. What a strange conversation. Was he always such a talker of empty nonsense?

She pushed her empty bowl aside and started on the fish. It was white fleshed, aromatic and cooked to perfection.

The door to the foyer opened, and a young man in apprentice uniform came in, saw Antho Tussamar at the table and sat in the corner. Probably one of his nephews. Mikandra felt like asking him *Is he always this full of shit?* She finished her fish and pushed her tray aside.

Antho waved the young man over. "This is my nephew, Thaeron." The young man nodded. "Thaeron, this is Mikandra Bisumar. She'll be going into the next intake for the Andrahar Traders."

"Oh?" The young man looked at her with a surprised expression.

"Thaeron will be graduating this year. If you have a problem with your gadgetry, my nephew here will fix it."

"Nice to meet you." The young man could not have looked less like an expert in anything had he tried.

Mikandra glanced at the tray with empty plates. Eating was

an excellent way of not having to say anything when you didn't know what to say.

"Have you entered the draw for your rooming arrangements yet?" Thaeron asked.

"Um—no." Was she supposed to have filled out something else? "I haven't seen any forms for that. I presumed the accommodation would be allocated by the Guild."

"Oh yes, it is, but you can request that you get placed with other people, if you're early enough."

"Oh. I thought part of the idea of housing all the students in the Guild building was to give them the opportunity to meet with people from other entities."

Antho Tussamar laughed, an action that made his belly shake. "And how welcoming do you think the Asto section is going to be to us? *They* all room together, and I'll tell you, you do not want to be mixed up with them. Or can you imagine being roomed with the Hedron section?"

"Oh, all right." She wasn't sure that she saw the problem. Aunt Amandra's lover Ydana Ezmi came from Hedron. But she was happy to play along. "Where do I apply to do that?"

"Ask the clerk on the desk. Thaeron can help you if you want."

"I'll think about it."

"No, young lady, I very strongly suggest that you do it. The academy is not a friendly place, especially not for a pretty young woman."

"I hear that the Asto and Hedron sections have more female students than male ones."

"But certainly you can't compare yourself to them? You're a noble lady."

"I'll think about it," she repeated.

She was getting irritated with this man. Why didn't he mind his own business? Why didn't he say what he wanted, like *I would really like it if you went out with my nephew because he needs to get married* or some sort of stupid thing. Because he wanted to get into Father's pocket, or, more importantly, she realised with a shock, he wanted to get a line into whatever happened at the Andrahar Traders.

He and Thaeron went into a discussion about subjects Thaeron would be doing, but it was mostly a monologue by Antho. Mikandra was starting to feel extremely tired with her belly comfortably full and her feet warm. Eventually, Antho heaved himself to his feet and said, "Well, I leave you youngsters to it. I have this afternoon's meeting to prepare." And he ambled out of the room.

Mikandra met the young man's eyes and couldn't help thinking that he looked younger than her. She felt sorry for him. He wilted under his uncle's shadow.

"Uncle and I were surprised that you signed with the Andrahar Traders." His voice said *disappointed* rather than surprised.

"I made a list of businesses I wanted to sign with, started at the top, and they signed me."

"The Andrahar Traders are in a lot of trouble."

Or do you wish them to be in a lot of trouble? "I don't think so."

"Oh? How so?" He really did that innocent adolescent very well.

"They're strong and they're determined to survive." That sacrifice by Rehan still gave her the chills, but it was Isandra who had suggested it. She, and Rehan, had a healthy attitude of what it meant to be in business. If times were tough, you cut your spending. Father always said similar things about the council.

Thaeron said, "I don't know that the Andrahar Traders can survive this."

"Why? They've done nothing wrong."

"Oh, it's not just this charge, but everything else as well."

"Is there more?"

He nodded, and leaned closer to her. "There are at least three court cases in preparation."

Three court cases? Hang on— "How do you know this?"

"Uncle sits at court."

That same uncle who had leaked confidential information to Nemedor Satarin. That same uncle who wanted her to room close to all the other Mirani students.

"I thought court information was confidential. My aunt used to sit at court, too."

"It is confidential. I'm just warning you. Between friends."

Friends? *My arse.* "Thank you." She rose. "If you'll excuse me now. I have some work to do."

She rose and left the room, smiling at him.

In the corridor, she blew out a big breath. Well, what the hell was that about? The politics Iztho had warned her about. Not hostility by non-Mirani Traders or the council, but undermining from within the Mirani chapter itself.

Within this building, every word, every deed had meaning and needed to be monitored. She was an empty slate, so people were trying to win her over to their side.

Mikandra went into the room where she had left her cloak. The notes had gone from the message slot. She had wanted to sleep, but the incident had wound her up so much that she wasn't tired anymore.

She sat down on the couch. Like all things in the building, it was a thing of quality, made from heavy wood and covered with lush red fabric. There was also a desk, empty except for a carafe and a glass—both empty. The small cupboard was empty, too. In the desk's drawer, she found a copy of the Trader manual. She had seen printed copies on the shelf in Lihan's father's office, but had never looked at one. She picked it up and leafed through the thick pages.

The first page contained the Trader pledge, and after that, there were instructions on ethics and how and what to report in terms of armed activities, rebellion and secessionism.

It said that Traders, especially those with arms licences, were to report to the Guild if they witnessed signs of organised rebellion or signs that supplied goods were used for purposes of war either against other entities or against groups of civilian or military nature within entities. Traders were to stop supplying arms to either party. They were to withdraw from all future deals.

She had seen all this before, and knew a lot of it off by heart. She put the book down.

The room had a tiny window which looked out over part of the noble quarter and the commercial quarter and one corner of the council building complex, the part that was disused and waiting for plans to rebuild it. It was still snowing. Over the other side of the ancient city wall, she could just make out the airport in the flurries of white drift. There was the low building where people waited for their flights, and the large open space on the other wide was where the craft would stop for passengers to disembark.

The Trader and commercial area was to the left, a group of smaller snow-covered aircraft parked in a grid pattern. The snow would make their operation erratic. The cold was very hard on the Asto-built craft, many of which refused to work in freezing temperatures. This was one of the reasons the Trader Guild headquarters hadn't come to Miran as it should have, because the Mirani Traders had a major influence on the foundation of the Guild. Also, people from other entities often found it hard to cope with the altitude.

A merchant's employee wheeled a trolley laden with boxes through the street below. A cart waited at an entrance. A bit further up the street, two people talked to each other, both hidden in fur cloaks that hid their identity or even gender.

There was a light on behind one of the windows of the disused wing of the council building. That made her do a double take. She didn't think that those buildings had been used for many years, not at least since she'd been a little girl. But there was definitely a light on, and someone moved in the room, too far for her to see any detail.

The person now came to stand in front of the window and looked out for a while before turning back into the room.

Strange.

There wasn't much else to see, so Mikandra sat on the couch again.

It was quiet in this part of the building, with the merest sound of voices drifting in from the corridor and the large room. It sounded like a lot more people had arrived in the common room.

She stared at the stucco pattern in the opposite wall. Her eyes felt scratchy and her head swam with numbers. She took off her shoes, lay on the couch and spread the cloak over her. The couch was too small to stretch out and the cushions too firm to be comfortable. There was no pillow. She should get up and unfold that bed, but then she'd have to put the sheets on as well, and she couldn't be bothered. She'd do that later, after dark.

The wind made odd noises when whistling around the outside windowsill. A Guild employee in red came down the corridor, looked into the room. "Mikandra Bisumar?"

"Yes, that's me." She pushed herself up.

"I have some items for you." He put a bag on the carpet—a familiar one that normally lived in the bottom of her wardrobe. Inside, she found her hunting clothes and all the other things she had asked for, as well as a small bag of sweets. There was also a silver necklace with a pendant in the shape of a flower. She recognised it as Liseyo's. A note in young handwriting said, *I will miss you so much. I will think of you every day. Please come back soon.*

Mikandra's eyes misted over.

Folded behind it, there was a second note. In the neat hand-writing she knew to be Mother's, it had a single sentence. *Go and make me proud.*

She stared at those words through a film of tears.

Here was she talking about courage, but how much courage did it take to be married at a young age to a dominating man who demanded a son to continue his business, but to give him two infertile daughters instead? And to remain married to this man for the sake of those daughters, and endure his rage and his domineering.

She held the note to her chest.

"I will, Mother. I will."

12

MIKANDRA LAY back down on the couch and somehow, she must have fallen asleep, because she woke up with a shock when a group of men walked through the corridor and came, talking loudly, past the door which she should have closed, but hadn't. One of the men looked suspiciously like Aithno Ilendar. The man walking next to him looked sideways and—

"Lihan!" She pushed herself up.

By the time she had stumbled to the door on legs that had gone stiff with sleeping in an uncomfortable position, he had already passed, but he stopped and backtracked while his colleagues and his father went on.

She felt groggy. No doubt her hair was a mess and she probably had the seams of the cushions from the couch impressed in her cheeks. Not how she wanted to face him.

"Mikandra? What are you doing here?" Since she had last seen him, he had grown visibly more mature. His face was all angles, his brow furrowed, and eyebrows heavy, with odd hairs springing up at irregular angles. No longer a gangly adolescent.

"I got accepted." It was the happiest thing she'd wanted to tell him.

He turned around and called to his father and colleagues, "You go ahead. I'll be along soon."

His cheeks were red from the cold and he smelled of outside air. There were still snow flakes in that part of the collar of his cloak that stuck up behind his neck. His hair was tied at the back of his head except for two thin plaits on either side of his head, which were intricately interwoven with green and blue ribbons. There was an engraved bronze bead on the end of each, which made the plaits swing. Through the opening of his cloak, she spotted his Trading medallion. The Ilendar licence number was 1110.

He said, "How did you manage to get into the academy? Your aunt told me that she wasn't going to accept any apprentices."

"I'm sponsored by the Andrahar brothers." Drat. He looked every bit as alert and smart as she wasn't.

His eyes widened and he whistled through his teeth. "Well . . . that is . . . interesting." She studied his face for signs of happiness, and saw none.

"Interesting?" Was that all? He'd promised to be with her and now "interesting" was all he could muster? "What is wrong? I thought we'd do this together. I thought . . ." But she no longer knew what she thought, except that she must have been crazy to think that she'd ever belong in his world.

Girls belonged in the theatre. Or in the hospital.

Why had she even thought that he was different? That he would treat her like a person rather than a girl?

He sighed. "You should probably come to the meeting that's been called. We're talking about the court case and the laws that are before the council." He looked down the corridor. A few others walked past, talking. "It's for all present Guild members. Let's go, or we'll be late."

Mikandra smoothed down her hair while they walked down the corridor. She still worried about her cheeks and wished there was a mirror somewhere. She probably looked ridiculous.

He stopped just before they reached the end of the corridor. "Mikandra, I have to warn you. I'm not sure if it's the best time to be involved with the Andrahar brothers."

He was going to play the jockeying-for-her-vote game, too? "It will be fine. I know about their problems." She probably sounded a bit more curt than she needed to, but damn, why was everyone fishing for what she knew?

"They're in a lot deeper than it looks on the surface."

"I know."

"I don't think you do."

"Stop acting like I'm just a little girl, Lihan."

He frowned in a what-did-I-do-wrong kind of way. "I'm not acting—"

"Yes you are. Everything you say implies that you think I'm just a girl and that I should go back home because I'm a girl and that I can't possibly understand what's going on and that I shouldn't get involved and let the men sort it all out."

His frown deepened. "I'm actually concerned about your safety. I don't give a damn about the gender of Guild applicants. You know that."

"You don't give a damn about me."

He pulled her aside into the entrance to the kitchen. He glared at her and she glared back.

"You never even spoke to me after you went to Kedras." Damn she was angry all of a sudden.

"I was busy."

"Too busy to talk to someone who's been your friend since we first went to school?" *Too busy to see a girl you kissed?*

He sighed and let his shoulders sag.

Another group of men walked past in the direction of the large common room.

One said, "Come on, Lihan, you're going to miss the action."

"I'll be there soon."

The men opened the door—the sound of many voices drifted into the corridor—and went into the room.

"I'm sorry." Lihan sighed again and shrugged. "Look, I haven't forgotten any of that." One corner of his mouth lifted and his eyes twinkled with that mirth she knew so well. For a moment she felt that everything was going to be fine. That he'd just been busy and would ask her to come and work for him when she had completed her apprenticeship with the Andrahar brothers, when their debt was paid, Iztho was married and their succession settled.

Then the smile faded from his face. "Thank you for that. You were a good friend and I will remember our times together fondly. As for what happened that last time when we were together . . ." He smiled again. "Let's keep that a secret between us, shall we? No need to tell anyone."

Mikandra wanted to scream, *But you promised . . .* but the truth was he had not promised anything after kissing her.

His mouth twitched. "We all have little immature flings."

Little immature flings? "You were my best friend for years." She hated how her voice sounded unsteady. Damn, she was tired and cranky and not in the mood for this.

He nodded, but his face betrayed no emotion. "I will continue to be your friend, and I will speak to you as a friend, after the meeting, because we really must go."

Mikandra could get angry and make a scene, but there was nothing left to be said. He'd moved on without telling her, and didn't feel in the slightest bit sorry about it, and didn't even understand why she was angry. A fight would not solve anything and would make her look like a needy girl, so she'd treat him like he'd treated her for the past few years: with ice cool and distant professionalism.

But damn it, was this what she'd been waiting for all those years?

She followed him down the rest of the corridor and into the large room, where more Traders had gathered than there were chairs, and most of them stood around the perimeter of the room. The vast majority of them were men, important-looking heads of families and their sons dressed in uniform, a wall of khaki shirts and trousers. Some wore heavy cloaks of thick and lush fur, Trader medallions and other decorations proudly displayed on chests. Several wore timers and readers on their belts. Faces were solemn.

There were also a couple of green uniforms from Bendara Traders. One of those was a woman. She smiled at Mikandra.

Still within the borders of the Mirani nation, Bendara was the vast agricultural area that bled into the western forests, the jungle and then eventually, the western coast marshes, and Barresh.

Antho Tussamar sat at the same table near the hearth where he had been sitting before, except that spot had now become the centre of the audience. Rehan Andrahar stood on the other side of the room. He met her eyes and his gaze lingered until she had to look away. There was no emotion in his face. Aithno Ilendar sat on the table next to Antho Tussamar, clutching a cup of tea.

Mikandra wriggled herself between all the men so that she had a better view, causing a few raised eyebrows. She should really have put on her apprentice uniform.

Antho Tussamar drummed his fingers on the table. "All here?"

"Yeah," said someone at the back of the audience.

While everyone was silent, the door into the foyer outside opened and someone else came in. People stepped aside to let this person through.

The newcomer was Aunt Amandra, slipping her cloak from her shoulders. She had clearly just come from council, with drops of molten snow in her hair and her face red from the cold.

"Sorry to keep everyone waiting." She pushed to the table at the front and sat down in the seat next to Antho Tussamar, dropping her cloak on the third seat. He pushed a cup of tea across the table to her.

"Thank you." She looked around the room and her gaze found Mikandra's. Her eyes widened.

Antho Tussamar cleared his throat. "So now that we are all here, we can start. There has been an unfortunate development overnight, with the court having suspended the licence of one of our members. For those who haven't heard, though I don't think there will be many, the Andrahar Traders have been asked to provide evidence that they didn't illegally import prohibited substances into Barresh.

"Aithno called this meeting to see if we as the Mirani chapter need to formulate a response to this charge. He seems to have some concerns about the process and what this means for the Mirani chapter in general. It's probably better if he explains this himself. Aithno?"

Lihan's father rose and stood in the middle of the room until there was silence. He was an imposing man with heavy eyebrows and a large and straight nose. Damn, even though his son was a spoilt dick, Mikandra still respected him.

"My argument is simple. I have known Jihan Andrahar and his sons for many years. We trained together, we worked together. When Jihan was killed in that accident, I helped his sons through the hard times. Although the Andrahar Traders are our competitors, I have high respect for them. Whatever people here may say about Iztho, I have always known him as hard worker who is extremely loyal—"

"Loyal to himself, yes." Someone at the back, the voice of a younger man. A couple of others shushed him.

"—extremely loyal to Miran, and a man whose word is worth more than gold. I know Rehan, Braedon and Taerzo as the same. There is no way that they would ever do anything wrong. I think most, if not all, of you here will agree."

There was some murmuring in the room.

"As I see it, this charge is motivated solely by politics. About a year ago, Iztho made a call of judgement based on Trader Law to suspend his support for a council plan involving the export from Barresh of locally-developed weaponry."

There was some muttering at this.

Aithno Ilendar continued, "The Andrahar brothers have an arms licence. There was nothing illegal about the deal in Mirani Law, but he judged it against Trader Law, because unrest was already brewing in Barresh, especially with the local Pengali people eager to establish their rights other than as domestic servants for the other local faction, the keihu people. Iztho judged that the money paid for weapons would go towards the ruling keihu party, who would use it for political aims to repress the rebellion, all with full support of the Mirani army who, at that time, controlled the enclave. He elected to pull out of the deal, which was a very wise decision. I would have done the same, and not doing so would have been a breach of Trader Law."

A few men muttered. Some voices sounded unhappy, but most seemed to agree.

An older Trader close to Mikandra said, "There was no weaponry."

The man next to him, probably his son, said, "He was asked to bring people against their will. Nothing to do with weapons. He was asked to bring unwilling victims. Slaves."

"Wait, wait," Aithno Ilendar said, looking at the men next to Mikandra. "Let's not repeat those unproven rumours."

"Well then let's prove or disprove the rumours," the Trader's son said. "Let's stop running circles around the council and trying to keep out of its way. If this business is as vile as the rumours suggest, *someone* has a lot of explaining to do."

"There is no explaining necessary," Aunt Amandra said. "Because there is no truth to any of those rumours of people smuggling. I speak for the council as well as the Guild. The contract with Iztho Andrahar was for weapons. I can show you the documents. I'm trying my best to uphold the Guild's position in the council, but this unfounded gossip is not helping our position in the slightest. Please stick to the known facts. Miran does *not* trade people."

The father muttered something under his breath about politicians.

Aunt Amandra continued, "Also, if Nemedor Satarin wants to banish all foreign influence from Miran, it would make no sense at all for him to import any."

The son snorted. "We heard that argument before. I still don't believe it. I spoke to Iztho, and he was pretty clear. He was to bring a prisoner to Miran. He refused on the grounds that it was people smuggling. That was the deal that fell through. Nothing to do with weapons."

Aunt Amandra said, "My definition of *prisoner* involves a convicted criminal and there would have been a formal charge against this person. In such cases, people can be exchanged. There is no formal charge anywhere. Not here, and not in Barresh. There was no prisoner. The rumours are without base. Please stop spreading these rumours."

"I agree," one of the Bisumar twins said. "The rumours were started by Barresh because they hate us."

The Trader's son next to Mikandra crossed his arms over his chest.

Aithno Ilendar continued, "Anyway, whatever the exact

issue, the locals in Barresh grew angry. They protested against what they saw as Mirani occupation. They started fights with our troops in Barresh, and lost. But while street fights were still going on, some very smart locals proceeded to apply to *gamra* to have Mirani protectorate status revoked, and they were granted this. We were not defeated as military. We were defeated with bureaucracy. Which brings us to the end of the two-day war.

"From that situation a year ago, we now have this smuggling charge, which becomes less credible the more you look at it. The Barresh council banned the import of menisha, our most important export to them—"

"We don't deal with dried menisha," Rehan said. "The entire charge is rubbish."

"—The charge is brought in the Trader Court, which freezes the accused's business until innocence has been proven. Someone clearly knew this, or they would have brought the case to the local court, which would have made more sense, legally, but would have allowed the Andrahar Traders to continue operating."

There was more muttering at this. Some suggested it was the doing of vengeful people in Barresh, others said it was the Coldi. Still others said that the Mirani council should come clear on the people smuggling allegations, to which others replied that is was a separate issue and that the council would *help* Traders, not drag them before court.

Antho Tussamar waved everyone into silence. "In my position as head of the Miran chapter of the Guild, I need to be assured that none of our members are treated unfairly by outside influences. I have requested, from the Barresh Exchange and the Miran Exchange, relevant documents of all the deals between the Andrahar Traders and Barresh. I will go through this information and assist the Andrahar Traders with preparing their defence."

Rehan said, "Thank you, Antho." But his face was hard. "I assure you that we are fine for the time being. We appreciate your support, but we can manage." An oh-so-chilly rebuke. "We are engaging our own channels to prove our innocence."

Antho Tussamar asked, "Any word from Iztho about what he's got to say for himself?"

Rehan gave him a sharp look. "Are you suggesting that you believe he's guilty?"

Antho Tussamar managed to look genuinely surprised. "Of course I'm not. Whatever makes you think so?"

Rehan said nothing, but there was a decided *watch your mouth* expression on his face.

The atmosphere turned decidedly cool.

A few men made for the door, talking about work they had to do.

Antho Tussamar said, "Are we done with this meeting?"

Aithno Ilendar exchanged an exasperated look with Rehan that said *Nothing has been decided!*

Rehan shrugged and met Mikandra's eyes. All the time he'd been inside he had never taken off his cloak, probably to disguise the fact that he wore no medallion, and drops of sweat pearled on this forehead and upper lip.

"We are not done at all, Antho," Aithno said in a low voice. "Not as long as you are a mouthpiece of that idiot on the High Council."

Antho Tussamar glared back. "It is the only way forward and you know it. The only way to stop Miran sliding into oblivion." He packed up his papers and strode out of the room.

Other men also streamed out the door, talking.

Rehan came to stand next to Mikandra. "Surprising to see you here."

"What'd you think, that I'd run home crying? I'm not that kind of girl."

"So I see."

"You don't see. Most of you are born into Trading families, but I chose to apply because that's what I want. I'm determined to make this work. I will fight if necessary."

All around them, men were talking and making their way out the door.

She asked, "Do you know of any other court cases in preparation against you?"

He frowned.

"Thaeron Tussamar told me there were three other cases being prepared."

The worried frown deepened. "Up until today. I would have said bullshit, but I don't know anymore. It could be bluff. It could not. Coming from a Tussamar, it probably is bullshit, but nothing is certain anymore." It was the first time she had heard him sound anything other than unemotional or angry. He looked tired.

"Before I forget, when you get your monthly bill from the Guild, there will be a charge for a meal and a courier to pick up my things from my house and an overnight stay here. I'm sorry about that, but they wouldn't let me pay and they said it had to be charged. I can give you the money—"

"Forget about it."

"Knowing that you need the money, I can't just forget it. It doesn't feel right."

"Seriously, I tell you the fuck not to worry about it. Don't. Worry. About. It."

"Sheesh. You don't make it easy for someone to help you, or even like you. Do you always run around like this, abusing everyone who's trying to be friendly?"

He glared at her and she glared back. She was highly tempted to say *I know what's wrong with you, Rehan Andrahar,* but the expression in his eyes disturbed her. It wasn't anger or hatred she saw there. It was torment, and fear. He put on a brave face to the outside world, but inside, he was all cut up.

She let a silence pass and said in a lower voice, "I'm leaving Miran tomorrow morning. I'm going after Iztho. I think I know where he is."

He nodded, and it was the first time in ages that someone didn't try to talk her out of anything she'd decided to do. She decided he probably was concerned for his brother's safety, but was too proud to admit it, or had been taught from birth that his first concern should always be the business. Or something.

He dug in his pocket. He produced a marker of the type merchants used in warehouses. "You have anything to write on?"

"Sorry, no. Write on my hand."

He grasped her wrist and held it steady while he wrote numbers on the palm of her hand. The tip of the marker tickled. His skin was clammy. "It's our account code at the Exchange. For communication." A waft of sweaty air drifted past.

She nodded, businesslike, trying to ignore her unease at being so close to him. At the other side of the room, she spotted Lihan looking at her.

Rehan let her arm go. "Good luck." And then after a small pause. "Keep safe."

Then he was gone, leaving her confused. Did he actually want her to go away or did he care what happened to her?

Mikandra turned to go back to her room with the intention of trying out the bathroom and the fold-out bed in the cupboard, but a female voice said, "Mikandra, wait."

Aunt Amandra. She followed Mikandra into the room.

Her eyes burned with the intensity of fire. "What were you thinking? Your parents are beside themselves with worry."

"My father kicked me out and told me not to come back. He told me that if I accepted the place, I would be disinherited and I would never be welcome at home. So I don't intend to go back there. I've sent a courier and told them that."

Aunt Amandra's shoulders sagged. The anger seeped from her. She shook her head. "Asitho really knows how to make enemies of people, especially recalcitrant girls." She sighed. "Your parents need you."

"No, they don't." Although Mother would, and she felt sorry for Liseyo.

"Go home. I'll come with you. Asitho needs someone to talk to him sternly."

Mikandra shook her head. "It's not going to make any difference. Fine, he might agree to let me go to the academy, until he finds something else that he thinks I shouldn't do. I made my decision. I want to stay here."

Aunt Amandra sighed. She looked at Mikandra's hands, and specifically the code that Rehan had written on her palm.

"It would really be better if you went home. I would be much happier knowing you are safe. The future is going to be rough for Miran and especially the Andrahars."

"Oh, is this about the three extra court cases that are coming up? I thought court information was confidential."

Aunt Amandra frowned. "Court cases? What do you mean?"

"Well, earlier today, Thaeron Tussamar said to me—"

Aunt Amandra put her finger on her lips. She rose, shut the door and went back to her seat.

She prompted, "Thaeron Tussamar said?"

"He said that there were three extra court cases being prepared against the Andrahar brothers. I asked how he knew and he said his uncle told him. He must have told a lot of people."

"*What?* Court cases are confidential."

"So confidential that Nemedor Satarin knows the details?"

Her frown deepened. "What are you talking about?"

"Nemedor Satarin came to the Andrahar house, offering them a loan because he knew of the court case and suspension." To be honest, he hadn't mentioned the court case or charge in so many words. "He said that the council had agreed to offer a loan for up to two hundred and fifty thousand credits."

Aunt Amandra's eyes had gone wide. "Bail out someone from the Trader Guild with council money? Certainly not. That's not even legal." She looked out the window, her expression concerned. "The only offer he could have made would be out of his private money, and that's a *lot* of money, and I very much doubt that he has that much."

"He left behind a card. That's what it said."

Aunt Amandra met Mikandra's eyes. Her expression was intense. "You're sure it was Nemedor Satarin?"

"I was there. He sat next to me at the table."

"Next to you," she repeated.

"Yes."

Aunt Amandra shook her head and her expression went hard. "You're right. Not much point going back to your family. You're already in too deep. You should go to Kedras as soon as possible."

"I'm leaving tomorrow."

"No, you should leave now. I'll go and check the bookings."

"I checked. The flights are all full." Wait, what was this about?

"I'll use my priority code."

Mikandra filled with panic. She wanted to go to Barresh, not Kedras. "Please, I'm fine."

"Have you told anyone about this flight?"

"No."

Aunt Amandra breathed out a sigh. "Then you might be fine. But promise me: please don't leave this building until that time."

"Are things that bad?"

"They may be. I wouldn't take anything for granted. You are the daughter of someone the conservatives thought they could trust. You signed with one of their most vocal opponents. If nothing else, they will be nervous and will be watching you." She looked tired. "I really didn't need any more to worry about besides this ridiculous law."

Mikandra was going to say that she was sorry, but realised that she was not. She had seen what the boycott did to the hospital and couldn't understand why anyone thought that was a good thing. "What exactly is going on in the council? What law?"

"There is a big power struggle going on. A section of the council has proposed a law limiting foreigners settling in Miran. This includes revoking residency rights for non-Mirani spouses. A lot of people, but especially the Traders and merchant class, are very angry about this. The vote is not due for a few weeks yet, but the issue threatens to split the council, because it goes to the heart of the deeper relationship between Miran and *gamra*. The import laws, the boycott. I'm guessing the flights are busy because many merchants are leaving, taking their import-dependent businesses and foreign-born wives to safety."

Mikandra nodded. This confirmed her suspicion.

She toyed with the idea of asking where her aunt stood in this debate, but was afraid of hearing the answer. "Would this law apply to everyone, even Guild couriers and foreign Traders?" *Like Ydana Ezmi.*

Aunt Amandra nodded, and sighed. "And before you ask, Ydana walked out on me when I announced that I would stand for election. I haven't seen him since. Will probably never see him again." Her voice sounded more angry than Mikandra had ever heard it.

"He left you just because of the election?"

"Oh, it wasn't just that, but that I live in this 'rotten place' as he calls it, where foreigners get shunned, called names and *murdered* on the streets." She was talking about the courier. So the news had already reached the Guild headquarters. "I've lost count of the number of times he's asked me to come to Hedron."

"Change colours?" Mikandra tried to imagine her aunt in the lilac and purple uniform of the Hedron Traders, and could not.

She nodded. "But maybe I'm just too damn stubborn for him, but I *believe* in Miran. I so badly *want* the council to see sense. With the Foundation treaty, we have something beautiful that has worked for a long time and should continue to work. We can't let it be ruined by some ill-informed people. We've got to keep our vision of Miran alive, and running away is not the answer to these proposed laws."

"I'm not running away."

"No, I know you're not. You're just playing with explosives." One corner of her mouth went up. "Pretty much like me."

Mikandra asked, "Do you think Rehan Andrahar is explosive? Do you think he . . . has a problem?"

Aunt Amandra frowned. Then she shook her head. "All right, here's my quick and dirty assessment of the family. Iztho Andrahar is . . . well I could probably have predicted years ago that something was going to happen, but no one would have believed me. But, once you've heard him sing, you know to the tips of your toes and fingers that there is no way that man is ever going to be happy as a Trader. When his father tore into him for playing music in the Guild bar at Kedras, something broke in him. Taerzo is spoilt rotten, doesn't take life seriously enough and could probably use a lesson in hardship. He's a good sort, but needs to grow up. Braedon is very gentle, probably a bit too gentle for his own good, but he'll do well enough. Talk to him about medicines and he's happy. Rehan . . . is quite something. I have hardly seen anyone more driven, focused and hard faced. Do something against him and he'll come down on you like a rock fall. Win his trust . . ." She met Mikandra's eyes. "And you could end up somewhere amazing. But winning his trust is the hard part."

"Does he trust you?"

"Not in the slightest. I'm too close to his enemies."

"He's not affected by madness?"

"Whatever makes you think that?"

"I don't know. He's just . . . strange." Then she added, "Something about him reminds me of the mad people I treated at the hospital."

Aunt Amandra fingered her upper lip. "Jihan's sister Dithiandra is as crazy as they come. She hardly ever leaves the house these days, and I don't remember a time I've seen her that she hasn't been talking complete nonsense. It seems to be quite strong in the family. Hmm, Rehan could be affected, but only a bit."

Mikandra's heart thudded. She'd been right about Rehan.

"But whatever affects him, do know that last year, Rehan Andrahar was the Trader with the greatest turnover in the Guild."

"I can imagine, if he's up against people like Antho Tussamar."

"No, Mikandra. He's the top of the *entire* Guild, not just Miran. Whatever you do, do not, *ever*, underestimate Rehan Andrahar."

After her aunt had left, Mikandra took her apprentice uniform out of her bag and went into the bathroom, or better said, the bathhouse. When she opened the door at the end of the corridor, she stepped into humid air. There were several connected rooms, each with a steaming pool. In the closest, largest pool sat two men she had seen at the meeting.

The next, smaller, room was empty. This room had no windows, and the light from lamps on the walls reflected in the mirrorlike water in the rectangular pool. Wisp of steam rose from the surface. A cabinet against the back wall was well stocked with towels and soap. She carried the soap basket and two towels to the pool, undressed and slipped into the water. It was beautifully warm. She lay back with her head on the edge.

The two men in the next room got out of the water and left. When their voices had faded in the echoing halls, there was blissful silence. For the first time in her life, she was alone and could do whatever she wanted.

She'd go to Barresh and find Iztho. She might even stay there until she had to leave for Kedras. Barresh was a primitive place, so living there would be cheap. Since it was no longer a protectorate of Miran, there was no way her father could easily find out where she'd gone.

But she needed to look less like a noble Mirani lady. It was time to get rid of that annoying hair.

After coming out of the bath, she dried and stood in front of the mirror. She held a strand of her wet hair up and cut through it with the nail cutter about two fingerwidths from her head. Then the next strand and the next one. As the wet strands of hair fell down at her feet, her satisfaction grew. The growing cover of short spikes on her head made her look like an adolescent boy. No more careful brushing, no more knots, no more tangled hair in clasps and buttons.

Then she put on her apprentice uniform and studied herself in the mirrored wall. No Endri from the city ever cut their hair, but plenty of people from other places did. If she wore her hunting gear, maybe she would look like one of the mountain nomads who came into the tiyuk market with their animals. Maybe she could pass for a merchant's daughter from any of those towns and then she wouldn't stand out so much.

13

MIKANDRA LEFT the Trader Guild building at dawn and walked through the streets which hid under a cover of pristine snow.

The building that was the terminal of the Miran airport lay outside the city wall. It was a low complex that spanned the side of the air field closest to the city. By the time Mikandra got there, a lot of people were already going into the building, dragging heavy bags over the icy ground. Overnight more snow had fallen on top of the half-melted and frozen snow from yesterday. It made for slippery ground, but fortunately, the snowfall had stopped.

Mikandra opened the door and let herself into the low-ceilinged hall and the crowds within. Inside it smelled humid, but cold, of damp stone and damp fur, like it did in the hospital. The floor was wet from people bringing in snow on their boots. Slippery too, in places. A poor cleaning woman walked around with a mop, but it was so busy that her work was almost impossible.

Flickering screens around the walls indicated which shuttles were coming in and leaving. Right now, for as far as she could see, the snow-covered airport was empty.

A lot of people were waiting for the passenger shuttle, and a huge check-in queue snaked through the hall. Most of the people were in family groups, many with children and lots of bags. Mothers snapped at children for playing in the puddles. Children cried, couples argued.

There were also a lot of young men, all of them Nikala workers. Their cloaks were of poor quality and their clothing was rough and patched. Their shoes were old, scuffed and re-soled many times. They moved in groups, talking and laughing loudly in terrible slang without much regard for people around them.

The queue moved slowly.

Although the walk to the airport had been cold, Mikandra was glad that she had left her cloak in her room at the Guild. She had no use for it in Barresh, and it was a big and bulky thing. Other people were wrestling with theirs, stuffing them into bags —that was very bad for the fur—or trying to keep them off the ground, which was hard because quality tiyuk fur was smooth and slippery.

The city guards at the desk were making a show of checking everyone's ID card. Signs with the destinations of various flights hung from the ceiling.

The Kedras queue next to her was the longest. She didn't spot any noisy young men travelling to the world whose most important function was the Trader Guild headquarters. Most of those passengers were merchants.

It surprised her how many people wanted to go to Barresh. In front of her in the queue stood a group of young men, friends talking and laughing. Two of the men walked on crutches, and one man had only one arm. Another's face was horribly scarred to the point that it made her shiver. She had seen men like these in the hospital. They looked like soldiers because they were ex-soldiers, retired for medical reasons, like so many of the young men in the hall.

Sometimes one of the men would cast her a strange look. The family behind her kept glancing at her, too.

Mikandra tried to ignore them. She shuffled along in the queue, feeling as visible as a massive hairy tiyuk bull in the snow. Even with her short hair, she didn't look like any of the other people. Her hair was straight, not curly. She was much taller than other women as well as many of the men, and her hunting clothes might be old and showing a bit of wear, but they were nothing like the poorly made and old-fashioned garments the people wore.

On the other side of the counter was a fogged-up window through which she could barely see the expanse of the airport, featureless white. A smaller craft had arrived, and a gaggle of guards in white and red went to meet whoever came down the steps. Mikandra recognised the thick mottled cloak and long gossamerlike hair of an Endri noble before he vanished amongst the guards. Who was it? Someone from the council having visited Bendara?

The line moved very slowly.

The guards took aside a mother who appeared to be travelling alone with two young children. She carried a couple of bags bulging with clothes, and a guard gestured for her to put her bags on a table. He proceeded to unpack everything, spilling an array of clothing, including women's underwear, on the table.

He took aside a pile of new-looking clothes and spoke to a colleague.

The woman protested. One of her children started crying.

"Please, these are clothes that my husband needs over there." She picked up the crying toddler, but the boy squirmed in her grip and broke into an earsplitting scream.

She put the toddler down where he tried to throw himself on the ground, but his mother held him up by the arm. "Shut your mouth!"

Over the top of the boy's screaming, the guard continued, "Since these items are not for yourself, you will need to fill in these forms—"

The mother belted the child on the ear. "Shut up!"

"—which are required for export. You need to take them over to the counter at the back of the room."

"But we'll miss our flight." The woman looked on the verge of tears. She probably couldn't write. Her face was red with the exertion of keeping the toddler off the ground, and he screamed his lungs out.

Mikandra shivered. If they were going to check her, she felt sure they would find something to object to, even if only because of who and what she was. Endri men travelled because they flew themselves or had the money for private craft, Nikala travelled because they had the numbers to fill up the larger craft and tickets were cheap, and the only ones staying at home were the Endri women.

Mikandra came up to the counter, the guard took her ID, looked at the screen displaying her details.

"Bisumar, huh?" He was a burly sort and his voice loud.

Several people turned and stared.

Mikandra's heart beat like crazy. The rumour that a Bisumar had flown out of Miran on a shuttle would soon be everywhere.

Mikandra bent closer to the guard. "I'm doing some work for my aunt." She kept her voice low. "I'm meant to travel on regular transport and not stand out. You're not helping."

His eyes widened. "Oh, lady. My apologies."

He let her through into the waiting area, where she put as much distance as possible between herself and the people who had heard him yell her name.

Fortunately, it was even busier here. She stepped over bags to get to the window, but came into view of another guard who also glanced at her. What else had the first guard seen on the screen about her? Had her status as *Trader Guild, Andrahar Traders* filtered through the system yet?

Her talk with Aunt Amandra yesterday had made her more nervous than she wanted to admit. The rivalry between the Endri families was something she understood. She had grown up with it, and the rules of engagement had been written in thousands of years of history. The Foundation agreement described how to handle disagreements between families. Nemedor Satarin, being a Nikala, stood outside that framework. His brash talk frightened a lot of people. He divided Miran in a way it had never been divided before.

Never in her life had she thought she would be glad to leave Miran, and now that was exactly the way she felt. She wanted escape from prying eyes and suspicious looks.

The windows rattled and from outside came a roar of engines.

A number of children ran to the window.

Mikandra felt, rather than heard, the shock wave of a large craft flying over. It vibrated deep inside her chest. She loved the roar of large engines, especially when they employed the downward jets for landing.

The shuttle came into view, slowly descending with landing gear outstretched. The downward jets blew up a huge cloud of snow which obscured the view of the craft. That engine sounded like . . .

The quiet field outside changed into a hub of activity. Airport staff wheeled two hot air cannons out of a shed. While a cart pushed the cannons across the field, staff worked to get them fired up. The craft touched down, shut the downward jets and the snow cloud dissipated, but the main engines were still going, blowing snow behind the craft.

Yes, she had been right about the model. The purple sheen of the exterior made this a Hedron-built shuttle. A Rhion model, the heavy-duty workhorse of the passenger movers. It had a Hedron-developed fusion chamber with three independently-controllable outlets on each side. The crew was two pilots and an engineer. The Rhions rarely came to Miran, because they did not handle cold and lack of humidity very well. This craft was working at the very edge of its effective operability. Why was it here? Because it could take more people than the regular shuttles?

Even while the cannons were directed at the engine chamber, the sound of metal ticking and cooling was audible inside the hall.

One of the guards went to unbolt the large double doors of the waiting area and threw them open. A blast of icy wind came in.

The first passengers already streamed onto the field.

The guard at the door yelled at people to hurry up.

A woman in front of Mikandra complained in a voice thick with Nikala speech.

"We's been sitting there since crack of dawn, what's th' hurry all of a sudden?" She lugged a number of heavy bags and limped heavily with one leg.

"Let me carry some of your bags."

The woman frowned while Mikandra took one of her over-stuffed bags. It smelled musty.

" 'S nice, dear, but really I'm fine. 'S with th' slave driver trying t' hurry us up."

Her accent was so thick that Mikandra had trouble under-standing.

"Aren't youz cold, dear?" And without waiting for the reply, "Why do those cannons have t' be so noisy?"

The hot air cannons went through a whole cylinder of fuel in the short time the craft stopped to offload and take on passengers. There were two cannons, and they each fed off two cylinders that were taller and broader than a person. There was a merchant downstream from Miran whose sole business it was to convert meltwater into fuel with a huge solar collector, and keep these cylinders full, just so that the shuttles could land here.

Mirani craft used the same fuel but in different tanks. Other *gamra* people always derided the Mirani craft as old-fashioned. They called them *rockets* or *missiles*, but they were robust and did what they needed to do: function well in cold weather and thin air.

The line of people progressed over the airfield, into the biting wind.

In the roar of the heaters and the engines, all other sounds vanished.

Up the stairs into the craft, past the roaring heat canons. By the time she entered the doorway, Mikandra's ears were ringing.

The craft was full of families, mostly with a lot of bags which people attempted to stuff in the baggage carriers.

The woman with the limp found a seat, and Mikandra returned her bag to a puzzled *thanks, dear.* Nobody else had helped any of the people with crutches or mothers with more children than hands.

It was so busy in the craft that it looked like all seats were taken.

She thought that Barresh was a backwater. That's what everyone always said. No Traders, no real autonomy, crime, street fights. Why were all these people going there?

Her seat was next to one of those young Nikala men who

seemed to be travelling by himself rather than as part of a large group. He looked slightly older than her, had longish curly hair and well-worn clothes. He looked up when she sat down. His eyes were startlingly dark blue. His face was quite round—not narrow as many Endri faces—and his golden curls danced around his head when he moved. His hands and arms were clearly a worker's: strong and sinewy, with the back of his arms covered in a thin fuzz of golden hair. His skin had a bronze tinge.

The man next to the window was a merchant, middle-aged, dressed in a traditional long robe. He leant his head against the back of the seat and pretended to be asleep.

Mikandra sat down, feeling self-conscious and holding her own—completely hairless—arms close to her side. The ex-soldier nodded at her, raising eyebrows at her short hair and hunting clothes. She didn't fit. Her clothes were too nice, her hands too cultured. She was a dead giveaway for an Endri girl.

The craft's crew—now trying to get all passengers to sit down—were all non-Mirani, mostly Coldi. They wore neat grey Pilot's Guild uniforms. Like the Trader couriers, they were employees, rather than members. She spotted one or two with goggles which frequent travellers used for going through the Exchange.

On this trip, of course, going as close as the western coast of the continent, they wouldn't be using the Exchange.

The doors were shut and crew came around to check people's safety harnesses.

Some people seemed anxious and one or two were crying. Maybe they were leaving behind family members, or maybe they felt like they had no option but to leave because of the boycotts, or something else. It was disturbing. Mikandra felt very small and ignorant. There was so much to learn about the world and how people's lives were affected by laws and government.

Finally, the crew members were happy and took their seats. The lights in the cabin went off and a mechanical-sounding voice in Mirani went through emergency procedures. It repeated the announcement in Coldi and then in a language Mikandra had never heard. She presumed it was keihu, the main language spoken in Barresh.

That made her uncertain again.

What if no one in Barresh spoke Mirani? That was a disturbing thought.

The engines roared. The air vibrated with power. Mikandra was pressed into her seat and let that majestic feeling of leaving the ground come over her. After a short while came a sense of forward movement.

Mikandra leaned over to see out the window. They were already quite high, and she had missed looking out over the noble quarter of the city one more time. Already, the outskirts of the city fell away to make place for the cloud-covered highlands. Alpine meadows and the occasional agricultural field. Meandering creeks in the valleys. Patchy and thin snow.

"First time away, huh?" the young man next to her asked.

She turned to him. Was it that obvious?

"Where's youz going?" He smiled, showing browned and uneven teeth.

She cringed at the accent. Yes, people spoke like that, but they swept streets. Not even the cleaners in the hospital were allowed to use slang.

"Me?"

"Yes, do youz see anyone else? Not him, eh?" He gestured at the merchant on his other side, who was leaning back in his seat, his eyes closed.

"Um . . ." It had not occurred to her that someone would ask her these types of questions, and she was sure that *I'm from the Andrahar Traders and I'm looking for Iztho Andrahar* was going to be an answer that was neither wise nor good for her.

"Visiting a cousin." She did her best not to sound too cultured, and probably failed miserably.

"In Barresh? Not many Mirani left there. Most of th' army got kicked out."

"Yeah, he's . . . a merchant." She was grasping at straws. She needed some story to tell him, and quick.

"Who with? I used t' work for the Menudin family, y'know. I know a lot of them."

Drat, next he was going through all the Mirani merchants and who worked for whom and it would come out that she knew nothing. "I'm not from Miran. I live in Bendara."

"Oh."

Fortunately, he seemed happy with her reply. She just hoped that he wasn't going to quiz her about Bendara, because it was a long time since she'd been there. She deflected the conversation away from her. "What are you going to do in Barresh?"

He laughed. "Jus' having some fun. Meeting some mates. I'm Jocassa by the way."

She so badly wanted to ignore him and turn away, but that would probably draw more attention.

"I'm Eydrina."

"Like th' hospital matron, eh?"

Her breath caught. "Do you know her?"

"Everyone knows her. That's where they send youz 'n fix you up if there's any fixing t' be done."

She frowned.

"I'm ex-army," he said.

"City guard?" Please, no.

He shook his head. "Used t' be on th' Kesilu coast." On the eastern side of the continent. "I signed up and was almos' sent out t' fight in Barresh, but that din' happen because th' Barresh Council threw Nemedor Satarin out. Turns out I's discharged from th' army after that. Din' need us anymore, they said. Turns out it's better this way—not fighting—'cause we get t' do what-ever we like, 'n there's no commander telling us what t' do." He laughed.

His words shocked her. These were the soldiers who defended the glorious nation?

"What about yourself? Youz don' look the type 's normally on this flight."

"It's a surprise visit to my cousin."

"Oh." He seemed happy with that, too. Really, she should come up with better excuses next time.

"Youz be staying with yer cousin, right?"

Mikandra shrugged. "I don't know yet." Now she wished she hadn't brought up the cousin. Next thing he'd want to know where this cousin lived and she'd done little more than glance at a map of Barresh that she couldn't even tell him a street name.

"Youz welcome t' stay with us. Th' mates are always staying in th' Market Street guesthouse. It's a dump of a place, but it's cheap 'n everyone else is there, too. If youz know what I mean. Unlike th' other places, th' upmarket places. Of course, if I'd any money, I'd stay there, too."

"Yeah." He was fishing for information, probably puzzled about her. A change of subject was badly needed. "At least it will be warm there."

"Hot, hot, hot all th' time. It's like being in a bathhouse, 'cept you can't get out. Then there's th' rain. It'll jus' come out of nowhere like pshhhhh." He flapped his hands up and down. "At leas' it's safe enough t' walk on th' street at night. They's meili, which aren't half as big as maramarang 'n they don' attack people. They jus' make a terrible racket in th' trees. Oh, and there's the ringgit, too. Youz won' get t' see them, but they's hide in th' reeds 'n make this horrible noise that's jus' everywhere 'n will hurt yer ears if youz unlucky t' get too close."

"That—um—doesn't sound like a lot of fun. Why do you go to Barresh if the place is that terrible?"

"Youz kidding? Where'd I say it was terrible?"

"How long do you stay there for?"

"What do youz mean? I live there. I jus' come t' Miran t' visit friends." He averted his eyes.

He probably meant that he came to sign his army retention notice that guaranteed him pay.

"How can you live in Barresh? Isn't the army banned from there?"

"Th' army is, but not private people. Th' locals say they don' need us, but they do. They's pay some of my mates t' train their guards. They's pay others t' protect their stores."

That was new to her. "But we're their enemies?"

"Th' command likes t' think so, but really, when people have been there's long as we have, they's bound t' be some friends. I have friends there. They's not all Mirani either. Some mates have married local girls. Some set up businesses. As long as youz stay clear of th' council, because they hate us."

"Is Barresh really as badly organised as they say?"

He snorted. "Dunno's you call it bad. There's no rules, you know. Or none that anyone's worries about. We get along fine there."

"But what about the two-day war?"

"Bah, don' believe what th' guys up top say. They's saying what suits themselves, 'cause they ordered th' army t' do things that were really stupid. I mean, really, really stupid. They din' mind 'cause they din' have t' do it, but th' whole business with th' tails was vile. Not saying anything but I see why th' Pengali were angry."

"Pengali?" Her knowledge was deserting her fast.

"They's the ones that live in th' forest. They's got tails, and there used t' be some local law that said that they's not allowed to work in th' city with their tails on. Because apparently some time ago th' Pengali servants of some rich family used their tails to steal things, or some rubbish thing. And then all th' babies born in th' city who'd be working for the keihu people had their tails cut off at birth. But no one's worried much about it for a long time. But the upper command found out about this law and told th' army t' cut any off when they's caught them."

What? Surely he was joking.

"Don' look at me like that. That's what they's did. Some of them at least. Most of th' men jus' refused t' do it, but some of them did. It was vile 'n stupid. Of course th' Pengali got angry."

"Did you see any of this happening?" She shuddered inside, almost feeling pain in a tail she didn't have.

"Not me. Happened before I came, but a mate told me he's seen it."

She gave him a sideways glance. In the hospital, ex-soldiers picked off the streets often told sensationalist stories because they were bored or because they wanted to make themselves look good. Most of those stories were bunk. She didn't know whether to believe this. On one hand, she very much wanted *not* to believe it. On the other hand . . . what was she letting herself in for?

"Is there anything to like about the place?"

"It's a fun place with lots of money, with all th' foreign folk coming in. There's lots of work. Good jobs, too. An' ye don' need many clothes either. Youz can sleep in th' streets and not freeze. Youz can party all night 'n not have t' go inside. Youz can go down t' th' river 'n there's no ice in th' water. An' th' trees—ye know what trees are?"

Mikandra nodded. She had once been to Bendara, Miran's agricultural district, where there were lots of trees. There were none in Miran, though, save perhaps the ones in the noble's conservatories. But the leaves tended to burn under Miran's strong sunlight. The highlands were covered with a yellowish green mat of tough-leaved rock creepers and other vegetation that grew barely taller than knee high. Higher up in the high-lands, like Estevan, nothing much grew at all except the shale-covered monotony of moss. And glaciers.

For all she heard of Barresh recently, she had never given much thought of what the place looked like.

"People say Barresh is unsafe?"

"Bah. They'll tell youz anything jus' t' keep youz away from a good place. There's a few people making trouble. Th' street gangs. Youz jus' stay away from them. Hint: they mos'ly have tails."

She felt stupid and scared. She had left on a whim and now there was no way back. What did she even know about Barresh?

Fortunately, she wouldn't need to stay very long. She'd go up to the local Trading office and ask for the name of the woman Iztho Andrahar was going to marry. Then she would find her, and he was probably there too, with the dress and the lute. And then she would clear up the situation, ask him what had happened to the missing money, ask him to provide proof that he didn't smuggle, ask him what he wanted her to do, and ask him to contact his family. Or whatever he wanted her to do.

14

BECAUSE THE SHUTTLE was flying west, the day dragged on forever. People grew tired and tried to sleep in their seats, but Mikandra couldn't get comfortable. No one else seemed to have this problem. She was too pampered. The workers were so exhausted, they slept wherever and whenever there was time. Even the crew members were nowhere to be seen.

She kept glancing over the sleeping forms of Jocassa and the merchant at her reflection in the window and the vast masses of cloud beyond. Occasionally, the craft would turn and sunlight from one of both suns would spear through the window, increasingly often as the day wore on and the light turned golden.

Once, the cloud cover broke and she spotted a landscape of rolling hills, small settlements and patchwork fields.

Probably some farming community near Bendara. The next time there was a gap in the clouds, the only thing she could see was solid forest. Not long after that, she thought that the craft was descending, and sure enough, they broke through the clouds and soon after, crossed the famous escarpment that she had only ever seen in pictures: a solid wall of rock with thick forest at the top, and a rocky beach at the bottom, descending into marshland, as far as she could see. The sunlight was now so low that it hit the cliffs side on in a bright display of gold.

The city of Barresh itself was spread over two islands surrounded by marshland interspersed with copses of trees. Mikandra was surprised to see how many houses could fit in a small space. Not just walled yards, but huge blocks of apartments in pyramid shape, especially on the first island.

How many people lived here?

"Th' closest island is Far Atok," Jocassa said next to her. She hadn't noticed that he had woken up. "That's where th' workers live."

The craft described a circle around the second island, much less densely populated, with red-roofed houses surrounded by walls.

She spotted the airport on the western side of the island and close to that, a complex of interlinked domed buildings. The roof in one wing of the complex had fallen in. The exposed ceiling beams were black.

"Is that damage from the war?"

"Youz mean th' council building? Nah, it's been like that fer a long time. They's all fixing it up nicely now. There's work going on in all th' town. Lots of work fer us cartin' bricks 'n things like that." He grinned. "Youz have sharp eyes."

Sharp eyes was one of the good things about her. They said that the watchtower attendant had often been Endri in the past, because they tended to have better eyes. Even Father had always commented on her eyesight when they went hunting.

The craft turned sharply and flew low over an expanse of water with patches of reeds and dammed fields of brilliant green leaves floating in the water. In one of the fields, a machine hovered over the surface, using a downward jet mechanism to blow all the floating plants to one side. People were raking these plants into huge nets, which went onto canoes.

The craft straightened and the view slid from sight. It was replaced with more fields and flat-bottomed boats in channels, and people standing in the prow with long sticks. All this went past at great speed because the craft was very low by now.

The downward and braking jets came on in a roar that made the floor shudder.

Then the fields and channels were gone, too, and the view

outside the window only showed cracked and weed-infested pavement.

Forward movement stopped, and a moment later the craft touched down.

Some passengers jumped up immediately and formed a queue in the aisle. Mothers admonished impatient children. People with bulging bags squished other passengers to the side.

Mikandra remained in her seat, looking disbelievingly at the expanse of cracked pavement, which was completely empty of any kind of aircraft. Was this the airport for the entire city? Where were all the shuttles and the Trader craft?

When the doors to the craft opened, a waft of humid air drifted in. Within a short time, it got hot and uncomfortable and with every step Mikandra progressed towards the door, she expected fresh air to come in, but the heat only got worse. Sweat trickled down under her shirt. The strap of her bag dug into her shoulder. The woman behind her was pushing a huge bag into her back. She wished that she had packed more thin clothes. Even her hunting clothes were far too hot.

At the craft's exit, the full force of the heat hit her. It was like a bath house or even worse with the biting force of the sunlight. The air felt like thick syrup. It stank of rotting plants and farts. She reeled and stood still at the top of the ramp until people behind her started muttering.

"C'mon missy, we don' have all day."

"Hey, I would like to meet my customers before evening."

Mikandra forced herself to take a step down, and then another one. Her head pounded. Her hand was sweaty on the railing.

She stumbled onto the cracked paving, where she had to stop or she would faint.

The air shimmered with the heat that burned in her nose with each breath. The stream of passengers walked down the ramp, across the field. Weren't these people hot?

One man patted her on the shoulder. "First time off th' mountain, huh?"

Mikandra nodded. The movement made her head hurt.

"Take it easy fer a few days. It gets better after that."

He laughed and rejoined the line of passengers that streamed past her. Mikandra concentrated on her breathing. The air scorched in her lungs. Her arms glistened with sweat. How could people live in heat like this?

Gradually, the roaring in her ears subsided. She raised her head and looked around, making an effort not to squint.

The first of the passengers were now at the gate ahead, where a single guard in black uniform waved them through.

Behind her, the shuttle was now being attended by airport employees. It was probably going back to Miran tonight for another load of passengers. No one waited to get on and no other shuttles had arrived.

There were only a few passenger shuttles parked on the far right side of the field, near the fence which ran in front of a line of bushes. One of those was a small craft bearing the emblem of the Pilot's Guild, all its doors closed. Those short-range craft were used in Miran to take people to other cities, like Bendara or Estevan. She wondered where this one would go, since there were no other towns in this part of the coast.

To the left, an open-sided shed masqueraded as maintenance station.

Three private craft sat in front of this shed, none of them of the familiar dark-coloured Mirani make. There was, however, a magnificent Hedron-made model with the characteristic purple sheen of Hedron steel. She stopped to look at it, taking in its elegant shape and curved wings. She had seen pictures of this craft before. Was she mistaken or was this really a Gazion? There were only about twenty or so of those made ever. What was it doing here on this poor excuse for an airport all by itself without guards which usually accompanied the craft of important people?

The low sunlight reflected off its side. The doors were closed and there were no family markings like there would be on Trader's craft. Who would own it?

Most of the Gazions were in the hands of Coldi people, because of the way their society worked with loyalty networks, and the way wealth was channelled to the top of each loyalty pyramid. The Chief coordinator of Asto, Thania Lingui, had a

Gazion. His immediate subordinates would have one. Most of the Coldi owners would be residents of Hedron because they made the things. The top of the Mining board at Hedron had them. And Ydana Ezmi, aunt Amandra's not-so-secret lover and leader of the Hedron chapter of the Trader Guild had one, although he had never used it to come to Miran. Chief Trader Maraiki Deni Evaros from Kedras had one.

Who had she forgotten? A powerful and shady Indrahui warlord? More specifically, who of that very rich and select group of people would visit Barresh?

She could come to only one conclusion: no one whose presence here wouldn't be bad news for Miran.

The single guard at the gate was looking at her while paying cursory attention to the passengers streaming through the gate.

Mikandra's heart jumped. So much for the craft not being guarded. She sped up to rejoin the queue.

The guard was a curious fellow, quite short with a solid build, with olive skin, dark curly hair adorned with thin plaits of various lengths and cut in curious stepwise fashion. This had to be one of the local keihu people. He asked for Mikandra's ID in passable Mirani—she deeply regretted stopping to look at the Gazion, since he had not asked anyone else for their ID—slotted it into his machine and looked at the screen. His face showed no emotion. He took the card out and handed it back to her.

Phew. So much for not drawing attention to herself.

Mikandra followed the other passengers through the gate and came onto another expanse of cracked and uneven paving. The air above the surface shimmered with heat.

The building she had seen from the air stood on the other side of the open space. It was a two-storey construction, surrounded by a solid stone wall. Some time in the past—but it must have been a very long time ago—the walls had been painted white, but now only fragments of paint still adhered to the rough stone, much of it chipped and cracked. An opening in the wall, not deserving the word gate, provided access to the entrance, a tall door under an arched porch, and a domed hall or staircase. Jocassa had said this complex belonged to the council, but Mikandra had seen this building entrance in pictures. This was the infamous Barresh Exchange. Illegal until recently, unreliable and therefore dangerous. As recently as last year, there had been a scandal when it accidentally transferred a craft that didn't even have an Exchange-enabled transmitter. The place should have been shut down over that, but no, they'd somehow managed to wriggle their way out of the mess.

It looked like they were even fixing up the building. There was a pallet of bricks, a pile of sand and various stacks of beams and wood placed in the shade of the trees that hung over the wall. A man shovelled sand into a wheelbarrow. A couple of others were building a structure outside the dome that looked like scaffolding.

The pictures that accompanied bad stories about the Barresh Exchange had never showed the rest of the building, the invading trees in the narrow space between the walls and the building, the exposed roof beams in the left-hand wing of the building and the missing windows. Was she dreaming or was the left-hand wing burned out? And were those gouges in the stone marks from explosives?

"Where are youz going?" a voice asked behind her.

She wheeled around. Jocassa. Damn, she had hoped that he'd gone his own way.

"I'm on my way to my cousin."

"Where does yer cousin live?"

"That way." She flapped her hand noncommittally at the other side of the square, where most of the passengers seemed to be going.

"Oh, he works for one of th' rich ones, huh?"

"Um—yeah." No one struck her as particularly rich in this town.

"What's th' family?"

"I—um—can't quite remember. The names are all so strange." *Go away.* She didn't want to lie any more.

"Youz know th' way? Youz want me t' come?"

"No. I'll be fine. Bye."

"Nice talking t' youz. Feel free t' come past if youz need help."

"Sure. Thank you."

15

MIKANDRA WAITED while Jocassa walked off in the direction of a group of huge trees to the right. In the shadow of the trees, there was a market, judging by the colourful canvas stalls. She probably wouldn't see him anymore.

A couple of groups of passengers walked past her and she caught snatches of conversation.

A man said, ". . . You said they'd keep the room until today?"

And a woman in the next group said, ". . . they had only a pile of bricks up at the entrance when I left."

Her companion said, "I don't understand why they don't just pull the entire thing down. It's such a dump."

"They're attached to their heritage . . ."

The next group of people spoke in strong Bendaran dialect and she had trouble understanding them.

All these people filed past her into a street on the opposite side of the square, oblivious to her standing to the side. Even the suspicious guard at the airport gate had gone. For the first time in her life, no one watched over her. No one waited for her, and no one expected her to do anything.

The feeling was strange and unusual, a bit scary, too. But exciting. Being a Trader would be a bit like this.

So, what next?

She dug her notes from her pocket and squinted at the paper against the glare from the sunlight. It was true that the light was different here. In Miran, the shadows from both suns were very crisp, blue edged on one side, gold edged on the other. Here, the air was so muggy that shadows from both suns almost blended into one, even in this time of the cycle when the suns were furthest apart.

Her note said, *Check the airport.* She had already seen that it was empty. There were no Mirani craft, and few other craft apart from that damn Gazion, of which she really should find out who it belonged to. So—where were all the private craft? There might be another airport, maybe on the other island, because she couldn't believe that no locals would own aircraft. On the other hand—where would they go? Barresh was very small and surrounded by Miran on three sides. The ocean was on the other side, and there were only some small islands, also owned by Miran. The only place people could go was offworld, and if offworld travel was extremely expensive for the people of Miran, it would be even more so for these people. So maybe there were no private aircraft. She still found that hard to believe.

Next on her list was *Trader Office.*

If she wanted the Trader Office, it was best to ask at the Exchange rather than trying to find it on her own. The Exchange was right here so she would start with that.

With a bit of luck, she would find what she needed today and she could book the return flight, and maybe enjoy this place a bit. The concept of "trees" and an ocean and rivers warm enough to bathe intrigued her. She had never seen hot springs, or any *flowers* that were not the size of her little fingernail and attached to little plantlets that confined themselves to within a finger-width of the ground.

She walked across the square trying to remain positive, but the heat sapped her energy. Her head was pounding. The paving was so hot that she could feel it through the soles of her boots. The air was almost too hot to breathe. A small breeze ruffled her hair but brought no freshness. Wafts of a bad smell drifted past. Her shirt felt wet against her back.

It was hot even when she got to the shade of the trees outside the building. There was more construction activity going on than she had seen at first, with building materials and ladders and tools stacked up against tree trunks and the ground underneath, which was uneven with knobbly roots.

Two men pushed a cart with bags to a place under a huge tree where a couple of people were mixing, in a giant vat, a white substance that could be plaster.

These workers were female, small and wiry, and had rough striped skin glistening with sweat. Their brown eyes were much larger than normal people's eyes. One of the workers had a tail, which she waved and curled at knee level as she worked. It looked like a giant banded worm. Fascinating. Mikandra found it hard not to stare.

The entrance hall of the building was two storeys high. The stairs to the top floor went around the outside wall. The ceiling dome contained a circular coloured-glass window depicting a five-pointed star set against a blue background with stars. Light fell through in shafts of brightly-coloured brilliance.

In a corner of the hall stood a bank of foldout tables with plans and drawings spread out over the top. A tall Damarcian in a tunic with the Masterbuilder Guild logo was speaking in Coldi to a chubby keihu man, pointing at sections of the plan with his Damarcian hands, with his index and middle finger much longer than the other fingers.

The far wall was hidden behind scaffolding, and a team of workers were painting the wall. Two of them were Mirani men, speaking what she presumed was the local language to others, a mixture of local keihu and dark Indrahui workers. One of them was Coldi even, hauling a big bag up the stairs with arms corded with muscle. He made a remark to two Kedrasi women who were sticking down mosaic tiles in the downstairs hall. The women laughed and repeated the joke to their helpers, a couple of Pengali.

Mikandra had never seen such a riot of cultures and languages.

She followed a stream of people up the stairs, but found her way barred by a very modern-looking sliding door with no signs of door handles. She stood there for a while, stupidly looking at it. A guard in black stood in the corner, his hands behind his back. He was Coldi, twice as wide as her with arms bulging with muscles. He turned his head slightly and looked at her from the corners of his eyes. His shirt, too, had the silver five-pointed star on the chest.

Actually, she couldn't be sure that this mountain of muscle was a *he*. Gender differences in Coldi were subtle enough to be masked easily. Apparently, the Coldi guards at Hedron were all women and they were the toughest and most feared in all of the settled worlds.

This guard had to be laughing at this Mirani bumpkin who had no idea how to open the door.

As she was about to give up and go back down the stairs, the door slid aside, spilling a waft of cool air onto the upstairs landing.

A local keihu man came out. He was short but less rotund than most of the local men she had seen. His hair was curly and short. Grey hair edged his temples. He wore a khaki tunic with a five-pointed star embroidered on the chest in silver thread.

"Lady, can I help you?" he asked in passable Mirani.

Mikandra tried not to worry about the *lady* tag and hoped that it was a sign of respect rather than the way it was used in Miran: only for Endri women.

"Yes, I'm looking for the Trading Office."

"The Trading Office? The Imports register is upstairs. The market is outside. You will most likely find a Trader in the guest-houses, and the Merchanting Cooperative has an office in the commercial district on the other side of the markets. Which do you want?" Actually, his Mirani was more than passable. She worried even more about his *lady* tag. She stood out even in a place as strange as this.

"I want the Trading Office."

"You are aware that Barresh doesn't have any local Traders?"

She'd known that, of course, but somehow had not expected that to lead to the absence of a Trading office. How else would Traders do business? Where would they meet and do their work? She forced a smile and glanced at the stone-faced Coldi guard who was no longer looking at her. "Well, wherever Traders register their imports."

"That'd be the customs office downstairs."

No, that wasn't what she wanted. She wanted the *Trading Office*, the home of the Trader Guild. Maybe he didn't understand. "I want to find a Trader's place of business."

"Just one particular Trader? If you can be a bit more specific, maybe I can help you."

"I'm looking for a Trader called Iztho Andrahar."

His brown eyes widened. Did she imagine it or did he do a double take? He shook his head. "I don't know him. A Mirani Trader, yes? He is supposed to be in Barresh?"

"He told me to meet him here." Time for her own little lie. "But he wasn't at the place where I was supposed to meet him. I'm trying to find out where he is staying or where he works."

A female worker came past, dressed in similar uniform to the man she was speaking to. She gave Mikandra a strange look before holding her hand up to the door, which activated the sliding mechanism.

Cool air wafted past. Mikandra was melting in this heat. "Please, I'm trying to find his place of business or wherever he is staying."

"His main business would be in Miran as I'm sure you'd know."

"Yes, I know, but he is here in Barresh. He told me to meet him." She was clutching at straws. She wanted so very desperately to be admitted into that cool room. The smell of paint made her head pound. She felt like she was going to be sick.

The man shook his head, oblivious to her discomfort. "Sorry, I can't help you. Maybe try the markets."

"Oh, all right. Thank you." She had to get out of here.

"If there's anything else I can help you with . . ."

"I'll be fine, thanks."

He nodded and crossed the landing, where a solid metal door slid aside to let him through. His khaki tunic was the last she saw before the door closed again. There were a couple of signs on that door, one in Mirani, which said *Authorised personnel only. Please use protective gear.*

The Exchange core had to be somewhere in that section of the building.

Mikandra descended back into the building site, thinking about that hesitant pause in his speech. He knew Mirani too well for any language problems to have caused him to pause. Her only conclusion was that he'd lied about knowing Iztho. Of course he knew who Iztho was. In Miran, she didn't know many foreign Traders, but someone who worked at the Exchange would remember all the regulars. If a high-profile foreign Trader was in town, they would know. Everyone knew when Ydana Ezmi was in town, which was why he had stopped coming long before his current fall-out with her aunt.

Mikandra went back out through the chaotic hall and the courtyard, where a couple of tailed locals were using a high-pitched whining saw to cut a metal beam. The one with the apparatus wore a mask and apron against the flying sparks, but little else.

Mikandra went back onto the hot and desolate square with its smell of humid earth, damp stone and farts. The strap of her bag cut into her shoulder. Her eyes were heavy. She hadn't slept all night, and it would now be night in Miran.

Miran. Snow. Cool crisp mountain air.

Damn it. She was *not* going to behave like a homesick child. She was going to show Rehan Andrahar that she was not a "pamby".

First, she needed a place to stay. Finding Iztho was going to take some time. Come to think of it, Iztho might well be staying in a guesthouse, although the fact that there were no Mirani aircraft at the airport didn't fill her with confidence.

If he'd eloped, he'd be trying to hide. Since a Trader's aircraft was a dead giveaway for his presence, he might have asked someone to fly it elsewhere. Maybe . . . She had images of herself inside the cabin of the Gazion. And then a cascade of thoughts about where the missing money had gone and—no, that was ridiculous.

Iztho would not take all that money and spend it on an aircraft he didn't need. Also, supposing he wanted to buy another aircraft, he would only get a Miran-made model.

That machine out there belonged to someone else.

But who?

She could see a glimpse of it between the bushes that surrounded the airport. It was probably stupid to worry about it and the least of her problems, but the craft's presence bugged her.

She walked past the wall surrounding the Exchange complex and turned into wide and tree-lined street that led away from the square. This had to be the Market Street Jocassa had mentioned.

There was a large building on the corner, with a moss-covered façade, unkempt garden and cracked steps leading up to the arched entrance. Windows on the top floor had no glass. Sheets and other bedding hung over windowsills. A young Mirani man—a Nikala with longer hair than would be allowed in the army—leaned out one of the windows, yelling at another group of young Mirani men stumbling up the steps to the entrance. When one of them tripped and fell to his knees, his friends squealed with laughter. They were drunk already and it wasn't even dark.

This had to be the guesthouse where Jocassa was staying. What a dump. The place even smelled like a sewer.

Past the guesthouse were shops displaying their wares under multihued cloth awnings. One sold clothing, and at the back of the shop Mikandra spotted many rolls of fabric; the next shop was an eating house, where two Pengali girls were sweeping leaves from between the tables and an old man attended potted plants that surrounded the outdoor eating area. Smells of food wafted through the street. More spicy than she was used to, but the smell still made her hungry.

Once she had gone past the shops, she found a much smaller guesthouse, also built from old stone with an arched entryway, but it had a well-maintained yard with neatly-clipped bushes on both sides of the entrance. Travellers of all types went up and down the steps. It was getting late and two lights on either side of the entrance spread a cool greenish glow that was typical of the charged pearl lighting that Barresh used.

This place looked more to her taste.

She pushed open the gate and walked up the steps. Inside the arched entry stood a desk where a woman sat behind a huge book. The opening on the other side of the entryway looked out onto a leafy courtyard where there were sounds of water splashing and people talking in muted relaxed voices.

The matron at the desk looked her over. "How can we help you?" She spoke heavily accented Mirani. Her face had that typical coarse look of keihu people, with a large groove-tipped nose and pore-riddled skin. She wore her hair on top of her head like the enormous fluffy nests that the mountain rats built from tiyuk hair. Her eyes were small, brown and beady. Disapproving.

"I'm supposed to be meeting one of your guests, but I forgot which room he's staying in."

The matron's eyebrows rose. "And who might this be?"

Too late, Mikandra thought of the implication of a young woman looking for a man's hotel room.

"Iztho Andrahar."

Again, a small pause. She leafed through her huge book, and shook her head. "Not here."

"But he has been here? Is this where he normally stays?"

"Maybe. I don't remember the names of all my guests. I don't give out names." She gave Mikandra a penetrating look that said, *and I'm not going to snoop on your customers.*

Mikandra shrugged. Tears were too close to the surface. She felt so incredibly hot and filthy and tired and that pool where people were talking and splashing sounded so welcoming.

"All right then. I'll need somewhere to stay for the night. Do you have a room?"

"Yes, sure. How many nights?" Her expression returned to one of business. She turned a page in the big book and ran her finger down a column of numbers. Her nails were long and painted purple.

"Um—two."

"Sure. A single room for one night will be sixty-five credits, and bookings of further nights will get a fifteen per cent discount if booked and paid for now. There is breakfast in the main court-yard for ten credits extra—"

"Sorry, did you say sixty-five?"

A frosty look came over the matron's face. "I did say that. If you're one of the army, ex-army or any of their girlfriends, I suggest you go to the place at the beginning of Market Street. You'll find all the other ex-soldiers staying there. We run a class establishment."

Mikandra's face glowed. "I'm sorry, I . . ." Tears pricked in her eyes. There was no way she could afford that much *per night*. Her money needed to cover a flight to Kedras later. "I guess I better go there then . . ." She backed away.

"Just turn left when you go out the gate . . . Pity, because you look like a nice girl."

Mikandra scurried down the stairs and out the gate. She was so embarrassed, she would prefer to sink into the ground and disappear. She was sweaty. It was so incredibly hot. She felt horrible. She was hungry.

This city was a lot bigger than she'd envisaged. It was a lot more expensive than she'd envisaged. People knew Iztho but pretended they didn't.

She trudged back past the shops and eating houses. If she went into the large guesthouse, Jocassa would laugh at her, and no doubt he would have large groups of friends. She knew the type. They jeered even at their sick and injured mates she treated in the hospital. Imagine what he would say to her. *We's not yer type, huh?* And they'd all laugh and offer money for certain services.

That would be insufferable.

Maybe there were other less expensive places where she could stay away from the rowdy guesthouses. A bed in a workers' dorm would do, nothing fancy. But she would have to hurry, because the light was turning golden and between these tall trees it was already quite dark. And who knew what nasty and sharp-toothed scavengers lived in those trees?

She wandered through the streets near the market and square. On the far side of the markets there were only warehouses. There was an alley that ran behind the Exchange building which connected to the next street. The whole block behind the Exchange was taken up by official-looking buildings that were in varying states of disrepair. There was a large domed building and a number of blocky ones, set back from the street behind a rusty and overgrown fence. On the other side of the alley were low buildings that looked too big to be private residences. But no other guesthouses.

She turned the corner into the street parallel to Market Street.

On this street she found two smaller guesthouses, both of them less appealing than the big place in Market Street. The first one was a badly-maintained building where noise and an awful smell spilled out the windows. A couple of Damarcians sat in the porch drinking, measuring her up with their suspicious gazes. Their eyes, with their black-rimmed yellow irises, gave her the creeps.

In the second guesthouse, a couple of women, two local and one Kedrasi, stood in the front porch leaning against the support pillars, eying every man who passed. A group of young men and women were walking up the steps laughing, one Mirani man with his arm around the waist of a local woman. She greeted the ones on the porch.

Urgh. Whores.

Mikandra could not bring herself to go inside. Maybe she'd walk around the block once more to see if there was a place she overlooked.

Like Miran, Barresh was almost on the equator and night fell quickly. In the shadows of the huge trees it was almost dark. The friendly shade of the trees from the daytime had changed to a spooky silence punctuated by shrills and shrieks that sounded too much like maramarang for her not to be worried. Things rustled in the branches. Animals chattered and squeaked.

Trees freaked her out. At least in Miran, you could see what was coming. Here, anything could fall on you without notice.

She clamped her arms around herself. This street behind the Exchange complex was too quiet. No one lived here. There were no shops.

Maybe she should go to the other guesthouse and pay the sixty-five credits and go back to Miran tomorrow. She could stay in the Guild headquarters. Or go to Kedras and stay there.

But then she remembered Rehan's face, *If she wants to be with us, she'll have to learn to take the heat.*

That was easy for him to say, with all his family's money

behind him. He could have come in here, hired investigators and would have found Iztho in no time. She had *told* him where she was going. He had offered no help.

And she had not yet found a trace of Iztho.

Mikandra spread her hands and looked at the small part of the sky she could see between the foliage. "Please, give me hint where you are."

There was a small sound behind her somewhere in the shadows, a scuff of a foot on the paving. Mikandra whirled.

The street behind her was empty. Lights burned in an upstairs window, but mostly the buildings were dark. When she walked on, the sound came again. Did she hear footsteps?

She stopped, barely daring to breathe. "Who's there?"

No answer.

A couple of shapes—similar to but smaller than maramarang —flew across the display of reds and oranges in the sunset sky and disappeared behind the dome of the building.

There was light in Market Street ahead. She could see people walking past carrying their purchases home from the markets.

There was another sound behind her.

She whirled around. A small figure ducked into the shadow of a tree trunk.

Children playing a prank?

"Stop following me. It's not funny."

Nothing.

Bushes against the rusty fence looked like ghostly fingers. There was no sign of movement. Had she imagined it?

She turned around to keep walking, but a couple of small figures had come out from under the trees in front of her, blocking her path. She whirled around, but there were people behind her, too. They were Pengali with long matted locks of hair, not wearing shirts. The last of daylight made the white pigment in their skin patterns stand out. Several were spotted, others striped. A tail waved at waist height.

"What? What do you want?"

None of them said anything, but they came closer. Mikandra looked for ways to escape, but there were a lot of them, and they had her surrounded.

The closest one had a head full of dreadlocks that hung to his waist. The pattern on his shoulders and chest was one of dark spots. He wore too-wide shorts held up with a piece of rope and did not have a tail.

His voice was rough as he said in heavily accented Mirani, "Tell me where it is."

Mikandra gasped. "Tell me where what is?"

"You know what I'm talking about."

"I don't. I don't have anything for you. Sorry, but you have the wrong person."

He said something in guttural tones that she presumed to be the Pengali language. A few more men came out of the shadows. One carried a stick with a greenish glow bulb on the end, and by its light, Mikandra could make out at least six men, all of them Pengali with huge eyes, long hair adorned with beads that glittered in the light. Her heart thudded like crazy. Jocassa had said that the streets of Barresh were safe except for groups of tailed Pengali. She should have taken this as a warning and stuck to the main streets.

"You come from Miran, don't you?" The man with the long dreadlocks came closer.

He held a knife in his hand, below the waist, the point directed backwards. Mikandra gagged with the smell of his sweat, a muddy, fishy scent. "You have the code word?"

"I have no idea what you're talking about."

"Rubbish." Something sharp poked her in the back and when she groped for whoever had sneaked up behind her, someone lashed a rope around her hands. "Your man is too much of a coward to come back here and now he sent you. Tell me where it is."

"I don't know who you're talking about." She hated how her voice spilled over in a squeak.

"Stop your acting. Your master sells the stuff. We have a lot of clients waiting and they've been impatient."

The fungus. Damn, had the allegations been true?

She straightened her back. "I have nothing for you."

"We'll see about that."

She struggled to pull her hands free. "Keep your hands

off me!"

The rope around her wrists tightened. Not a rope at all, but someone's tail.

Her captor laughed. His hands were rough-skinned and felt hairy. He patted her belt and pockets. Then squeezed her breast. Mikandra held her breath. If they were going that way, she'd give them a fight. Someone else pulled her bag off her shoulder.

"Hey, there is stuff in there I need."

The man spoke to his mates in his rough and guttural language and started rummaging through the bag.

Mikandra tried to yank her hands free.

"Look what I found." He held up her pouch.

Mikandra saw spots. Everything she needed was in there. Her account cards, her identity cards. Without it, she couldn't go home, she couldn't live.

"No. Please."

He opened the clip and rummaged through the contents, muttering in his language. Several others laughed. Then he closed the pouch and tossed it to one of his mates.

"No, please! I can't get home without it." She couldn't go to *Kedras* without it.

"Then you stay here." He laughed. "There are ways of making money, especially if you're a pretty girl."

Someone at the back yelled. Heads turned. Ears pricked up and they all ran and jumped on top of the wall surrounding the council complex and then down the other side, tails held high. One of them had her bag on his shoulders.

"Hey, stop!" She ran up to the wall, but it was too high for her to climb. "I'll go to the guards."

The sound of laughter drifted from the yard beyond. Then they were gone and Mikandra stood at the wall, her head pounding.

This was unbelievable. This couldn't be happening to her. She'd teach them. She'd get her things back. They might laugh, but she would set the guards on them.

Angry, shivering, she walked as fast as she could around the block. Into the Exchange building. The building activity had wound down but the Damarcians were still at work under the light of a couple of glowing bulbs on stands. They didn't even raise their heads when she walked past.

Mikandra went up the stairs, onto the landing and the metals doors that said *Authorised personnel only.*

The glass door to the left slid open when she held her hand up to the panel. The corridor beyond was dimly lit with bluish light. A glass wall on the left-hand side allowed her to see into the Exchange control room. A couple of circular benches surrounded the hologram of the anpar lines, a blue web of constantly moving threads that represented the anpar energy lines as they snaked through the galaxy, zapping in and out of existence as the Exchange network created them. Some were semipermanent communication lines, others represented the anchor lines of shuttles in the process of transfer.

The room smelled brand new and the equipment more modern than any she had ever seen.

According to the rumours in Miran, they had a new core, too. *Someone* obviously had money.

On the other side of the Exchange room, she found the public desk. A young keihu woman with masses of curly hair sat behind it.

"Can I help you?" she asked in decent Mirani.

"Could you please tell me where to report a crime?"

The woman frowned. "I can call the city guard for you. What happened?"

Mikandra told her as much as she wanted to share.

"In the alley behind the building? That is not very smart to walk there alone."

"Please, I need to have my things back."

"That's going to be hard. The Pengali are quick and will probably already have sold a lot of your possessions."

"Please. I have no money. Nothing. I've got nowhere to go." Tears were awfully close to the surface.

"Unfortunately, I can't help you with any of that. Do you have any relatives here?"

"No."

"Friends?"

"No." Mikandra swallowed. "Please. What can I do?" In

Miran, people like her came to the hospital, feigning illness. Or sometimes they just sat in the hall only to vanish again before their turn came to see a healer. Sometimes kindhearted people would feed them their leftovers.

"You could go to the guard's office, but it doesn't open until tomorrow morning."

"I have nowhere to sleep." All of a sudden, she was incredibly hungry.

"You could ask someone for a loan."

"Who can I ask?" Strangers? That was begging. Endri didn't beg. "I can do . . . things for you, here. Please. I have nothing."

The woman gave her a strange look, and Mikandra sensed that she would probably call the guards soon. Jail was not a good place to end up in a strange city.

So she left, muttering something about going to see the guards tomorrow morning. But while she went down the stairs, despair closed in on her.

What was she going to do? She had no money to buy food, no money even to stay at the cheap guesthouses.

Outside the building, she rounded the corner into Market Street and plonked down on one of the stone benches in the part of the street between the guesthouse and the shops. She buried her face in her hands, wanting to disappear and never come back. How could she have been so stupid?

What was worse, it seemed that these thugs had been expecting a delivery from a Mirani Endri. What would they have delivered if it wasn't menisha, and who would it be from if not Iztho?

She and his brothers had been wrong. He was guilty.

There was no point to anything anymore. She'd die here without ever being able to go back home, let alone take up her position at Kedras. She'd be a beggar on the streets for the rest of her life. No one in Miran would ever know where she'd gone, except Rehan Andrahar, but he didn't care and wouldn't look for her. She did still have the number on her hand, but asking him for help would be the ultimate embarrassment.

No, she would try to solve this herself.

But how?

16

MIKANDRA HAD no idea how long she'd been sitting there when a group of about twenty people came walking up the street. They were loud, yelling and laughing, pushing and jostling each other. One of the shop attendants started pulling baskets of clothes underneath the awning of the shop.

Because they might steal or ruin their stock? Because they meant trouble?

Mikandra rose and slipped into the safely-lit area outside the shops, where tables and baskets displayed wares for sale by the light of hundreds of glow bulbs strung up in the trees. She went into a fabric stall and feigned interest in the wares to let the group pass.

"Can I assist the lady?" The shop's owner had come up to her. He was quite rotund and dressed in a robe of similar colourful design as the fabrics in the stall. Damn why did all these locals speak Mirani so well?

"Um, I'm just . . ."

Her stomach rumbled. She glanced over her shoulder. The men were all young, of Nikala descent, mostly male. Ex-soldiers. There were a number of girls with them, local keihu and Pengali and a Kedrasi girl with brilliant red hair. As they passed, her eyes met those of one of the group.

Jocassa.

His eyes widened. He called out, "Hey!"

Please, no.

"Eydrina!"

Mikandra did her best to ignore him.

On her other side, the fabric vendor continued, "Would the lady be interested to see our choice of quality fabrics?"

"Um—no, thank you, I was just—"

Jocassa yelled, "Come on, Eydrina, join us!"

There was nothing for it. Mikandra didn't want to go back to telling him lies, but what was the alternative? Maybe he could lend her some money so that at least she could pay for somewhere to sleep. Maybe he could share some food.

"I'm sorry, I just . . ." She fled the shop. The vendor muttered something about Mirani louts behind her back.

She joined the group of young men and women. Jocassa clapped her on the shoulder. "Hey, I knew I'd see youz again. We were jus' having fun on th' town. What 'bout youz? How's yer cousin?"

She shrugged, for want of a better response.

"These are my mates."

He gestured to the man next to him, a mountain of muscle a head taller than Jocassa. He wore a singlet shirt that accentuated his massive shoulders. An ugly scar ran down his cheek. His grin revealed several missing teeth.

"This is Thasep."

"Hi," the thug said, and his grin widened. His hands were the size of a normal person's head.

Compared to the giant, the next man looked like a midget. He was also Mirani, with too-long hair held back in a messy ponytail and the fringe hanging into his eyes. He was dressed in a local kaftan which was too wide for his thin frame. His hair was curly, but his face was narrow and long-nosed.

"This is Dalit."

Dalit squinted at her. "Oh. Hallo." His eyes were dark blue and focused somewhere over her shoulder. "Nice to meet you."

"Nice to meet you," Mikandra said, feeling uneasy. He didn't look like an ex-soldier. He didn't sound like an ex-soldier either.

Jocassa raised his voice. "Everyone, this is Eydrina. We met on th' shuttle. She's visiting her cousin in Barresh."

Mikandra cringed.

There were mumbles of hello and how are you doing while the group started walking again.

Jocassa said to her, "I thought you'd be staying in th' more fancy streets?"

Mikandra felt like sinking through the ground. She had behaved like an idiot. "I was robbed. I have no money and nowhere to go."

Tears pricked in her eyes. She was so tired.

"What 'bout yer cousin?"

Mikandra shrugged, not trusting herself to speak.

"There was no cousin, right?"

She shook her head.

" 'N yer here by yousself running away from some sort of marriage with an old guy 'n youz have never been here before. Never left Miran."

She nodded. Close enough to the truth.

"And th' scum that robbed youz were 'bout this high 'n had tails, right?" He held his hand at shoulder height.

She nodded again.

"Man, I shoulda warned youz, but I thought youz had someone t' look after youz. This is no place t' roam th' streets alone at this time of th' day, specially not at th' alleys that connect th' streets. What'd they steal?"

"Everything."

"Money?"

She nodded.

"ID?"

She nodded again. "My clothes, spare shoes, everything. I have nothing left." Her voice cracked. "What am I going to do? I can't even buy anything to eat."

"Don' worry."

"How can I not worry? I've lost everything."

"Calm down, calm down. Youz will be fine. We's here t' help youz out. Fer starters, we's a large room in th' guest-house. No one counts how many of us sleep there because we rent by th' room, 'n we's regulars there. Youz can stay there."

"Thank you. Can I borrow some money for food? I'll pay it back when they catch the thieves. I'm going to see the city guard tomorrow."

He laughed. "Don' like yer chances there. Th' guard's not interested in arresting their own citizens. Th' Pengali gangs rule th' streets at night. You'll never see any of it back."

Panic clawed at her heart. "But how am I going to go home?" Worse, how was she going to get to Kedras?

"We'll solve that problem when we get to it. Mos' of us had ID stolen before. We's still travel when we want. There's ways and means."

"Illegal."

"What d'youz think?" His eyes went wide.

She couldn't work out if his shock reaction was in mockery or real. She guessed the former, but only because she couldn't imagine many legal things went on in this place.

Jocassa said, "Don' worry about th' ID for now. Youz need money 'n there's plenty of us t' chip in." He yelled, "Hey, guys!"

The group of men and women gathered around him. The men were all ex-soldiers, and the women mostly locals, but one Kedrasi, one Damarcian. There was even a Coldi girl on the arm of one of the Mirani men. All their eyes, blue, sandy-coloured, brown and black with gold specks, were on her.

"Eydrina here's new 'n she's been robbed already. She's got no money left."

Mutters went around of *fucking gangs* and *kill them all*. Everyone in the group spoke Mirani, including the Coldi girl.

Jocassa cupped his hands and went around the group. Men dug in their pockets and handed him donations.

Jocassa came back with both hands full of coins, pearls and whatever else passed for small change in various currencies. She spotted triangular Mirani tirans—only used in Miran by the street vendors because all the families had accounts—a number of pearls of various sizes that Barresh used for small change and even some Asto chips, which travelling people carried because they were accepted form of payment at most airports.

"Here. That should keep youz going fer a bit."

"Thank you so much. I swear I'll pay it all back." The truth was on the tip of her tongue, that she was from an old Mirani Endri family and she'd reward them later, but that was stupid because she was no one and she wouldn't have much money for a long time. She had nothing to give.

Jocassa shook his head. "Youz go 'n find a job or do what-sever youz s'pposed t' do here. Next time someone else's in trouble, youz pay yer bit 'n that's how it works. All of us fall on hard times every now 'n then. Th' important thing about being one of us is that we's friends to help us out, not t' give us more debt 'n we need."

He dumped the whole bundle in Mikandra's hands with a chinking of coins. A few went rolling on the floor. He picked them up and added them to the weight in her hands.

As Endri, Mikandra rarely handled physical money. She carried a chip with her wherever she went, and bought only at places that accepted payment by account. It was a long time since she handled Mirani tirans and she didn't even know how much the other currency was worth.

Mikandra worked the whole lot into her pocket, too ashamed to meet anyone's eyes. These were the people who, by contract of the Mirani Foundation, she was supposed to look after. The Endri were supposed to give the Nikala work and shelter, to look after education and health. Instead they patched up problems in the hospitals by treating the symptoms and never the cause, and neglected everything else.

The Endri of Miran would never look after each other like this. They circled each other looking for an opportunity to pounce on each other's wealth and undermine each other's power, or profit from it if they couldn't undermine it.

Like Geonan Takumar wanted a young girl and her father would have been looking for an opportunity to get an entry into the wealthy and conservative Takumar family. No one in the Endri ever did anything that didn't benefit themselves in one way or another. Sending your wife or daughters to do unpaid work in the hospital was just another way of increasing one's standing.

Around her, the group debated where they were going. Mikandra wanted only a bed and something to eat.

Jocassa said he'd come with her, Dalit said nothing and seemed to go wherever Jocassa went, but the others wanted to go to some other place where apparently there was a party. Maybe one of the other guesthouses, she didn't know.

So the three of them made their way down Market Street. After falling away completely, the wind had again picked up and occasional squalls blew clouds of pink petals from the trees. The wind was oddly warm.

Jocassa peered into the sky, at the orange-tinged clouds that scudded over the city.

" 'S gonna rain soon."

Dalit nodded. "Better hurry up."

Even this late at night, the markets were a hive of activity with vendors yelling for attention, people cramming to get the best deals. Under the cover of the huge trees, there were people selling spike-finned fish, people selling strange types of bread, or the most unusual types of fruit.

Others sold fabric and even furniture. There was a barber doing brisk trade combing and plaiting the hair of middle-aged men.

There was clothing in varying styles, fabrics, carpets, cooking pots and utensils. Beautiful glass-stone bowls. Woven cane chairs, engraved mirrors, baked and coloured pavers like she had seen in the mosaics being restored in the Exchange building. Everything was a riot of colour and nothing like she'd ever seen before. Were these wares locally made?

Who again in Miran said that Barresh produced nothing?

While they walked through the crowded aisles, many people greeted Jocassa with handshakes and claps on shoulders. He talked a lot, and laughed a lot and introduced her as Eydrina to a lot of merchants, some local, some Kedrasi or Damarcian. A stocky Coldi woman behind a food stall gave her an icy stare after having smiled to Jocassa. Her stall boasted a large vat of smoking oil in which she and a few helpers, most of them Indrahui, fried a variety of unidentified things. The smell was heavenly and the stall was doing a brisk trade from all different kinds of people.

At this stall, Jocassa bought a dish wrapped in folded leaves. There were chunks of something in a sauce with red strips of some vegetable over the top. The sauce was dark brown and smelled of strong spices.

"It's fish," he said and tucked in.

Even so, Mikandra couldn't bring herself to buy from a Coldi vendor. She bought a couple of rolls of fish bread at a much less busy vendor, because they were cheap, she gave as excuse.

It was true, they *were* cheap, but tasted doughy and she had to work hard in trying to swallow the bread. They were nothing like Rosep's freshly-baked bread. Or Gillay's. Or the bread at the Guild headquarters.

"I should have warned you that the fish bread is no good," Dalit said while the three of them sat eating on a bench between the trees, overlooking the square. "To bake the bread requires an oven and you can't make fires in Barresh." He was still squinting at her and by now she wondered how much he saw and if poor eyesight was the reason he'd been discharged by the army.

Mikandra vaguely remembered something about not being able to make fires in Barresh. "Because of the oil from those trees —whatever they are called." Megon trees, that was it. They exuded a fine mist of oil that settled on everything and made it pretty much impossible to light a fire.

"Yes, the oil gets sold to makers of aircraft and firefighters." Dalit licked his fingers. "There's a merchant who makes a bit of money doing that."

That left her to wonder how the Coldi woman heated her oil, and where she got the ingredients. If they came from outside, there would be Traders involved, yet she had seen no sign of Traders in all the time she'd been in the city. It seemed to her that if a Trader decided to set up business in Barresh, there would be a great demand. However, those decisions were in the hands of the Trader Guild, because they had to release new licences.

She finished as much of the bread as she could stomach and stuffed the last bit into her pocket. "Where do they get all this?"

"What d' youz mean?" Jocassa asked around a mouth full of food.

"All this food, all these things for sale. Where does it come from?"

"Most of it, around here. Other stuff's imported. There's a lot of foreigners in town. Damarcians want Damarcian stuff. There's not so much Mirani stuff here these days, 'n whatever th' stalls have, they mostly can' give it away. Most of us don' want Mirani food anymore."

"Barresh is a free market," Dalit said. "There are no restrictions on imports, unlike in Miran." There was a political undertone to his comment and he met Mikandra's eyes while he said this. Fishing what her opinion was.

She was tempted to ask why he cared, and why he was ex-army while he belonged there just as much as she did. He might look like a Nikala worker with his curly hair, but he sure didn't speak like one. A merchant's son?

A spy?

She shivered. This was no time for such thoughts.

"So," Jocassa said while scrunching up the leaves of his empty food parcel. "What about this guy youz s'pposed t' marry?"

Mikandra cringed. Was there no end to his innocent curiosity and his endless ability to recall her lies and repeat them to her at any inopportune moment? She shrugged. "He's old and ugly."

"Old 'n rich's not so bad. At least youz only need t' keep him occupied fer a bit until he carks it." He laughed at his own joke.

Dalit glared at him. There was an expression in his eyes that chilled her.

Jocassa's laughter faded. He looked away and shrugged. "Oh man, can't you let off?"

"No, I can't." Dalit's voice was intense.

Jocassa sighed and shrugged again.

An uneasy silence followed. Mikandra stared at her hands folded in her lap. She was about to ask if they should perhaps go to the guesthouse so that she could have a bath when she remembered that she had no spare clothes and no soap or towels or any other toiletries and then she was about to propose to go back to the stalls so that she could buy them when Dalit said, "You promised."

Jocassa spread his hands. "It wasn't so easy, right?"

"You promised to bring my mother back." Dalit punctuated each word with anger.

"I gave youz back th' money."

"This isn't about money. It's about my mother's life. They threatened to kill her. My sister is missing. Mother sits inside that house too afraid to set foot outside the door. She needs to leave Miran."

Whoa. Mikandra revised her estimate of Dalit. He might be ex-army, but someone whose family attracted that sort of attention had to be somewhere high up, someone who had fallen foul of the upper command.

Jocassa's shoulders slumped. "I said I's sorry 'n I meant it. I tried, man, I really did, but th' house is guarded all th' freakin' time. I couldn' even get close enough t' throw a rock into th' yard."

Another uneasy silence.

"I really tried, man. I said so many times. I mean it."

Dalit's mouth twitched. He did not meet Jocassa's eyes.

After another tense silence, Mikandra asked, "Your mother?"

Jocassa began, "Dalit's pa's a nasty piece of work. His ma din' agree with some of th' stuff that th' council's been doing. She was telling people t' vote against—"

Dalit said, "For once, hold your mouth."

"But I's only explaining."

"And do we know what connections she has?"

Jocassa swallowed visibly. "But Eydrina's only—"

"We don't know. She could be a spy for all I know. As long as my mother is alive, I won't trust anyone with the full story."

Jocassa shrugged again. "Fair enough, man, but give a fellow a break, right?"

Dalit sighed.

A squall of wind blew his hair to one side. A flurry of petals drifted past. There was a rumbling noise in the distance.

Mikandra frowned at the part of the sky she could see. "Was

that thunder?" It was an unusual growling sound, different from the echoing rumble of thunder in Miran.

"Sure is," Jocassa said.

Dalit pushed himself to his feet. "Let's go, before we get wet."

In fact, a few big drops were already splatting on the pavement.

At the markets, merchants were running around with ropes and sheets of cloth, bringing in exposed wares. More drops of rain fell, big and wet on the pavement, releasing a smell of earth.

A rushing sound came towards them from the dark side of the square. Mikandra thought it was the wind, but Jocassa said, "Uh-oh, run."

The wall of rain hit.

17

M IKANDRA HAD never seen rain like this before. Water came down in solid sheets. It was as if someone threw buckets of water from the sky.

People ran for cover. A merchant shouted at a woman—his wife?—who was dragging baskets of wares under cover.

Mikandra ran after Jocassa for the relative shelter of the leaning wall that surrounded the Exchange building. Behind her, Dalit tripped and fell. Mikandra ducked out of her shelter to help him up. Rain pelted on her back and head. Her hair dripped water into her eyes. Within moments, she was soaked to the skin.

Dalit said something, probably *thanks* but his words were lost in another clap of thunder, this one so close that the flash and the sound arrived at the same time, and the ground trembled with the noise.

They made for the guesthouse at a run. Every time Mikandra thought it couldn't possibly rain any heavier, the rain found new intensities. It was hard to see. Gutters overflowed in huge water-falls. Now Mikandra understood why each street was shaped like a gutter with a depression in the middle. Water collected in yards and gushed out into the street taking with it a collection of leaves and fallen flowers and discarded food wrappers and other rubbish.

The middle of the street turned into a raging torrent. The stairs into the guesthouse had become a water feature and the entrance hid under a waterfall that cascaded from the roof two floors up.

Under the arched entry a number of sodden refugees from the weather stood huddled together. Mikandra wondered if she needed to register as guest, but there was no desk, and Jocassa didn't seem to worry about it. He led her through the hall.

Like many of the buildings she had seen in the city, this one centred around a courtyard, which seemed to be used as a dining area. Sets of mismatched tables and chairs stood in the rain while their occupants had sought refuge under the over-hang of the upstairs gallery. They had dragged some of the tables there, but most people sat on the ground, leaning against the pillars that supported the floor above.

Several of them greeted Jocassa. There were cries of "Pull up a chair." Someone ducked into the rain to pass three chairs into the covered area.

Mikandra sat on the chair a Mirani youth gave her. The seat was wet, but couldn't possibly be any wetter than she was. Something squelched in her pocket. When she checked it, her fingers met a soggy mass. Oh yes, the fish bread. Wonderful.

"What are we waiting for?" Jocassa asked. "Where's th' party?"

Another man said, "Thasep was gonna get supplies, but he's probably got distracted."

"What, youz trusted Thasep with th' money?" another said.

"He offered t' go out."

"Yeah, because all of youz 're afraid of a bit of rain?"

One of the Mirani men went to sit on a table, carrying a battered lute which he proceeded to tune while others talked and laughed. Mikandra wondered if it was polite to ask where the bathroom was.

The lute player launched into a popular folk song about men serving in the army. His playing was moderately competent, but he was so drunk that he didn't remember half the song's lines. She was neither Nikala nor soldier, but even she knew that the line was *and I give my life if fate decides, for freedom and for better tides* but he sang *I give my life for better tides, to serve the man and get free rides.*

One or two people thought it was funny.

Then she got it, and felt disgusted.

She was cold and tired, and wondered where she would sleep and if someone could lend her any clothes while these ones dried, but she didn't want to draw attention to herself. In this town, if you were Mirani, you were ex-army, and if you were ex-army, you came here to party.

The lute player meanwhile had started a Mirani ballad. It was a beautiful piece that she had never heard before and would have sounded much better if he hadn't been so drunk.

His mates laughed.

One yelled, "What're youz tryin' t' be, singing that song? All primmed up 'n noble?"

Another added, "Comb out yer hair 'cause it's gone curly."

The man put down his lute, walked into the rain to the middle of the courtyard while undoing his pony tail and dunked his head in the overflowing fountain. Dripping wet, he smoothed his hair. "This better?"

Everyone laughed.

He went to one of the potted bushes, broke off a slender branch and wove the twigs around his fingers, then snipped off some flowers, stuck them in his "rings". Like the ornate Trader's rings.

The men laughed harder.

He straightened his back, stuck his chin in the air and strutted back to his lute, dripping water, all the while his friends were doubled over in hysterics. He picked up the lute and continued the song, trying to mock a very deep voice and failing miserably.

The giant Thasep entered the courtyard, carrying two bottles. He gave them to the keihu girl who had come in with him, and she plunked both bottles on one of the tables. Several men cheered. One lunged for a bottle and unstoppered it.

The singer put the instrument aside, and, still holding his back straight, bowed before the keihu woman and made a movement like he took a cloak off his shoulders to drape it over hers.

Mikandra's heart thudded. They were making fun of Traders.

Offering the cloak was how Traders asked a partner in marriage. Mikandra had seen it a few times with her friends and had often dreamed of Lihan doing this for her. The official offering of the cloak was usually a prearranged occasion and performed before as large a crowd as possible for maximum impact. But there were the occasional surprise marriage proposals.

The young woman also straightened her back, falling into her role. The lute player remained bowed, trembling and pleading, still trying to mock a deep voice. The young woman took the pretend cloak off her shoulders, flung it down and left the courtyard.

The crowd's squeals of laughter hurt her ears.

Mikandra didn't know where to look. This was a re-enactment of something that had happened. Iztho had come here to sing. He had offered marriage to a local woman. She had refused. Was it the same woman he had told her he would marry?

Jocassa held a bottle under her nose. The glass was brown and the liquid inside looked slightly darker, but by the oily way in which it stuck to the side of the glass, she knew what was inside.

Mikandra shook her head.

"Ow, c'me on, everybody drinks. Don' spoil th' party. Jus' a bit."

"No, I'd rather not."

"Why not?"

Mikandra grasped for reasons. *Because I've seen people drink themselves to death in hospitals? Because when I smell that stuff, I remember old Leitho and his orange eyes and orange piss, and his hallucinations. And I think about how he's probably dead by now.* But she said, lamely, "I'm not used to it. I . . . never had any."

"Youz never had any? Youz kidding? They don' have it in Bendara? Youz gotta try this. C'me on, pass us a glass." He held out his hand and someone else passed him a chipped glass. He poured—

"Not so much."

—and handed her a good glass full of the bright orange oily brew. "Here ye go."

Mikandra took it from him. It was not entirely a lie that she hadn't had any, but not entirely true either. She *had* tried the brew, but didn't like how it made her feel strange and lightheaded. She had been at one of those parties with her old friends who had all moved onto businesses, quite inappropriate companions for her now they were all considered adults, but she had still hoped to hear news from Lihan in Kedras. It had been a rather awful occasion because one of the boys had been trying to chat her up, and she spent most of the night fending him off. Someone had put a glass of brew in her hands and she was trying to work out how not to embarrass the party's host while drinking as little as possible. Her father would be furious if he found out that she'd been drinking.

That horrible party was about a year ago and she hadn't tried drinking brew since. Nor had she ever been to similar parties again.

By now everyone near her was watching so she could do nothing but take a sip. People cheered. The brew tasted sweet and made the inside of her mouth feel warm. She remembered that feeling. It made the hairs on the back of her arms stand up. As if Father was watching.

Jocassa smiled. "See, there ye go. 'S not so bad, is it?"

No, it wasn't so bad. It was kind of naughty. By far the majority of people who drank brew handled it well and did not slide into addiction. Endri drank brew, but mostly men, as it wasn't considered a thing for ladies to do. They might drink a little bit, and giggle a lot afterwards, but not in public places. Father didn't approve of those "tea parties", but Father couldn't see her here. Father might never again look over her shoulder and tell her what to do. She took another sip. As long as she didn't drink too much, right?

The bottle passed further into the courtyard. Jocassa took a big swig from his glass and leaned back in his chair.

"Why would a man want t' be anywhere else but here? We's got all th' good things 'n none of th' bad things. Ye know, sometimes I jus' need t' go back t' Miran 'cause I forget how good th' life here is."

He took another swig from his glass, closing his eyes.

"Jocassa, that man who was just playing the lute, what was that about?"

He opened his eyes. "Oh, sorry I's already forgotten that youz are new here. 'S about this stuck-up Mirani Trader, Iztho Andrahar, youz know him?"

"Heard about him." Her heart thudded.

"Well, he wanted t' marry this woman from here. Youz know how Traders do that thing with th' cloak?"

She nodded.

"Well, he did that, but he din' know that she's already taken. Rule number one fer any place youz visit: don' mess around with th' Chief Councillor's woman, not even if youz are a rich Mirani Trader."

"He didn't know that she was married?"

"Not married, no, but spoken for. Rule number two if youz visit a strange place: don' mess with th' Chief Councillor."

Her heart thudded even louder. "So, what happened after that? She refused the cloak, and then, what did he do?"

"He left with th' army at th' end of the war. Then he came back fer a bit. Some people said he asked her again, some said he's even bought a house. He was here a lot, always tryin' t' tell th' Mirani how t' behave. People said th' council was buying lots of stuff off him, like stuff t' fix th' buildings 'n that. Th' Exchange got a new core. They's said that he got a good deal fer them. I dunno what's true, but we's always poked fun at him fer sharing th' woman with another man. Y'know . . . there's rumours I could tell, but t' be honest I's no idea if any of them's true. Probably not. They's pretty colourful." He laughed.

Shivering, Mikandra asked, "Is he still in town?"

"No. Haven't seen him for a while, t' be honest."

"One day, your big mouth will get you into trouble," Dalit said while sitting down on Jocassa's side with a glass containing something that looked suspiciously like water.

"What trouble? I was jus' filling Eydrina in. She wanted t' know what Arit's singin' was all about." He upended the glass into his mouth and lunged for the bottle in the middle of the table. "She's gotta know all these things or she won' understand any of th' jokes. I did what youz said 'n not told her any of th' rumours."

Dalit sighed and rolled his eyes. "If one day, someone decides to follow you around and frame you for something you didn't do, they could get you into jail in a heartbeat."

"No, they can' 'cause I tell everyone everything. I got no secrets, mate. Secrets are fer people with money. I got none of that, either."

Jocassa poured and then held out the bottle to Mikandra. "Here, youz half-finished the glass."

Before Mikandra could say anything, he had refilled her glass. She protested. "I don't know if I can—"

"What's wrong with a bit of drink 'n fun?"

"It's poison." She put her glass down, feeling cold all of a sudden. "The fungus contains a poison that accumulates in the body's fat and only slowly leaves the body. If you drink too much, it builds up. There is a limit you can drink before you die."

He frowned at her. "What are youz, a healer of some kind?"

"Of some kind, yes."

"Hey, I din' know that." Then he raised his voice. "Hey, boys, youz can have Eydrina here look at yer bad bites 'n she can give youz something t' put on it."

Mikandra cringed and looked away, trying desperately to think of a change of topic. This was way too close to home.

Jocassa started to talk to Thasep, and Dalit seemed lost in his own world.

Thasep related a story about how he had outsmarted the liquor vendor who had tried to charge too much, but when pressed about amounts of money, it was clear that the vendor had the better of his Mirani customer. Thasep didn't get it. Jocassa didn't get it either, but Dalit looked in Mikandra's direction with a sad expression that said *they can't help it* and the sense of failure hung between them.

By now, her glass was again half empty, but she guarded it so that no one could put any more in. In fact, she was already looking for a way to wriggle her way to those potted trees over there so that she could empty the rest of the vile orange stuff over the soil.

Her head swam and it was as if every time she moved her head, the rest of the world took a while to catch up.

The rain had stopped, the courtyard had filled up with people and more were still coming in from the street. Many of the newcomers were also locals and tailed Pengali, many of the latter barely dressed, dancing and singing and talking. Mikandra studied all of them carefully, but most of them were young and many female and none looked remotely like the wiry criminals with dreadlocks who had robbed her. Pengali, she decided, did not come in one flavour.

One group brought a strange instrument that looked like it was made from hollow pieces of wood. They set it up in the middle of the courtyard. One of the Pengali mounted it like a riding beast and beat a sweeping rhythm on the hollow logs. Each piece was a different length so their tones were different and formed a tune. It was strange music with an uneven rhythm which she couldn't place, and one which had certainly never been covered in her general music classes. Mikandra had never been good at music, and this type didn't fit what she'd learned about beats and bars. Liseyo would know. She knew all about music—

Liseyo—

—looked at Mother as she sat at the table. Mother was biting her lip. A tear rolled down her cheek.

She said, *I can't stop them. Father is trying, but I don't know that he can stop them either.*

Mikandra wanted to shout out, *stop what?*

Then I will go by myself! Liseyo rose from the table and made for the door.

Mother cried, *Liseyo, please, it's bad enough that we lost one of you already.*

Liseyo met Rosep who was coming into the dining room, carrying a tray. *Mistress, you don't know what these men will do to young and pretty girls like you.*

I don't care! Liseyo's cheeks were wet with tears. *I want Father to come home.*

Liseyo! Mikandra reached out for her sister, but instead hit a Mirani soldier sitting next to her in the courtyard. He yelled out, "Hey!"

"Sorry." She shifted away from him, her vision still blurred. Her heart thudded like crazy. What in the ancestor's name was *that?* Not a memory, because she had no idea what Mother and Liseyo were talking about. Father couldn't come home? What had happened in Miran?

She remembered that meeting of Mirani Traders and the speech by Aithno Ilendar at the Guild. Maybe the political movement behind him spanned more than just the Trader Guild. Was this what Dalit's mother was involved in?

Aunt Amandra had been concerned that militant supporters of Nemedor Satarin might try to harm her. Could they be trying to harm her family instead? Had she misunderstood Father's objection to her joining the Guild?

Heart thudding, she stared into the crowd, heaving to the music. No one seemed to have noticed her dizzy spell.

18

THERE WAS a commotion on the other side of the courtyard, men's voices yelling somewhere near the entrance which was obscured from Mikandra's view because of the crowd.

The music stopped. A male voice yelled a few words that sounded like an order in keihu. The light under the balcony behind Mikandra went out. A number of people, mainly Pengali, pushed between the tables, into the shadow of the overhanging balcony. A number of them went up the stairs.

A group of about ten men came into the courtyard. The golden curls gave the leader away as a Mirani Nikala, and although he was not in uniform, he walked like a soldier, held himself like a soldier and gave orders like a soldier. The others in the group were mixed: some Pengali with matted dreadlocks—Mikandra shivered—some keihu and a few mixed-race people.

"What's going on?" Mikandra asked, but she couldn't see Jocassa in the dark and none of the bystanders responded to her question.

The group's leader barked an order in Mirani, "Disperse."

The men fanned out through the courtyard two by two. Each of them carried a pearl light on a long stick, holding it aloft over the heads of the partygoers. Its greenish-white light showed sweaty faces and eyes wide with fear. No one said a word.

For a while, the thugs merely walked backwards and forwards between the partygoers as if they were looking for someone. Mikandra held her breath. They could not *possibly* have been sent by her father, could they? He would be crazy enough to do something like that. She looked over her shoulder. People stood jammed together on the stairs, hiding in the dark.

Then there was a protesting squeal from amongst the crowd.

Two thugs dragged a young man into the centre of the courtyard, one of the tailed Pengali, who protested loudly in his language. No one dared move to help him. While one man held his arms behind his back and dodged his whipping tail, another man held the pearl light close to his face. There was a moment of silence as if they expected a reaction, but nothing happened. They let their captive go without speaking a single word. He scurried into the arms of a Pengali woman.

Another duo plucked someone else from the crowd, also Pengali. The same thing happened: they held the light to his face and waited, then let him go. No words were said. And so it went on. The thugs walked through the crowd in a zigzag pattern and picked out some of the locals, Pengali or keihu, to subject them to this curious treatment.

Mikandra whispered, "What are they looking for?"

People around her made shushing noises.

Now a couple of men struggled out of the crowd with another Pengali, a woman, who fought and kicked the men wherever she could.

Her shrill voice echoed in the courtyard. "You filthy worms. You childfuckers. You mother-raping slime!"

Pretty impressive knowledge of Mirani obscenities.

Her tail lashed one of her captors in the face. A third thug came to help his mates. They forced the woman to her knees, shone the light in her face, and *something* flashed in her face.

Someone shouted. Any Pengali and keihu still around Mikandra started pushing away from the thugs, except there was no room for them to go. The space under the balcony and leading up to the stairs was full and the way across the courtyard blocked by the thugs. At the back of the crowd a Mirani voice yelled to stay calm.

Meanwhile the thugs pulled a blindfold over the woman's eyes and dragged her towards the entrance, still struggling and screaming obscenities. They'd tied her tail to her leg. The brown and white banded tip of it wriggled furiously.

The remaining thugs came closer to where Mikandra stood. They picked someone else out of the crowd, about three rows before Mikandra. This was a young keihu man, protesting loudly in keihu while they held his arms behind his back.

They shone the light into his eyes—

—and a beam missed his face, cut across the crowd and hit Mikandra's face.

Her vision blurred. Her legs went weak and the world spun around her.

She was falling—

She was drifting in a stream—

Flying through the air where there was no up or down—

Her knees hurt. She sat on the ground amongst a forest of legs. Her hands and knees were muddy from a puddle. Someone was pulling her under her arms, trying to get her up. Mikandra looked up. Jocassa's face was blurry before her eyes.

"Eydrina, please get up or they's take youz, too."

Mikandra struggled to her feet, feeling sick and panicked that she might throw up on someone. Her head hurt so much.

Jocassa said, "C'me on, get up, quick—let us through, all of youz. Let us through!"

People parted. Jocassa dragged her through the crowd, pushing people aside until they were in the shadow of the balcony and then to the stairs to the upper floor. Here it was so crowded that they could go no further than a few steps. Someone whispered that the upstairs balcony was full and mentioned a door being closed.

So they stood on the stairs, Mikandra still feeling unsteady on her feet, and Jocassa sheltering her from view of the courtyard.

It was hot here, and smelly with the sweat of many different people.

"What was that?" Mikandra still felt dizzy. She stood jammed up against Jocassa and a few keihu women, whose eyes were all wide with fear.

Jocassa said in a low voice, "With some people, when they's been drinking, they see things when they's in a bright light. In some people, it's so strong, th' light shines back. Those ones they want."

"Only when they've been drinking?" Her thoughts went to Leitho.

"Yes, th' Pengali call it *avya*. It happens with them 'n th' keihu. Never seen it happening in a Mirani before." He squinted at her. "Is it because youz are from Bendara? Youz have any keihu blood?"

Mikandra shrugged, wishing he'd stop repeating her own lies back at her.

"Who are these men?"

"Mercenaries."

"Who pays them?"

"Dunno, but th' Barresh guards are always absent when they's come so they's probably have something t' do with it."

"Do you mean they have these raids often?"

"Mos' nights they come t' one of th' guesthouses. Mos' times people know where they are so they make sure they get out of th' way. They don' normally come here until late at night."

"Does no one do anything about it?"

"Like what?"

"Like go to the guards?"

"When you's Mirani, th' Barresh guards are not yer friends."

"That woman was Pengali. The others they tested were keihu. Doesn't anyone care about them?"

"They's don' belong t' th' families anymore. They don' have jobs that th' people call respectable. No one cares about them."

The homeless of Barresh. It hit her like a shockwave. She'd worked amongst them in Miran and had lived amongst them here without recognising it.

"What happens to the people they take away?"

He shrugged. "There's rumours they's get paid money but no one's been able t' tell for sure. Not sure what they's get paid for either."

"Don't they ever tell you when they come back?"

"They's don' come back."

"Never?"

"No one's seen any that they know of—careful." He pushed her head down while a beam of light lanced over the heads of the people jammed on the stairs. Between the people on the step below her, Mikandra could make out the Mirani leader standing at the bottom of the stairs, looking up. The light angled on his face, and she saw that she'd been wrong: he was not Mirani. The bottom half of his face was covered in a fuzz of dirty-looking *hair*. His eyes were cloudy grey, not dark blue. He stood with his hands at his sides. His hands were hairy, too, as were the parts of his legs below the knee that poked out from under his short trousers that were stained with grime.

Who was this disgusting man?

She closed her eyes and held her breath, sheltering behind Jocassa's body. No one spoke. No one dared move.

When the light vanished and the man moved on, Mikandra could almost feel the relief in the people surrounding her.

Down in the courtyard, the thugs completed their lap and held a few others in the light, but none showed any reaction. They left in total silence, taking their charge with them.

When they were safely gone, people streamed off the crowded stairs back down into the courtyard. Voices of protest went up, and someone wailed. Most others just looked scared.

A breeze of cool and humid air over Mikandra's wet clothes made her shiver.

"Come on, we's safe now." Jocassa started down the stairs. "They's gone fer th' night."

But going back to the party was the last thing she wanted. "Jocassa, I'm extremely tired. Can you show me where I can sleep, please?"

Jocassa gave her a strange look, and she realised she'd forgotten to tone down her speech and had spoken to him as she would speak to Rosep.

Poor Rosep.

Poor Liseyo missing her sister.

Poor Mother, worried about her oldest daughter.

What was happening in Miran? Who would hurt Liseyo? What was Father trying to stop and why couldn't he come home?

"All right. This way."

Jocassa took her across the courtyard and up another set of stairs, out onto the upper floor gallery, where there were more tables and chairs and where doors opened into dormitories.

The dormitory at the very end of the balcony was surprisingly large and airy, with a huge window looking out onto another courtyard on the far side. The room held three rows of beds and a couple of mattresses on the floor between the beds.

"Youz can have this bed." He indicated a low bed by the door. It had only a mattress—quite disgusting probably—and no blankets. She tried very hard not to think of her comfortable bed at home.

"You all sleep in this room?"

"My bed's over there." He pointed. " 'N Dalit's next t' me. If youz need anything, y'know . . ." He spread his hands.

"I'm fine." Perhaps a bit too harsh, but she sure wasn't going where he was hanging out his fishing line. Jocassa was a lot of things, but dumb wasn't one of them. He knew, or suspected, that she wasn't a merchant's daughter. So how could you tell someone of the Endri? They had no significant hair anywhere except on their heads, and the women didn't bleed.

His cheeks had gone red. "But youz might want t' wait to try t' sleep. There'll be a racket when everybody comes in."

"I'm fine, really." *Please go away and stop being nosy.*

Jocassa nodded and left.

Mikandra sat on the bed. It was quite hard and there were no pillows. A squally breeze came in through the far window and went out the door.

Two people sat talking on a bed in a corner, but Mikandra was too tired to care. Too tired to contemplate the happenings, too tired even to worry about having to find a job. Or about having no clothes other than those she wore. Which were still wet, and smelly.

She took off as many of her clothes as she dared and sank

down on the bed. It didn't take long before she slipped into a dreamless bliss.

19

MIKANDRA WOKE UP feeling disoriented. She turned on her back, looking at a ceiling with cracked plaster spotted with age. It took her a while to remember where she was, why she was here and what had happened last night.

The light in the room was still blue and dark as on Miran's snow days. An unfamiliar rushing sound came in through the open door behind her.

She lifted her head. Her muscles hurt from lying in a fixed position on that hard mattress. She had barely moved throughout the night, and whatever noise the partygoers had produced when they came in, it had not woken her up.

She had no idea of the time of day except it had to be early because all the beds around her were occupied with sleeping people. A young local woman slept next to a Mirani ex-soldier, using his shoulder as pillow. Both were stark naked. She had to stop herself staring, but on the other side, Jocassa lay asleep on a mattress, also stark naked, curled up with his back to her so that she had a direct view of his backside. At school, the girls used to whisper and giggle about this, but did Nikala men really have such hairy backsides? Then a fleeting thought of panic. They could tell what she was the moment one of them woke up and saw her hairless body.

As quietly as she could, she climbed from the bed—it was made of woven wooden twigs and it creaked—and found her trousers. They were still damp from the drenching last night and the thick fabric was starting to smell musty. She shuddered with the disgusting feel of the fabric on her skin.

She walked to the window.

The courtyard pavement glistened with wetness. The sky was a mass of low grey clouds shedding sheets of rain which lashed the roof. Water overflowed from the gutter and clattered onto the paving two floors down.

The only time it ever rained in Miran were a few drops in spring sometimes. Almost all water—and there was a lot of it—fell as snow. Nothing like this. At least, it would not be so hot today.

A blast of droplet-laden air wafted in. There was no glass in the windows and the people sleeping closest to the window would get wet. She wondered whose bed she had taken and whether she was supposed to have slept closer to the window. Maybe they'd tried to move her while she was asleep. That was an embarrassing thought.

She turned to the door and picked her way through the narrow spaces between the beds, avoiding limbs that hung in the aisle.

In the courtyard, the tables and chairs where everyone had partied last night stood abandoned in the rain. A few empty bottles lay on the ground and in flower beds. The flowering tree in the pot drooped, all its branches laden with water, the flowers wet and floppy. There was no sign of people anywhere.

What exactly had happened to her last night?

Her head still echoed with the voices of Liseyo and Mother. They were scared. Something was happening in Miran. It freaked her out.

She wondered if this was the same thing as what the Endri called not being right in the head. Like the old guy Leitho in the hospital. He saw things and heard voices, but she'd never considered that he might hear people he knew. She tried to recall things he said, but felt ashamed that she had never listened to

him or even attempted to take any of his hallucinations
seriously.

She had always suspected that there was a link between
drinking brew and hallucinations, but the link with light was
new. Yet, now that she thought of it, she couldn't remember
anyone with hallucinations ever having come into the hospital
after dark.

Yet, the problem was not defined solely by addiction to
menisha brew. Light affected some people who had been drinking, but not all. Why Pengali and keihu but not Mirani Nikala?
Why Mirani Endri?

Were two of those affected Rehan and Iztho Andrahar?

She remembered Rehan's absentminded expression. The
memory chilled her. Almost every Endri family had a member
who wasn't right in the head. Could their disease have been
avoided only if those people had not drunk so much brew?

But that didn't make sense either. One of the worst affected
with hallucinations was Dithiandra Andrahar, Rehan's aunt and
Jihan's sister, and she never left the house and would never have
had the opportunity to drink. Endri women didn't drink, and
especially women of that generation would obey their fathers
unconditionally.

So what? The hallucinations happened in some people, but
drinking menisha brew made them worse? What would happen
if Dithiandra Andrahar drank?

And why would someone pay a bunch of thugs to go into
guesthouses to find these people? Who sent the thugs? Someone
in Barresh, Jocassa seemed to think. Had these people taken
away Iztho?

An icy chill went over her back and she was glad no one here
knew her real name and why she was here.

Mikandra walked across the upstairs gallery and went down
the deserted stairwell. There was no one on the ground floor, not
in the courtyard, not in the corridor and not in the archway that
led to the street. When she walked through the entrance hall,
there was a shimmer of movement in a room off the hall—this
was probably the guesthouse's cranky owner and she had no

desire to speak to him, especially not about any payment she might owe him.

Going out into the street presented a different problem: how to stay dry? Locals walked around wearing peculiar hats with long flapping sides that directed the water off the wearer.

Mikandra had no such gadgets, not even a cloak to keep her dry. But it wasn't far to the shops where she wanted to start asking for work so she went into the rain, skipping over puddles.

But she might as well not have tried. The very air seemed liquid. The trees dripped big and fat drops onto the street whenever there was a bit of breeze.

At a street stall, she bought the cheapest breakfast she could find—some sort of porridge goo that consisted of little balls stuck together with white gel. It tasted . . . funny, like everything in this place smelled funny either of farts from hot water wells or of the all-pervasive soapy smell of the megon oil. The porridge was probably a bit more watery than intended, because the rain became heavier while she was eating and the trunk of the tree at her back did not give much shelter.

A stall in the street sold rain hats. Mikandra counted out her money—Jocassa's friends' money—and decided against it. Surely it *had* to stop raining soon.

It was still too early to start asking merchants for jobs. Many of them were only arriving at their stalls or shops. She walked past the guard office in Market Street, but it, too, was still closed.

The only thing Mikandra hadn't lost in the robbery was written on her hand. She would rather die than ask the Andrahar brothers for money, but Rehan had given her the code so that she would use it, right? *He* wanted to keep up with what she was doing, and she could ask about what was going on in Miran.

The foyer of the Exchange was quiet at this time of the day. The builder's table still stood in the corner, and bags of sand and piles of wood lay in piles at the bottom of the stairs, but the workers had not yet arrived for the day.

With all the humidity, the upstairs corridor beyond the

sliding doors felt positively frigid. That thought made her smile. Only yesterday, she would have died to be allowed into this room.

When Mikandra asked for the communication booths, the woman behind the counter pointed her to a large room with cubicles, each with a comfortable chair facing a wallscreen.

Mikandra sat down and, when the woman had left, punched the code. She wrote a short message which she hoped would sound businesslike.

Iztho does not seem to be in Barresh. I have potentially identified the woman he wanted to marry and will make an attempt to talk to her. Well, that sounded a bit more positive than reality. She had yet to set eyes on the Chief Councillor's wife, but she knew who this woman was. *I'm hearing disturbing rumours about things that are happening in Miran. I hope you are all well.*

She scrubbed the last sentence out and rewrote it three times, but she didn't like *Please let me know if my family is all right* because it sounded too desperate. She also didn't like *What is going on in Miran?* or any of the more formal wordings. These messages weren't always completely confidential and she didn't want to sound like she was interested in politics in case someone was keeping an eye on her.

After signing off, she went to the guard office in Market Street where, as Jocassa had predicted, the man at the counter could not have been less interested in the robbery. She mentioned Iztho's name, but they seemed neither to care nor to recognise the name. So—maybe the Pengali thug had been talking about someone else. After all, he had not mentioned Iztho's name when he'd said, *Your master has sent you.*

While she answered stupid questions on exactly how many men there had been and what each of them looked like without using the word *Pengali*—because we don't make assumptions based on suspects' ethnicity—she grew more determined.

Solving her situation, getting herself to Kedras in time for the academy year, was her responsibility and hers alone. She would not ask the Andrahar brothers for money. She would not beg. This whole trouble was her own stupid fault, and she would work her way out of it.

If people wanted money, they found a job, and she had best get started on that.

The shops were right here.

The business closest to the guard station was a seller of baskets and rugs, who had set up a large blue tent to shelter his wares from the rain. He was middle-aged, rotund like so many local men and when she entered the tent where the rain thundered on the roof, he barked orders to a small child who toddled around and was surely too young to understand.

Mikandra felt nervous and silly facing him soaking wet. The water dripped from her hair into her neck. She swore she would buy better clothes as soon as she earned some money.

He asked, "Can I help the lady?" She could barely hear him over the noise.

"Yes, I was wondering if you have a job for me."

"I'm sorry, lady, but we don't sell any—wait, did you say job?"

Hope surged in her. "I did. I can help pack things and unpack things and deliver—" What *did* shop owners do?

He stared at her like she'd slapped him in the face.

Her hopes deflated again. "If you can't help me, maybe you'll know someone who is looking for workers. I am reliable and—"

"No, we can't use anyone. I'm sorry."

"Do you know anyone else who—"

"Sorry, no. We don't give jobs to foreign louts."

What the. . . ?

She was so surprised she couldn't think of anything to say. Louts? If she looked like a customer, he called her a lady. If she asked for a job, she was a lout?

Seething, she walked to the next shop and found an owner who didn't speak Mirani. In the next shop, she was more formal and direct.

"A job?" The owner scratched his head.

"I can help you pack and unpack stock and—"

A voice came from behind her. "You dare ask us for a job?"

It was the owner of the fabric store where she had met Jocassa yesterday. He went on to rant at his colleague in keihu. The man's previous friendly but guarded look turned suspicious. What was this other idiot telling him? That she stole or was a spy?

Anyway, with that vindictive idiot around, it would be useless to keep trying in this block of shops. Maybe she would have better luck at the markets.

She slunk back out into the rain.

The cloth merchant yelled after her, "Get out, Mirani filth. Get out, before I send the guards after you."

Shaken, Mikandra made her way to the markets, where only a few stalls operated in the pissing rain. She asked all of them, but none seemed to have a need for workers who were Mirani and female.

Feeling dejected, Mikandra trudged back to the guesthouse, wondering if she could possibly ask to borrow more money so she could go back home. But what would that achieve except confirm to her father that she was good for nothing and needed to be married off? It would certainly not get her to Kedras to start her training. It would not convince Rehan that she was worth supporting.

But then again, what would either of those two men have done in the same situation? Swear at the merchant probably. Much as swearing profusely was said to be the Trader's style, it wasn't hers. She didn't think Aunt Amandra swore either.

Courage Iztho had told her.

Well, that was great, but didn't solve many of her problems. For one, where was he and why had he left the family in such a mess? Who really had courage?

She went back to the guesthouse at midday, and found Jocassa in the courtyard. It had stopped raining and he sat at the table closest to the fountain counting money out in little piles.

He glanced up as she dropped at the table. "Bad day?"

She sighed and wiped sweat from her face. How could it be wet and cloudy and still so hot?

"I hate this place. I hate it."

"Ah, so youz are in that stage. Yup, we's all go through it." He chuckled and continued counting his money.

Mikandra felt annoyance that she owed him. She had been

such an idiot. She was hot, she smelled and she couldn't stand this place. She should never have come here.

"I've been trying to get a job, but everywhere I've asked they say they don't like foreigners or they have some other excuse. Some of them are really rude. This is stupid. I've never seen as many foreigners as in this place. There's even Coldi working in the council building. So they don't like foreigners, and the streets are full of them?"

"I said I can give youz some money. Looks like youz be best off going back home."

His expression said, *Give up, you're too soft for this place.*

Oh, home seemed so attractive. But there was no home for her to go to.

"I can't." Emotion welled up in her. What had gone from a simple task had become a struggle to survive. But she remembered what Rehan Andrahar had said. *If she wants to be one of us, she'll have to handle the heat.* She balled her fists under the table. "I won't."

He let a silence lapse, in which he swiped all the money off the table into a bag. "Bein' stubborn is stupid. What for, anyway? Youz take what life brings. Y'know, I din' ask t' be born t' a poor mother who'd drink herself t' death. I wanted a nice family. But all th' nice girls got married while I was in th' army t' make money so that my mother could eat and pay th' healers, and th' drink, too, whenever I din' look her way. I tried t' get out of th' army many times. I tried merchanting, but th' boss was an old perv who jus' wanted a playboy. I tried t' get into the agricultural co-ops in Bendara, but bein' from th' city, I had no 'xperience. Youz would know all about that. I's still tryin' t' get out when they found my mother frozen in th' street."

"I'm sorry."

"Don' be. Life goes on."

"You seem to be doing fine now." She nodded at the bag of money.

"I's jus' making small change. Enough t' pay my way."

She wanted to ask what he did, but was half-afraid to hear the answer. With every word he said, he further broke down the picture she'd built of him as a frivolous happy-go-lucky lout. Yes, that was a face he put on, but underneath was a very damaged but cunning young man.

"Anyway, what I's goin' t' say is that youz can' have ideals if youz really want t' work."

"I don't have any ideals. They still won't give me a job. I'm broke. I need clothes. I need a bath, I need to pay for my bed—"

"What sort of jobs have youz tried?"

"Some shops. Warehouses. Merchants. Some of them were really rude."

Jocassa said, "They won't have youz. Yes, they will be rude. They's not impressed with the Mirani right now. There was a *war* here 'gainst our army. There was fighting in all th' streets. They won 'n kicked us out. They hate us. They's take our money but they still hate us. Th' people on th' street are not goin' t' give youz jobs."

"What else can I do?"

"Youz going about it all wrong. Youz need t' look for better or smarter jobs."

"I can't see what else I can do."

"Don't you see? Whatever youz are and whatever yer family does in Bendara, it's nothing like any of us. They don' like us, but they'll have us men for luggin' heavy things, 'cause we're soldiers 'n we're dumb."

"I can't lug things." And he wasn't dumb either.

"Precisely. You'll have to tell them what youz can do."

"But I can't do anything. Even my healing knowledge is useless. They would have none of the medicines." Neither was she skilled in sewing, cooking or childminding or anything of the sort. She was annoyed at feeling outsmarted by him. Here he was, saying that she was too dumb to get a job. How had she ever made it into the Trader Academy?

"Youz can read 'n write Mirani. Add up sums. That's what youz can do. That's more than any of us can do."

Mikandra stared at him.

Heat crept up in her cheeks. Who was the dumb one here?

He broke a piece off his roll and held it out to her. "Eat this. Youz look starved."

"Thanks."

" 'N then youz should rest 'n have a bath."

20

MIKANDRA DIDN'T KNOW how she extracted herself from that conversation but it was certainly not with her pride intact. She felt thoroughly humiliated by a person to whom, a few days ago, she wouldn't have given any time. Even in the hospital, she never thought about the lives of the men she treated. She cared little about the reasons why they were in the hospital other than that it was their own fault. She never considered the reasons why they signed up for Nemedor Satarin's army other than that they were Nikala and that's what Nikala did. She had never questioned any of it. She had, self-righteously, assumed that they couldn't look after themselves because that was the task of the Endri. She'd been stupid, an arrogant rich kid who needed to be taught a big lesson.

Lesson taught.

Humility accepted.

Look, Rehan, I'm out of the sheltered world and into the heat.

Jocassa's last bit of advice was strange, though. Rest and have a bath? No way she could relax until she had secured a job and income. A bath could wait until later.

When Mikandra went out again, she knew exactly where to go: on her walks through the nearby city block she had spotted a shop that sold readers and other office equipment.

The place looked fairly new and, besides paper, pens and readers, had shelves bulging with other gadgetry.

The owner was a Damarcian woman, typically tall and graceful with black glossy hair done up in an elaborate bun. Hers was the first smile Mikandra saw that day. Mikandra asked her whether she knew if anyone needed someone who could read Mirani. The owner didn't need anyone but she told Mikandra to go to a woman who worked on the ground floor of the Exchange in an office that was called "Data Archiving" and this woman told Mikandra to go around the back of the complex to the council buildings. "There is a narrow street that runs the length of the block. You will find the entrance to the council complex there."

Mikandra nodded. Sadly she knew the street and knew where the council buildings were; she'd been robbed in this street.

"Ask to speak to the librarian," the woman added.

Mikandra left the building again and walked around the corner into Market Street, along the side walls of the complex to the back. Contrary to last time she had been here, the alley was filled with light and there were plenty of people in the street, strolling or carrying purchases. The rusted gates into the council complex stood open and builders walked to and fro carrying materials inside. Inside the gate in the building's forecourt, a couple of Pengali were mixing cement under a tent shelter. One was shovelling sand into a large drum that turned around by itself. In Miran, builders would either use a noisy engine or do this by hand. Miran made a point of not using energy pearls, because the devices, charged with the power from sunlight, were not all that useful in Miran, where it was clouded over or misty a lot of the time. But the main reason Miran didn't use them was because the pearls were a Coldi invention, which was a lame reason, seeing how easily people lit their homes with pearls and how people in Miran fumbled about with oil lights.

Mikandra went up a couple of steps to the only entrance that was in any state to be used as such. It led into a dome-structured hall which functioned as foyer, with a boarded-up door to one side and an open entrance into a corridor on the other. A couple of builders walked past into this corridor without taking any notice of her.

There was no one else in sight, so Mikandra followed them.

She came out into a passage with one open wall that gave access to a courtyard, with columns supporting the roof.

A significant part of the wall on the other side had been adorned with an intricate mural, painted a long time ago, judging by the faded colours and chipped paint. Even so, it was an amazing piece of work.

The painting depicted a city with numerous gold domes protruding from a sea of roofs interspersed with large spreading trees. A building in the foreground sported a five-pointed star on its façade and in the background sunlight glinted off marshlands. Wow, was this really Barresh?

She had heard something about this having been a great city in the past. Then again, prior to the Coldi invasion, Miran had been great, too. Neither city had done too well since. And the Coldi hadn't even stuck around.

The painting was a thing of great skill and so detailed that she could see the individual flowers and leaves on the trees and the jagged shapes of the creatures that were related to the mara-marang silhouetted against the sky.

On a balcony in the middle of the painting stood a dark-skinned man overlooking the city. His tunic was deep turquoise, heavily embroidered with silver. He wore his dark hair combed back and held in a ponytail at the nape of his neck. On his chest he wore a glittering insignia that looked suspiciously like it carried the Trader Guild's symbol, but she had to be mistaken. Barresh had no Traders. Yet his strong face seemed familiar, even though the groove in the middle of his nose indicated that he was a keihu local—

"Can I help you?"

Mikandra whirled around.

The man who had spoken to her in flawless Mirani was taller than her—unusual for locals. He had a fine-featured face—almost feminine, with a full and curved mouth. Soft black curls tumbled carelessly to the collar of his shirt.

"Um, yes. I was told by someone at the Exchange that

someone here might have a need for someone who can read Mirani." It seemed a pretty silly thing to say, especially since his command of Mirani was so good.

He cocked his head. His skin was much too pale to make him keihu, and his eyes were the deepest black she had ever seen. In comparison with him, the eyes of the locals were light-coloured. She couldn't even begin to guess his ethnicity.

"Omarion Baku," he said.

"Excuse me?"

"Omarion Baku. The man in the painting."

Mikandra had definitely heard that name before. She eyed the turquoise-clad figure on the balcony. "But . . . he wears a Trading medallion. I thought he was a pirate."

"Yes."

"What yes?" This guy was weird and the intense way he looked at her gave her the shivers. Who was he?

"Omarion Baku was both a Trader and a pirate. He was the only licenced Trader Barresh has ever had, and became a pirate later in life out of protest for the Mirani annexation of Barresh as a colony." His black eyes continued to meet hers, as if throwing her a challenge.

The Mirani annexation of Barresh. What a load of rubbish. Barresh had *asked* Miran to help them deal with riots in the city.

He continued, "It is interesting how different entities have their own versions of events in their shared history. You should read what the Trader Guild histories have to say about Omarion Baku. In Barresh, he's a hero. For the Trader Guild, he's a villain."

Mikandra's heart thudded against her ribs. It was as if he had *known* what she was thinking.

But he was right. Asto's invasion in Miran had probably been nothing more than a small blip on their aggressive colonisation record, and Coldi children would never learn about the events that had destroyed a great city and broken the backbone of a proud country when a civilisation invaded that was so much more advanced than they.

He continued, "Because Omarion Baku would not surrender to the Mirani occupancy, the Trader Guild revoked his licence and cast him out, but he continued both Trading and wearing the medallion. He held the people of the city together under occupation. They hid out in these buildings, which is partly why they look so battered and run-down today."

"But it was two hundred years ago." His continued use of *Mirani occupation* grated on her.

"Yes." He let a pause lapse and added, "I guess it's time the damage was fixed up."

His black pools of eyes met hers, but she couldn't gauge if he was serious or not.

Then he said again, "Yes." And let a silence lapse. "I wish it wasn't so, but the problem is that the occupying army left behind hundreds of years' worth of documents, and it is essential that we know what is in them before we can make a decision to keep or destroy them."

What the heck was he talking about now?

"Don't look like that. You asked if we could use people who read Mirani."

She had asked, yes, a few questions ago.

"I can read Mirani. I can help."

"Excellent. Do you have a name?"

"I'm . . ." She almost gave him her real name. "Eydrina."

"Are you related to Eydrina Lasko, the medic at the hospital?"

Oh, ancestors! "No. No. I don't know her. I mean—I know *of* her, but I never met her or anything like tha—"

"Never mind, *Eydrina*."

Damn, he did not believe one word of what she said. She wanted to ask *What is your name?* but didn't dare do so for fear of being called out on her lying. It was as if this man looked straight through her.

There was a voice further down the corridor and a second man came from an entrance in great strides, but stopped when he saw Mikandra.

"Ah. Lady." He nodded. He was keihu and dressed in black, which Mikandra had come to know as the colour of the Barresh council, with the five-pointed star emblem on his chest in gold thread.

The tall man said a few words in keihu to which the council worker replied, with a slight bow.

Then the tall man continued to Mikandra in Mirani, "You will have to excuse me. I would tell you more about the history of this city, but I am required elsewhere. If you continue down this passage and turn left, you will find the library."

"Thank you."

The tall man went off with the council employee and Mikandra continued down the corridor. What a weird, *creepy* man was this. And then the way he spoke. His pronunciation was flawless, but his language excessively formal. It reminded her strongly of how Ydana Ezmi spoke, but Aunt Amandra's lover was both Coldi and from Hedron and this man was . . . she didn't even know. What was he? Who was he?

The passage opened into a domed hall that was a junction of five such passages. A number of chattering Pengali workers crawled over the floor using fine brushes to clean the mosaic tiles. Like almost everything in Barresh, it depicted the ubiquitous five-pointed star in a coloured panel directly under the highest point of the domed ceiling. The chemical they used smelled foul, but where they'd scrubbed away the grime, the floor came out in brilliant colours. The star was golden, the background was vibrant blue. Where had the people found those pigments all those years ago when this mosaic was made?

Turn left, the tall man had said, but there were two left-hand turns. There was a left-opposite and left-behind. The left-opposite turn led into a corridor with featureless doors on either side. The floor was grey with dirt and grime and looked like the last person had passed that way at least a hundred years ago.

She chose the left-behind passage, which led through a corridor where the floor had already been cleaned and where the air smelled of fresh paint.

It turned out to be a good choice, because she found the library at the end, through two double doors that stood wide open.

The library was a huge hall, pentagonal, with rich wood-panelled walls which looked new—hence the smell. A team of builders was working to build a mezzanine floor around the outer perimeter of the hall. The wooden structure was finished in the sections opposite and to the left of the main entrance. Here, other people were setting up shelves both underneath and on top of the mezzanine floor.

The layout of the place reminded Mikandra of the Miran library, which also consisted of a large hall with balcony-like floors surrounding the perimeter.

That hall in the Miran library was an ancient, sacred place, with the faint smell of leather-bound books, precious wooden shelves and cabinets displaying significant items, like the four Foundation stones. Like this hall, the floor was an intricate mosaic of coloured tiles. Like this hall, noise echoed off the domed ceiling.

Maybe one day this library would be as stately as the Miran library, but all the building activity made it a noisy place.

Apart from the builders and shelf construction, teams of burly men in black council uniform wheeled in trolleys full of boxes which they offloaded in a huge pile in the middle of the floor.

On the other side of the pile, a couple of women were unpacking these boxes. They took stacks of books and papers to yet other people at a long row of desks. These people were leafing through pages, writing out details. Different people again were putting books away on shelves.

Um, so she needed to find a librarian here?

Mikandra wandered, looking around for someone who had the air of being in charge. A couple of young keihu women halted their chatting and giggling when she came past. A Coldi man in black uniform—What? Since when did foreigners work for the council?—came the other way carrying a huge box. Mikandra stepped aside to let him pass. He said something, but whether it was a greeting or something else Mikandra had no idea. She didn't *think* he spoke Coldi.

A small woman crouched while rummaging through another box. She also wore black. Tiny plaits adorned with beads swung about her head. When Mikandra walked past, she looked up. Her tail swung over her head. Huge brown eyes met hers. Pengali.

Mikandra couldn't see anyone who looked impressive enough to hold the title Librarian. She asked a Pengali man, but he didn't speak Mirani and pointed her to the side of the hall where shelves were completed and filled with books. Here she found a group of keihu women sitting on cushions on the ground. One woman sat in the middle, reading from a book. A couple of young children played with empty packing boxes in an aisle.

"Excuse me."

The woman in the middle stopped reading and everyone in the group looked at Mikandra. Their expressions were reserved, suspicious.

"I'm sorry to disturb you, but I'm looking for the librarian."

In broken Mirani, one of the women explained that Mikandra should find someone called Pakine, or something that sounded like that, and that this person was the librarian. Mikandra couldn't even guess whether that person would be male or female or whether she'd be able to tell.

She set off into the suggested direction which took her to the part of the hall where the floor was being built. Here, she found a tall Damarcian standing over a table with plans, talking to builders in rapid and badly-accented Coldi. The builders, Kedrasi, Coldi, Indrahui and a few other kinds, listened and asked occasional questions. Then he gave a command and they set off.

"Excuse me? Are you Pakine?" Mikandra tried to reproduce the name as faithful as possible.

He frowned and looked her up and down, from her short hair to her dirty clothes.

She was afraid that he was going to send her away, but he called out.

From the other side of the library came the wiry older Pengali woman with the plaits. Mikandra had walked past her a few times.

"I'm Bakimay," she said. She pronounced all the vowels short. Her voice sounded quite angry and her tail swished and curled as if to accentuate that impression, although Mikandra had no idea what she had done wrong.

Mikandra began, "I was told that you need people who can read Mirani—"

"Ah, I see. You are one Daya sent." Her accent was harsh and clipped, like the Pengali language.

"Um . . . I think so." She guessed the tall man she'd met at the mural was Daya, but how had he communicated with this woman while having walked in the other direction?

"If looking for people like you, looking in wrong place."

Um—what? "I'm not looking for anyone. I only want a job. I can read Mirani. I was told to come here."

"Read Mirani, hah?" She looked Mikandra up and down again with those huge eyes and repeated, "Read Mirani." She said nothing for a while and Mikandra wondered if she expected her to continue the conversation, and had no idea what to say. The tip of the woman's tail wriggled.

The woman continued, "Do you have . . . ID pass?"

Mikandra shook her head. "It was stolen."

The woman raised her eyebrows in semi-annoyed fashion. Then her tail flicked. "Why Mirani never have pass? Always stolen, hah! Stolen, lost. Is all the same. Excuses, excuses! You have name?"

"Eydrina."

"Ancestor name?" Oh, she could see in one look that Mikandra was not the same as the soldiers in town.

"Avarin." A very common merchant name in Bendara.

Again that suspicious look. Then a sniff. "Very well. You tell lies, we don't trust. But. We need people can read Mirani. You work here. Take books out, read, write down what's in books. Someone come to take books away. Someone come to bring new ones. You write. Is boring. Accounts. Boring, boring, boring, hah."

Mikandra nodded. "I can do that." Boring suited her fine. She only wanted to earn enough money to get out of here.

The woman continued, "Boxes are from army. They leave and we find mess. Paper, books everywhere. Scribble, scribble, no one can read. We don't know what they mean. Is a mess, hah! We don't know what to feed to fish and what is useful. You read.

You write down. You put days, years. We give to translator. We put in order, hah."

"Yes, sure." Guess this meant she had a job. "What about pay?"

"We pay. Five days you work. Five days you come on time. You do work. Five days, then we pay." She held up a hand with her fingers outstretched.

"How much?"

"Questions, questions. We treat people fair. No pay more because Mirani. No pay more because Coldi. You get five credits morning, five afternoon. Pay after five days. We pay any kind of money you want. You come tomorrow morning. Here." She pointed at the ground and her tail did the same. "Come on time. Come in clean clothes."

"Sure. I'll be there." The pay was pretty ordinary, but better than nothing. And yes, she did get the message about being clean. She was probably getting used to the smell, but she had to be surrounded by a bubble of sweaty air.

21

I T WAS STILL mid-afternoon, but the light had turned ominous, reflected off a huge bank of clouds that gathered over the escarpment. Enveloped in greys and darker greys, cloud castles reached for the zenith of the sky. Filaments of white took turns to block one or both suns, casting ghostly half shadows when only one sun vanished.

Mikandra went back to the guesthouse where Jocassa was no longer at the table in the courtyard. A few Mirani men she vaguely remembered from the party last night sat on the fountain's edge. They fell quiet when she came into the courtyard. One of them lifted his hand in tentative greeting. Oh no, they didn't trust her.

"Do you know where I can find the bathroom?"

One of them pointed. "Dunno that you call it a *room*."

Another man guffawed.

Mikandra went to the other side of the courtyard where he pointed. Behind the planter box and the fountain, she found an arch which led to yet another, smaller, courtyard. A couple of huge trees spread their branches over the entire space so that it was quite dark on the ground. In the middle of the courtyard was a steaming pool. A couple of people sat on a shelf that surrounded the pool perimeter under water. All of them were Coldi with thick fleshy arms and slicked-back metallic-looking hair. Their bodies looked white and distorted in the dark water.

"Um. Do you mind if I join you?"

None of them replied. Clearly they did mind. Or maybe they didn't understand Mirani. Well at least they wouldn't know the difference between a Mirani Endri and a Nikala and would care even less.

She turned away from the pool and stepped out of her hunting trousers and pulled her shirt over her head. The sweaty smell lingered in the air.

Under the eyes of the Coldi spectators, she slipped into the water.

She let the warmth seep into her while she lay back against the side of the pool which, admittedly, was hard and rough and not very comfortable.

The Coldi continued their conversation. Mikandra listened. Their dialect—somewhere from Asto but not Athyl—was hard to understand for someone who had only heard the archaic Trader dialect of Coldi.

Even with their clothes off but seated in the water, it was hard to figure each person's gender. There was very little difference in voice between men and women, and Coldi women didn't grow breasts until their first pregnancy.

She figured out that the group was talking about people in the guesthouse, not in a nice way. One person in the room smelled bad, apparently, and another made too much mess. Of course *those stupid Mirani* were at fault.

They clearly had no idea that she understood Coldi. She hesitated a few times, preparing Coldi words that she had never spoken aloud. But she said nothing, because she wasn't sure if she had the syntax right or whether the way she had learned Coldi grammar was specific to the Trader dialect, because it was definitely not the same as they spoke. And she could probably do without making enemies of random people.

The group left soon after—she noticed that Coldi bodies were hairless, too—and as soon as Mikandra was alone, she grabbed her clothes, emptied her pockets into a little pile of coins, and dunked her shirt and trousers in the water. She had no soap and wasn't sure how to wash clothes anyway—Rosep looked after the laundry at home—but she scrubbed until her knuckles hurt and hung her things over a bench to dry.

She was so incredibly tired. It was so quiet here. Voices of the men in the other courtyard sounded far off. Thunder rumbled in the distance. A stone duct trickled steaming water into the pool. If she sat really still, steam rose in curls off the water's surface.

Hot water springs. She had seen those in Bendara. This was where the smell of farts came from, not because the place was dirty.

She should probably get something to eat before it got dark or started raining.

Her clothes were still soaking wet, so she grabbed a towel from the stack that she hoped was there for the use of all guests. It was a thin cloth of loosely-woven fabric. She wrapped it around herself and took her clothes upstairs to the dormitory where she hung them over the end of her bed.

Already, the courtyard downstairs was filling with people in preparation of tonight's partying and the sound of talk and laughter drifted through the building.

Damn, she should have bought food *before* making her clothes all wet. She sat cross-legged on the bed and spread her collection of coins before her. Would it be enough to buy more clothes?

While she sat there, two small figures slunk into the door and past her bed to the corner of the dormitory. One of them lit a pearl on a stand next to the bed. Both were women, Kedrasi with brilliant red hair and sun-kissed faces with large brown markings around the eyes and hairline. She had seen them before, quietly going about their business while the guesthouse's Mirani guests were being loud.

The women spoke to each other in low voices. One of them had brought something wrapped in crinkly paper which she unpacked on the bed. The women sat down at either end, reaching inside the crinkly parcel and popping things in their mouths. Crunchy things.

A heavenly smell spread through the room.

Damn, she was hungry.

The woman facing Mikandra noticed that she was watching. She said something and held out her hand. She was the oldest of the two, with flecks of white hair marking her temples.

The other woman turned around and beckoned. "You want some?" Her voice was soft and gentle. She was much younger and her fine-featured face was almost childlike.

Mikandra was going to say no, but what else was she going to do? Sit in the dark and listen to the drunken singing downstairs while waiting for her clothes to dry?

So she went to the bed. One of the women made place for her and gestured to the paper parcel.

Mikandra hesitated although her mouth was watering. "I don't want to eat your dinner."

"Is too much for us anyway."

The paper contained a mass of curled crisp-fried stringy things which she had never seen before.

"What's this?"

"Nice. From the markets."

Mikandra picked up one of the fried curls. It was thin and crispy, and reddish brown. "Is it safe?" But it would be, because like Mirani, Kedrasi also ate the yellow-coded food.

She put the end of the curl in her mouth and bit a tiny piece off. A strong taste—spicy, tangy, salty—exploded in her mouth. Nothing like she'd tasted before. Mirani food was refined. It wasn't such a *riot* of tastes.

She knew the signs. "It's Coldi, isn't it?"

The older woman said, "Machizu has the best stall in the markets. She makes up her own dishes and they're all green-coded, so everyone can eat them."

Coldi indeed. She remembered the Coldi woman in the markets and her very popular stall.

She wondered what the curly things were. Coldi didn't eat vertebrate animals, but they would eat slugs and worms and snails.

Mikandra bit off another piece. The taste was so strong that it made her eyes water, but she kept eating just for the thrill of eating Coldi food. What would her father make of that? Who cared what it was? Worms, snails, grubs. If it was green-coded, there would be no harm. And it tasted good.

She smiled at the women and stuffed the rest of the piece in her mouth. "It's nice." She chewed and picked up another piece.

A short time passed in silence. Both women were also eating. They wore local dress, the loose tunic and wide trousers she had seen a lot of people wear and that were sold at almost every stall at the markets. You could get many different colours, but the Kedrasi women had stuck with the reds and pinks that Kedrasi usually wore.

After a while, the older one said, "I'm Melvi and she is Ariani."

The younger woman smiled. "She is my mother."

"I'm Eydrina." Mikandra cringed. She wished she had never started using a false name. All these lies were getting her deeper and deeper into trouble. "What are you doing in Barresh?"

"We work for the masterbuilders who are contracted by the council."

"It seems like everyone is working for the council."

"Yes, Barresh put out calls for workers, because they need to fix a lot of things."

Mikandra couldn't disagree with that. "Do you get paid or is this a sightseeing trip for you?"

"Oh no, we get wages. Everyone else does, too. I'm pretty sure our employer gets paid for his work in the normal way, because Damarcian builders do not work for nothing."

That was true, too. She took another curl from the paper, since it didn't look like the two women were still eating.

Melvi smiled at her. "Go on. It's too much for us. We're not very big."

It was true; they weren't big. Kedrasi would only come up to well below Mikandra's shoulders.

"But then who is paying for all this?"

"The council."

Mikandra didn't ask further because it was clear the women didn't know more and didn't care where the council got the money. They spoke instead of both women's husbands who were at home in Kedras. The younger one seemed too young to be married, but maybe she was older than she looked.

Mikandra asked about their family customs. When she went to the Trader academy, she would live on-site and not have much to do with the Kedrasi society but many of the Guild's employees were Kedrasi.

They talked about life at Kedras and the differences between that and Barresh.

"They use so much water," Melvi said. "All this washing and washing and washing."

"The people in Barresh think it is rude to be smelly and not to bathe after going to the private room," Ariani explained.

Damn.

That explained Jocassa's odd advice earlier today and Baki-may's displeasure.

～

That night, Mikandra discovered why she'd been given the bed near the door. When it wasn't raining, it barely cooled down at night, and with no thunderstorms to push it along, the breeze didn't reach far into the room. She lay sweating, without any covering, and too afraid to take off the towel. The cold mountain air of Miran seemed impossibly far away.

By the time the sky showed a faint tinge of light blue, she couldn't stand it anymore. It was still far too early to go to the library, but she'd go to the Exchange on the off chance that Rehan had responded to her small message.

Her clothes were still damp but they were no longer smelly. Mikandra went for a quick dip in the pool—thank goodness for her short hair—and got dressed. The stack of towels had grown overnight. She couldn't see anywhere to leave the dirty one, so she put it in a little heap on the bench next to the clean ones. Someone would probably think that was rude, too.

Well, she was doing her best. If they wanted her to be perfect, they should provide her with a manual.

At least the Exchange operations were the same everywhere. Mikandra was given a cubicle and when she turned on the screen and typed her code, she found a message for her. The communication was marked security-encoded and had no identifying features but when she opened it on the screen, it was definitely from the Andrahar Traders. From Rehan, to be precise, and the length of it surprised her.

Thank you for your update and your concern. We are safe for the time being. I managed to sell the aircraft for a good price, and have already paid off the Hedron account, as well as a few other dues. The only thing that galls me is that the Tussamar brat Thaeron gets to use it.

We hope to avoid having to make other sales, but if necessary, we will sell Braedon's aircraft, then the office. For now, Taerzo will be supplementing our income by doing aircraft maintenance. Braedon is negotiating with the hospital to set up a service doing simple home visits to sick and elderly of the Endri who don't want to visit the hospital for minor problems. The hospital doesn't want him charging for it, but he's not interested if he can't.

I am over my ears into the court case. I've been going through the Exchange documents to try and find out what happened and what the charges are. I've engaged a Guild Lawkeeper and an investigator. I'm not leaving any evidence on the table, but I don't trust the Mirani Lawkeepers Guild, because their political motives are too mixed up with their work ethic.

Yesterday, the council went through a long day of debating the new residency laws. I wasn't there, but apparently, there were a lot of people in the gallery. According to those who were there, at some point in the debate, a group of protesters against the law grew too rowdy and were asked to leave. When they refused, scuffles broke out which spread to the street after the guards finally managed to get the detractors out of the assembly hall. The protesters congregated in an area of the lower Endri quarter, and prevented a number of families leaving or returning to their houses.

That explained what Mother and Liseyo had been talking about. But—since when could she hear the things people were saying from this far off? The thought that Leitho's hallucinations might be real chilled her.

All of a sudden, this climate-controlled room was too cold for her, and the presence of a screen made her nervous. The

Exchange's communication links were not completely secure, that was the first thing people always said about them. *If you need to send something absolutely confidential, send a courier.*

He ended the letter with, *I sincerely hope that you are doing better than we are, because the shunning and scorn is getting to all of us. Walking into the Guild headquarters has become a very unpleasant experience with all the disagreements that rage about whether we should actively oppose the council's request for cooperation with their laws or invoke the noninterference clause. The battlefront continues at home. Taerzo continues to think that we can take the easy way out and accept Nemedor Satarin's money. Give me strength not to assault him the next time he brings it up. Please keep in touch.*

She stared at that line for a bit. How could such a curt and standoffish man write such an honest letter with details he would never share with her face to face?

Did this mean that she could be chatty to him as well? Probably not.

She replied in a formal way, explaining that she was going to stay until she had to go to Kedras, and that she was investigating some leads. Her reply sounded a lot more positive than she felt, and she regretted it the moment she'd sent it. She should have asked directly for the wellbeing of her family. She should have told him of her problems. She should have asked him for more details about Iztho.

Maybe tomorrow.

Right now, she had to go to work.

In the library, the pile of boxes to be sorted appeared to have grown since yesterday, and there seemed to be even more builders in the hall, if that was possible. They were putting floorboards on the structure they had built, and the hall was filled with sounds of hammering and shouting, of whining winches and saws.

While she stood a few paces inside the door, looking for a Pengali figure with lots of bead-adorned plaits, someone behind her said, "You came, hah?"

Mikandra whirled around. Bakimay had entered the hall behind her. She stood with her hands at her hips, as if in a challenge.

"You thought I wouldn't come?"

"Mirani. Never know. Sometimes they come, sometimes they don't."

"I stick to my promises. If I say I'll come, I'll come." What was it with these people never trusting her? "I'll work, too, and I'll come back. You'll pay me, not once but again and again. Because that's the kind of person I am."

Bakimay met her eyes in a silent challenge. "We'll see. We'll see, hah."

Her huge eyes studied Mikandra's clothing, but, finding nothing to complain about, she jerked her head and led Mikandra to the area under the completed mezzanine floor. Her tail moved at knee level, which Mikandra had deduced signified a neutral state of mind. The more angry or emotional, the higher the tail.

Bakimay showed Mikandra a desk half buried under a huge pile of musty old books and told her that each book needed a summary of its contents, written on a page and attached to the outside. The books were then to go to someone who would translate her Mirani into keihu and the books would be put away in other boxes.

Mikandra sat down and took the first book off the stack. If she had hoped to be given material that might tell her something of interest, she was disappointed. It was an account book more than thirty years old. Moisture had affected the cheap covers, creatures had sharpened their teeth on the edges and the pages were spotted with grey dots. The writing, in hasty scrawls, was untidy and barely legible, full of spelling errors.

She leafed through pages disintegrating with moisture, hardly knowing where to start. She asked Bakimay whether these books were worth keeping, but was told that initially everything should be catalogued. Make a summary, note dates. That was easier said than done. The books were a mess.

Bakimay said, "Never said it was easy. You work. Get paid. Five days. Leave early, no pay."

Trader's Honour 217

"Yes, I get that you don't trust me." Didn't like her, even.

"I tell you, so no surprise if you stay two days and ask for pay." She accompanied this with a snap of her tail.

"I will surprise you." Damn, this tiny woman was starting to get under her skin.

"I seen everything from Mirani. Cannot surprise me."

"You want to bet?" She gave Bakimay a determined look and started working.

The work was mindless and boring, but at least it was dry in the library, because judging by the noise on the ceiling window, the sudden downpours continued outside. One moment the weather would be fine, the next it would be pouring.

At night in the guesthouse, Jocassa said that this was normal. Mikandra resolved to buy one of those rain hats as soon as she got paid. That, and two sets of clothes that were more comfortable and dried quicker than her hunting gear. And sandals, because her shoes were wet and smelled disgusting.

There was another message from Rehan the next morning, this one even longer than the previous.

Nemedor Satarin came back to the house yesterday morning. Unfortunately, none of us were home except Mother. The first thing I knew about it was when the High Council secretary sent a message to complain that his boss objected to being called "a bloodsucking leech" and a "selfish prick" and suggested that we should consider appointing a carer for Mother if she was so obviously mentally unstable. It was most embarrassing, because I could hear Mother's words as I read them, and was trying very hard not to laugh. I did manage to say that we'd look into it, although I'd rather have told him that there is nothing wrong with Mother's sense of perception and that she does tend to be rather honest about her opinions. Part of me wishes that I could have seen that confrontation.

That said, her run-in with Nemedor Satarin has not made things better for us. Disagreeing with the council is one thing, abusing them quite another. We have to be inconspicuous and inoffensive. If we make too many powerful enemies, the situation will blow up. If Nemedor

Satarin gets into a fight with the Traders, your aunt will get involved,
Antho Tussamar will get involved. You haven't heard Aithno Ilendar in
full flight. His speeches are scathing and lethal. He doesn't care about
unity of the Mirani chapter. He just cares about his rights as Trader.

The Trader Guild has the power to force Miran into sense, but only
if they are united. Miran has the power to destroy the businesses of
individual Trading families. They have the power to divide the Guild.
They are flexing their muscles and trying those powers on us. Support
our laws and we will give you money. Don't support them and we will
not help you at all or might even cut you loose. Some of us want to
fight back because the residency laws go against everything the Guild
stands for. Of course Antho Tussamar says that we should support the
council. Rumours are that the first Traders are ready to pack up and
leave Miran.

Mikandra guessed those Traders would be men who had
brought foreign wives or adopted heirs to Miran, because there
were a number of Traders who, for the lack of heirs, appointed
an apprentice as heir. Most of those apprentices were Mirani, but
she knew at least two Traders who had foreign apprentices.

He also wrote a detailed commentary on the Guild Lawkeeper's work so far in making a case for Iztho's innocence. He had
opened the entire business archive to the Lawkeeper to show
that no one except Braedon dealt with menisha fungus, and that
he only sold medicinal extract. He said that the Lawkeeper was
applying to get all the import and export records for the relevant
day for all the relevant Exchanges, but that this was going to
take some time.

When she finished reading, she noticed that the time stamp
on the message was very recent. She wondered if he was still at a
place where he could reply to her, probably the Andrahar office.
They would have an Exchange hub there. She wrote a short
message on her efforts, which said nothing more than that she
had little news to report.

He replied immediately. *Are you surviving well there?*

She typed, *As well as I can.*

I hear the place is extremely hot.

Boiling. You can barely breathe.

They exchanged some comments about the weather. Rehan

said that he'd never been to Barresh. *No reason to go,* he said. *No Exchange, no money. They produce nothing that we sell.*

He'd be surprised if he knew the truth.

Then he continued, *I would appreciate if you could get your hands on the original import logs from the Barresh Exchange. The ones we have been able to get are from the central Guild log at Kedras. They show the alleged illegal imports, but I want to see the original logs to see if they match the times given by Kedras.*

She replied, *I will try.*

Mikandra had assumed Iztho's innocence up until the moment she was robbed and the Pengali thugs asked her *Tell me where it is.* Right now, she didn't know anymore. There was no proof that whoever the thugs bought their wares from was Iztho and no proof that they were expecting menisha. She could still not believe that Iztho would have been so stupid, but the possibility had been awakened.

She hesitated and typed, *What would you do if Iztho was guilty?* She rubbed that out twice, but eventually took a deep breath and sent it. Because, as far as she could see, they should consider the possibility, however unpalatable.

I fail to see why Iztho would have done this. Our regular business makes a lot more money than he could ever make illegally, and none of us ever touch the stuff. Menisha brew gives me such bad dreams that I once ended up in a guard cell after drinking. Apparently, I assaulted a guard while drunk, but I don't remember any of it. True story. It is vile stuff.

She could just about hear his angry and defensive tone.

I'm sorry. I've heard some disturbing stories here that may point to his guilt. You may need to consider that this is indeed the case, unlikely as it seems. She rubbed out the *to you* at the end of the sentence.

Point taken. Sorry. A small pause. *If it would turn out that he is guilty or we cannot prove his innocence, we have to apply for the licence to be transferred to me. We have to prove our character. That will take much longer than a simple court case.*

Could you set that process in motion if the court case does not go in your favour?

We are doing that. The Lawkeeper suggested it.

Was he peeved? Was he just being businesslike? She took

another deep breath and sent another question that would puzzle him. *Forgive me a very strange question, but your Aunt Dithiandra, did she ever have a drinking problem that you know of?*

That is indeed a strange question. Not that I know of, no. What is this about? I thought you were looking for Iztho.

Mikandra hesitated. *This town is awash with menisha brew. There seems to be a link between it and hallucinations in certain people. I'm not sure how secure this communication link is and how much more I should say. I don't understand it yet. Iztho may have played a role. I don't know yet. I haven't found him yet.*

She had to wait a while for the reply. *The link is not secure. Don't say anything that could cause problems. If there is an important message, please use a Guild courier.* Then another pause. *Please, be careful. The Andrahar Traders will survive. This case isn't worth dying for. Iztho will turn up. He's gone offline for a few days before.*

The pattern continued. In the morning, before going to the library, she would go to the Exchange and communicate with Rehan and he would rattle out his frustration. The case preparation wasn't going well. The Lawkeeper he had hired was having trouble securing some documents. He used a lot of legal terms of which she wasn't sure what they meant. She wasn't sure if he cared that she didn't understand, but she found a Mirani dictionary in the library, looked up the words and asked him about the process. He seemed surprised by her interest, but responded by elaborating in more detail. She had to ask him several times if it was all right to share that information over the link and he said that none of it was information that people couldn't obtain elsewhere.

On the fourth day, lacking important news and not wanting to go into detail about her own situation, she started talking about the faded glory of Barresh and Omarion Baku. He dug out some history books and diagrams—she bet they were from Iztho's room—to prove that the five-pointed star had been of significance in the past of Miran as well. The Foundation monument had five pillars. There were five Foundation families.

She described the mural as best as she could, and he sent her the life history of Omarion Baku as recorded in the Trader Guild histories. Apparently, he had been a rather brash and obnoxious man, a loudmouth who had made few friends in the Guild.

Then she apologised for talking to him about this unimportant stuff.

Please keep talking. It's not much fun here at the moment. Everyone here either yells at us or tries to wheedle information out of us, and that is just the people we trust.

She agreed that this bit of communication with her home town was the highlight of her day, one moment when life seemed almost normal, and when she didn't have to watch her back or pretend to be someone else.

She looked forward to the chats during the day, when her mind was dulled by the mindless work in the library. True to Bakimay's prediction, it was boring. In those first five days, two of her fellow first readers left.

But she stayed, as promised.

At the end of the five-day week, Mikandra lined up with the library's other guest workers for payment. When it was her turn, Bakimay gave her a suspicious look.

"I stayed. You pay," she said in imitation of Bakimay's clipped tone.

Bakimay said nothing and handed her the chip with a sullen expression on her face. Her tail, waving at shoulder height, told the real story.

"Not all Mirani are fickle and untrustworthy. Judge the person, and not where they come from."

Walking out into the light-filled corridor, the small victory made her steps light.

~

Mikandra took her chip to a credit booth where she obtained a handful of pearls that people in Barresh used as currency.

In the guesthouse, Jocassa refused to take back the money he had lent her. He said, "Jus' pay your dues when someone else is in trouble."

So in the dying daylight, she went to one of the clothes shops and bought two tunics and two pairs of loose trousers. She chose ones with a pattern of red swirls on white. They were a bit more expensive than the plain ones, but those were the Mirani colours. Being less tight than her usual clothes, they felt more comfortable in the heat. She bought sandals made from local leather which she had learned was made from fish skins. She bought soap. She paid for a barber to dye her hair dark. And at Machizu's stall, she bought a big bag of crunchy worms and ate them all.

Time flowed into her new routine and one day bled into the other.

Although there were parties in the guesthouse almost every night, the thugs did not come back. Neither did the woman they had taken.

At the council buildings, Mikandra did not see the tall man again. She heard nothing more about Iztho Andrahar because most of the workers in the library were not locals, and she saw nothing more of her stolen bag.

She went to the account keepers and opened an account— although the employee frowned deeply at her paltry collection of pearls. The thing was, she wanted the money to be safe for when she needed to go to Kedras.

A merchant and a couple of men at the guesthouse paid her to write letters of reference. The ex-soldiers needed to reaffirm their availability to the army and the merchant was a Barresh local, bitterly complaining how the new Mirani import laws stifled his business. She nodded and listened, and agreed with him.

The money in her account grew. Slowly, Mikandra climbed out of the hole she had fallen into when her bag was stolen. Slowly, she started to think again about the reason she had come here, and about other things than pure survival.

In the library, she and Bakimay had agreed on a sullen stand-off. Bakimay no longer reminded her that she was supposed to be fickle and unreliable because she was Mirani, and seemed more grumpy about having been wrong about this with every pay day.

Mikandra had now been working in the library for a couple of weeks. More than a sun cycle had passed. In that time, she and her fellow assessors—a selection of itinerant Mirani men of varying intelligence—worked through a substantial pile of musty books that were becoming progressively newer and less musty. Some were even legible. It was amazing what extravagant nonsense the previous Mirani council had funded. *Dinner and entertainment for the members of the Barresh council. Fish bread flown in fresh from Miran.* Really?

Today was the day that the group of local women came to the library that had also been there the very first time she had come. They came every week to take part in some kind of tuition. An elderly woman would sit in the middle of the group giving instructions while the students wrote in their books.

Mikandra walked past on the way to the shelves several times and made out lines and scrawls on the pages of the women's books. She had been curious about the strange alphabet they used. People in Miran said that keihu was not a written language. Since coming here, she'd seen it written using Mirani characters, but the script the women used was unlike any she'd seen before. Their speech sounded like keihu. So, it was a written language.

It seemed that people in Miran, including the council, severely underestimated Barresh and its people.

No one ever said that Barresh had once had a Trader. Every time Mikandra came into the building she couldn't help looking at the proud face of Omarion Baku. Sometimes she would linger and hope that the tall man would appear again. From over-hearing discussions between library workers, she made out that this Daya was the Chief Councillor of Barresh, the man who had married the woman Iztho had wanted, but she never saw him again. She sometimes wandered the corridors at midday trying to find him, but when going into the depths of the building, she always came across a section of corridor closed by vicious-looking Coldi guards and she didn't want to draw attention to herself by trying to get past.

As usual at the weekly women's meetings, many of the women had brought children. The older ones sat with the women, writing in their own books, but the younger ones ran riot between the shelves. It annoyed Mikandra. In Miran, children had to be quiet and out of sight. They had to behave and do as adults told them.

These children were plain ill behaved. A couple of the brats were pulling books from trolleys.

Mikandra had already told them a few times to stop it. They looked at her, frightened, and ran away, but she didn't think they understood Mirani, because they came back as soon as she turned her back. What were all these children doing in the library anyway? It was a place of quiet, for study.

Now two boys were collecting some of the empty boxes which had contained the documents that Mikandra was working on. Oh, yes, the rascals would build forts out of those boxes while their older siblings and mothers were attending their lessons.

But those boxes were not rubbish and she would need them for putting the books back in when she'd finished with them.

"Hey!"

The boys froze. One clutched the box he was holding to his chest. He backed away from the pile.

"Give that back. It's not yours."

The boy dropped the box and he and his little friend ran away, but as they rounded the corner, one of the boys crashed into a toddler who had just learned to walk. They both went tumbling.

The bigger boy scrambled up and ran after his friend. The toddler started wailing.

Mikandra yelled after them, "Now look at what you've done! Ill-behaved brats!"

She picked up the child and set him back on his feet. He cried big tears which ran over his chubby cheeks. Where was his mother?

She lifted him up and he stopped crying out of surprise. Tear-filled big eyes met hers.

His irises had a very unusual light brown colour, sandy almost. The only other people who had eyes like that were Kedrasi. The boy's fine hair hung past his ears, straight, unlike that of most local children who had curly hair. It was very black, almost unnatural for a child this age . . . yes, the roots of the hair were light. Dyed? Whatever for?

She had dyed her own hair to be less conspicuously Mirani.

This boy . . .

His eyes were not Mirani, but his face was quite narrow, Endri-like, even for a child that age, serious looking and intense. A chill went over her as she recognised the set of his jaw. The boy didn't yet have the long and sharp nose, but the shape of his mouth and chin were familiar. She'd seen a much older version of that face before, in a comfortable room by the fire in Miran.

Unless she was very much mistaken, this little boy was the heir to the Andrahar business. The oldest son of the oldest son.

At that moment, there was female voice and a woman came around the corner. She was taller than Mikandra, pale skinned but with black hair which she wore loose over her shoulders. Not keihu, not any type of person she had ever seen before, except perhaps that mysterious Daya.

She froze, and looked from Mikandra's short hair to her tunic. Was she looking for the Trading medallion or a family emblem?

The boy held out his hands to her, making sounds like *mama-mamamamamam*.

"Is he yours?" Mikandra asked. Her heart was thudding.

"Yes, thanks." Quite curt.

"He's cute. Looks a bit like my nephew." Well, she couldn't straight out ask about Iztho, could she?

A flick of her eyebrows. "Thank you." Oh so cool. She took the boy from Mikandra's arms while not breaking eye contact and hoisted him on her hip, above the slight rounding of her stomach. Pregnant?

Mikandra wanted to ask, *Are you the woman who refused an offer of marriage from Iztho Andrahar?* but there was no need to ask. This was the woman. Anmi Kirilen Dinzo was her name. That little boy was Iztho's son. And the child she carried, was it Iztho's, too?

She wanted to ask, confront her, but all of a sudden, she felt like she had walked into a wall at full speed and her head was spinning from the impact.

She had to steady herself by holding onto the shelves. What was that?

A male voice sounded, and a man came around the corner of the shelves. Oh crap, this was the creepy Daya guy she had met the first day she'd come here when looking at the wall paintings.

He said something to the woman, and she replied, but Mikandra had no idea what language they spoke. Not keihu. His voice sounded cautious. Mikandra tried to listen through the woolly feeling in her head. Now her ears were ringing. Her chest felt constricted, like she couldn't get enough air, but she stood stoically, although her heart was racing.

Daya and Anmi each wore one dangling earring of fine silver filigree with an inset amber stone. As far as she knew it was a Coldi custom that married couples adhered to, although Coldi didn't marry but had contracts. But these people weren't Coldi. Whatever language they spoke to each other wasn't Coldi.

The pressure in her head abated. Mikandra took a deep, unrestricted breath.

The little boy held his arms out and the woman passed the boy to the man. He lifted the boy to sit on his arm. The woman nodded coolly at Mikandra. "Thank you. He won't disturb you anymore."

They both walked away, leaving Mikandra behind in a thick silence. She leaned against the shelves, shivering all over. What the hell was that? Maybe she should start looking after herself better.

She returned to her work, but while she filed away moisture-eaten books under their respective dates, anger grew inside her.

So, this was how she saw things:

Iztho had fallen in love with this woman, fathered her child, but she had chosen to marry this other man Daya. This had been her own choice, since Iztho had offered marriage, but she had refused.

Why? Because the other guy offered more power and a better deal?

So, the child had been born and—oops—the boy turned out to be Iztho's. So, this woman was stupid enough to think that dyed hair would hide his identity? Maybe she had hired some of the black-clad guard thugs to drive Iztho out of town and falsify the Exchange records so that she wouldn't have to deal with the Andrahar family ever again.

This woman was evil.

22

THE MORE MIKANDRA thought about it, the more angry she became. This was what Iztho had meant with situations Traders had to deal with. Large-scale bullying by people backed by governments that seemed so overwhelming it didn't look like you had any chance to fight back. Ganging up of entire communities conspiring to rid themselves of a Trader who they thought had wronged them. Likely, Iztho had suspected that some of this might be happening by the time she met him in his room, but likely even he had misjudged the depths to which the Barresh council would go to get rid of him.

After finishing at the library, she went to the markets and bought a notebook and a pen. She hadn't owned either of those since going to school. Everyone used readers, but although she lingered at the shop that sold those for longer than she should, she couldn't afford them just yet, or at least not if she wanted to have money to travel to Kedras.

At night, after sharing a meal and chatter with the two Kedrasi women in the corner of the veranda, she sat down on her bed. A few days ago, she had also bought a small metal stand with a light pearl. It was a strangely cute little thing, resembling an eyeball on a metal spring, and when it stood on the shelf next to the bed, she often half-expected it to come to life and start jumping around.

It gave a surprising amount of light, and the pearl hadn't yet needed recharging. But if it did, she knew a little shop where she could exchange this pearl for a charged one.

By its greenish light, she sat cross-legged on the bed and opened the book.

On the first page, she wrote the day that the Trader academy would start and counted the days—just forty-two.

On the next page, she wrote down two lists: one of all the things she had learned so far, and one of the things she hadn't.

The second list was much longer than the first, and contained important questions like: who is the strange man Daya? Where is he from? Why is he in Barresh? Why does Barresh care about the Andrahar Traders?

The next morning she asked Rehan for specific dates that Iztho was said to have brought in illegal fungus. He gave her a couple, but also said that his Guild Lawkeeper had discovered that in transferring dates from the Trader calendar to the Ceren one, someone had made mistakes and records might be out by a day. Mistakes, her arse. That was not an innocent error. No one working with Exchange data all day would make stupid mistakes like that. The problem was made worse, he said, that the data came from before the Barresh Exchange installed a new core and came online with the rest of the Exchange network. According to the main Exchange node at Damarq, Barresh didn't exist to the network before that time. All their data were entered manually and the person who did that could easily have been bribed to enter something else.

Preparations for the court case were still frustratingly slow, he told her. The Guild Lawkeeper he had hired had trouble securing almost every document needed.

Have you considered that you're working against the entire Barresh government? she asked him.

Or the Mirani one, was his reply.

That made a chill go down her back. To her shame, she hadn't thought of the situation in Miran for a while, and had stopped noticing the shuttles that came in daily and no longer scrutinised the passengers for signs that they left Miran permanently. *Did the council approve the foreign residency law?* She had almost forgotten the restrictive, claustrophobic feel of living in the city.

He replied, *Not yet, but a group of merchants have staged a protest in the council hall. The council ordered the guard to remove them and there were fights. Part of the guard refused to obey their orders. They were, they said, not fighting their countrymen and joined the protest. Aithno Ilendar went to speak up for them. I'm not sure what possessed him, because the Guild can certainly not use another front on which to disagree with the council. Anyway, he persuaded the protesters to leave the council hall, but now they have set up an exclusion area around the Ilendar house. Their territory spans a couple of blocks of the adjoining merchant and Endri quarters where they say anyone doing real business is still welcome. Some people from elsewhere in the city with foreign wives or business partners have sought refuge there. From where I sit, overlooking the square, I can see a couple of the young guys patrolling the boundary of this area, which runs just behind the markets. Amandra Bisumar has been going in and out to negotiate a compromise that would get everybody back to work, but hasn't been successful so far. Everyone knows that it's only a matter of time before Nemedor Satarin orders the army to clean it up. The situation worries me. We don't need any wars or enemies to bring us down. Miran is tearing itself up from within.*

She asked about her family, but he said that the Andrahar house was within the area, and her family's house was on the other side of the boundary and he didn't know much of what went on there, save that all people who lived there supported the council.

I'm worried for my mother and sister, she confessed to him.

He replied that he'd ask Gillay to keep an eye out for them, because the house staff could mostly still move around unhindered.

∽

Now that she had the dates of the supposed imports, Mikandra went to the imported goods counter at the Exchange after work and tried to get a list of approved imports for that day. She told the man behind the counter a story about lost data from her merchant family.

"The data were destroyed in a fire," she said, and even the lie made her see flames in the snow and that image made her shiver.

The man gave her a sympathetic smile. "I'm sorry, but I can't give out these data to everyone. Only if you have authorisation."

"But we have nothing left, and we need the information."

"I'm sorry. Really, I am. Look, why don't I help you fill in the application? There's not much to it. We only need your ID. Then they can process it overnight, and you can have your list tomorrow." He smiled.

She sighed. "I don't have my ID on me."

He raised his eyebrows.

Mikandra mumbled something about going to get it and fled the room.

Well, so much for that. Head, meet tail.

This tactic of boldly walking up to someone and demand what you wanted appeared to have worked only once. She should think of another way to approach people, because this trick had worn out. Worse, each time she tried this, the lies multiplied.

Coming down the stairs of the Exchange and into the yard, she noticed that the airport had grown noticeably busier. A couple of private craft sat to the right-hand side of the gate, and some building activity had started there, too. A couple of workers were clearing bushes. Through the new gap in the vegetation, she spotted a Damarcian craft, probably belonging to one of the builders, and . . . there was a second Gazion. Well, it seemed they were breeding.

At a closer look, this craft was slightly smaller than the other one, looked more used, and it carried the emblem of the Trader Guild with the number 8515.

This craft belonged to Ydana Ezmi, Aunt Amandra's lover.

Mikandra rushed to the guesthouse, in and out of the bath in a heartbeat. She rubbed her hair dry and put on a clean tunic. She wished she still had her apprentice uniform, but it had been stolen with the rest of her things. She wished she had something else that would impress a foreign Trader.

Jocassa came in and joked about her getting dressed to see a boyfriend.

Mikandra felt like a huge flashing beacon that said *homeless person* when she walked up the stairs to the guesthouse where not so long ago she'd been embarrassed by not having enough money. That time seemed like a world away. How rich had she been back then, and how innocent and self-conscious.

The same cranky matron with her ridiculous hairdo stood at the desk, leafing through her big book. She looked up when Mikandra came in, but if she remembered the embarrassing encounter in which she had told Mikandra *It's a pity, because you look like a nice girl*, her expression showed none of it.

"I have to deliver a message for Trader Ydana Ezmi," Mikandra said.

The woman nodded. "He's having dinner in the courtyard. I'll ask if he will see you."

Mikandra had to give her name—the real one this time—and the matron waddled off into the courtyard giving Mikandra a good look at her enormous wobbly behind. She came back a short time later and said that Trader Ezmi was happy to see her.

And so it was surprisingly easy to get access to that sanctuary of the guesthouse's leafy courtyard with its neatly clipped bushes and perfectly matched tables and chairs where neat and civilised people sat. What a difference with the guesthouse on Market Street. What a . . . totally boring, stuffy and suspicious kind of place. There were lots of people middle-aged and older, lots of merchants wearing expensive clothing and jewellery, and a lot of sideways looks from under carefully maintained brows. Expressions of *What is she doing here?* or *Why is she wearing that ridiculous outfit?* and *What did she do to her hair?* that reminded her of being at home amongst her mother's noble lady friends.

Trader Ydana Ezmi sat by himself at a table in the corner of the courtyard. As customary, he was in full uniform, a lilac tunic and trousers and dark purple cloak, which, in the case of the Hedron Traders, had a mere cosmetic function. He was reading from his reader which lay next to his plate.

He looked up, met her eyes. She had been afraid that he wouldn't have any idea who she was, but he smiled and gestured for her to come over.

Mikandra did and greeted him politely. Hedron was the last entity chapter to have been added to the Trader Guild, and their licence numbers were all really high, 8515 in his case.

He said, in his curiously accented Mirani, "Would you like anything to eat?"

"I would love to, thanks." When a Trader offered, you did not refuse.

Surprising how she'd gotten over her hangup about accepting help from other people. One day, when she was rich, she would buy everyone dinner, and buy the poor people of Miran heaters. Today was not that day.

She sat down and the matron scurried off to order another meal from the kitchen. People around them resumed eating and talking. The smells drifting through the courtyard were mouth watering.

"I'm surprised to see you here," he said.

"I am surprised for the same reason." She replied to him in Coldi, the Trader dialect.

"Ah." His gaze went over her. He had aged a fair bit since she had last seen him, which had been long before Aunt Amandra ever considered running in the election. His hair, which for Coldi people was normally thick and black with iridescent spots in blue, green and purple, had gone white at the temples. He wore it in the typical Coldi ponytail. Like many Coldi, his irises contained a smattering of golden speckles. She remembered how gorgeous Coldi eyelashes were: dark, thick and long with metallic highlights. "I was wondering if you were the same Mikandra Bisumar listed in the Guild intake."

"I am. I'm going to work with the Andrahar Traders."

"Ah," he said again, and repeated, "Ah." As if that explained it all.

A Pengali waitress brought a tray of food. It contained local rolled-up bread cut in slices so that the brown coating of spices formed a swirl in each slice, a bowl of sauce and a plate of vegetables.

Mikandra started eating while he drank tea. She was looking for an opportunity to ask whatever questions would not make him suspicious, but he did nothing except observe her. It was strange and uncomfortable.

Finally, he said, "You look famished. What have you been doing all day?"

"I work in the library."

"For the Miran library?"

"No, for the Barresh council."

He frowned at her. "That's . . . unusual. Why not wait in Miran until the court case?"

"I came here to meet Iztho. He is my mentor. But he's no longer here. I had some . . . misfortune, and rather than go back to Miran, where my parents are angry with me, I thought I'd wait here."

He nodded, his expression thoughtful, and let another silence lapse. "Amandra has mentioned her brother at times. He is . . . very traditional."

Mikandra wasn't sure how she was supposed to take that. She didn't like the thought of discussing her parents with this man. She'd come here because she wanted to see what he knew about Barresh, the court case or anything else that might help her figure out what was going on, not to discuss her family. So she asked him, "Do you have business in this town?"

"I do. I've had talks with the council about supplying pre-made buildings for the airport."

"Pre-made buildings?"

"They come in modules. Hedron manufactured. You can put them up in a few days. This place needs a lot of buildings quickly."

True.

Then he added, "I'd hoped while I was here to pay a visit to Miran, to—you know . . ." He shook his head and sighed. "How is she?"

Mikandra debated saying *just fine*, because she really didn't want to talk about her family, but with him here, it was probably unavoidable. Also, if there was anyone who had the influence to help Aunt Amandra out of her obvious unhappiness, he was sitting at the table with her. "Last time I saw her she looked tired and harassed. She's boxing against the majority."

"I told her that it was a bad idea to take the position. I never liked the way that Nemedor Satarin spoke. Next thing she was running with him. I don't understand."

"I don't think she was ever fully with him. She ran the election alongside him because she hoped to be a voice of unity. But it hasn't worked very well."

He shook his head. "I've only heard bad news since the election. Riots, merchants leaving, rumours of prisoners held in Miran. Now we have a Guild courier murdered and news has come out that Trading businesses are leaving Miran—"

"Traders leaving?" Rehan had said nothing about that this morning.

"Haven't you seen this?" He turned his reader towards her. It displayed an article from the Trader Guild Bulletin.

. . . *attempts by the council to quell the riots have only had an adverse effect. Our Guild representatives affirm that most of the part of the city known as the merchant quarter is off limits to those supporting the council. Our local members can still move freely throughout the city but are advised to exercise extreme caution when going into the lower-central region. Any of our members not of the Mirani chapter are strongly advised to reconsider their need to travel to Miran. We cannot guarantee their safety.*

This advice supersedes any advice issued previously. A warning is in place for all Traders wanting to visit Miran. For more details see the Guild's warnings list.

This trouble has been fermenting for some time but came to a head after the high-profile wedding of Foundation family Trader Lihan Ilendar to Damarcian high-profile Trader Roisieli Takani Temuran . . .

What? Mikandra's heart jumped. She reread, but there was Lihan's name in clear letters. There was no mistaking him because he had no brothers.

There was even a picture of him, smug-faced, on the arm of this woman, a tall, dark-haired Damarcian beauty wearing the Ilendar traditional wedding gown that—damn it—if Lihan wasn't going to care about succession, should have been hers to wear. That woman wasn't going to give him any children either.

Mikandra felt like someone had slapped her in the face.

The arsehole.

He knew. He knew when he was speaking to her in the Mirani Guild building that he was about to get married. He knew she had been besotted with him for years. He never meant anything with that kiss. Never took her seriously, probably even wanted her to go away.

We can be friends, huh?

And then she got angry with herself for even letting the issue distract her. It should have been clear that he wasn't interested, but she had stupidly kept hoping. Stupid, stupid, stupid.

She looked up.

Ydana Ezmi must have seen something in her face, because he asked, "Are you all right? I know it's a shock to hear this about the town you thought was safe—"

"I'm fine. Just give me a moment."

She breathed through flaring nostrils, ready to belt something. Seething.

Arsehole. The fucking arsehole.

She swallowed hard and read on, but her heart was racing. *The wedding had been a private ceremony so as not to stir already-frayed emotions. The family said that while initially the couple had planned to remain in Miran, it had proven to be impossible within a few days. Every time any of the family left the house, they had to run a gauntlet of hostile people in the street. The city guard refused to guarantee protection—*

Ydana Ezmi continued, oblivious to her inner turmoil. "With these riots going on, I'm not going against Guild advice not to visit Miran. A Guild courier was murdered in Miran. I have no intention to become the next victim. I have no indication whether Amandra supports the Mirani authorities. I feel that I'm just deluding myself. She probably doesn't want to see me again. I've wasted thirty years of my life waiting for her."

That made her look up. Even though he meant Trader years and not Ceren years, it was an awfully long time.

He stared into the distance, his face haunted. "You know, I'm not getting any younger, and this is not where I'd envisaged our relationship to go."

"I'd be surprised if she didn't want to see you again," Mikandra said.

The look of hope in his eyes almost made her cry. What a way to waste most of your adult life: waiting for a lover to make a decision about the relationship.

"Has she talked to you about any of it?" His expression was wary. "Your father—"

"My father and his sister don't get a long too well. Anyway, I'm no longer at home, and my father doesn't want me back, so you can tell me anything you want, because it's not going to get back to the family in the form of gossip."

He sighed. The tense position of his shoulders relaxed a little. "Amandra has been . . . very distant. We had a very bad argument. She told me she wanted to run in the election and I didn't take her seriously enough. You'll probably know that she often has grand plans and I'm afraid I'd become used to the fact that she usually forgets about them after the buzz of the idea has died down. So I made a joke about it, and she said that I never support her and that I only ever try to pull her away from her home. I'm afraid that part is true. I've been asking many times if she wants to come and live with me, because there is no way I can live in Miran. I'm afraid I may have driven her to running in the election with that despicable man. I was surprised at how angry she got with me. It's like she put a lifetime worth of annoyances in that argument."

Mikandra spoke carefully. "She told me that the reason she went into the council was to save Miran from taking unwise turns."

"That sounds like my Amandra." He sighed. "Her heart is too big, but she can't hold the entire world in it."

Yes she remembered now: Coldi loved their proverbs. "I don't know that she can do much. It looks like she has a minority position."

"I really don't understand the Mirani voting system. How can someone be voted in if no one supports her?"

"The Traders support her." Most of them, at least. "The High Council is elected by all the people of Miran." And most of the Nikala who supported Nemedor Satarin never bothered to vote, therefore, her vote was an artificially inflated measure of her support. The truth was that most people in Miran didn't support her aunt or the Traders. They didn't care about foreign imports; they only liked the way Nemedor Satarin spoke, and he was a very good orator.

"I'm going to get her out," he said. "I'm worried. All right, she had her opportunity to make the world a better place. Now I want her home." He laughed, but there was little humour in his voice. The fact that he missed her badly was etched in his face. He sighed and folded his hands on the table. "You made a wise move to come here. Miran is imploding. Even your employers will have to leave."

The Andrahar Traders leave Miran? That would be the day the city ended. "I'm not sure if this would be such a good place." Considering what she'd just found out about the Barresh council, it might be a worse place to be than Miran.

"Don't think about today, think about the future." He held up his finger. "This will be an excellent place. Mark my words, Barresh will have the future. It is nothing now, but wait a couple of years, and it will be a very different story."

Sadly, she had to agree with him. "I don't understand who is in charge of this town. Yes, there is the council and the guards, but they seem to come from all kinds of different places, not just locals."

"The Barresh council went through some major changes last year. Previously, they had a family and class-based system like Miran's, and only the keihu section held positions of power. After the changes, all sections of the population have seats on the council, including the non-natives. It's an interesting concept that other places with mixed and large transient populations could learn from."

"But who pays for all these new buildings? Because Barresh used to be a Mirani protectorate and got its money from Miran. Now that the Mirani army is gone, I had expected Barresh to be poor."

"Each family contributes according to their abilities."

"There must be some pretty rich families here, judging by

their transport." That Gazion that still sat in the private aircraft space at the airport and continued to bug her.

"You have sharp eyes." He laughed. "That one belongs to Daya Ezmi. He has made Barresh home, and yes, for now holds the position of Chief Councillor of Barresh."

She had never heard the Chief Councillor's last name. "Ezmi? How did he end up with that name?" Like Ydana, all Coldi at Hedron were from the Ezmi clan, and the tendency to only use first names in public life was Coldi. But this man was definitely not Coldi, and like the Mirani Endri, Coldi didn't crossbreed with any other type of people.

"Yes, he's a compatriot of mine. I'm surprised you haven't heard of him. He's styled himself into the leader of the free *zhadya*-born movement."

The *what?*

"You haven't heard of them either?"

She shook her head. His air of incredulity annoyed her. She might agree with him that the Mirani council's hostility to foreigners was not helpful, but she didn't subscribe to his brand of *everything Miran does is stupid* either. He hadn't always been that way either. She remembered him being in Miran, dressing as a local and looking happy and relaxed. Maybe he had changed more than her aunt.

"For a long time, and I'm talking hundreds of years, and possibly more, there has been a group of children born from Coldi parents who are different. They are smaller, sickly and, on Asto, usually die a few days after birth. The ones who survive are always completely crazy, and rarely make it to adulthood. If they do, they never have any children. It wasn't until our clan moved to Hedron and these children all survived that we understood: these children don't have the built-in Coldi resistance to heat. In fact, they are not Coldi at all. Most of them used to live in the outer rings of the cities on Asto, in poverty, ignored, often in prison. Out there, people called them *zhadya*-born.

"It was not until recently that we understood them to be throwbacks to the people who used to live on Asto before the meteorite strike and the New Beginning. In fact, they are the same people as the ones we called the *buried children*."

Mikandra vaguely remembered being taught the very basics of Asto's history: of the meteorite that obliterated an advanced society, and of the rise of the Coldi people since then. Coldi were an artificially created race of people who had survived the disaster where their creators had not, except for the very few babies left in life-suspension chambers underneath the earth in Athyl, the largest city on Asto. These babies were the buried children.

"Asto is their home, but they cannot live there," Ydana said. "There are many of these people on Hedron, but even there, they are not well liked because of their unusual tendency to collect energy in their bodies and release it at the most inopportune moments. A hazard, as you can understand, and they cannot work in an industrial environment—"

"Energy?" She saw a flash across a woman's face in the dark courtyard of the guesthouse in Market Street. Jocassa had said something about it. But that woman had been Pengali, hadn't she?

"A potential in energy, like the Exchange uses, but a lot less powerful. I've seen *zhadya*-born who are in full control of it and it's most disturbing. Daya is one of them, and never fitted in at Hedron or anywhere else, so he's decided to make Barresh his home. That is where you'll find that a lot of the Barresh council's money comes from: Daya's paid-out inheritance."

When she gave him a puzzled look, he said, "He owns half the Hedron Mines."

"But I thought the mines' owner was Edyamor Ezmi?"

"Correct, and he is the manager. But when the mines' founder Xiya Ezmi died, ownership was divided between both his children: Edyamor and his sister Seveyu, who had to relinquish her inheritance on behalf of her children when she married offworld to Thania Lingui. Daya is her son."

Oh crap, Thania Lingui was the Chief Coordinator of Asto. Daya Ezmi was the son of two very powerful people across the two main Coldi worlds: Asto, their home world and the heavy industry powerhouse of Hedron.

That answered all her questions of where the money came from. And the Gazion, and why there were Barresh guards who looked like elite Asto guards, because they *were* elite Asto guards and they probably reported back directly to Asto.

"Does that answer your questions?"

She nodded. It more than answered everything. This Daya was a man who was extremely dangerous, who had the money to buy his way into everything, and clear all opposition, including entire nations. Including rivals who had set their eyes on the same woman.

She asked, "Why Barresh?" A man like that could buy anything he wanted. Why Barresh other than that he wanted to annoy Miran and get a foothold into Ceren?

"Why not?"

Oh, how could he say that in such an innocent way? "It's only going to inflame old conflicts."

"Daya could not predict the reaction by the Mirani council, nor the recent spate of anti-foreign decisions."

"But surely, the presence of Thania Lingui's son is what the Mirani council is reacting to, isn't it? He was here before the election. Nemedor Satarin was elected to the Mirani council after his military defeat in Barresh, and his election victory was based on border-tightening promises. Are you sure this Daya Ezmi didn't *cause* the two-day war?" Or funded it, and that was why it had been unexpectedly successful. *Weapons of fire* the soldiers in the hospital had said, with burn injuries likely to have been caused by Asto-made imported weapons.

He gave her a disturbed look. "What makes you think that?"

"When a Mirani Endri girl grows up, the first thing she is told is that her first child is the nation. That she must nurture it and take responsibility for its wellbeing. Barresh was a Mirani protectorate and falls under our responsibility. Picture this: a man who represents an enemy of Miran comes into town, instigates a rebellion of locals that results in the expulsion of the Mirani army. Tell the Mirani council that is not an act of subversion, espionage or plain war."

"Yes, I can see your point, but Daya hasn't done anything of the sort. He is here because he can't live on Asto and doesn't get along with his family, and didn't fit into Hedron either. Besides, he married a woman from this town."

"Someone who was already spoken for."

He frowned. "I don't know anything about that."

"I do. She is the lady Iztho Andrahar wanted to marry."

His frown deepened. "You're sure?"

"As sure as I can be." She decided against mentioning the boy. That toddler was too important for the Andrahar family. "Now Iztho is gone, the Andrahar Traders are facing a trial for importing something that Barresh made illegal but that comes only from Miran, something the Andrahar Traders don't normally deal with. And—"

He gave her a sideways, sharp, look. "What are you suggesting?"

"At the moment, nothing, because I have no proof. Except that an important Mirani family is in a lot of trouble, and none of it is of their own making."

"You're saying that the smuggling claims are false and that someone is trying to frame the family?"

Mikandra said nothing, but met his eyes squarely.

He said, "If that is true, it will come out in court."

"I hope so." But only if she or Rehan could find evidence. "Whatever the outcome of the court case, no one in Miran likes this development. Many of us do not agree with what Nemedor Satarin is doing to the city, but that doesn't mean that we're not loyal to Miran. The wounds of the past are deep. There is rarely a day in my family's house that the invasion is not mentioned."

He looked even more disturbed. "But certainly that was—"

"A long time ago, yes, but it has shaped every part of Mirani life. Miran was a beautiful, proud place—still is. People in Miran want progress, but they don't want to have it forced on them from outside. Some people have stronger opinions on this than others. Whether we're Traders or conservatives, progress to us doesn't mean that we'll just walk away from our traditions and give up on them, because *giving up* is not in our blood."

"I know, I know. I've battled this 'never give up' mentality for twenty-five years." He sighed and met her eyes. "Is there a solution? One that does not involve conflict and hurt to people we love?"

23

A T NIGHT in the guesthouse, Mikandra didn't join in any parties and didn't even join the Kedrasi mother and daughter, because she had already eaten. She sat in the corner of the upstairs balcony with her book and her light, and stared at the pages, seething with anger.

She couldn't stop thinking about Lihan, about how cool he'd been to her when she met him in the Guild building in Miran.

Well, fuck him, to speak like Rehan. She mouthed the obscenity that she had never let cross her lips. Traders had a reputation for swearing a lot. She might as well be true to the cliché.

"Fuck him, fuck him." It felt good to say it.

He hadn't even had the courtesy to tell her that he was getting married. *We can still be friends,* he had told her. What a load of crap.

Never would she be friends with him again. Never, ever.

She had hoped to transfer to his business once she'd finished the apprenticeship. She'd wanted to work with him and his father, but they had simply abandoned Miran when things became a bit tough.

That was not the way she wanted to live.

She was going to do the apprenticeship with the Andrahars. In Miran. And when she had her licence, she would work either with the Andrahars, or separately in her own business, and outcompete Lihan in everything.

Fuck him.

She went to bed when most people came into the room, and although she had finished being angry with Lihan, her mind now went over the political situation and Ydana Ezmi's last question. Would there be a way out of the ever-increasing madness of the Mirani boycotts and the council's responses that did not involve conflict? If Asto had its sights on Barresh, could Miran stop them? If Barresh wanted to be independent, could they do so without compromising the security of Miran? If the Mirani chapter of the Trader Guild could not live with the import restrictions and new residency rules, would they all leave Miran, and if they did, could they do so in peace?

She didn't think any of those things were likely.

There would be more fighting. The Mirani army would continue to try to influence Barresh, *gamra* would continue with the boycott until something broke in Miran. Until the Traders left, until the huge body of Nikala people in the city were fed up with the lack of everything and staged a revolt against the council. And surely, Asto would continue to make use of that situation to push into Barresh.

Sooner or later, there would be a proper war, not a lame two-day one. Based on technology, there was no way Miran could win. It was in Miran's interest not to let a war happen.

In the darkness of the night, her worries grew into wars that spanned the continent, her fear for her family grew into massacres, until the snowy mountainside was drenched with blood and no one could possibly have survived.

Miran would die. History would be wiped out. A beautiful city would become frozen over and empty of life.

She had to remind her wayward imagination that she was exaggerating. It wouldn't be like that. The council had more sense than that. The Traders would never leave. Miran would never be so stupid to challenge any other entity in war.

But her mind continued to conjure up ever more horrible images.

When she realised that sleep wasn't going to happen she got

out of bed, ignoring the muffled noises made by some lovers on the other side of the room, and took her book of notes downstairs in the courtyard amongst the remains of the night's party. She cleared glasses and bottles off a table and opened her book. The light in the holder above her had almost burned out but gave just enough glow for her to write down all the new things she had learned.

On a blank page, she drew a diagram that showed Barresh as a small circle within Miran. It used to be that the Barresh Exchange operated illegally and every traveller or legal freight had to come through Miran. No more. She drew a line from the Barresh enclave to the left-hand edge of the page to symbolise the direct line out of the city-state.

It used to be that the Barresh council was a group of decadent fat keihu men who had no power because all their decisions had to be approved by the Mirani council. No more. She drew a jagged circle around Barresh to symbolise a real, effective border.

It used to be that the Mirani army sent troops there to "keep the locals under control" but effectively to misbehave with as much decadence as they pleased. It used to be that people from outside couldn't visit Barresh unless approved by Miran.

Now everyone could visit. She drew a lot of arrows into Barresh.

Some of those arrows were from Asto—she drew a little circle in the corner of the page to represent that world and a few arrows from there to Barresh. The page was getting pretty messy by now, and that's what the situation looked like in reality: messy. Barresh was like the leak in the waterbag that was Miran. No matter how much Miran fortified its controls, undesirable people would come in through Barresh.

Why would Daya Ezmi set up this group for whatever-they-were-called people in Barresh if he wasn't interested in spying on Miran, especially considering he was someone said to be able to look into other people's minds?

That was a disturbing thought. Anyone in the street could be scanning her on behalf of the Barresh council. They possibly already knew everything about her.

She took a few calming breaths. *Well, let's not worry about that,* because it would be the end of her.

So.

Iztho.

She drew a little circle on the adjacent empty page.

And his lover.

Another circle.

The lover was in this group of Coldi throwbacks, and Iztho found out things he shouldn't have.

Hmm. What things?

They were either things that the Barresh council did—she drew a circle for the council—or things someone in Barresh did, or things the Asto leadership did in Barresh.

This Daya was *Thania Lingui's* son.

She drew lots of squiggly lines between Barresh and Asto.

In any case, Iztho, loyal to Miran, had too many fingers of influence with the new power in Barresh and had to be taken out of the picture.

Or something.

Of course, the suggestion that someone had falsified Exchange documents to frame Iztho was just that: a suggestion.

But there was no shortage of people with motives to do this.

She turned over the page and listed them all:

Barresh council

Daya Ezmi and his woman Anmi

Thania Lingui

And then, a bit further down, the ones that were much less likely, but should not be discounted:

Miran council

Nemedor Satarin

Antho Tussamar and rival Traders

There, that list "only" mentioned the six most important people or groups in the system, or even all of settled space. The more she looked at it, the more it gave her the creeps. If any of these people had done something to frame Iztho, the consequences would be serious and ramifications felt throughout *gamra*. There *would* be major conflicts, none of them within her control.

But the most likely people to have wanted Iztho out of the way were the first two. She drew a circle around *Barresh council* and *Daya Ezmi and his woman Anmi.*

She stared at the page for a while, but it didn't bring her any insights. Then, because it was starting to go light, she closed the book, put it in her bag and went to the Exchange.

Like most days, Rehan was waiting for her by the time she'd settled into her usual cubicle.

There were times when she wondered what else he did in a day and how many people still worked in that office. She wondered if he sat there alone because they couldn't afford to keep the other staff and because it was too dangerous for them to traverse the streets anyway. She wondered about Trimon and Zimana and what a hungry winter it would be for them if Trimon lost his job.

After the usual chat about the weather—it was snowing in Miran—she asked him, *Have you ever heard of a group of non-Coldi people born from Coldi parents?*

She expected questions, but his reply came back immediately. *The Aghyrians. I've heard of them. There are a lot at Hedron.*

I hadn't heard that name for them before.

Coldi use the term zhadya-born, but I don't think they like that description. They're not just zhadya-born either. The buried children are of the same people. They are the people of the old Asto city of Aghyr. They call themselves the most powerful people who ever lived. They say that they invented the Exchange and that there would have been no human settlements other than on Asto if it hadn't been for them.

She detected a tone of wariness.

Have you met these people?

Some. They're odd, maybe dangerous. I don't know that anyone knows what they want.

They have made Barresh their home. Their leader is a man called Daya Ezmi.

The same Daya Ezmi who is Thania Lingui's son? I didn't know Thania Lingui had a zhadya-born son.

Yes. He is the man who has married the woman Iztho wanted to marry.

There was a short pause.

She typed, *You are allowed to swear.*

He responded immediately. *Fuck.* And a bit later, *Can you come home?*

That question surprised her. She typed, *I have no money,* but then remembered her vow not to ask him for any, so she deleted it again and wrote instead, *Do you think I could be more useful in Miran?*

There was a pause. *Probably not.* Another pause. *But if what you're saying is true, I don't like you being there. If you're found out, they might think you're a spy. You do not mess with anyone within a whiff of the Asto leadership and come away without damage.*

I'm fine. Mikandra frowned at the screen. Why the concern all of a sudden? *There are lots of Mirani here. No one knows who I am.*

Maybe he was right about the danger, but if the Barresh council suspected her and wanted her out of the way, they could have arrested her on some made-up charge a long time ago.

Please, listen to what I say and pay it more attention than you usually do with advice. These people are dangerous and have ways to find out what they want. They know your identity no matter how careful you are. They will observe you and learn things they have no business to know. Leave that place as soon as you can and come home.

Despite the heat, she shivered. She remembered that pounding feeling when meeting Daya and Anmi in the library. What had Ydana Ezmi said again about the abilities of these people?

At home, she could look after Mother and Liseyo. She could ask him for money. In the overall scheme of things, the price of a ticket was a piddly amount for him. Nothing was more tempting.

But going home was giving up. Going home was not *courage.* Going home was going back to having nowhere to live and having no money unless she asked Rehan.

Living cheaply independently was a lot easier in Barresh than in Miran. But oh, she smelled the heavenly scent of freshly-baked fish bread, she felt the warm glow of a fiercely burning fire and the comfortable warmth of a cloak.

She blinked pricking eyes and typed, *I'm fine here for the time being. There are some things I want to do.* And then, to distract herself, she added, *I didn't know Lihan Ilendar got married.*

I didn't know that before yesterday either. It surprised everyone, even in the Guild. When people on the street heard, they were angry and tried to set the house on fire.

I guess this wasn't because they didn't get their invitations to a wedding party?

Hahaha. No. They called the family traitors and scrawled all over the outside walls. Most people think that these people were hit gangs hired by other Traders, but there is no proof for that. The family are gone now, and the riots have spread to the next block. It's tricky to navigate the exclusion zones when going to the office.

Is there any way you can do work at home? She had a sudden vision of flames in the snow, rioting men throwing burning sticks and kicking down a gate. Their voices echoed through the night.

She shivered as if a blast of cold hit her.

What was that? There was no menisha brew in sight.

A reply had appeared on the screen *I can work at home, but we need to keep access to the airport. I need to keep an eye on who these people are and what they're doing.*

Would they stop you trying to get through?

At this point, I have no idea what they will do. Most of them are young Nikala men who wear scarves over their faces. I don't know who they are and why they're not working. I don't know if they're there because they want to be or because someone pays them. They're probably just bored and looking for trouble for the sake of having something to do. I don't know that the city guards can stop them. I don't know that they want to. At the moment, the city feels hostile to us.

Be careful.

Funny you should say that.

That made her smile. She couldn't picture what his face looked like when he sat there alone in the office while Braedon helped Eydrina Lasko out and Taerzo fixed aircraft, but she could feel his loneliness. The Rehan she had met was a stiff, rude and abrupt man with a hard emotionless look on his face. His written words showed an entirely different person.

After telling him that she planned to stay in Barresh and

promising him several times that she'd be careful and not to do any stupid things, she announced that she had to go to work or be late. She signed off with a feeling of despair and regret. Nothing she could do made much of a difference. Investigations of Exchange data with the authorities were way over her head and needed to be done by Lawkeepers. He hadn't mentioned the court case for a number of days. She didn't think that it was going well. While Taerzo and Braedon busied themselves with other activities, he sat alone in that office, being eaten from the inside by his own destructive thoughts.

The brothers would have been much better off having assigned Braedon to this task, not Rehan with his highly-strung mind.

She wished she could do something, because if this went on, there would be no apprenticeship for her and then what? She would be stuck here forever.

How long could Rehan hold out before he ended up like Leitho? And what could she possibly do to help the court case?

24

W HILE WALKING around the block to the council buildings, she had a thought so obvious that she hit herself in the head for not having thought of it before.

She worked in a library. Libraries held information. The stupid mess that passed for the records and accounts of the Mirani army was only part of the library's holdings. While walking through other parts of the hall, she had spied sections with beautiful maps and old books. There were also new books that contained all the transcriptions of council meetings. Sure, somewhere in the library there would be information about this group of people, *zhadya*-born or Aghyrians, whatever they called themselves, why they were here, and what they stood for. If she knew what they wanted maybe she could hand the brothers information that might back up whatever their Guild Lawkeeper could find. Possibly, even, Iztho had been mentioned in council meeting transcripts, and she knew the shelves where those stood.

During the midday break, she would normally sit in one of the many courtyards or go to the markets where she had become addicted to Machizu's food, but this time, she remained in the library. There were a lot of people in the library, but the section with council meeting transcripts remained deserted. Mikandra walked through once and spied the dates on the spines. Anything prior to independence had been written in Mirani. She took one book off the shelf and opened it. On the pages was an account in neat print of a meeting discussing a new regulation. She flipped a few more pages, but then noticed Bakimay looking at her, probably shadowing her and reporting everything to Daya.

Damn, she would have to wait until there was no one here. She put the book back and wandered into another section. Bakimay went back to her work. A bit later, Mikandra again walked into the council meeting section. The books she'd want would be those from around the time of the two-day war. There were a couple of gaps on the shelves. Mikandra didn't dare linger and went to the adjacent section, which was all about local produce and contained books about plants and trees and fish and other creatures Mikandra had seen at market stalls. Ringgit, the noisy animals that lived in the marshes, turned out to be air-breathing, winged fish. They floated on the surface of the water. The noise was their mating call.

Bakimay walked past a few times with her eyebrows raised. She stopped once without asking anything, but the second time, she couldn't contain her curiosity.

"You can go outside. Is not raining."

"I know." The locals had found her reluctance to go out in the rain amusing.

"Work finished. Work again this afternoon."

"I'm not working. I'm looking for something. Maybe you can help me?"

"Oh?" Bakimay raised her eyebrows. Pengali eyes were very expressive and it amused Mikandra to see carefully cultured hostility warring with curiosity.

"I'm looking for information about the history of Barresh, especially about the different groups of people who live here."

"Pengali were first. Everyone else come later."

"I'd like to read about when all the different people came to live here, if I can."

Barely hiding her curiosity, Bakimay pointed her to a section of the library that had already been finished and that held many beautiful old books so different from the disintegrating volumes from the Mirani army headquarters.

Mikandra found a wealth of information on history, most of it in Mirani script, but in an ancient syntax that hadn't been used in Miran for hundreds of years, though she had learned it at school. Apparently, Barresh had once spanned a couple more islands than the current two, and those old settlements had been abandoned. There were old plans of proposed bridges between the islands, and grandiose buildings, even trains.

Newer books were beautifully illustrated histories written in the script she had seen the women practice in the library. It seemed that keihu had been only a spoken language until independence.

To her huge surprise, Pengali was a written language, and a very ancient one at that, although several books referred to the legal requirement to write everything in Mirani "to appease the occupying force".

Apparently, the cliffs of the escarpment held many caves and passages where ancient histories of the Pengali tribes were carved into the stone. Apparently, too, the beautiful glass-stone eating bowls and other carved objects were Pengali-made, as was most of the fabric, the felt and the woodwork. The Pengali *looked* primitive, but their culture was ancient, rich and productive. In contrast, the keihu had never done much more than provide lazy and corrupt government.

Interesting.

But the history section was so big and there was so much material that she could spend days going through it before she found something that even vaguely related to Aghyrians. All she could figure from the old materials was that they hadn't lived in Barresh until recently.

Then she had another thought. On the morning she left home, Father had been grilling Liseyo over her knowledge of Mirani history. If she wanted the short version of the history of Barresh, the place to go would be a school.

She went to see Bakimay, who usually left the library at midday, but had probably stayed to keep an eye on her strange Mirani employee.

"What? Already finished? Not happy? History is boring, hah. Not like Miran, hah."

Mikandra clenched her jaws. "The books you showed me were interesting. But it will take me a long time to read all those books. I don't have much time. I'm wondering if you could do something else for me."

The suspicious look didn't leave Bakimay's face. Mikandra wondered whether, instead of going to the markets, Bakimay had gone to the Chief Councillor to inform him of this new development in this suspicious Mirani woman who was probably a spy.

She imagined the two of them sitting at a table—looking suspiciously like the one in the guesthouse where she had sat with Ydana Ezmi—talking about her.

"I would like to know what kind of history is being taught to children in Barresh. I'd like to visit a school."

"You ask strange questions."

Mikandra bet she meant strange not in a good way. "We are interested in history in Miran. History is what makes a place. History helps us understand a place."

Bakimay's eyebrows went up. "You not like others. You come on time. You work. No complaining. Work is boring, yes? But you come and come."

Was she dreaming or did she hear Bakimay give a compliment? "I need the money. My family taught me to honour my promises."

Bakimay shook her head, which made the beaded plaits dance around her head. "You not like others. No drink, no? No party? No selling foul orange brew?"

"Not all Mirani are like that. I'm sorry if you've been treated badly by the ones who do these things. At home in Miran, I am a student of history." More lies. Liseyo would be rolling on the ground with laughter if she heard this. "I want to visit a school. Could you take me to one?"

"Schools are in Pengali parts of city. You find Pengali people no friend of Mirani. Only old ones speak your language because when occupation we had to learn. Mirani used Pengali as servants. Mirani think Pengali are stupid. But Mirani soldiers happy to fuck Pengali girls as whores. Mirani fight Pengali men. Mirani cut off tails. Mirani kill a lot of our people. No friends. Pengali not nice to Mirani. Still want to come?"

Mikandra cringed. She lived with all these soldiers who indeed—save the tail-cutting—did just that. Was it a surprise that the only Pengali at the guesthouse parties were women? "If you can be my guide and translator, yes, I would."

Bakimay told her to come to her desk at the end of the day. She handed Mikandra a khaki tunic. "You put on. Look like one who lives here."

Another blunder. All Pengali had probably found her white and red tunics offensive and proof that she was the same as the type of Mirani people they knew.

After she finished work, Mikandra went into the library wing's bathroom, a courtyard pool surrounded by cubicles where water from hot springs ran through stone ducts. A worker had explained to her that steam pressure from the heat of the earth drove the water.

Having a bath in Miran was a formal occasion performed no more than once a day. In Barresh, you were considered dirty if you didn't bathe and rinse each time you visited the private facilities. This was a habit down to the very poorest people in the city who bathed in the open-air pools if their houses didn't have hot pools. Every building she had visited had a bathing facility with towels and flasks of megon oil to stop smells and skin infections.

If you smelled, you were dirty. In a place with a climate like Barresh, not smelling was a constant challenge.

So she jumped in the pool, dried and rubbed oil on herself and went back to Bakimay, wearing the khaki tunic with the council emblem. By this time, it was starting to go dark.

To her question if school hadn't finished for the day, Bakimay snorted and said that she didn't understand the Pengali at all.

Bakimay took her through the tree-lined streets of the main

island, where the keihu families' stately houses stood behind walls with ornate gates.

On the far eastern end of the island, many of those old houses were either being renovated or expanded into complexes of three or four floors with many rooms.

It was into one of those complexes that Bakimay took Mikandra.

What had been the old house's gate now opened into a tunnel, a dark maw leading into the depths of the building. Inside, with the approaching night, it was almost too dark for Mikandra to see. The ceiling was so low that Mikandra had to bend to get into doorways. Surely the original house didn't have ceilings that low. Bakimay said that as soon as the Pengali took possession of an empty house, they divided each floor into two so they had more room for people to live. A mansion that would have housed a rich family and their servants was now the home of hundreds.

It was warm in this tunnel, with a riot of smells competing to be noticed. Mikandra sensed the presence of people in the darkness. There were soft voices, and giggles. When Pengali weren't shouting at each other, their language didn't sound quite so harsh.

The first time a rough-skinned hand touched her arm, Mikandra jumped. Then her eyes became used to the darkness, and she noticed people around her. It was too dark to see their faces, but the white pigment spots or stripes on their shoulders and tails stood out in the low light.

Sweat trickled down Mikandra's back. All those Pengali bodies might be clean, but the Pengali had a curious odour of wet mud that Mikandra's nose, used to fresh highland air, found unpleasant.

Bakimay took her to a room on the building's ground floor. There was no window, but air and light trickled in from a couple of shafts that stood out like glowing tubes in the ceiling. Groups of Pengali children sat on mats on the ground underneath these light tubes. They looked up when Bakimay came in. Several of the older children rose and made what sounded like an official greeting.

The only adult in the room was a young male. He spoke to Bakimay in Pengali and Mikandra stood to the side, feeling like a big awkward smelly giant.

The kids all looked at her with their huge eyes. The skin patterns that adults had on their shoulders and backs covered their entire bodies. Their tails were shorter than those of adults, but much more vividly coloured and moving constantly. The white portions in their skin patterns almost glowed in the light.

One of them waved a tail at Mikandra and she waved back. The children in the group giggled, a soft snorting noise. She dropped to her knees. Within moments, the children had forgotten about their work or about sitting still. They were all over her, patting her hair, feeling her skin and her ears. They were small, lithe, bouncy, striped or spotted all over, and they tangled and tumbled, using their tails for everything.

The teacher gave a sharp order, accompanied by a snap of his tail.

Several of them scurried back to their previous spots. The teacher snapped his tail at the remaining ones.

Mikandra said, "Leave them. They don't bother me."

Three little spotted children had settled themselves in her lap, having a tail fight for the best position. A little girl was at Mikandra's back, trying to plait the too-short strands of her hair and another one was trying to jump onto her shoulders.

The teacher snapped another command, and the little ones drooped off, back to their mat. The little rascal who had tried to climb her shoulders pulled his knees up against his chest and glared at the teacher.

Mikandra tried not to laugh.

Along the walls hung quilts and knotted tapestries of intricate detail and beauty. There were ornate glass-stone plates with carvings and panels of wood with fine lettering across them. She couldn't imagine that these small children had made these things. The tubes in the ceiling were made from glass-stone and throughout the part of the tube that protruded from the ceiling, there were intricate carvings in the surface. Light glowed at the end of the tube and in the carved grooves. These were true works of art.

On the other hand, she could see no books or other teaching material. Maybe this was a school for craft?

"Do they sell any of this produce?" she asked. Mikandra remembered walking past stalls with glass-stone eating bowls and other products for domestic use, all very plain and none as elegant as the tubes. There should be much better markets for this craft.

Bakimay answered the question herself. "We sell at markets. Only some things. Is not for selling. Glass-stone come from here." She held her fist to her chest. "Stay here. Not selling."

"You teach the children to make these things?"

Bakimay gave her a strange look. "Not understand. You want history. I give history. You not see. You think writing is on bits of paper or screens. That's not real writing. Real writing is on things that don't disappear when you turn off."

Now Mikandra saw. The tapestries and the carved glass-stone were not pretty artefacts to decorate the classroom. They were class materials. The quilts and tubes were the Pengali children's books.

"I see. This is the history of the Pengali," she said, nodding at the closest quilt. It consisted of a couple panels of finely embroidered figures with tails.

"Yes, history of Pengali," Bakimay sounded satisfied, as if she had well and truly won the round of the debate. "You come because you want to learn history. So. Learn history. You want hear about Pengali? You listen. Pengali are not like you. You listen to story. You be patient."

She spoke to the teacher, who told all the students to sit in a circle.

Mikandra's stomach made a growling noise. A couple of children giggled. They clearly had sharp ears. She wondered if these children had to go to dinner or something. It was late afternoon and she was getting very hungry herself. But there was no sign that class was about to end.

The teacher asked the pupils to come forward one by one and read off the collection of quilts, tapestries and panels on the walls. Bakimay translated while each child spoke.

The Pengali history began with the tribe living in a village at the bottom of the escarpment until one day, people fell from the sky in a silver machine. They were hungry and lost and the Pengali offered them food and shelter, which they accepted gratefully.

Each night, the visitors would look at a new bright star in the sky and cry, until the light faded and the star went back to being its wandering self.

Their silver flying machine wouldn't work again and the people settled on one of the islands in the marsh. The Pengali called these people *Akkar*. They learned to grow their own food. They built big houses. They taught the Pengali lots of good things. How to cut glass-stone. How to make better boats. How to hunt better. But they had few children. Pengali had lots of children so a few Pengali females went to offer themselves. The next year, there were a few children born with no spots or stripes and very short tails. The children of those children had no tails at all. Some of them came back to the Pengali. There was a brief time when the people interbred freely, then the Pengali went back to being Pengali, the hybrids went to live on the island and the Akkar refugees slowly disappeared.

That was until a year ago.

Bakimay translated the teacher's words. "We knew Anmi was Akkar when she walked out of the forest into Pengali village. Like Akkar, she crashed in a flying machine, only her machine land in forest. Like Akkar, she has name written on arm. I saw it. Like Akkar, she has *avya*. I saw what she could do when Ikay—the tribe's female elder—" Bakimay added, "—taught her. Pengali found Akkar man for her. The Mirani wanted to take her away. Pengali fought them. Mirani are gone now. Akkar is not gone. Akkar lives in all of us. We can put all of us—keihu, Pengali—together and we bring Akkar back because is in our blood. We give Anmi and Daya family." She stuck her chin out as if daring Mikandra to challenge. "Anmi have children. They belong to all of us."

Mikandra had to bite her tongue not to mention who was the father of the young boy. On the other hand, there was no way that these smart people didn't know that already. They just chose to ignore that blot on their favourite queen.

"Where did you learn all these stories?"

"They are written on the walls of the Akkar homes which they dug into the rocks."

"Old paintings?" She thought of the mural in the council building, which was obviously much more recent than the time of the meteorite strike on Asto.

"Carvings in stone. On walls. We copy for children to learn."

"These original carvings are still there? Can I see these caves?"

"No, can't. Pengali and Akkar only. Is sacred."

"Are there any images of the carvings?"

"Paper rubbings only."

❧

By the time Bakimay and Mikandra came out of the building, a glimmer of blue light hung over the eastern horizon. Mikandra asked if she hadn't disturbed the children's dinners and sleep.

Bakimay snorted. "You strange and stupid. Pengali live at night. See better in the forest. Too much light hurts eyes."

Damn, like the maramarang, they were nocturnal. Well, that explained a lot.

"How do you manage to work all day and all night?"

"We manage. We work."

She was beginning to build up a healthy respect for these people. Never mind the rich keihu families, these people were the driving force of Barresh.

She went back to the guesthouse for a quick rest and bath.

Mikandra sat in the water thinking about all she had learned. It was a story very different from the one she had expected. The keihu were an *artificial* race. Like the Coldi, they had been made by the old people from Asto.

Back in the library, she found Bakimay and asked to see these rubbings of the ancient writing.

"You no give up, hah?" A few days ago, that remark would have sounded angry, but no longer.

"I like to study history."

"Come at midday. I show you something better."

Mikandra wondered what "something better" was and when she was going to run into questions from the council about why she wanted to know all this. How about *Iztho found out something in Barresh that he wasn't supposed to know, and I want to know what it is?* Or *I'm looking for data to use against Barresh in the court?*

For most of the day, she kept looking over her shoulder, nerves raging in her each time someone came up from behind her.

But nothing happened and at the appointed time, Mikandra arrived at Bakimay's desk.

Bakimay rose without a word and took Mikandra further into the building, down the corridors Mikandra had wandered once or twice, where all the doors were open and rooms empty, the restoration activity already finished but where no one had yet moved in.

Bakimay stopped at a door to the left to hold her hand up to a panel next to a metal sliding door. Lights blinked, the panel showed Bakimay's large-eyed face and the door slid aside. Lights blinked on. Mikandra followed her into a room with an arched entrance which opened into a bare pentagonal space. Pink granite covered the floor, walls and ceilings.

It was rather dark here, with just two lights on the walls. Bakimay's and Mikandra's footsteps echoed in the empty space. No, the walls weren't empty. They were covered in carvings. There were shapes of people and trees and various objects she didn't recognise. Some panels were small, others large, and others again contained only text.

"What is this place?" Even Mikandra's whisper sounded too loud.

"Cannot go to caves, because sacred. Also, far away and not easy to get to. So build caves here."

A replica.

The place smelled of dry stone and although it wasn't ancient, it *smelled* ancient.

She stopped in the middle of the room, studying the carved panels on each of the five walls. Damn, she felt like she had been here before.

Of course that was impossible, but she had seen a very similar room.

In Miran, there was a tunnel that ran from the library to a chamber directly underneath the Foundation monument. This chamber had five black marble walls with ancient glyphs, lit with flapping oil lights. In the middle of the room stood a table with a glass-stone panel in which were carved the names and family trees of the Mirani Endri who had first come from the highlands.

After the Foundation monument had been built, there had been a long period of neglect and disrepair, during which the tunnel had fallen in and the citizens of Miran had forgotten about the chamber. It had been rediscovered in her grandfather's lifetime and painfully restored until it was reopened when Mikandra was little. Important Mirani historians were still working out the meaning of the characters.

These days, every Mirani Endri child went into that chamber once. Mikandra remembered the chill that crept over her in there, the way the teacher's voice echoed. She remembered the flowing look of the glyphs on the walls. She and Liseyo had tried to copy them from memory and had played "old people" for weeks.

The symbols, the style and the characters in this chamber were identical.

"This is the day Akkar arrived." Bakimay pointed at a carving that showed a curious shape half-hidden by marsh reeds and bushes. It was an aircraft of some description, but not one she recognised. Its curious position confirmed the story, as told to the children, that it had crashed.

In another panel, a number of tall people faced a group of Pengali on the beach. A Pengali man held a bowl which he offered to a tall woman. She was thin, with untidy long hair. Her shoulders were bent. The people behind her were men and women of all ages, some children, some injured with bandages or crutches. The artwork was so detailed that it showed pain in their expressions. In comparison, the Pengali looked magnificent and proud.

The two suns were low on the horizon, and above in the sky blazed a bright star.

Underneath the image was a panel with the elegant curled script.

"You can read what it says?" Mikandra asked, almost whispering in this sacred place.

Bakimay ran her finger along the lines of characters.

"They came because their world was a wasteland. They were hungry and tired. We gave them a home."

The point of view surprised her. "A Pengali wrote this? You used this writing for the Pengali language?" She would have thought that the visitors had written this.

"We change some characters. Pengali has sounds that Akkar does not. Our people write this after Akkar came. Wanted to write which people belong in this place." Her eyes met Mikandra's. "So that when other people come, we prove the islands and the coast are ours."

Creating some sort of legal record, even back then.

Mikandra stepped back and studied the carvings.

The panels were better made and had more pictures than the ones in Miran. Maybe the type of stone lent itself better to carving, or maybe the people here had more peace for craft. Or the forefathers of the Pengali had more skill and cared more about their history.

But the characters they used were the same. In the Mirani version of the carvings, there were no images to help the translation of the ancient language.

Historians assumed that the cave dwellers who were the ancestors of the Endri had always lived on the highlands because there was no indication that it had been otherwise, and no one had ever questioned why this civilisation had started up there.

When you thought about it, those people who lived in caves and grew their food in underground chambers were not suited to the climate, especially compared with the hunters and forefathers of the Nikala who lived in the canyons and had hands with claws that helped them climb to catch food. They lived off fish from the rivers, moss and fungi off the cliffs, and maramarang. Some of those tribes still lived there. They were hardened, strong and tough. They were, like the Pengali, an ancient people. The cave dwellers were far too refined and weak for living like that. Like the refugees depicted on the carving, they were sickly and hungry. Like the visitors who had come to the Pengali, they had used the local people to create a hybrid race. Mirani Nikala had hands with long thumbs and little fingers. They were exceptionally strong in their shoulders. On rare occasions, a child was born with a claw on the pinky.

She asked, "It may be a strange question, but are there ever any keihu babies born with tails?"

Bakimay smiled, showing her carnivorous teeth. "You understand. Yes. That happens. Parents don't like. They cut off before anyone can see."

In Barresh, the hybrid race that was the keihu had won the stakes in wealth and power. The Pengali had reverted to their original form and the visitors had died out or merged completely with the keihu.

In Miran, the hybrid race had become a type of people by themselves, had fought with the visitors, who had responded by closing themselves off and grabbing onto all wealth, power and land they could get, only to find themselves too isolated to survive.

The teacher at the school had said *Akkar live in all of us.* That was true in Barresh where Aghyrian traits, like the telepathic ability they called *avya* was equally spread across the population.

In Miran, it hadn't happened that way. The Aghyrian traits had inbred and become stronger. This was why the Endri now had such bad fertility problems. This was why so many people were going mad and were hearing voices, not because they were mad, but because they actually could hear other people. She bet that the menisha fungus had something to do with it, too. She bet it stimulated that ability. Was it a contamination that had ridden on the refugee ship from Asto?

Miran's Endri were pure-blood Aghyrians. This was why they didn't interbreed with anyone else. And this was the secret of the little boy who shouldn't exist. The oldest son of the oldest son was a resurrection of an ancient race.

Bakimay touched her arm. "You all right?" There was genuine concern in her eyes.

"I think so," Mikandra said. But her head pounded and she fought a feeling of dizziness.

At the time of the disaster on Asto, at least two ships must have left in time. One of those ships had come to Barresh. The other had come to Miran. The Mirani Endri were direct descendants of them.

So, if the Barresh council scoured the streets and guesthouses for people with mental abilities, it would be much better for them to use Endri. This was what Iztho had discovered and the Barresh council didn't want anyone else to know.

Bakimay stared at her, and at that moment, Mikandra knew that Daya Ezmi knew, because Bakimay was one of those gifted mindreading Pengali—she could hit herself in the head for not seeing this earlier.

At that moment she knew that her life was forfeit and there was nothing she could do about it.

Mikandra was still dazed by the time she came back to her work. The book she had been working on lay open on her desk. She sat down and stared at the pages without seeing anything. The columns and figures of the Mirani accounts danced before her eyes. Wherever she turned, there was danger.

She had to get out of here or meet the same fate as Iztho, wherever he was—and the unspeakable answer to that loomed large in her thoughts. Who said he was still alive? Those thugs could easily have killed him. If you wanted to hide a body in Barresh, you only needed to dump it in the marshlands and the fishes would do the rest.

It was simple: Barresh had been sending thugs to guesthouses to round up people with this ability to use them as defence for the Asto-funded stronghold in the city. Think of it: people with telepathic abilities made the best spies. Sharp shooters with the ability to mentally guide their shot never missed. That was how they had defeated the Mirani army.

Weapons of blue fire.

She had seen the "fire" flash across the face of a Pengali woman. Now she understood the position of the Mirani army and she understood why Nemedor Satarin wanted to ban all foreigners and she understood what Iztho had discovered.

On the Mirani side of the border, what would Nemedor Satarin do when he found out that these *scary foreigners* also lived in Miran, and worse, occupied most positions in his own government? He was already waging a war against the Traders.

She had to warn Rehan.

What about herself?

It was a couple of weeks before the Academy year started. She needed to keep working until then to have enough money to go—and have the whole thing fall through if the Andrahar court case dragged out. She couldn't go home because she had nowhere to live.

She would be trapped in Barresh under the eyes of people who imprisoned people like her.

What could she do to get herself out of this situation?

After a night of almost no sleep, Mikandra should have been tired, but at night, the worries exploded in her mind. She also realised with horror that because of her nightly escapades, she had forgotten to go to the Exchange to talk to Rehan that morning. She lay in bed, sweating, cursing herself and staring at the dark ceiling. By the sound of things, there was a party going in the courtyard.

She sat up on the edge of the bed several times, thinking to go and join them, but each time she lay back down because she couldn't afford to get involved in trouble. If she went down, she would have to drink. If she drank, and the thugs came, then next thing would be that she'd find out in which of the old and abandoned buildings the Barresh council hid these people.

She wanted to go to the Exchange to speak to Rehan and couldn't believe that she'd been so stupid to forget him, but she was too scared to go out into the dark streets and it would be the wrong time of day. Rehan wouldn't expect her yet.

When the sky started to turn blue, she had enough. She got up, bathed and dressed and made her way through the nearly deserted streets to the Exchange.

However, when she typed the code into the screen at her usual cubicle, Rehan had only sent a message of a single line. *I have to go now. Something has come up. Keep well.*

Panic rising in her, she stared at the screen and the unresponsive dot at the bottom.

She'd gotten *used* to him being in the office to chat. How could he not be there?

Had he said anything about going somewhere? He couldn't work, so he wouldn't be travelling. What did he mean *something has come up?*

She thought of fights in the streets, barricades, people setting fire to houses. Rehan unable to get to the office and unable to leave the Endri quarter. Braedon and Taerzo unable to work. She rose from her seat. All other cubicles in the room were empty, and the only person in the room was the keihu woman who attended the desk who probably reported everything that happened in this room straight to the council. When Mikandra left the room, the woman smiled cheerfully and said there was no charge.

Mikandra left the building again, despair clawing at her. There were no Traders' craft at the airport, no one to ask until the passenger shuttle from Miran arrived later in the day, if there would be a passenger shuttle.

25

WHEN SHE CAME to the library, someone sat at her desk.

Daya Ezmi.

He leant back in her chair, casually flipping through a book from the pile that she intended to tackle this morning.

Mikandra stopped, and considered running before he noticed her, but in retrospect realised why there had been a particularly vicious black-clad guard at the door. A Coldi woman, with arms thick as jungle vines, not the juvenile keihu type that usually patrolled this part of the building. Daya was the reason for her presence. There was no way Mikandra could leave the library past this guard.

Daya looked up from the book and his eyes met hers.

He rose from the desk and gestured for her to come.

Mikandra did, because there was nothing else she could do. Her heart thudded against her ribs.

"So we meet again. I heard that you have an interest in history."

Mikandra nodded, listening in his voice for any signs of emotion, but finding none. Her mouth felt too dry to speak.

"So do I. Bakimay told me that she showed you the replica of the cave we've built here. That room is not quite ready yet, but we're planning to take students into that room. The Pengali have maintained these caves for thousands of years and we understand their objection to letting large numbers of people visit. I also understand that people in Miran do the same thing, that there is an underground chamber underneath the Foundation monument that all school children visit. I've applied to visit it, but the Mirani council won't give me the permit." The statement sounded like a challenge. Hell, of course the Mirani council wouldn't allow him to visit that room under the Foundation monument if they knew who he was.

He rose. "Come, I'll show you something."

Mikandra hesitated. She didn't want to go *anywhere* with him where she wasn't in view of at least two other people.

He said, "I've told Bakimay that I'll be talking to you for a while. You don't need to worry that she'll be angry with you."

Just as she feared. Mikandra looked around the library. She couldn't see Bakimay anywhere. She glanced at the door. The menacing guard still stood there. She carried her gun Coldi-style on her right arm. The male Coldi guards were scary, but it was the female ones who were truly petrifying.

Daya paused. "Is there a problem?"

"Um. Yes. I want your guarantee that wherever we go, you'll bring me back here." Even to herself, her voice sounded strangled.

He frowned. "Of course I'll bring you back here. Bakimay will have my hide if I keep you."

He smiled, and again she tried to judge his expression, but couldn't.

That creepy, shivery, head-pounding feeling crept over her again.

Then a scary thought: what if that feeling was caused by his mind reading?

She met his intense eyes. Could he see inside her thoughts? Did he know who she was, why she was here and what she wanted?

Sweat rolled over her back.

The vicious Coldi guard was looking at her with an intense expression.

Nothing for it. She didn't trust him in the slightest, but there was no way she could run from that guard and as far as she knew, there were no other usable doors into the library.

"All right. But I have nothing to hide." *So don't even try any of that mindreading stuff on me.*

Daya raised his eyebrows, but said nothing. He led her into the corridor. They walked past restoration parties who all greeted him, into the passage that provided access to the assembly hall. In her wanderings through the building, Mikandra had peeked into this door once when it was unguarded. The assembly hall had already been restored, with a mosaic floor, wood-panelled walls and wooden benches, a magnificent combination of old keihu style and Pengali craft.

They passed a guard station where Mikandra had always had to turn back. The huge keihu guard nodded politely. Then Daya turned left, up a broad flight of stairs.

At the top was a set of wooden doors where two Coldi guards stood sentry, both of them women. One of them opened the door to let Daya pass. She wore a singlet-type shirt and her bare arms bore scars in a pattern of triangles. Her expression remained blank. Both women were Hedron guards, most definitely.

The room on the other side was huge, more like an apartment than an office. The far side consisted entirely of windows over-looking the square and Market Street—they were in the room on the very corner of the complex. A set of comfortable couches stood so that visitors could admire the view.

A glass wall separated off two other rooms. The one closest to the main door held a neatly made bed. The other room was a library.

Daya bade her to sit and Mikandra sat, looking around the room and searching for clues as to why she was here and finding none.

A restored mural on the wall behind a desk showed an image of the Barresh council in session. All the men were handsome, none with a voluminous stomach or a couple of chins. An image on the other wall showed Pengali at work in what looked like a quarry where they cut stone and fashioned it into ornamental tiles.

The five-pointed star was everywhere: on the ceiling, in the carpet and engraved in the glass separation to the library.

Daya went to the desk and rummaged in a stack of folders that lay on a cabinet against the wall. His back was turned to her. The guard had remained in the foyer and the door had shut. Mikandra wondered what would happen if she attacked him.

The library on the other side of the glass partition held books that were much older than those in the main library where she worked. Not all of them were in Mirani either. She spotted titles in Coldi and Kedrasi and other languages she didn't recognise. She spied several works on the history of Barresh.

To her surprise, there were also several volumes with the emblem of the Trader Guild. The manual, a book on navigation. There was also a book about the history of Miran which was exactly the same volume as sat on her father's bookshelf. The book next to it was unmarked but there was a note stuck on it that said *Iztho Andrahar* in Coldi writing. And there were the volumes of council transcripts that were missing from the library shelves.

Her heart was thudding. *Those* were the books she wanted.

Daya came to sit opposite her and put a reader and a folder on the table between them.

"I've been wanting to talk to someone who has been in the chamber that's underneath the Foundation monument in Miran. Everyone I've asked has been too old. Apparently they only started taking school children there recently."

Mikandra shrugged, wary. This was not just about history, was it? He wasn't stupid and strongly suspected the truth behind the Mirani Endri. Any moment now he would come up with some question or remark that was at complete right angles to the history issue. He'd distract her and get into her mind and would find out what she knew. Or something.

He picked up the reader and thumbed the screen into life. For a few moments, he flicked through images, then he said, "Ah."

He passed the screen to her.

The screen showed an underground chamber fairly similar to the one she had seen in replica, except this one was circular.

There was a stone tablelike structure in the middle, also covered in carvings.

"Press the corner," he said.

She did, and the next few images showed details of stone friezes. One was a view over a city. Another looked like a street map with tiny characters indicating names of streets or buildings or people who lived there. The pattern of streets didn't look familiar.

"The text on the walls in the Miran chambers, does it look the same as this?"

"Where is this? Are these from the caves in the escarpment?"

"No. These are from under the foundations of Athyl." The current biggest city on Asto.

Yes, things were exactly as she had suspected. But what was she going to tell him?

She flicked through a few more images with details of carvings until coming to one of a frieze that was unfinished. The left half of the picture was intricate and beautiful, with flowers and trees and flying creatures. On the right-hand side, there were roughly carved outlines of intended work, with a carved panel over the top.

Daya said, "With the help of the Pengali, who have used our script all this time, we've been able to picture together the Aghyrian language. This sad story describes what happened. The author of this panel says that he heard news of an impending collision between a meteorite and the planet. He says astronomers discovered it by accident when they were observing an eclipse of Beniz by Yaza." He used the Coldi names for the two suns. "The meteorite came from between the suns. The planet had three days warning. He says that there are only three space-worthy ships and that people are fighting over who gets to go on them. He says chaos has broken out in his beautiful city. People are fighting in the streets for places in cellars and in the underground aquifers. He says that authorities are not giving out details about where the meteor will hit or how much will be destroyed and he thinks that this means that they expect no one to survive."

The air in the room suddenly seemed cold. Mikandra

repressed a shudder. Some worlds were notorious for being prone to strikes from space.

"Some people did survive. There were the Coldi, made to be a tough kind of human to settle worlds with hostile climates. There were the three ships. We've now found the likely location of the one that came to Barresh. My question is: it makes sense that the second ship came to Miran. Did they?"

"I . . . I don't think so." Her mouth felt dry. Sweat ran down her back, but she shivered at the same time. Her head felt like it was filled with sawdust. She licked her lips and plunged further into the lie. "I went into the chamber underneath the Foundation monument. It only lists the members of the people who witnessed the Foundation agreement." She bade silent forgiveness from the Mirani historians.

"Are you sure? How old were you when you went in there?"

Mikandra put both her hands on the sides of her head. "Stop it!"

"Stop what?"

"Whatever you're doing. It makes me dizzy." The pounding in her head stopped. Mikandra glared at him. "Don't you already know what I'm thinking? Can't you see what's in my mind?" She clamped her hands between her knees to stop herself shivering.

He gave her a sharp look.

In the silence that followed, the feeling vanished completely.

Daya breathed out heavily through his nose. "If you must know, this supposed 'mindreading' doesn't quite work like that. Communication requires input from both parties. None of us can plainly see what other people are thinking."

That was a lie.

She met his eyes squarely. Neither of them spoke.

After a tense silence, he went on, "We in Barresh are trying to piece together a viable population of Aghyrians. This is a private project of mine and has nothing to do with the Barresh council. Apart from the *zhadya*-born of the Coldi, which is where I come from, and the buried children, of which there is only one, my lady Anmi, I have found Aghyrian genetic material in keihu and Pengali. I'm trying to piece this genetic material back together.

We have severe fertility problems. Zhadya-born are mostly male. Besides Anmi, we have two women of fertile age. Three children were born this year. All of them are male. We have two pregnancies. Those children are male, too. We need to find more pieces of our genetic heritage. If there is anything in Miran . . ." His eyes looked genuinely pleading. ". . . anything at all, we want to know about it. If people suspect that they have Aghyrian heritage, I'll pay for them to come here and have us look at it."

So that was why he was interested in scouting out people with a lot of Aghyrian blood and picking them up off the street? Use them as breeding factories? She thought of that Pengali woman who had been taken away from the guesthouse party. Was she now locked up somewhere and pregnant with some experimental child?

And what about his wife? Was she a prisoner?

Was he peeved that the father had turned out to be one of those Mirani he hated, and was a boy to boot? Or had he attempted to keep Iztho here, and when Iztho would not let himself be restrained, had he taken steps to get rid of him?

He was still talking about how people from Miran were welcome in Barresh. That it was a safe haven for those who fled the residency laws. That Barresh had no laws about the ethnicity or origin of its people. That he would help any businesses that wanted to shift from Miran.

Blah, blah, blah. The man was a criminal.

She had to get those books to see what secrets they hid. He clearly hadn't counted on the fact that she could read the titles from this distance. Sometimes it paid to have very sharp eyes.

26

R EHAN WASN'T THERE the next morning either.
Mikandra sat in the cubicle staring at the screen but
it remained unresponsive. When she went to sign off
at the counter, the woman said for the second day in a row that
there was no charge to the account in the same cheerful voice she
had used the day before. Mikandra had trouble meeting her
eyes, and refraining from asking what could have happened.
Was anything bad going on in Miran? What had Rehan meant
Something has come up?

She went to work in the library, replaying horrible scenarios
in her mind, and she had to slap herself for getting worked up.
Likely, the truth was simple. Maybe the unrest had spread and
he couldn't reach the office anymore. Maybe he was busy with
the court case.

At midday, she wandered around the marketplace hoping to
catch some news from people coming in from Miran, but there
were no arriving shuttles and all the Mirani she saw at the
markets were the usual crowd, those who lived in Barresh. There
were no visiting Trader craft.

She needed to do something. Check on the Andrahar brothers, get out of here before anyone questioned her.

She stood in front of the Exchange building, and her attention
went to that library room in the corner. The only thing that sepa-

rated her from that curious folder with Iztho's name was a glass window. All right, it was on the top floor of the building. And there was lots of security—on the inside of the building.

What about the outside?

One of the windows had a small box balcony. It was an odd construction that suggested that the window in question had once been a door. There was a large spreading tree whose branches reached over the wall. Not quite to the balcony, which was a pity. A group of painters was working on the ground floor. They had ladders.

The answer to what had happened to Iztho was in that room, and it was perhaps already too late for her to find it. Rather than being too brash, she had been too timid. She should have barged into the Exchange, given them her name and who she worked for, and demanded to see the records and whatever else they had relating to Iztho.

They probably would not have given it.

No, probably not.

She went back to the library, and back to worrying. If she did something stupid, like break into that office to see what was in that book, she wanted to make sure it was worth the risk and not already too late.

At the end of the afternoon, she was working on packing away books she had finished assessing when she spotted a Pengali man in council uniform come into the library. He was not one of the regular guards and Mikandra's nerves jumped up a notch.

He went to speak to Bakimay, and she pointed in Mikandra's direction. The Pengali crossed the hall, walking around the stack of boxes with Mirani army archives that had become a lot more organised. He stopped at Mikandra's table. By that time, her heart was thudding.

Mikandra met his eyes, but saw no emotion in them.

He said only, "Come."

"Has anything happened?"

He shrugged.

"What is going on?"

He gave her a blank look. Damn, she got the one council worker who didn't speak Mirani. She had learned some keihu, but hardly enough to hold a conversation and her command of Pengali was nonexistent. She understood their tail gestures better than their speech. This man didn't have a tail.

She bet it was that creepy Daya Ezmi again, with his mindreading and friendly-threatening-aloof conversation that freaked her out. *You can all come to Barresh* indeed. Come and never be heard of again.

She accompanied the Pengali out of the library, down the corridor with the mural to the alley outside, where the ground was wet with large puddles from a recent shower. They went into Market Street and around the corner to the entrance of the Exchange.

Her thoughts about the nature of the matter changed. There was bad news from Miran, about her parents, or about the Andrahar brothers. That was why Rehan hadn't contacted her.

Upstairs in the communication room, the Pengali took her to one of the cubicles next to the door, the ones she didn't like because the light from the corridor glared in the screen.

She sat down. He gave her a code and an earpiece, which she put on. Then he left and on the screen appeared—

"Rehan! What's wrong?" He looked his usual distant, well-groomed and businesslike self. His hair hung loose, combed forward over his right shoulder in a glossy curtain of platinum.

"Wrong? Apart from the usual, nothing—"

"Nothing? Why do you freak me out like this? I was *worried* about you." Damn, she was angry all of a sudden.

He looked taken aback. "I thought you'd like having a real talk."

"Why weren't you there this morning or yesterday? I didn't hear anything for two days—"

"The Lawkeeper called me to Kedras. He wanted to go over some documents and discuss the case. We've been crazy busy."

Yes, now she noticed that he wasn't in the office, but sat in a comfortable aircraft cabin. She could see the controls behind him, and out the window, golden light reflecting off the glass façade of a building. The Guild headquarters.

He continued, "I didn't hear anything from you on the morning I had to go. I left a message. Did you get it? I was worried about you."

Crap. She breathed out heavily. She was being stupid. He wasn't her brother and she didn't own him.

"Sorry that I didn't come. I was out with some Pengali. Did you know that they're nocturnal? I didn't, and it messed up my normal day. I came back, and I didn't have time to come to the Exchange before going to work." It sounded like a lame excuse. She breathed out heavily. "I'm sorry."

"I missed our chat."

Mikandra nodded. Damn, she'd missed it, too. "I found out some things, but nothing important that relates directly to the case." Yet. She didn't want to say anything about the book. She didn't want to say too much about anything else either. Someone was sure to be listening. "How did you go with the Lawkeeper?"

"The case is weak. There are small discrepancies between the Exchange data from the central node and the one from Barresh, but it seems that is due to a logging error and there is no evidence of manipulation. The exports don't show up on the Miran Exchange, but anyone who wanted to smuggle would use a third locality anyway. They would have used a high-volume port like Kedras to hide the shipment and lump it with something else."

"So basically, you have no evidence against the charge?"

"Pretty much. I'm applying for transfer of licence. I wish . . ." He stared into the distance.

"Yes?"

He let a small silence lapse. "I'll talk to you about it later. You *are* coming back to Miran at some point, aren't you?"

"Well, I guess, but . . ." She'd been planning to go to Kedras. Was he saying that there was no point in turning up for the start of the academy year? "Can you do anything to hurry the application up?"

He shrugged. He had lost his businesslike air. "It will take the best part of a year to go through the process. I won't be able to work all that time." She could feel the pain in every word. "Before you ask, I don't know yet what it means for you. I'll look into that after the court session the day after tomorrow."

"Is anything going to be solved on that day?" Her course started soon. There was no way she could fund herself.

"Probably not. The process will probably drag on for some time." He must have seen the expression on her face. "I'm sorry."

"I want to start at the academy." Her voice cracked.

"I know. I'm sorry."

And it wasn't fair of her to keep thinking of herself while he was in so much trouble and was still missing his brother as well. But damn. If she couldn't start at the academy, her whole future collapsed.

He sighed and wiped both hands across his face. "I was hoping that we'd be in a better position this close to the trial. Our entire business is about to be dealt a huge blow. I don't know if we can survive this. This is my father's business, my grandfather's business."

"You look tired."

He blew out a breath. "I *am* tired." He rubbed his face again. "I can hardly think straight. You know, sometimes I feel like I understand what my aunt is going through all the time. I think I can hear people talking in the room and then I turn around and there is no one. That's how tired I am."

"You didn't fly yourself?"

"No, Braedon did. Taerzo has been here for a few days already. Bartering for a deal on aircraft parts or something. I hate to leave Mother alone, with the situation in Miran as tense as it is. If anyone comes to the house, she's likely to take Father's gun that she has told us she can't find and start shooting at them."

Mikandra remembered Isandra's harsh words at breakfast. "I can imagine her doing just that."

"She asked about you the other day."

"Did she? I thought she didn't even see me."

"Mother never misses a thing." He gave a wary smile which faded quickly. "I worry about her. What happens to her if we're unsuccessful? Her pride won't survive that."

His pride wouldn't survive that. He was worn out, worn down, close to despair and on the brink of madness.

She wanted to tell him to take it easy, but understood why he couldn't. She wanted to tell him what she had discovered, but didn't trust the link. And what were the implications of her discoveries for him anyway? That was, any except *We have more enemies than we thought we did?*

"I presume Gillay is at home with your mother?"

"Yes. But if Mother has it in her head to do something stupid, Gillay won't stop her."

"I'm sure they'll be fine. You're better off concentrating on the case. Can you let me know how it's going?"

"I will."

When he'd signed off and the screen had gone dark, she remained in the cubicle for a while, his pained expression etched in her thoughts. She had failed at everything she had set out to do in Barresh. She hadn't found Iztho and the only evidence she had—questions asked by the thugs who had robbed her— suggested his guilt rather than his innocence.

There had to be a way for her to prove that Barresh had changed the records.

Rehan looked like he was going to pieces. He was a proud man and would not ask for help, even though he was at risk of sliding into madness for reasons that had nothing to do with his intelligence. Reasons he wasn't aware of and she wanted to talk to him about.

He needed help and she could help him.

But damn it, he was a grown man and wanted no babysitting. She didn't own him.

She stared at the opposite wall without seeing anything. The warm feeling from seeing him alive and well still lingered.

Damn it.

The last time she'd felt like that, the man in question had betrayed her badly. Sold her out to some Damarcian airhead. A trophy wife from an influential family.

Crap.

This wasn't the time to admit to herself that Rehan Andrahar had grown roots deep inside her heart.

Powerful men made lousy partners. They were ambitious, selfish.

No. It wasn't worth the pain. She was not going to wait for another man. She didn't *need* another man.

But they *would* be a crack team, working together. There were many great Trading couples in the Guild.

Working together. Nothing else.

But first Rehan and his brothers needed to win this case. It was time for desperate measures.

When Mikandra came back to the guesthouse after work, she found Jocassa sitting by himself at a table in the courtyard. Normally she would go up to the two Kedrasi women and they'd go to the markets together, but this time, she sat at his table where, as he often did, he was counting his money. She sat down opposite him and watched. He had an ingenious system where he put one Mirani tiran for each lot of five pearls and then counted those off on his fingers, placing a finger on the table for each set of five.

His face was scrunched up with concentration.

"What *do* you do for all that money, Jocassa?" Because she had never come close to finding out.

He didn't take his eyes off his work. " 'S not that much money. 'S mosly scrap metal."

"Enough to live here. I never see you do any work."

"I do work."

"Business that can't stand the light of day?"

"Whoa, whoa, watch out what youz are sayin'. It's honest business."

"If it's so honest, tell me what it is."

"I protect things." Evasive as hell. *Honest business? My arse.*

"Things. Like illegal things? Like brew? Like weapons?"

Now he looked up and frowned deeply at her. "Why all this askin' all of a sudden?"

"Because I want to ask you something and I need to know if you're reliable."

"Oh? What for?"

"I can't tell you yet."

He raised his eyebrows at her. "Something illegal, I'm guessing?" His face was completely humourless, but she was sure that he was poking fun at her.

"If it turns out that I can trust you, and if I've solved the problem I need to solve, I might tell you why."

He froze with his hands on top of a pile of coins. "What are youz? A spy?"

"If I was a spy, would I be asking someone in a guesthouse for help?"

He shrugged, probably conceding her point. He glanced at her from under his frown. "So what?"

If ever Jocassa was going to be busted for anything, it would be through his curiosity.

Mikandra lowered her voice. "Say if I wanted to get into a place . . . that's normally closed, could you help me? I need to get in through an upstairs window."

"Youz get a ladder 'n jus' climb in."

"There is glass."

"Oh." Another frown. "Youz want a burglar."

"I guess so. That's why I'm asking you."

The eyebrows went up further. "Why d'youz think I'm a burglar?"

"Because whenever I ask how you make the money, you change the subject."

"I don' change th' subject!"

"You do. You 'protect things' or 'deliver things'. Vague replies like that. If you were really proud of what you were doing, you wouldn't be saying that."

"We's ex-soldiers always get th' jobs other people think we's stupid enough t' do. We's stand guard fer their warehouses. Sometimes . . . stuff happens."

"*Stuff*," she repeated. Not that there was any need for him to explain. She bet that, as in Miran, competing merchants got into each other's stores. She bet that merchants employed guards, and that those guards were easily bribed.

"So. If you're not a burglar, do you know any?"

He shrugged. "S'ppose I know some people . . ." Then he looked up at her. "If youz are tryin' t' crack the Exchange, forget it."

"Not the Exchange. I need to get into a room at the council."

"That's as bad as th' Exchange. Din' I tell youz t' forget it?"

"I have two days. I've run out of friendly options."

"Two days t' what?"

"Until there is a court case. I know exactly where the thing is that I want. I just need to get it. Then I'll leave Barresh and you'll never see me again."

He shook his head. "Dunno how many poor buggers have said that t' me before. I'm hard t' get rid of."

"Jocassa, please. I'll pay."

"I thought youz had no money."

"I got paid all this time I've been working."

"But that wouldn't give youz that kind of money. Th' thieves 'n burglars for rent are not cheap."

"I'll pay back everything later." Heat rose in her cheeks.

Jocassa's frown deepened. "All that on credit? Youz know th' rates fer pay-later jobs? Seems a bit . . . radical for a nice girl like youz."

"So where? Can you tell me?"

"Listen, I'm serious, youz do not want t' be messing with th' Exchange or th' council or th' guards there. There's Coldi ones, too. There's a reason there's no jails in Barresh. As a woman, if youz are not a whore, keep yer head down and hope someone bigger 'n you doesn't take a fancy if youz know what I'm talking about. I don' know who youz are but I don' know that youz could tell th' working end of a gun. Whatever's yer aim, it's not worth it."

"Tell me." Mikandra returned his stare. "Because I'm going to do it, whether you help or not."

He looked at her, shaking his head. "No way. Youz are not going. I'm not helping. That's that."

He glared at his piles of money. "Now look what youz've done. I lost count." He swiped all the money back into a large pile.

"Jocassa, have you ever felt that your family didn't care if you were alive or dead? Have you ever found someone who believed in you, and wanted to give you a chance? Have you ever seen that person be hurt badly because of injustice done to them?"

He gave her a suspicious look. "So there were no man, right?"

"There was, but he wasn't the only reason I came here. My parents wanted to marry me off because they didn't want the burden of paying for me." The web of lies grew and grew. "I ran away. My mentor gave me a chance, but now these people are trying to frame him. Please Jocassa, I have no one else to ask."

He didn't say anything for a while. His dark blue eyes took in her short hair, her clothes.

"Youz are a good sort," he said. "Youz are no good at lying. If I's t' do stuff for youz, I need t' know what's going on. The truth. I's not as dumb as youz think."

"I never said you were dumb."

"No, but youz acted like it plenty times." He fixed her with a look more angry than she had ever seen from him. No, he wasn't dumb at all and she *had* behaved like he was. "Youz want me t' do some seriously risky stuff. What can youz offer that would make me even think about it? What can youz say that's make me think that youz are not goin' t' report all of us t' th' Mirani council?"

"Why should I?"

"Youz got t' be joking, Eydrina from Bendara." His eyes met hers squarely. Oh no, he didn't believe her. "Youz want t' pay us for doing illegal things so that youz can report us to th' council."

"What? Why would I do that? I have nothing to do with the Mirani council." Mikandra stared at him. "If that is what you want to believe, I can't say anything to change your mind. And I'm not going to." She rose.

"Wait, where are youz going?"

"I'm going to do this myself. I changed my mind. I don't want your help." She turned and walked away, her steps becoming more heavy as she went. She had no idea how she was going to get into the building. Without help, she was nothing.

"Wait."

Jocassa swiped all the money off the table into a bag, ran across the courtyard and caught up with her on the stairs.

"What? Leave me alone. Go back to believing I'm a spy."

He sighed. "All right, I'm sorry. I don' really believe youz work fer th' council. I'll help youz. Although I'll live t' regret this."

"Why the change of mind?"

" 'Cause youz are stubborn 'n if I don' help, youz are goin' t' ask people youz shouldn't be messing with."

She let her shoulders sag. He was probably right. It also irritated her that he still thought of her as needing protection.

They went back into the courtyard and sat at the same table. A couple of ex-soldiers on the next table raised their eyebrows.

Jocassa lowered his voice. "I'll do this fer free, but we will need t' hire people. First lesson about this kind of business: youz never do the big jobs alone. When does this need t' be done?"

"As soon as possible." *Hire people?* This was turning into a bigger fuss than she planned. She'd just wanted to bring some ropes and some tools to remove a window from the frame, practice with them and go in alone.

"We can go get th' gear tonight 'n then do the job tomorrow."

"So, what do we need?"

"Most importantly, a thug lookout. Thasep can do that, but he'll want payin'. Dalit can do th' security system. We need weapons and signal-jamming gear. I know where to get them, too."

"Weapons?" A chill went over her.

"Youz said Council. They's one the second floor. Youz don't jus' walk in through th' front door without setting off all th' alarms in th' entire block. Youz climb in through th' window. Youz need gear for that. Th' builders can lend some t' us. Youz need weapons in case something goes wrong."

"Yes, I'd figured that."

"But apart from the climbing gear, we're going t' need someone who can turn off the security system."

"System? There's only the door into the foyer and there are guards on the other side. As long as we are quiet—"

"Don' be mistaken by looks. That place has th' best security there is, came in with th' new Exchange. All Hedron built. Youz know the Chief Councillor has lots of ties with Hedron? He's got th' whole pace wired up. They'd have filmed youz from th' first step you set into that building."

She felt sick. "How do you know all this, Jocassa?"

"I used t' work in th' army security, but here I keep doing th' same for whoever pays. Mosly protect Barresh businesses against thieves. Mind, some of th' merchants are thieves themselves. Gets real complicated 'n messy 'n all th' stuff that goes on could get me killed. I tried t' get work in Miran, but th' merchants in Miran don' have th' money."

For their nightly trip, Jocassa told her to get dressed in a neutral, nondescript colour. Up in the dorm, Mikandra could hardly do up the buttons of her shirt because her hands were trembling that much. If it came out that she had done any of this, she could wave goodbye to her place at the Trader academy. Licence holders had to have an impeccable record.

It was raining heavily by the time they left, which made the air even more steamy than usual.

The streets were dark and slippery. The few people out on the street all hid under rain hats, making them look like ghosts. Hordes of meili squawked in the trees above them. Their screeches made Mikandra think of the maramarang and she kept looking over her shoulder just in case any of them decided to attack.

Jocassa took her further into the city than she had ever been, further even than she had gone with Bakimay.

At the far eastern end of the main island of Barresh, the street opened out into a gentle downwards slope from which she had a view over the bridge between the two islands, a place she had only seen from the air.

On the other side, silhouetted against the moonlight, was the second island of the city. From here, in the haze of the rain, it looked like a giant heap of light. Mikandra had learned that the island was called Far Atok and it was where the Pengali and a lot of the permanent foreign workers lived. The keihu upper class thumbed their noses at anyone who lived there, but judging by the many lights, the population was much greater than that of the main island. The closer they came, the more lights, windows and apartments resolved from the darkness.

They crossed the bridge and the dark churning water underneath. Groups of youths lurked in the darkness of the unlit pavement, speaking in soft voices that followed them as they went.

Mikandra walked as close to Jocassa as she dared.

"Don' act scared. Jus' pretend youz come here all th' time," Jocassa said. "Youz can't see them, but they can see youz. They can see everything in th' dark."

Not acting scared was easier said than done. She felt so big, so helpless, so *obviously not a local*. It would be easy for a group of people to overwhelm both of them and steal everything she and Jocassa had. But they made it across the bridge in safety, and back into the glow of street lights and reflections in puddles.

There was a lot more activity on the streets in this part of the city. Small Pengali sat and talked on the street oblivious to the rain. Brightly lit passages led into the hollow hills. Occasionally, a soft breeze would bring a waft of food and the muddy scent of Pengali bodies.

Jocassa turned off the main street into a dark back alley that led between solid, multihued walls that surrounded courtyards of crowded houses. There was no space for trees here, only for pots and garden beds full of trailing and climbing plants. Voices rose from over the walls. People talking, yelling, singing. The scent of cooking was everywhere.

The little alleys were a veritable maze of passages, with stairs going up or down. The walls on either side made it very hard to see where they were. Mikandra used the moonlight to try to orient herself, but realised that if Jocassa left her here, she would possibly never find her way back to the guesthouse. She was in his hands, and he had placed his trust in her, that she wasn't a council spy. He must never find out who her aunt was.

He stopped to knock on a solid wooden door. Three knocks, a pause and then another three.

There were footsteps in the yard beyond, a bolt was shoved

back and the door opened. Jocassa spoke in keihu to the man who opened the door. Mikandra caught no more than a few words about the weather.

She couldn't see the man's face, but his size and smell gave him away as Pengali. He wore dark clothing including a hood that covered his head and hid his face in shadow.

He opened the door further to let her and Jocassa into the courtyard. Huge eyes glittered in the darkness of his hood.

The yard was dark and areas under the cover of a roof cluttered with stuff: old furniture, boxes, piles of wood and many other items without any sign of order.

The man shut and bolted the door and preceded her and Jocassa into a door from which low light emanated. Inside the house, the light was barely strong enough t0 reach the floor, let alone in the narrow passages between boxes and furniture that was stacked up against both walls. Mikandra felt her way forward.

Inside a plain room, there was a low table with pillows around it. An oil lamp produced a fitful light that left the edges of the room shrouded in darkness.

Jocassa bade her to sit down, so she did.

The Pengali man lowered his hood. He was a lot older than she had expected an arms dealer to be, resembling a wizened grandfather with his white hair and wrinkled skin. When she looked at him, she saw herself reflected in his eyes. His shirt hung open, showing his striped skin and a variety of beaded necklaces. Curiosity was evident in his face.

Another man came from a dark entrance at the back of the room carrying a box. He set it on the table and took out a number of ridiculously modern devices. Metallic, flat, smooth, with a small display and a few buttons. Mikandra had no idea what they were for.

Jocassa went into discussion with the man, picking up each device in turn and studying it in great detail. He put two of them on the table, and the others back in the box.

Mikandra met his eyes.

"They's signal disrupters like we gonna need to disable th' security. Th' Hedron-made ones are th' best you can get." He turned over the devices so that the screens faced Mikandra. "What d' youz think." His expression said *act knowledgeable.*

Mikandra picked up one of the devices and turned it over in her hands while taking care not to press any of the unfamiliar buttons. It was much heavier than it looked. She picked up the other device and weighed both in her hands, while the awkward silence lingered. Hedron made, huh?

Jocassa said in a low voice, "I'm going for th' cheaper one, but don' tell anyone yet."

She couldn't see how, not speaking keihu or Pengali, she could.

Next, the old man set another box on the table. He opened the lid. Inside lay a gleaming charge gun of the type that Traders were allowed to wear and usually did so under their cloaks. It had a Coldi-style arm bracket.

Jocassa was again talking to the man.

Mikandra reached inside the box and lifted the weapon out. The metal felt cool and heavy in her hands. This was serious gear. This was what she wanted.

But while she admired the weapon, Jocassa and the dealer spoke in raised voices. With her limited understanding of keihu, she had no idea what they were talking about. The dealer seemed annoyed so she put the gun down.

As soon as she did so, Jocassa pushed the box away and shut the lid.

"But I want this," she said.

"It's no good," Jocassa said. "It's a charge gun. Th' people youz are after are not harmed by charge guns. Worse, they's collect th' charge and fire it back. No. We don' want charge guns."

"Then what are we going to do to defend ourselves? You said we needed weapons."

"Hope we don' need t' defend ousselves. If something comes up, we's use knives 'n crossbows."

"What's the good of a knife against an elite Coldi guard?"

"Nothing. But jus' so that youz don' have any illusions: if any of th' council's Coldi women guards get involved, we's dead. They's all ex-Hedron guards."

Mikandra felt weak. What had she started?

"Sure youz want t' go through with this? Youz can still back out."

"No, I want to do it."

In the end, they got a disrupter, a handful of tools for levering windows out of their frames—Barresh glass-stone did not break and you couldn't cut it with hand tools—and protective jackets. While the Pengali man packed it all up, she wondered who was going to pay for all this stuff, but he seemed happy enough to let her and Jocassa depart with the equipment.

"You didn't pay for any of this," she said as they made their way back through the maze of alleys.

"Nope."

"You said all this stuff is very expensive."

"It is. I's getting it on credit."

"Why, Jocassa? Why stick your neck out for me? I said I could pay. You don't even know what I'm doing."

"I's curious." He let a silence pass and added. "Besides, th' Pengali scum owes me money. I jus' wanted t' see his face 'n make him scared. Now, because youz were there, he thinks I got friends in high places. He might pay me. If he doesn't, I's keep th' stuff."

"I don't want you to get into trouble over this."

"Youz kidding? He's had it coming fer a while. We's all in it, 'n I hope t' hell that whatever youz are doing is going t' pay off. Fer both of us."

It was true and he was right. If she'd wanted to play nice, she would have stayed at home with her parents. She could always go back to being doomed a spinster for life and working in the hospital. It was this, or nothing.

They walked in silence until they had crossed the bridge back to the main island. There, finally, Mikandra dared ask the question that had been on her mind since the negotiation.

"What did you mean back there about people who are not harmed by charge guns? I've heard of people surviving being shot, but thought that was a fluke or a low setting."

"No, these people actively take th' charge 'n fling it back at th' gun that's shot it. Usually not much good for th' shooter."

"You mean—they do this on purpose?" She saw light flashing across the face of a Pengali woman.

"On purpose and then some. Th' good ones can even kill you with it. Th' Chief Councillor 'n his wife are th' best. Th' bet is we won' run into them. They'll be at home with her being pregnant 'n all that. But they's likely t' have some people on guard that's not too bad at it either. It's th' *avya* that th' Pengali talk about. Hedron guards are jus' a piddle compared t' these people."

This was starting to look like a more and more crazy venture with every step she took.

"Youz look doubtful. Youz want t' continue with it?"

"I do. Someone I admire told me never to give up and to have courage."

"Yeah, but words like that are fer noble fools who don' want t' live, 'n think *survival* is some kind of code of honour."

27

JOCASSA'S WORDS made Mikandra so angry that she barely spoke to him on the way back. All right, so she was a noble fool who didn't want to live. *Survival* was a noble word. She almost told him who she was and what this was really about and that he and his mates got his retention payments from the Mirani army *because* of the levies paid to the Mirani council by Traders.

When they arrived in the courtyard, he went to join his friends and invited her to come.

"No. I'm going to bed."

"What's up with you? Youz been cranky all th' way back here. What'd I say?"

"Some people do things because they feel it's the right thing to do. Not everyone does things only if they benefit themselves. Not everyone is that selfish."

He frowned at her. "I's helping you, right?"

Not without a benefit to himself. If this went wrong, he would suffer less than she would. "I'm talking about honour being for fools."

"Youz are not doing any of this fer yousself?"

That mock-innocent look of his made her even more angry. It went against everything she had been taught all her life, about Foundation, about responsibility. And these people, these selfish creatures, were the ones she had sworn to protect and feed and give jobs?

"What? What'd I say wrong?"

"I cannot expect you to understand."

She ran up the stairs into the dorm, but it was so late that Melvi and Ariani had already gone to sleep. She undressed and lay in the dark, staring at the ceiling.

Sleep, of course, remained elusive.

The party in the courtyard got going and the sound of laughter drifted up from the courtyard. All of a sudden, she was sick of this place without morals, this place where everyone did as they pleased and no one cared about the future, about their home towns, about education.

Jocassa was right in a way, she did do this for herself, but she did it for the Andrahar Traders, so that *they* could employ people and pay their council dues so that the council could provide for the workers and the soldiers. She could not expect them to understand the weight of that responsibility. *That* was the difference between Endri and Nikala, and she would never bridge that gap, no matter how long she spent in this stinking cesspool.

In a way, Mikandra was glad that she couldn't talk to Rehan the next morning. Times at Kedras and Ceren didn't overlap in a convenient way at the moment and he would be asleep. That was just as well, because she didn't want to tell him, or even make him suspect, what she was going to do.

That day in the library might well be the last day in her job ever. She couldn't tell anyone, and she hoped Bakimay wouldn't pick up anything.

What she was about to do would certainly destroy Bakimay's respect for her and, somewhat proud of the way she had turned around Bakimay's low opinion of her, she hated to do that.

After work, she went to the guesthouse and bathed. She bundled up the protective jacket because it would raise too many eyebrows if she walked the streets wearing it. Also, the thing was quite heavy and hot. She re-dyed her hair, put on her dark clothes and strapped on the belt with the knife. It seemed such a ridiculously old-fashioned weapon that offered her no protection at all.

Jocassa, Dalit and Thasep were nowhere to be seen, and she hoped that they would be true to their word and turn up at the agreed meeting point.

By the time she arrived at the spot under the trees, Mikandra was so nervous that she could barely move.

Jocassa and Dalit sat on the ground under the tree, Dalit with his back leaning against the wall that surrounded the complex. They shared food from a paper bag between them.

Jocassa gestured. "Sit down." He looked way too relaxed. Exactly how often did he do this kind of stuff?

Both men were similarly in dark colours, Jocassa with a shawl to cover his hair. Dalit wore black like the Barresh city guards but couldn't look less like them. He was far too small and thin for that. Next to him on the ground lay a leather bag which would contain the disruptor and knives.

She glanced at the part of the building visible over the top of the wall at Dalit's back. The tree they would climb later was a bit further down the street. Its spreading branches cast a deep shadow in the gathering darkness. A couple of Pengali girls stood talking at its base.

"Don' be nervous. There won' be any action fer a while."

"Why?" Her heart thudded. Had anything gone wrong?

Jocassa jerked his head behind him. "We need t' wait until th' building shift finishes."

Mikandra looked at the building again. A light was on in the yard, and there was the sound of voices on the other side of the wall. "They's jus' packing away th' gear."

Fair enough.

"Besides, Thasep's not here yet."

Her heart jumped again. "Is that a problem?"

"Na. He's thick. Can't tell th' time. We got all night t' do this, right? We's not in a hurry."

She nodded. Right. *Calm down, silly girl.*

But if it was all the same to them, she'd like to have it over and done with as soon as possible.

She sat down and took an offering of fried worms from Jocassa's bag. But she was so nervous that they tasted like nothing and when she'd had a couple, her stomach seized up into a hard ball and she couldn't eat any more. She was afraid that she was going to be sick.

Dalit didn't eat much either. Every now and then, he would look up in Mikandra's direction, his expression distant.

Jocassa didn't seem to be similarly inflicted. He was well underway to polishing off the portion of fried worms, jamming one handful after the other into his mouth. "Hmm, that woman could make millions if she found a way t' sell this stuff in places where there's people with money, like Damarq."

He crunched loudly through another handful of worms.

"All present," came a voice from behind and there was Thasep, also dressed in dark colours. He carried the rope, with the anchors and the other climbing gear in the bag over his shoulder. He also wore a belt with a hammer and a knife and was probably the only one of them who looked convincingly like a builder.

Jocassa patted the ground next to him. Thasep grunted while lowering his huge frame to the ground. He dumped his bag and peeked in the paper wrapper.

"What? Worms again? When are youz gettin' real food fer a change?"

Jocassa rolled his eyes. "Maybe when someone in this place sells fish bread that isn't dry as dust I'd think about it."

Thasep snorted and took a handful of worms anyway.

Meanwhile, Jocassa went over the plan they had discussed in the morning and repeated what everyone would do. "We change one thing: Dalit's coming into th' tree, keeping an eye on the street 'n th' outside of th' building. 'S too busy in th' street otherwise. He's t' create a fuss if we need a distraction."

Did he realise that Dalit hardly saw anything?

Eventually the Pengali girls moved away from the tree, the shoppers went home, and the street became quiet. Jocassa scrunched up the paper wrapping from the worms and tossed the ball over the wall into the yard. Mikandra heard it bounce on the pavement twice before coming to a rest. No one on the other side complained about people throwing rubbish.

Jocassa got to his feet. "Let's go."

They went to the tree, where Thasep took up position with his back to the trunk.

"Got th' light?" Jocassa asked.

Mikandra nodded.

"Th' knife?"

She nodded again and patted the pocket of the jacket she had put on. Her stomach twisted uncomfortably. She had wanted that gun, badly.

"Thasep will lift youz up first, then me 'n Dalit. Go."

Thasep interlaced his fingers and Mikandra stepped onto them, wobbling awkwardly. It was rather embarrassing being so close to this thug. He smelled of bad teeth and unwashed clothes.

Up into the tree. The branch was a lot smoother than she had expected, and was covered in moss and other slippery stuff. She could only walk slowly, holding onto adjacent branches. Jocassa climbed up directly behind her, while Dalit sat near the trunk and Thasep was climbing in. For his size, he was surprisingly quiet and agile.

Mikandra crossed the point where the branch went over the wall. Jocassa lashed the rope with the knots onto the branch and looked around before he let it dangle down. He quickly slid down the knots and into the yard. He jumped down the last distance, and disappeared into the dark. He came back, whispering, "Can any of youz see th' ladder?"

Mikandra's heart was thudding. They'd counted on the builders' ladder that had been in the yard this morning.

Jocassa went the other way and fortunately came running back with the ladder. He put it against the balcony and climbed up. Now Thasep lowered himself down the knotted rope into the yard and helped Mikandra down. He was to stay in the yard to ward off trouble in the same way Dalit was to stay in the tree. Dalit had already pulled the rope back up. She couldn't see him anymore in the darkness between the tree's branches.

Jocassa had reached the box balcony. He gestured. Mikandra

followed up the ladder, but she wasn't half as strong or agile as he.

"Hurry, there's people coming," Thasep said.

Mikandra clambered up as fast as she could and more or less flung herself over the railing. Thasep took the ladder away and disappeared with it into the shadows.

Jocassa was already at the window, peering inside without touching the glass. A line of lights blinked in the darkness of the room. The feeble glow showed the outlines of shelves of the library.

"In here?" he whispered.

"Yes."

He turned around and signalled to Dalit in the tree. Mikandra could see the red light of the interruptor flashing between the branches. Something buzzed near the window.

Jocassa started working at the corner of the window with his knife. He prised it at straight angles between the frame and the glass. Bits of cement fell onto the balcony.

He whispered *watch it* and the next moment, there was a small snap and a glass pane came out. He caught it in his hand as if he did this every day.

So he wasn't a burglar, right? Like she believed that.

He reached into the window and undid the lock. It opened outwards. Silently, Jocassa climbed onto the windowsill, gave her the thumbs up and vanished inside the room.

Mikandra followed him, not half as quick and graceful as he had been.

In the dark, it was hard to see anything in the office except the desk that stood immediately inside the window.

Jocassa's disembodied voice said, "Do youz know where this thing is that you're looking for?"

Mikandra flicked on her light and walked quietly to the shelves against the back wall. The book stood where it had been when she had been sitting there on the other side of that glass partition. She took it out and slipped it in her bag.

The book next to it was indeed a copy of the Trader manual. What was that doing here?

She took it from the shelf and opened it at the first page.

A label was affixed to the page like she had seen at Lihan's house. *A gift from the Trader Guild to apprentice Daya Ezmi on the completion of his academy training.*

Crap.

Daya had been to the academy. Traders swore loyalty to each other. They swore to uphold the truth. What if he . . . told her the truth when she had been sitting there?

Jocassa whispered, "Can youz hurry up? I want t' get out before someone comes."

"Yes, coming."

She slung her bag over her shoulders and ran back to the window.

28

MIKANDRA CLIMBED on the windowsill, onto the balcony. Up the railing. Whoa, it was a long way down there. She turned around and dangled her legs over the railing. One foot found a rung.

Jocassa had picked up the glass pane and was sticking it back into the window with a couple of globs of putty.

Mikandra shifted over the railing until both her feet were on the ladder. She put her full weight on the rung and climbed down. Her hands trembled.

Thasep whispered from the bottom, "Hurry up."

Jocassa swung himself onto the ladder above her. His movement made the ladder shake.

The light went on in the room upstairs, flooding the yard in light.

Jocassa swore.

Mikandra reached the bottom, and ran for the shadow of the tree. A small light blinked amongst the greenery where Dalit sat. He'd already let down the knotted rope. Thasep pushed her up the rope ladder. Dalit stuck out his hand and helped her onto the tree branch.

There she sat, panting, while Jocassa and Thasep scrambled up.

Two guards had come into the office and walked around.

Both were Coldi and looked female. Mikandra shivered. Because Jocassa had stuck the glass pane back, they hadn't yet seen that someone had come in through the window, so the guards stood at the door into the foyer, studying the panel next to the lock.

Thasep pulled the rope ladder up and undid the knot. Dalit was already on the other side of the wall and dangled off the branch by his hands. He let himself drop and hit the ground with an *oof*.

"Shhh!" Jocassa hissed.

The guard who had been outside the main entrance to the building was coming in their direction.

"Come." Thasep reached down and pulled Dalit up again with one arm.

The guard, a solidly built keihu man, walked past. He glanced up into the tree. Dalit pressed himself against the trunk, and Mikandra was squashed up between him and Jocassa.

She held her breath.

The man stood very still as if he was listening, then he turned around and walked back to the building's entrance.

Phew.

"Quick, let's go," Jocassa whispered.

Thasep dropped out of the tree and helped Dalit down. Then Jocassa.

A light went on in the ground floor of the building, casting a yellowish glow in the courtyard. Someone opened a door. Two people came into the yard, one of them with a torch, which he directed up to the top of the wall.

In panic, Mikandra let herself drop from the tree. On the way down, she hit a branch which snagged on her shirt. Something ripped. She landed hard on her feet. Ouch, her ankle.

"Run."

Jocassa didn't wait for the others to act on his command.

They ran. Pain spiked through Mikandra's ankle. With every step, it felt like she trod on knives. She clamped her teeth to stop herself from screaming. She didn't look back, but ran. Her whole future hinged on getting out of here without being caught.

Around the block, into Market Street. They stopped to catch their breath at a bench between a couple of large trees.

"We did it." Jocassa laughed. "We did broke into th' council!"

He clapped Dalit on the shoulder and then Mikandra. "Youz were a real pro. Are youz sure you've never done this before?"

"What are you taking me for?"

But actually, she had done this before. She'd climbed the kitchen roof and down to the back gate to sneak out of the house to see Lihan. Most Endri kids, especially girls, were half-decent at getting out of places without anyone seeing them.

"Eydrina, look at youz." Jocassa laughed. Thasep laughed, too.

Mikandra looked. There was a huge rip in the front of her tunic, showing her skin.

"Oops." She pulled the sides together.

Jocassa laughed harder. "We's a bunch of real bunglers 'n we even fooled th' guards."

Even Dalit was laughing. "You should have heard Thasep's squeak when the guard looked up in the tree. It was something to behold."

"Come on, let's go 'n celebrate." Jocassa started moving again.

Mikandra clutched her bag with the book inside. She was so happy that it had been successful and that it was over.

"What's wrong with yer foot, Eydrina?"

"It's not so bad. It twisted when I fell out of the tree. I'll be fine." She tried to demonstrate, but within a few steps it was clear that she was not fine.

"Let me help you." Dalit took her arm.

Walking up the steps into the guesthouse, Mikandra was struck by the odd feeling that she felt happy for the first time since leaving Miran, and possibly a long time before that. This odd band of men and their unconditional camaraderie was growing on her. From the moment she had met him, Jocassa had been helpful. Sure, he probably hoped to gain something from his association with her, but he'd been friendly. Not once had either of the men ogled at her or made lewd remarks.

In the courtyard the usual party was winding down. Many people had already gone to bed, with just a band of diehard drinkers remaining. The musician sat on one of the tables, playing chords on his badly tuned lute.

"I think this deserves a drink," Jocassa said.

"All right, I'll go get th' bottle," Thasep said.

Mikandra felt like saying no. Her skin crawled at the idea of having to drink brew again, but she knew she couldn't refuse. These men had trusted her and she should repay that trust.

"I'll get changed into something that doesn't have big holes in it."

Thasep grinned a gap-toothed smile.

She turned to the stairs, which proved more of a challenge than she thought. Pain spiked through her ankle with each step. Ouch and ouch.

She stumbled up to the balcony and into the dormitory. A group of people must have gone out, because it was quite empty apart from the Kedrasi women, already asleep. Jocassa and Dalit must have joined the group in the courtyard, because the sound of Jocassa's laughter drifted up from below.

Mikandra picked up the box from under her bed that contained her possessions and sat down on the bed with it, rummaging for a new tunic. She put the bag with the book next to her, pulled the ripped tunic over her head and slipped on the new one. Then she put her bag back onto her shoulder. She was not leaving it unattended. Her hand closed on the book inside. If only she could have a look. Surely, Jocassa wouldn't mind if she came a bit later? She took the book out of her bag and opened it on her lap. But damn, the pearl had almost run out and she needed to take the stand onto her bed to still see something. It wouldn't stay up by itself, so she had to use her bedsheet to try and prop it up—

The floor creaked. Mikandra gasped and looked over her shoulder. There were heavy footsteps behind her and a hand clamped over her mouth.

Mikandra struggled, trying to twist out of the person's grip, but the arm that held her was much too strong. Another hand— gloved—grabbed her upper arm just under the shoulder. She was pulled up and backwards off the bed.

Ow, her ankle.

Mikandra tried to look over her shoulder, but all she could see was dark clothing. The hand across her face felt very warm, like the high body temperature of the Coldi. Oh damn, this was one of those ex-Hedron guards.

There was a second person in the room, also Coldi and dressed in black. As with many Coldi, it was impossible to determine gender, even by voice. This person picked up the book.

Mikandra tried to scream.

Please, she needed that book, or everything she had done in Barresh would have been for nothing. She thumped her good foot on the floor as hard as she could, relying on the guard's grip on her arm to keep her up.

People were always going in and out of this room. There were usually people on the veranda. Surely *someone* would hear it, walk in, or wake up and disturb these thug guards? Where was Jocassa?

The guard pushed Mikandra out of the room, across the gallery and down the stairs. Her ankle hurt with each step.

Jocassa, Dalit and Thasep sat at a table in the middle of the courtyard surrounded by a few more guards, in a pool of light cast by a couple of light pearls carried by guards. Everyone else —mostly curious regulars from the guesthouse—stood in the shadow of the overhanging balcony. They were Mirani youths and their keihu and Pengali girlfriends, Kedrasi guest workers, Damarcians, Indrahui, Coldi. One look at their blank faces and Mikandra knew that none of these people would help her. As they had done when the thugs came to take away the Pengali woman, they would prefer to watch and keep themselves out of trouble.

The guards pushed Mikandra to the table. She met Jocassa's eyes. His expression was apologetic.

Someone else waited in the darkness, flanked by two enormous Coldi mountains of muscle, a tall figure in a light-coloured tunic with a hood covering the head and hair.

Mikandra held herself straight and proud. Whoever this person was, either Daya or the lady, she knew one thing: she would never make it out of this courtyard alive. Bakimay had said that Aghyrians with strong abilities and good training could kill a person just by looking at them. Maybe she was going to be the subject of a demonstration.

The person came forward and lowered the hood.

It was Anmi, her face emotionless.

Mikandra held her breath, waiting for the inevitable. Her heart was thudding like crazy.

Anmi spoke, softly but commandingly, in a language Mikandra didn't recognise.

From between a gaggle of guards came a second person. Daya Ezmi. He replied to her in the same language and the melodic tone of the words belied the meaning Mikandra detected behind the words. *Are you going to kill her or do you want me to do it?*

Someone muttered, "Oh, crap." It sounded like Jocassa.

Daya glanced at Jocassa, a bemused look on his face.

The thugs made Mikandra sit down on a chair. The guard released her mouth, but both guards remained on either side of the chair, holding her shoulders.

A few onlookers tried to leave, but the whole courtyard was full of guards and all the entrances were shut off.

Anmi came closer, pulled back another chair at the table and sat down. So this was one of the buried children? For that she would have been born thousands of years ago and lived in stasis all that time, she looked strangely normal, and was much younger than Mikandra had expected, maybe even younger than herself.

She met Mikandra's eyes with a penetrating look that made her shiver. The irises were the blackest of black. Her skin was pale and almost translucent.

One of the guards handed her the book he'd taken from Mikandra. She opened it and flicked through. A frown crossed her face.

"I'm puzzled by you. You have been following us for quite some time now. You asked around town about my former lover. You asked about the history of the city and you asked about us. We cannot detect any signs that you are a spy. Only yesterday we decided that you were harmless and were going to ease off on the surveillance. But now this. What are you doing here and what do you want?"

"Am I not allowed to visit and work?"

"And steal things? Is this book worth breaking into the Chief Councillor's office for?"

"I haven't stolen anything." But she was talking nonsense and she knew it. These people knew precisely what she had done, either through their surveillance or other means.

The lady gave her a hard look. Mikandra went dizzy again. She recognised the feeling and this time knew it for what it was: the probing of mind reading. She shivered, but couldn't look away from Anmi's eyes.

She continued, her voice intense. "My partner became interested in your story, because it confirmed something that is very important to us. We had not spoken to anyone from Miran who had been taken into the chambers under the Foundation monument, because Mirani people we have spoken to are older and when they were at school, the chamber was still being excavated and restored. He showed you the chambers on Asto, which have sacred values to us. But it seems your interest in history masked a different agenda. Who are you and who do you work for?"

"I work for myself. My name is Eydrina Avarin."

"That is a lie." Her voice was soft and menacing. "I checked after you first came in. There is no such person as Eydrina Avarin. Not in Miran, nor in Bendara as you've told everyone."

In the darkness, Jocassa said, "That's fine. No one here talks about who they are. 'S self-protection—hey, ow! Keep yer hands off me."

"Leave my friends alone. They have done nothing and they are not involved with any of my business."

"They're accomplices."

"I paid them. Let them go." Mikandra stared back at her, defiant. "And don't try to intimidate me. There is no way you can know that there is no Eydrina Avarin unless you have access to the Mirani population registry, and there is no way Miran would give you access to that from here. You're lying."

"You're a Mirani spy."

"If I wanted to be a spy, then why would I be so obvious about it? I'd pick a name and identity with a history. I left Miran because I fled a marriage with an old man. I came here and I was robbed on my first night in Barresh. I have no money to go back home and my ID was in the same bag that was stolen. I'm working to earn money. You can ask anyone at the guesthouse. That is the truth."

"Yes, your ID was taken." Her voice was chilling. She took something from her pocket and flipped it in the air. The light reflected in the shiny surface of an ID card, which she put on the table. "Enough with the lies now, *Mikandra Bisumar.*"

"Bisumar? Oh crap!" Jocassa squeaked.

A ripple of talk went through the curious onlookers. Several people looked at her with wide eyes. She could see what they thought, that she was a spy for the council. With her name, with her family, she had to be.

Mikandra's head reeled with anger. She'd spent all her time in Barresh gaining the trust of these people. "You sent the thugs who stole my money? You, as official of the Barresh council. You dare call me a criminal?"

"The guards arrested your attackers soon after they must have robbed you. They recovered most things."

"I went to the guard office the next day. They said nothing about it. They didn't even talk to me properly."

"A supervisor took your things to the council as a matter of security. You were at the Exchange asking questions. We did not know who you were, except that your name is marked with the Trader Guild flag."

Another gasp from people in the audience. Murmuring voices, the tone not friendly. Out there in the dark space underneath the gallery, there were a lot of people who would now be angry with her. Even if she could escape the thug guards, she would probably not be safe. She heard Iztho's words *people trying to screw you because they think you're rich, or people thinking you're trying to screw them because they think you're rich.*

She didn't dare meet Jocassa's eyes.

Sweat ran down her back.

"I have nothing to hide and I did nothing wrong." Oh, ancestors, this would not end well.

"Obviously you do. So I'll ask the question again. What are you doing here? Specifically, what do you think you'd find in that book?"

"The truth." And then she added, because everything was lost anyway, "Out of all things, proof of your son's birth."

"My—" She frowned, no longer looking unequivocally angry.

"Your son. My sponsor's son, who is the heir of the family. Iztho Andrahar's son."

The murmur of voices increased.

The lady let a small silence lapse. An expression of confusion came over her face. Had she seriously thought that no one would notice the boy's dyed hair?

When she next spoke, her voice was soft. "Wait—you say you're working for the Andrahar Traders?"

"Yes." Mikandra straightened her back. "I'm Iztho Andrahar's trainee. Iztho got framed for smuggling menisha fungus into Barresh, which he didn't do. The Andrahar licence is suspended and Iztho is missing. That's why I came here: to look for him. The remaining brothers are fighting this in court very soon. They have no proof of his innocence." Panic clawed at her. The trial would begin the day after tomorrow, and she was back to having nothing and would be lucky to get out of this alive. "No one knows where Iztho is. His family is in chaos and mourning. I was accepted as apprentice just before all this happened. I am due to start at the academy this coming intake. The Andrahar Traders are the backbone of the free trade movement in Miran. The Mirani chapter of the Guild is split over this issue. Everyone is afraid for the future. Some Traders—" *Lihan Ilendar, the bastard* "—have already left. This is more than just a court case, it's a political fight, for my aunt, who's trying to uphold sanity in the Mirani council, for the Traders, who want proof that justice still exists. If Nemedor Satin gets full control of the country, what will Miran do? He's hardline and he will not let Barresh be happily independent. I thought you in Barresh knew that well enough before you started framing people who could have been supporters for a peaceful resolution. You do not want a war. Miran does not want a war." She glanced at Daya. *He* had gone through the academy?

Anmi let a few moments of silence pass. Her expression was still confused. "Iztho told me he had his family sorted out—"

"Nothing is sorted out."

"—he set up an account for their survival and explained the situation. You didn't know any of this?"

"Any of what?"

Anmi glanced at Daya, who looked incredulously back at her, and then she opened the book. She took out a document and handed it to Mikandra.

It was an official note, a message recorded by the Exchange. The header said that it was confidential, to be delivered to Iztho's family on the same day Mikandra had received her acceptance. A line across the top said *duplicate* in Coldi. The main body of the letter was written in Mirani, in what was unmistakably Iztho's classic, old-fashioned handwriting.

Rehan, Braedon and Taerzo,

By the time you read this, I'll be gone. Do not try to look for me because I do not want to be found. After years of trying to please you and our parents, I am bowing out and taking the step to make a living from music. I fear my reputation as Trader has been damaged too much from events in the recent past. This letter serves to formally hand back my licence.

Very soon, you will receive a court summons on a charge of smuggling. The summons will be aimed at me, but brought against the Andrahar Traders. This is a fabricated charge that is the result of a long association that has gone sour.

There is something you need to know.

Many years ago, I befriended a young merchant Nikala man. He and I shared a passion for history and spent many a night in the library with ancient books and scripts. He was also passionate in his belief in our nation, and when he rose to prominence, I believed that he could make a difference. His name, of course, was Nemedor Satarin.

But over the past years, I grew increasingly uneasy with his actions. While we both acknowledged the potential of the powers of the ability that people in Barresh call avya, *I was horrified with persistent rumours that he is sweeping up poor and disenfranchised people from*

Barresh and zhadya-born from Hedron. He is obsessed with this avya. *He calls those people* human explosives.

*Things came to a head last year when he appealed to me to do him a favour as a friend, to pick up a person who he said he had contracted to come to Miran for 'research'. The woman in question was Anmi and not only had she not agreed anything, she knew nothing about any settled worlds other than her own, which is an isolated, non-*gamra *world. I saw that I had been blind to his obsession and had to make a stance. My change of mind came too late to save my relationship with the lady, but it was the main cause for the two-day war. Which, with the help of the lady, Barresh won.*

Nemedor Satarin has been on a mission to discredit me ever since.

In this envelope you will find evidence you need to prove that the Exchange data was tampered with at the Miran Exchange on the order of certain elements in the Mirani council.

Attend the court. Make sure you take Mother. While you are at court, stay at the Guild complex. Do not return to Miran, but pretend that you have work to do. Then quietly arrange for the business to be relocated elsewhere. Barresh will have us. Over the past year, I have relocated a lot of our accounts to Barresh. One of the attached sheets will include instructions on how to open these accounts. You can trust the Barresh council.

Do not look for me, because you will be watched. Nemedor Satarin will not stop until he finds me. I will be happy, playing and singing and will contact you as soon as it is safe. You know I have never enjoyed the life of the Trader, and it is time that I act on it. Give my medallion to the young Bisumar girl when she completes her apprenticeship. Mother insisted that we accept her as apprentice. She's probably right in that things need to change. Farewell. Iztho.

Mikandra looked up.

Her heart thudded. It was not at all how she'd thought. The Barresh council had *helped* him. Iztho had sent the courier who had been murdered in Miran. That murder was not a random attack, but someone knew about the message he carried. Someone had made sure that this message never reached the family.

The person who had tried to bring the Andrahar Traders down was Nemedor Satarin. Because the Andrahar brothers were the only ones who still held a foundation stone. Because only the Andrahar heir could wield that power. And because that little boy was Iztho's son. The heir. The oldest son of the oldest son.

And if this was true, Rehan and his brothers were in immediate danger.

Anmi spoke in a soft voice. "Do you see now that we are not at fault? After the two-day war, Iztho initially left Barresh, but he came back after the Mirani council found out that he had acted at a crucial time, which caused us to win the war. I didn't want to speak to him because I felt betrayed by him, but Daya got on well with him. Daya is also very much interested in history." She exchanged a glance with him, and he smiled. "They had many meetings and established that we can't communicate mentally with the Mirani Endri."

"You mean—you can't see into my mind?"

She shook her head. "Not at all."

"And that dizzy feeling I get, that's from people trying?"

"Iztho complained about that, too. Anyway, when the first accusations of smuggling came out, Iztho realised that his old friend in Miran was never going to forget how he had refused to hand me over to the Mirani army."

"Couldn't you forgive him for that?"

Her mouth twitched. She looked into the distance. "Eventually, maybe."

Then a shrug, not as careless as she pretended to be. "Also, Iztho now knew what you also know: that the Mirani Endri are also targets for Nemedor Satarin's obsession. Iztho realised there was no way he could win, as long as his former friend had the backing of an entire government, so he decided to disappear, after setting up a way out for his family. He'd been dreaming of becoming a musician for a long time."

Mikandra's head was still reeling. "The family never got his message. The courier was murdered. His satchel was empty." She had sat by his bed watching him die. Someone in Miran had removed the message to the Andrahar family. Isandra had said *have you heard from Iztho?* She had *expected* to hear from her son.

She knew at least some of what was going on. Trimon had said something about Iztho getting on well with his mother.

"What about the boy?"

"I never knew the child was Iztho's until after his birth. It was not thought to be possible. If anything, it proves the heritage of the Mirani Endri. It means a lifeline for our project to restore the Aghyrians."

"Yet, you've hidden his parentage."

"I don't want the Mirani council to know. I understand what he means. This is a very powerful boy. I want him to be safe."

True. "What's his name?"

"He carries my father's name, Vayra Perling Dinzo."

There was nothing familiar in those names, although she thought of the Mirani of old, who also used to have three names. "He should have the Andrahar name. The family should have a say in this."

"Yes, when he's safe. When all of you are safe. Please, believe me and trust us." She gestured.

A guard in black approached the table and placed Mikandra's familiar bag on it. She opened it and dug inside. Her pouch had been ripped to shreds. Whatever small change was gone, but her notebook and account details were still there. Her apprentice uniform was still there. Anmi placed the ID card on the table.

Mikandra took it and held it against her chest. "Thank you."

"I'm sorry that we didn't speak to you earlier. I hope you can understand that we thought you might be a risk to us. Barresh is too small to annoy any of its large enemies, especially Miran."

Mikandra nodded.

"I have the details to the accounts that Iztho set up with the family's money. If you come to us tomorrow, we can supply you with new codes. You can use the funds immediately."

Mikandra shook her head. "The brothers can do that later. First, I have a court case to attend."

29

MIKANDRA HAD THOUGHT she'd miss the court session, what with her missing ID and lack of money, but now everything had changed. She even had her clothes back.

She could go to Kedras and prove the setup. She had Iztho's evidence and could save the business.

She ran from the guesthouse to the Exchange where she booked the first flight to Kedras, which, unfortunately, didn't leave until the next morning. After paying for it, she had exactly three credits left in her personal account.

It was going to ruin her, but this was worth fighting for.

After she came back, she found Jocasssa and Dalit in the courtyard. They looked at her when she came in, but didn't greet her.

"The Trader Guild, huh?"

Mikandra sat down at the table with a sigh. "I'm sorry about telling you lies."

"Why din' youz say who youz were?"

"And stay here? With no money?"

"Surely youz had money somewhere?"

Mikandra shook her head. "The thugs took everything I had. My father disowned me after I accepted my offer for the Trader Guild. I didn't lie about being alone and running away from home."

His mouth twitched. He looked like he might not believe her. "So who exactly is yer father?"

"Asitho Bisumar."

A flicker of distaste went over his face. "That makes sense." In an if-he-was-my-father-I'd-run-away-too kind of tone.

Dalit said, "That makes High Councillor Amandra Bisumar your aunt, right?"

Mikandra nodded. "I asked to apprentice with her, but she didn't want to sponsor me, so I went to the Andrahar Traders."

Jocassa stared at the table, his mouth twitching.

"Mind you, no one expected me to do that. Our family isn't up there with the Andrahars at all. I was astounded that I was accepted." Which had been Isandra's doing.

Jocassa kept staring. All the politics in the Endri were so far removed from him that the differences between the families meant nothing to him. The only emotion the Nikala felt towards the Endri was distrust. While the Endri held up ideals, the Nikala had stopped believing in Foundation long ago.

Mikandra felt horrible. These men had trusted her. In a strange sort of way, she'd come to like Jocassa with his mock-innocent ways and the raw intelligence that lurked under the surface. He'd certainly changed the way she thought of Mirani Nikala. She'd been just as selfish as she accused them of being.

"I'm sorry," she said again. "I don't know what else to say."

"What else t' say? Youz can tell all yer friends that youz lived with th' real poor people 'n joke about it."

"No, I'm not going to do that, and you know it. I will fight for what's fair."

Jocassa shrugged. "Give it a few days 'n you've forgotten us already. Fair t' youz means that youz get t' feel good about unimportant stuff."

"I told you I'd pay back what you gave me."

"It's not about th' flaming money. That's th' problem. Youz think it's about money, that youz can fix anything by giving money and telling us what t' do. We don' want t' be told what t' do. We want t' be treated as equals. That's what Nemedor Satarin wants: he wants us t' have th' same chance as th' Endri people. No, don' say anything 'cause youz don' get it. Youz go back to th' rich life, 'n we jus' work our guts out 'n die young."

They sat in silence for a while. Mikandra was lost for anything to say. In a horrible way, he was right, and there was nothing she could do.

She rose. "Anyway, I better go to bed. I have a very early flight to catch tomorrow."

He looked up at her, unblinking. "Where?"

"Kedras. I'm going to deliver the letter she gave me to the court."

He didn't say anything for a while. His face showed how he was processing the emotions—anger, disappointment, jealousy. "Good luck." He regarded her with sadness in his eyes.

She nodded, and almost reluctantly, broke eye contact.

As she walked up the stairs, that bitter tone in his voice continued to haunt her. He'd probably hoped that by helping her, she'd give him a chance. That might have been the sole purpose of his friendship, and it was a friendship of sorts. Jocassa had taught her more than she had taught him.

Yes, she owed him.

She stopped on the stairs and listened to their voices in the courtyard, the meaning beyond her hearing.

Damn right, she owed him, and once again, she had nothing left to give.

I'll pay him back later. When she finished at the Academy, she would need employees.

But then again, would he still be around, or would he and his mismatched band of friends have shifted to some other place. Or, more disturbingly, would they have died?

She went to the dorm, undressed, but lay awake all night, listening to the sounds of other people snoring.

She had thought she would be happy to solve the Andrahars' innocence, but the truth it revealed about Miran was so ugly that it would shake her life, and that of many others, forever. She would never be able to go home. If the Andrahar Traders left Miran, where would that leave her? What about her family, about Liseyo, and what about Aunt Amandra? Did she even know about these captured people? Did she know about the cruelty?

Leitho had foreseen all this. He was always telling her to free his people. The hallucinations didn't make people see nonsense; it made them see the truth of things that happened to their kin.

After she went to court with this document, Miran would never be the same. There would be a wedge driven in the society that had functioned well for thousands of years. The contract was broken. Foundation was useless. Everything she knew and loved about Miran was coming to a hard, merciless crash.

Eventually, she got sick of staring at the darkness and got up. She dressed in her plain apprentice uniform—which was much too hot for this climate—and packed up her bags by the light of the small light pearl. Everyone else in the room was still asleep, so she sneaked out as quietly as she could. Then she dropped her bags at the door, sneaked back and placed the cute pearl and its stand next to Jocassa's bed.

She *would* be back, and she *would* do the right thing by these men.

When Mikandra walked down the end of Market Street and crossed the square to the airport gate, the bluish glow of coming daylight gathered over the edge of the escarpment. The marshlands ahead were shrouded in filaments of low-hanging mist. The air was so still that not a leaf moved on the trees.

A handful of bleary-eyed people had gathered at the airport gate. Local businessmen, all keihu in various degrees of rotundness, a few Kedrasi returning home, a couple of Damarcians who looked suspiciously like builders, a Mirani merchant. When she joined the group, there were a few respectful nods. People glanced at the Guild emblem on her tunic.

So, Barresh had no Traders.

How about she changed that? There were plenty of offices, and plenty of workers. It might be hard to find good ones, but they could be trained . . . whether they were uneducated Mirani ex-soldiers or nimble Pengali.

Of course the airport was a disgrace and would need upgrading, but that work was already underway. The new Exchange was very good and there were plenty of builders in this place. The city was vibrant with opportunity instead of laden with responsibility.

While she waited in the line, she built dream cities in her mind. She paved the airport and painted lines on the ground. She cut down the bushes and ripped out the fence and gate to make way for an airy modern building. One section for general passengers, one for commercial. There could be an upstairs office complex for the to-be-formed local chapter of the Trader Guild. It would be a large open structure with a common room that looked out over the airport and the marshland. There would be a hub fed directly from the Exchange. The square outside, that horribly bare and hot place, would be covered with shade roofs. There would be shops and eating houses. Machizu would occupy a huge stand with lots of tables. There could even be an aerial walkway between the airport and the Exchange. Of course there would need to be better guesthouses for all those visitors, but there was room for those on the northern side of the square.

Market Street would remain the same, only better, cleaner, and tidied up. She liked Market Street. The cheap guesthouse would become a meeting point for young artists and musicians.

Barresh needed trains. Kedrasi were good at building trains. They—

—a shuttle came down and landed not far from the gate with a roar of downward jets. The first rays of sunlight peeped over the escarpment reflected in its brilliant metallic surface. This was a common Asto-built model, in service for many years, reliable in a wide range of conditions.

The door opened. The passengers streaming out of the craft were mainly Kedrasi, a lot of them women. More workers for the council.

The guard opened the gate to let them through. Mikandra waited behind him while he checked the incoming passengers. He gave cursory looks at the ID card reader. However, when two keihu people came past, he ignored them altogether. The data storage unit on his reader, which he carried on his belt, flashed briefly when they passed.

Barresh *looked* a low-tech city, but, like in Hedron, locals carried ID chips. It accentuated everything she had learned about the city. Everything here said, *we do not yet look like much, but do not underestimate us.* She vowed she never would.

The craft had emptied and now the new passengers could get on. Mikandra followed the others across the cracked paving, up the ramp and into the craft.

A polite crew member—Kedrasi—collected her bag at the entrance and took it to the luggage compartment at the back.

Mikandra found her seat right at the front of the craft. A Damarcian with the Masterbuilders' logo on his tunic sat next to her and gave her a polite nod. He pulled out a reader. The screen displayed plans and maps.

Mikandra did up the harness with sweaty hands. It was stupid and embarrassing, but she wasn't going to admit that this was her first anpar flight. While she was wearing the Trader Guild uniform, no one would believe her anyway.

The doors shut and the ventilation system came on.

With a burst of power from the downward jets, the craft lifted off the ground.

Both suns had cleared the horizon and cast a golden glow over the masses of rainforest at the top of the escarpment. The land looked like some giant had pushed the top layer of rock off the marshlands and onto the highlands. The terrain rippled like a curtain pushed to the side. Mist clung to the treetops in the valleys, still in slumber, sheltered from sunlight. The forest stretched out towards the east as far as she could see, but she knew that the border with Miran wasn't that far away. In Bendara, people considered the wild forest from Barresh an ugly invasion of their farmland. Mikandra thought it was beautiful.

From there, the land sloped up and up, coming first to Bendara with its patchworks of fields and many roads. Further up again were the large grain fields that were the driving engine of the Mirani export to Asto. Further east, the land rose above the tree line, and this was the country of the huge tiyuk herds and their nomadic minders. Above that, there was only highland vegetation, ground-hugging plantlets and in the right season, snow. On the eastern side of the capital, the land dropped again to the gorges which fed rivers that tumbled off the eastern escarpment, an even more massive break line with cliffs so high that the smaller waterfalls evaporated before they reached the bottom.

The Mirani continent bore hallmarks of an extremely violent geological past, which had thrust the centre section of the plate up.

It was also incredibly beautiful, and as the land receded under her, Mikandra knew that there was not a planet in all of the settled worlds more beautiful and diverse than Ceren.

The detail of the ground receded, and the clouds over the forest became little white puffs. The shuttle flew in broad circles so that it would stay over Barresh terrain. At times sunlight came into the window, casting double-edged shadows in ever-increasing sharpness.

Slowly, the sky turned dark with a brilliant azure blue over the horizon. From up here, the curve was obvious and then she could get a glimpse of the massive polar ice cap. Crew in the cabin walked around inspecting for loose items and seatbelts. They already wore their harnesses over their uniforms. They were handing out pillows to secure passenger's heads in the headrest.

The jump was near.

It was only a single jump to Kedras, along a single anpar line. She'd seen those lines at the Exchange, massive fluxes of energy that linked up one point in the galaxy with another.

The businessman next to her looked at his hands in his lap. Clearly, not everyone was relaxed with the process of Exchange transfer, when whatever object was the focus of the anpar lines would be disassembled in one place and reassembled at the other end. It was best not to think of all the things that could go wrong with this process.

A white light started flashing at the front of the cabin, counting down to the jump. People fell silent.

Then a red light flashed as well.

Three . . . two . . . one . . .

Everything went white.

Mikandra floated in nothingness. She had no hands and no eyes to look at her body.

When her vision reassembled, everything around her had a rainbow-hued aura. Slowly, the discordant colours overlapped and her vision returned to normal.

The crew were already walking around. Maybe in a year or so she, too, would have become used to this process.

The craft's engine hummed steadily. Outside the window was the bright azure glow of the atmosphere. A single yellow sun.

Kedras was smaller than Ceren but orbited closer to the sun. Most of the planet's land was red-burnished desert but while also quite cool, there were lush oases with azure rivers and green ribbons of forest and cultivated fields. Little specks of settlements dotted the valleys.

The shuttle turned and she could already see the huge complex that was the Trader Guild headquarters. It was a giant glass-and-metal building, surrounding the airport on three sides. Part of it was a shared airport facility for the inter-connected townships that dotted the green delta, but most of the building was off-limits to non-Traders.

Nerves returned. She had read that the courtrooms were accessible to all Traders, and right now, she hoped with all her might that her status as apprentice was enough to let her into that inner sanctum.

30

THE SHUTTLE touched down not much later. Passengers started moving around as soon as the downward jets cut out and the craft sank on its landing gear.

The doors opened and let fresh and dry air into the cabin. A bit like Miran but not as cold.

From the cabin, passengers left the craft over a raised walkway that slowly sloped to the building, a huge glass façade that reflected the deep blue sky and the pavement with its neat pattern of signals and lines.

Mikandra peered at the section on the other side of the space enclosed by the building's two arms. This area was a gaggle of small craft that extended past the wing of the building. All of them carried the Trader Guild symbol. Each licence holder had their own designated area, a neatly painted square on the pavement, with broad laneways for manoeuvring and landing craft.

People rode in open-cabin carriages or walked to and from the building.

Mikandra spotted a couple of the almost black Mirani craft, but no clear indication which one—or two—belonged to the Andrahar brothers.

One of the main reasons Kedras had been chosen for the Trader Guild headquarters was that the climate was very reliable and business days lost to closure due to weather were almost nonexistent.

In the hall, many people gathered, waiting for their flights or arriving passengers. There were numerous stairwells leading from the hall into other parts of the building. Signs in the Trader dialect of Coldi pointed to various services. Passenger office, freight office, tickets.

This place was massive. She had tried to calculate the time, but her only approximation was that the court session was this morning. Depending on the local time—and what was that?—it might have already started. There were so many signs, so many of them in Kedrasi, which she couldn't read. She was still in the public area of the building.

"Excuse me, do you know where the courtroom is?" she asked a woman who looked like she worked in the hall.

"The court?" She spoke Coldi with a strong accent.

"The Trader court."

"Ah." Then a frown at her uniform. "The Trader section is the wing on the other side." She pointed out the window, across the airport.

"How do I get there from here? As quickly as possible."

The woman pointed her to an exit to the hall that led into a wide corridor where the glass wall that looked over the central airport made up the right hand side. The doors on the left-hand side led to offices. It was not very busy here, so Mikandra walked as fast as her sore ankle allowed. She had to stop when she became too out of breath. The air at Kedras was thin, resembling Miran but not quite as cold. After living in the soup of Barresh, she wasn't used to it anymore.

Through the window, she spotted someone outside between the parked aircraft walking in the same direction she was going. Someone in a khaki uniform with silver hair. It didn't look like Rehan or Braedon. She wasn't sure about Taerzo, but now the man had vanished again behind an aircraft.

Mikandra kept walking and the man continued as well. She slowed and he slowed, too, hidden from view behind another aircraft.

Crap. Someone following her?

She stopped altogether and peered at the busy section of the Trader craft area outside the window. People walked past the window and stood talking. Colours were bright and shadows sharp in the clear air. Various types of refuelling robots trundled over the paths between the lots. The Mirani man was nowhere to be seen.

Maybe he just happened to walk fast in the same direction. And she had other things to worry about.

At the end of the corridor, she came to a foyer with a glass wall at the far end. A pair of sliding doors had the Trader Guild emblem engraved. They slid aside at Mikandra's approach.

In this hall, there was a second glass partition with sliding doors. Next to those doors, a woman in the carmine Trader Guild uniform sat behind a desk of which the top consisted entirely of screens. She was talking to someone via her earpiece, and when Mikandra came in, she looked up and cut off the conversation. She nodded at Mikandra.

"The entrance to the apprentice accommodations is on the far side of the building."

"I'm here because I need to deliver something to the court."

"The court is in session."

"I know. I need to deliver evidence."

"Do I have your name on the attendants list?"

"I'm Mikandra Bisumar, for the Andrahar Traders."

The woman trailed her finger over one of the screens. "I can't see your name here."

"Please, I have very important information," Mikandra said. She was sweating under her tunic. She hadn't come all the way here only to be stopped by bureaucracy. She was going to get into that courtroom. "The court sessions are open to all members." Beyond the desk and the shoulder-height partition, in one of three corridors that led from the hall, she could see a sign that said *Main Courtroom*.

"That's true, but you need to have registered, because the number of seats in the room are limited. I'm afraid the session is booked out."

"I'm not a spectator. I carry extremely important information." She had to stop herself from shouting. "All right, I don't need to go in myself if someone can take it in for me." Although she didn't want to let go of the letter, she'd do it if there was no other way.

The door slid open again behind her. The woman glanced up and quickly looked away.

A young male voice said, "Well, look at who we have here."

Mikandra turned around. Thaeron Tussamar. The Mirani Trader she had seen outside?

He gave her a cultured smile that felt as fake as it looked. "You've changed a lot since I last saw you. I hardly recognise you. You caused a pretty big fuss in Miran by disappearing. Your poor father doesn't know what to do with himself."

"Sorry, I don't have time to chat." Mikandra turned to the woman. "Please, let me through."

The woman just stood there, staring from one to the other. A look of horror came over her face. Somewhere in the Trader manual there was a section about employees of the Guild having to maintain absolute neutrality in disputes between Traders.

"What's this?" Thaeron said. "If you want the Mirani apprentices to treat you well for the next four years, you can't afford to be rude to anyone."

An Asto Trader, in maroon and blue came into the hall. The woman pressed an orange square on one of the screens. The partition door slid aside, letting him through.

Mikandra said to Thaeron, "I don't mean to be rude, but I'm in an extreme hurry. I need to get into the courtroom."

"I've registered, I can take whatever you need to have taken inside." He held out his hand.

Oh no, he wouldn't.

"I'd rather do it myself." Mikandra clutched her bag to her chest. There was no way she'd let *him* touch the letter from Iztho.

His expression hardened. "If you're going to be like that, you won't last long here. I can guarantee—"

Mikandra turned to the woman at the desk. "Please, I need to get in, now."

Thaeron said, "Let an employee deal with it. That's why they're here. They can still get in even if the court is closed. Why don't I show you the apprentice accommodation. You can meet the others. Many of them have already arrived." He grabbed her arm.

It triggered memories of her father grabbing her in the same place and dragging her off somewhere she didn't want to go, yelling in her ear to behave herself while the nails on his fingers dug into the soft skin of her underarm.

Mikandra acted without thinking. She twisted her arm. He clearly had no experience in restraining naughty little sisters and lost his grip. Mikandra lunged over the desk, and slammed her hand at the orange square. The doors opened and she ran through. Ouch, her ankle wasn't up to running.

Thaeron yelled, "Hey, what do you think you're doing?"

His footsteps thudded behind her. He had not ordered the woman to contact security. Mikandra had been right. He was desperate to stop the information reaching the courtroom. Did this mean that *he* had tampered with the log file of the Miran Exchange? She heard Antho Tussamar's voice *If you have a problem with your gadgetry, my nephew here will fix it.*

Mikandra ran. Pain spiked through her ankle with every step.

The sign that said *Main Courtroom,* however, merely pointed into a corridor.

She charged in, past many doors. Most were closed but every now and then, one was open and she glimpsed the office inside.

The carpet muffled her footsteps. She couldn't hear Thaeron anymore, but he was sure to be behind her. She didn't dare look, because she might trip. Her ankle was going to give in.

There was a marble-pillared foyer at the end of the corridor, and at the far end of that, two heavy wooden doors. That had to be the courtroom.

Mikandra ran past a door the very moment it opened. She almost ran into the Guild employee who came out. He uttered a startled noise. Mikandra tripped. Someone screamed, and there was a huge flash behind her.

Mikandra dropped to the carpet. She hid her head under her arms while purple spots danced in her vision. The corner of the book poked her painfully in the ribs. An alarm went off.

Doors opened. People came into the corridor.

A man yelled in Kedrasi over the wailing of the alarm.

Mikandra pushed herself up. Someone dressed in red lay face down on the ground at the door where she'd almost crashed into the employee. Two people bent over him, one trying to undo the man's shirt. Another man was stomping out a fire on the carpet.

A male voice yelled, "Stop him! Stop him!"

A lot of people ran down the corridor towards the foyer. There were sounds of yelling, and a crash.

The alarm stopped wailing.

"Are you all right?" A woman asked Mikandra.

Mikandra looked up into her spotted Kedrasi face. She whispered, "He shot at me." And hit the poor man who'd walked unsuspecting out of his office instead. Her ears were still ringing.

She tried to get up but her ankle wouldn't cooperate. Ouch.

"Take it easy. A medico will be here soon," the woman said.

"No time." Mikandra got on her uninjured foot and heaved her bag back onto her shoulder. "I have to go to the courtroom." Ouch, her ankle.

"Miss, stay down. You need medical attention."

"No. I am here for the court. My ankle can wait."

"You are not allowed in once the session has started."

"I'm going in anyway. I haven't come all this way for nothing."

She took a couple of hobbling, uncertain steps. Every time she tried to put weight on her foot, pain spiked up her leg. It felt like she had broken something, but she had to keep going.

People around her backed off. Most of them were Guild employees, who lined up on both sides of the corridor.

Mikandra took one step, and then another one and another one, mostly hopping on her good leg. She arrived at the courtroom door and pushed down the handle. It creaked badly. The door was so heavy that she had to use her whole weight to open it.

The room was packed. One of the court judges at the long table at the far end of the room had been speaking, but fell silent. Many in the audience looked over their shoulders. Almost all of them were Traders in a riot of uniform colours.

Whispers went around the room. Mikandra could almost feel

the meaning of their words. *What is she doing here? Who let her in? Can someone please alert the guards?*

An employee in red scurried to the door. "Miss, you are not allowed to come in here. You should wait outside—"

The judge, a stern-looking Damarcian Trader in her dark blue uniform rang her bell. "Silence!" She met Mikandra's gaze with her black-rimmed yellow eyes. "What is the meaning of this? Who let you in? This court is for Traders only."

"I'm an apprentice." Mikandra glanced at her uniform. Big splatters of blood marked the front. *What?* She raised her hand to her face and it came away covered in blood. There was a cut in her cheek. She must have cut herself when she ducked for cover. Well, that explained the stares.

"I have travelled from Barresh, and have risked everything to get here in time." She raised her voice, and everyone in that room stared at her. Where were the brothers? "I've been kicked out of my home, lived in poverty. I've been robbed and just now, shot at, all in the name of this case and my determination to prove injustice. I have important evidence that will change this case, and I'm here to present it to the judges. Anyone who tries to stop me will be accused of trying to obscure the truth."

A wide aisle sloped gently towards the far end of the room and the desk where the judges sat.

Mikandra hobbled down while everyone in that room watched her. There had to be at least five hundred Traders in that room, all of them from the most influential licence holders. No one spoke. Her progress was slow with her ankle.

Her eyes met those of Aunt Amandra in the crowd, wide and horrified.

She reached the judges' table and bowed as far as her ankle allowed her. "Your honour. My name is Mikandra Bisumar. I am an apprentice of the Andrahar Traders."

She spotted Antho Tussamar in the audience. He was looking not at her, but at the door she had left open. His expression was worried. Wondering where his nephew was?

The judge frowned.

"The reason I look like this is that someone just tried to shoot me. One of the employees is wounded."

People started talking.

"Quiet!" The judge rang her bell again. "Is this true?" She was looking over Mikandra's head to the door, where a number of Guild employees stood.

"It is. One of the office staff was hit. We have a gunman loose in the building."

"This is ridiculous!" someone shouted.

Several people rose from their seats and a heated argument broke out in the far right side of the room.

Antho Tussamar had risen from his seat and was working his way out of the row of seats to the path that ran along the far wall.

The judge rang her bell until everyone fell quiet. Antho Tussamar strode out the door.

The judge asked the employee, "Is there a need to suspend the session while the guards deal with this incident?"

"It's safe to continue. This part of the building is secure. He went into the public section."

"What about the injured employee?"

"He is being looked after. The charge glanced off. He will be fine."

"Thank you. Then we shall continue the case."

The man shooed his colleagues out and shut the door behind him.

"Sit down everyone." She rang the bell again.

People sat and Mikandra now spotted Taerzo and Braedon on a bench at the front of the audience, immediately facing the judges' table.

Both watched her with wide eyes.

Rehan stood in the accused box, an area surrounded on three sides by a wooden railing and guarded by a tall Indrahui man in the red and black Trader security uniform.

Rehan's eyes met Mikandra's over the heads of the crowd. His face was serious, but his eyes were wide.

"Let us have a look at your evidence," the judge said.

Mikandra slid her bag off her shoulder, dug inside, and gave the judge the copy of Iztho's letter as well as the Exchange listings which she hoped would make more sense to the judge than they did to her.

The judge read, while a deepening furrow grew on her forehead. The murmur amongst the spectators increased. Mikandra wondered when she would be allowed to sit down. Her ankle throbbed.

The judge turned over the sheet and studied the Exchange listings. She handed the documents to a colleague next to her, a Kedrasi judge, who also read, the expression of unease on his face increasing.

He passed the letter to the judge on his other side and met the chief judge's eyes. A few words were exchanged between them.

She nodded and rang her bell again. "We have seen the documents and decided that the accusation needs serious reconsideration. The case is adjourned."

A murmur of talk went up. Mikandra heard some angry voices, but had no idea who they belonged to. Rehan watched her over the heads of the audience.

The judge rang the bell. "Quiet everyone!"

The talk died down.

The chief judge looked at Mikandra. "This duplicate comes from where exactly?"

"The Barresh Exchange. The original of this letter never reached the family, because the courier who carried it was murdered in the streets of Miran."

Someone said something that sounded like a protest, but she couldn't hear the words. The man was definitely a Mirani Trader.

The judge gestured to the court assistants and one woman in red rose to take the letter from the last of the judges and gave it to Rehan.

His face showed no emotion while he read. Then he looked at Mikandra and while he kept his face blank, his eyes radiated happiness.

The judge rung her bell. "Following this new evidence, the court will adjourn, and the judges will deliberate *if* the Andrahar Traders have to answer the accusations—Yes?"

An elderly Coldi judge had raised his hand. She spoke briefly to him. Then the Kedrasi judge commented, and the Coldi judge shook his head.

The chief judge spoke to them, and both nodded.

"We've already made a decision. The current case is void. The evidence before us casts serious doubts on the reliability of the documentation brought by the accusers. It includes evidence of tampering with the Exchange logs in Miran. I end the court session. We will deliberate the next step. Any outstanding issues will have to be brought in a new case. You may go."

In the uproar that followed, a Guild employee came from the scribes' table to the stand and handed Rehan a small bag.

With that, the session was closed. People rose from their seats and started streaming out the back of the room. There were reporters yelling questions and soon the buzz went around: *The Andrahar family has been cleared of all suspicions.*

31

MIKANDRA STOOD in the aisle while people streamed out of the room. Standing still and hoping that no one would step on her foot was the best she could do. Several Traders, much older and mostly male, came out to congratulate her, saying things like *good work* and *extraordinary courage*. All of them were non-Mirani. The Mirani Traders eyed her with suspicion from the other side of the room. They didn't congratulate her. She felt dazed.

Eventually, most of the audience left through the back door. Braedon was the first of the brothers to reach her.

Instead of showering her with praise, he squeezed her shoulder in a strong grip. His lips were pressed together. His eyes said more than words could have done. He made her sit down in one of the aisle seats. "Look at you. You're injured."

Mikandra protested. "I'm fine."

"Not while you have blood pouring down your face." He opened his document case, found a face towel, screwed the cap off a small bottle and poured a good amount of the contents over the fabric. The air filled with the scent of Mirani herbs that reminded her so much of home that tears pricked in her eyes.

All of a sudden, she felt exhausted.

Braedon wiped her cheek, turning the towel red. "Did you get hit in the shooting? You look terrible."

"I didn't notice. It doesn't hurt." She didn't even know where and when it had happened, presumably when she had fallen onto the carpet. She must have cut herself on something, maybe something sharp on the outside of her bag.

He worked quickly cleaning up the blood and then wiped some disinfectant on the cut. Mikandra thought of the hospital. One part of her wanted to go back and apologise to Eydrina for using her name and to Liseyo and Mother that she had run away. She *would* go back and make Mother proud.

Taerzo and Rehan still stood at the front of the room in the company of two Mirani Traders whom she didn't know. Their faces were grim and determined. Rehan glanced at her several times. An employee in red came in and spoke briefly to the men.

"Let me have a look at your foot." Braedon twisted her sideways in the seat so that her feet poked into the aisle. He took off her shoe. Her ankle was swollen and blue.

While Braedon was wrapping a bandage around it, Taerzo and Rehan joined Mikandra and Braedon.

Taerzo said, "The guard said that they've caught Thaeron Tussamar. He got caught in the public bathroom."

"Good." Braedon shook a spray bottle and sprayed liquid on her ankle. It smelled odd and made her skin go cold. He snorted. "Shooting inside the Guild building. I don't know that I've ever heard of that happening. Why?"

"They've been desperate to hide the truth," Rehan said. "That's why Nemedor Satarin came to our house. That's why the Tussamars tried to chat up Mikandra."

Mikandra met Rehan's eyes.

She thought about how rude she thought he'd been when she last met him in person, and how open, almost intimate, his correspondence was. How much she knew about him, and how she— embarrassingly—thought she had fallen for him. Now, facing him and his formal Trader ways, those thoughts seemed ridiculous.

He sat down next to her. He had his hand clamped around the bag he'd been given. His knuckles where white.

"I just wanted to say . . . thank you. You were . . . just

awesome. Fucking awesome. This is probably the only time I'll ever say this, so take note. I'm a hard teacher."

He was going to take over her mentorship? "Does it mean I can stand the heat?"

One corner of his mouth lifted. "You want heat? I'll give you forty, fifty years of slow torture. I'll give you so much heat that you'll beg to be treated *like the other apprentices,* the soft ones."

"After Barresh, there is nothing I can't handle," Mikandra said. "Bring it on, brother, bring it on."

"The fuck I will."

"Can you two lay off?" Braedon said, while putting the med kit back into his document case. "Brother, she's just got us all off the hook, and you're still trying to make this into a bluffing contest."

"Leave him. He enjoys it," Taerzo said.

"She enjoys it," Rehan said, while still meeting her eyes.

Braedon snapped the document case shut. "Come on, let's go and eat something. I'm starving."

Food was good. She hadn't thought about food for a while.

Mikandra let Braedon help her to her feet. The bandage felt snug and already the spray he used had made her ankle numb.

They walked out of the courtroom.

Taerzo and Rehan went first and then Mikandra with Braedon nearby, but she didn't need to lean on his arm.

"Does that feel better?"

She nodded. "What is that stuff?"

"It's a new treatment based on a plant extract from Indrahui. You have to be careful, though. Even though you may not feel anything, it doesn't mean that the damage has healed. You must rest your foot."

For a while, they walked quietly, listening to Rehan and Taerzo's talk.

Taerzo joked that with Thaeron facing trial and punishment, Rehan could buy his aircraft back.

"Are you kidding, brother? I wouldn't touch anything that piece of shit has touched. I'll get a new one."

Their banter belied the seriousness of the situation they'd still face at home. The brothers wouldn't have missed the glares from

Mirani colleagues. Those Traders would think that the brothers had betrayed Miran.

Mikandra turned to Braedon.

"Have you been all right? I mean—with the riots in Miran and all that?"

"I guess, although we've been holed up in the house or the office. It's taken a toll on all of us, including Mother. I can't say it's been very pleasant in our house since you left. We've had many fights. All of us have been sick with worry at different points in time. I'm so glad it's over."

"Is it over? Is the council going to accept being blamed for tampering with the Exchange records or will they take it out on all Traders? Are they going to defend the Tussamar Traders or let them take the blame?"

He shrugged. "Who knows? The council are cowards. I don't think they'll try to spar with the Guild. You've heard about the Ilendars?"

She nodded.

Here in the airy corridors of the building, the oppressive atmosphere in Miran seemed so far away.

"I don't know what the future will hold for Miran," Braedon said. "But whatever happens, the Andrahar Traders can now withstand the blizzards the universe will throw at us. We must take things one step at a time. We cannot solve the bigger problems yet, but we are stronger."

She nodded. Braedon was so cool and composed, so utterly pragmatic. Why had she ever thought that the three brothers were similar?

They had been walking down the corridors following a stream of people who were going in the same direction. Those people now queued up before a set of double doors. Inside, Mikandra could see glimpses of a large, multi-storey hall that she recognised from pictures as the famous Trader bar. A Guild employee stood in a stiff position with his hands behind his back at a small table where people had to sign their names in an old-fashioned book. The Guild employee turned the page when necessary.

Mikandra sensed movement next to her. Aunt Amandra had

caught up with them. In the harsh desert light that came in through the window, her face showed more wrinkles than Mikandra had ever noticed.

She spoke softly. "I take back everything I've said about you being too soft to be a Trader. If you have the ability to get out of Barresh better than you went in, you have to be smart. Not even Nemedor Satarin managed that. That was a fine performance. I'm proud of you." She put a hand on Mikandra's shoulder.

"Have you heard any news about my family?" Mikandra asked.

"That stupid oaf of a brother of mine has dug himself in. He's lent his house and yard to the guard and elite army corps supporting Nemedor Satarin. I'm very unhappy and worried about it."

Mikandra's heart jumped. "What about Mother and Liseyo?"

"They weren't at the house last time I was there. I presume they're staying with your mother's sister."

"Are they all right?" She thought of Dalit's story. What if Mother had left the house and left Father? It happened, not very often, but it did. The thought chilled her. How would they get money to live?

"Sorry, I don't know much more than that."

Panic clamped around her heart. She remembered getting that odd note of support from Mother after she had sent the courier to pick up her clothes. "I have to make sure that they're safe."

Aunt Amandra nodded. Her expression was grim and distant.

The line shuffled forward.

After a brief silence, Mikandra said, "I spoke to Ydana in Barresh."

Aunt Amandra whirled and gave her an intense look. "What was he doing there?"

"Selling prefab buildings for the airport construction. He didn't come to see you? He told me that was his plan."

Aunt Amandra shook her head and stared out the window. "Things may be . . . irretrievably broken between us. I haven't seen him for so long. I attended the court because I was hoping that he'd be here. I want to speak with him. We had a really bad fight. I was stupid and said some stupid things." Her face had a painful expression. "Especially now."

Mikandra was curious what she meant, but they arrived at the door and had to sign in the book. Rehan and Taerzo went first.

Inside the room beyond, people sat at tables. A heavenly smell of food drifted from the entrance.

Then it was Mikandra's turn. In the book, Traders had written their names, licence number and place of residence. She wrote *Mikandra Bisumar, 1101* and then hesitated. The Mirani council didn't want the Traders anymore. What if she wrote something else, like *Barresh?* But of course, it wasn't that simple. She added *Miran* to the line she'd just written.

The Guild employee studied her face.

"He knows every Guild member," Braedon said, while Aunt Amandra wrote in the book. "That's his job."

The man dipped his head at Mikandra. "Lady, welcome to the Guild."

She felt uneasy. In Barresh, she had been friends with Melvi and Ariani, who were ordinary Kedrasi people like him. She didn't want to be treated like she was better than them.

And, as the family was admitted into that inner sanctum of the Guild, the Trader bar, she realised that all her life, she had been treated like she was worth more than other people, even when she thought she wasn't. Even her unpaid job in the hospital had been unquestionably advantaged. At night, she went to a comfortable home while the homeless slept on benches, unheated apartments or in the streets.

Her time in Barresh had profoundly changed her.

The central hall of the bar was three floors high, and furnished in classy wood and stone. The ground floor was covered with tables and chairs, and so were the separate sections of the balconies on the two floors above, which looked out into the central hall. It was already quite busy and the huge space hummed with talk and laughter.

Rehan chose a table in the middle of the hall. Mikandra ended up in a seat between Braedon and her aunt. Rehan sat opposite her. He met her eyes, and she didn't know where to look.

Apart from the brief joking conversation, she had barely spoken to him. After all his intimate correspondence, she had expected . . . she didn't know what, but definitely more than this awkward dance. It was like he felt embarrassed about all the things he had told her.

A waiter in red came, and all ordered meals and drinks.

Mikandra let the sounds of talk and laughter wash over her. She was so tired.

Rehan produced the small bag he still clutched in his fist. When he upended it, four medallions fell out. He gave one each to Braedon and Taerzo, put one on top of his reader, set the fourth one in the middle of the table and met Mikandra's eyes. "That one will be yours."

She nodded, and couldn't bear to keep looking at him. There were probably thousands of things she should ask or talk about, but they had all slipped her mind. How was she going to work with him when he kept awkward silences like this?

He pinned the medallion back on his tunic.

Braedon had already put on his, and was checking something on his reader. "Oh, crap."

"What's up?" Taerzo, who sat on Braedon's other side, looked at the screen.

"The news has just broken in Miran. There are protests all over the streets. Off-duty army troops staged a protest in support of Nemedor Satarin and clashed with the pro-import group. People in the council are feral. Listen to what Nemedor Satarin had to say. *Today is a black day for Miran. When our citizens turn on us and use outside influences to 'prove' that we are guilty of fabricated charges, it is time that we reconsider what these citizens mean for us and how we are going to react to this action of treason.*"

"What a load of fucking nonsense," Rehan said. "Even now he's saying that they've done nothing. Like the Exchange can't possibly be right because they're controlled by evil foreigners. What a fucking dumbwit."

Aunt Amandra glanced at Mikandra in an *are-you-all-right-with-the-language?* way.

"He's going to want revenge," Taerzo said.

Rehan balled his fist. "Then we fucking give him revenge. We'll show what he's done, to all of *gamra*. The man's a fucking criminal."

Braedon shook his head. "If we do that, we'll be fighting instead of working."

"Should we just play nice then?"

Braedon shrugged. "I don't like fighting, brother. I sell medicines that fix people up, and I'm not interested in injuring them. If we fight Nemedor Satarin, the ones injured will be us, or we can join the Ilendar Traders here in Kedras."

Rehan snorted. "Miran is our home and it has always been. Trouble like this comes up every couple of years. We've always pulled through."

Aunt Amandra said, "It's different this time. The Traders don't enjoy the wide base of support they used to. Even a lot of the Endri don't support the Guild. Traders need a stable base. The Ilendars are gone for good. They'll probably end up going to Damarq."

"Changing colours?" Taerzo frowned.

"That's what I think they'll do."

"I'd rather die than go to Damarq." Rehan's expression was angry.

Braedon said, "If things are really bad, we could stay here for a while, until things calm down."

Mikandra took a deep breath. "Would you consider going to some place new, that doesn't have Traders? Start up a new chapter?"

Rehan frowned at her. "I thought you were relatively sane after all, but I think I misjudged. Why would any Trader go to a place without support?"

"There is support in Barresh."

His eyes widened. "Barresh? It's a dump."

"Have you been there recently?"

"Yes, I—"

"I lived there. In fact, I came straight from there. A lot has changed. They have a brand new Exchange with a new core."

"That's true," Taerzo said. "Much better than the Miran Exchange."

Mikandra continued. "They have a lot of people who are interested in investing. The Barresh council is behind it. They have people who are very quick with numbers and good with tools."

Rehan snorted. "I can't even believe that we're talking about this. Enough people in the Mirani chapter of the Guild will support us. We'll get through this."

"Barresh is there in case you need it. That's all I'm saying."

Rehan glared at her.

"It's going to be interesting with those two," Braedon said. "I get the feeling that we'll never again have a dull moment—" His gaze went to the middle of the hall.

Mikandra turned to see what he was looking at.

Ydana Ezmi stood a few tables away, his gaze roaming the tables on the ground floor and the lower balcony.

Mikandra sensed her aunt stiffening next to her. She whispered, "Ydana."

Beams of light from the ceiling cut through the air and made the purple cloak over his shoulders shine with brilliance. His chest heaved with breaths as if he had been running.

His gaze found their table and he came over in large strides, holding out his hand. *"Amai, shinu eysh' mazhayu."*

Mikandra frowned at Braedon. "What did he say?" Hedron Coldi had so many different words and pronunciations.

Braedon didn't reply, but stared, his mouth open.

Ydana took Aunt Amandra into the downward beams from the ceiling lights. The glow made her hair shine like silver. Ydana took a few steps back and bowed.

At the table Taerzo groaned. "He's not going to do it again, is he?"

People on surrounding tables had stopped talking. Some twisted around in their seats to see what was going on. Silence rippled through the hall.

Ydana raised his hand to the clasp of his cloak. He undid it and swept the cloak over her shoulders.

The silence intensified.

Aunt Amandra looked funny, with the thin purple cloak over her thick fur one. For what seemed like a long time, she didn't move. Hardly anyone spoke.

On a table next to Mikandra, a man whispered, "Not again, she's refused him twice already."

Mikandra held her breath.

Slowly, Aunt Amandra raised her hands to her neck. Any moment now and she would return the cloak to her lover, saying that she belonged in Miran. Mikandra thought of what Ydana had told her seated at the table in the courtyard in Barresh. He was a wounded man who would not live with another refusal. If she turned him down, he was likely to do something stupid, like kill himself.

Aunt Amandra fiddled with fastenings and tangled chains around her neck. Her hands trembled. She let her own cloak slip from under his. Slowly, she raised it and draped it over his shoulders.

His mouth fell open. His eyes widened. Then he laughed. He lifted her off the ground and turned a pirouette, narrowly missing a chair with her boots. He let her down and kissed her.

The cheer that went off hurt Mikandra's ears.

At the table, Taerzo smiled like a madman. Braedon was talking to someone on the next table, both of them laughing. Rehan sat quietly, chewing the nail on his thumb. He was still watching the embracing couple. His lips were pressed in a thin line.

Taerzo rose and was the first to congratulate the couple. Ydana smiled and clapped him on the shoulder in a *now it's your turn* manner. Braedon also rose to congratulate the couple.

"I'm very happy for them," Mikandra said, fighting a pricking feeling in her eyes. "They should have married long ago."

Rehan whirled towards her in a way that reminded her of his outbursts she had witnessed. His eyes glittered.

"Rehan? What's the—"

"Don't you fucking dare—"

"It's all right, it's all right. I'm not going to think there's anything wrong with you if you get emotional when two people find happiness after so many years."

He looked away. His mouth twitched. He blinked a few times, but a stubborn tear leaked out of his eye and ran down his cheek. He wiped it away angrily.

"No, I won't and you know it. I might even come to believe that you're the same person as the one who wrote me long personal messages when I was in Barresh."

He breathed in deeply, as if he were going to say something, but at that moment Taerzo and Braedon came back to the table. Aunt Amandra and Ydana followed, holding hands. They were still wearing each other's cloaks.

A waiter came to bring the food they'd ordered earlier. Ydana told him to bring his order over to the table as well. There was laughter and happy talk. Their odd group of all-Mirani Traders and one Coldi one attracted looks from others in the hall. One older Mirani Trader outright stared at the purple cloak on Aunt Amandra's shoulders.

Then, when they'd all sat down and dragged over chairs, Braedon said, "I can't imagine that both of you will live happily in Miran, so what is your position about the council, Amandra?"

"You haven't heard the news yet?" she said.

He shook his head.

"I've resigned from the council. I drew up the letter two days ago."

"Why? What changed two days ago?"

"A friend sent me some information that he thought I had. It shattered every last shred of trust I still had in my colleagues at the council. I heard some of it confirmed in the court today."

"Friend?"

"A long time ago, when I was still young and keen and a sharp-sensed Trader, an important man asked me to mentor a wayward young nephew of his. He wanted to send the young-ster through the Trader academy to knock some sense into him. The boy had grown up in a very privileged family in an environ-ment to which he was unsuited. He'd run away from home and turned up at his uncle's doorstep. He was drifting into that dangerous territory of loneliness, potential criminality or madness—"

This was starting to sound familiar. Mikandra said, "You mean Daya Ezmi?"

Her aunt's eyes met hers. "How do you know?"

"I met him. He told me some of his story, although nothing about you."

"What did you think?"

"He creeps the hell out of me."

"He creeps the hell out of everybody. He knows it. That's why he tends to keep to himself. He's got this mental ability—"

"Avya. I know."

"He can't help being the way he is. He sees into people's minds. He doesn't want to. His uncle—"

"Edyamor Ezmi."

"Yes, Edyamor Ezmi, he asked a Mirani Trader to be his tutor because Daya mentioned to him that he can't see into the thoughts of the Mirani Endri."

"You know why that is?" Mikandra asked.

Aunt Amandra and Braedon shook their heads. Ydana held his head cocked, listening.

The waiter had brought Ydana's food, a bowl of sizzling fried curls and one with noodles and sauce. Mikandra wondered. . . .

If Endri were Aghyrians and they both came from Asto, and Asto's high acidity and richness in fluorides made for red-coded food, then in theory . . . She reached out and picked up a curl.

Taerzo batted her hand away. "Hey, what are you doing? That's Ydana's. It's red-coded—"

Mikandra put the curl in her mouth and ate it, while everyone watched, horror on their faces, until she'd be sick or start bleeding from her nose or whatever rumours went around over eating red-coded food.

The curl was hot. It burned in her mouth worse than Machizu's spiciest food.

They waited and stared at her, and Mikandra stared back at them.

Eventually, Braedon said, in a low voice, "Nothing."

"Nothing," Mikandra repeated. "A small piece like this

would make a Nikala's mouth blister. Red-coded food is probably not very healthy for us, but we can eat it, because we share the Coldi's heritage."

There were frowns all around the table.

She went on to tell them of everything she had found out with Bakimay and how Daya was trying to piece together a viable population of Aghyrians where they could support each other. "And not lock people away because of their supposed madness. People like your aunt Dithiandra are not mad. They have a type of this ability called avya, which can be controlled. There was an old man in the hospital. His name was Leitho. He was one of the Endri, but no family claimed to own him. He lived on the streets and was an addict. Menisha brew makes the hallucinations stronger. I wouldn't be surprised if it turns out that it *came* from Asto with the ship. In the hospital, we failed Leitho in every possible way. We didn't listen to him and didn't take his hallucinations seriously. He was talking about people being imprisoned and mistreated."

Her eyes met Rehan's. He nodded, once. His expression looked haunted. Had he seen these people, too?

She continued, "There *are* people being imprisoned and mistreated. Thug gangs roam the streets of Barresh rounding up people who have *avya*. No one is sure what happens to these people, but they are not seen again. Daya says that *he* was imprisoned and mistreated during a visit to Miran. He says Nemedor Satarin is behind it."

Rehan said, "There have been rumours for a long time. This is what Aithno Ilendar was referring to during that meeting you attended. He seemed to think that he had some proof, but I've never seen it."

"I asked about these rumours, repeatedly," Aunt Amandra said. "I never got a straight answer. I treated the rumours as untrue until proven otherwise, but what Daya told me leads me to believe that it's true. Daya is a lot of things, but a liar isn't one. His story is horrific and he should have told me earlier. That was what finally swayed me. He contacted me the day before yesterday. He also told me that you'd been to see him." She met Mikandra's eyes. Well, *coming to see him* was one way of putting it. "I've failed Miran. I thought I could make it a better place by maintaining unity and dialogue between the opposing camps, but no one else seems interested." She stared into the distance. Ydana put a hand on her shoulder.

The conversation turned to places to live. Mikandra had expected her aunt to move to Kedras but was surprised to hear that she planned to move to Hedron.

"Change colours? It's not necessary. There are mixed couples."

"That's true, but the Mirani chapter never knew what to do with me."

"That means I'll be the only female Trader in Miran." A chill went over her.

"Yes, I'm sorry. But you'll be in good hands, and you won't have to face everything alone, as I did—" She turned to Braedon, who was again looking at the news on his reader, a deep frown on his face. "Any other developments at home?"

Braedon put the reader in the middle of the table so everyone could see it.

A big headline said, *Miran on the brink of chaos.*

Mikandra read snatches of it upside down.

Protest in response to Nemedor Satarin's call for action against the traitors . . . taking possession of the streets in the lower part of the Endri quarter of the city . . .

Taerzo swore.

Rehan rose abruptly from his seat. "We should be home with Mother and Gillay in case something happens."

No one disagreed with him. Mikandra felt cold. Iztho had said to *take* their mother to the court. He had foreseen this.

Mikandra and the three brothers made their way out of the bar after saying goodbye to Aunt Amandra and Ydana. The last glimpse Mikandra had into the hall was of the two of them talking to a waiter—presumably to order more drinks—while still holding hands.

The three brothers had come here with both Taerzo's and Braedon's aircraft, but they decided to leave Taerzo's here for safety.

Braedon's aircraft was a common well-used Mirani model,

nothing fancy but comfortable and tidy. There was a Trader saying that you could tell a Trader's character by looking at their aircraft, and in the case of Braedon that was true.

Braedon slipped behind the controls and Rehan told Mikandra to sit next to him.

"Into the fire, huh?" she said.

"You must stand the heat. Whether times are good or bad, there is work to be done and it must be done well. Your training starts now."

32

THEY FOUND MIRAN shrouded in grey, cloud-filled, misty dusk. Snow drifted from the sky, whipped up by the ever-present wind. The snow sweepers had kept the airport fairly clean, except for the thin trails that had blown over the paving since the passing of the sweeping machine. Mikandra peeked out the window, but could see no people and no visible changes since she had left.

Mikandra no longer had a cloak. Braedon gave her a spare from a cupboard at the back of the craft, which was much too big for her.

Rehan had been asleep on the bed against the back wall. He was rubbing his face furiously, but nothing made the impressed folds of his sleeve disappear from his cheek. Mikandra tried not to look because if she did she would laugh.

While they were collecting their bags from the various cupboards, Braedon opened the door. The air that came into the cabin was bitterly cold, and sucked out the warmth and all feelings of comfort with it.

Mikandra stepped onto the ramp holding both sides of the cloak. It was a beautiful, heavy thing of quality, but because it was too big for her, icy fingers of cold prised underneath. Her shoes, too, were not suited for walking in snow, and while Braedon walked around the craft pulling the covers over the engine exhausts and landing gear recesses, she jumped up and down.

Rehan stared over the city on the other side of the passenger building. Lights were already on, both in the building and in the streets.

A group of three grey silhouettes was walking towards the craft across the snow-swept field.

"Who the fuck are they?" Rehan said.

"You tell me, brother." A gust of wind swept Braedon's hair aside. He stood on the ramp just outside the door, with his arms crossed over his chest and his cloak draped over his shoulders. He squinted against the snow. "Taerzo, Mikandra, you best come inside."

Mikandra went back into the cabin and took up a position from where she could see out past Braedon and Rehan's backs.

The three figures resolved out of the snow and mist. The men wore the white and silver uniform of the city guard. One of them came up to the bottom of the aircraft ramp. "Good day, Trader."

Another said, "Congratulations on the outcome of the trial." But there was nothing happy in the man's voice. "We need you to come into the office for some formalities."

Braedon gave Rehan a sideways look that said *Formalities, my arse.* "Just me or all of us? Can our apprentice go home?"

"It's *about* your apprentice. The lady is registered with us as a missing person, possibly abducted."

"She's with us," Rehan said.

The man looked past Braedon at Mikandra. "Do you have any ID, lady?"

Mikandra handed Braedon her card and he gave it to the man, who inserted it in the reader that dangled from his belt. He addressed her directly.

"Lady Mikandra Bisumar, your father wants you to come home."

"I am an independent member of the Trader Guild. If he wants to see me, my father knows where to find me." Oh, the pompous coward that her father was. He now let the guards do his dirty work for him? That only showed how little he cared. He cared about his *authority* being challenged, not about her.

The man took one step onto the ramp. "You defied your father's orders. You—"

"Mate, back off." That was Rehan. "You're on Trader Guild territory."

The soldier backed off the ramp until his feet were once more on the ground.

Rehan continued, "You heard the lady. If her father wants to see her, he can come to our house. I trust he knows where it is."

"We have orders—"

"I told you to back off, mate. If you dare touch the lady, there will be consequences."

"Whoa, no need for that sort of talk."

"Good, then we understand each other. We'll go home then." Rehan turned around and offered Mikandra his arm.

He was so formal that Mikandra felt tempted to giggle like a girl going to a ball. This was a façade, a game, and she played it, putting her hand on his arm.

He guided her off the ramp, past the three guards. Rehan's arm felt tight under his shirt.

Behind Mikandra, Taerzo kept both his hands under his cloak. The guards could not be so stupid that they didn't know about the gun he had there. All Traders carried arms. To attack a Trader was an act of war against the Guild.

In complete silence, Braedon pushed the button in the door panel that retracted the ramp, then shut and locked the panel and the door.

They set out across the snow-blown field, watched by the three guards.

"Don't look back," Rehan said next to her.

"My father sent them."

"Maybe, but that's not the only reason they're here."

Mikandra could think of many reasons. Asking her to return to her father could be a ruse, or an excuse for them to approach the brothers.

Snow became more heavy and the sky darkened alarmingly.

They reached the building and walked through the corridor that bypassed the departure hall with its light behind steamed-up windows. Through the fog of condensation, she spotted people with bags seated on the benches. A cleaner walked through the aisles, moving his mop to and fro. Last time she had come here, the cleaners had been unable to work because of the crowd.

"It's not busy," she said.

"New travel laws," Braedon said. "It's become hard to leave for anyone who's not on business."

Without her aunt, the council would be even more restrictive.

Outside the airport, a blast of wind pelted snowflakes in her face. The cold fingers of the wind reached in the spaces underneath her too-big cloak. Her thin apprentice tunic, which had seemed impossibly hot in Barresh, was no match for the biting cold. At least Rehan was warm on one side of her and his body blocked some of the wind.

A sled with two tiyuk waited outside the building. The animals, two magnificent spotted bulls, stood with their heads lowered against the snow. Steam blew out their bristled noses. The driver, a highland boy, sat huddled in the driver's seat, using his cloak as tent. He gave the group one glance and went back to staring. The people who used his services were Nikala from lower parts of the city who lived too far away to walk.

One of the animals lifted its shaggy head with a great tinkling of the harness. The boy whistled. The animal snorted and continued moving its head up and down. The boy jumped to his feet and grabbed the rope that was attached to the animal's earrings. The bull snorted and rolled its eyes. The head tossing was a defensive display that the males of the herd used to ward off animals from a different herd.

Sure enough, another sled came into the street at a trot. The two magnificent beasts snorted when the driver pulled up the reins and stopped in front of Mikandra and the three brothers. Steam rose off their pelts.

"Tarlen!" Taerzo called.

Yes, the driver was the Andrahar groundsman. She had seen him before, an unusually tall and wiry fellow for a Nikala. He probably had highland blood, which would explain his skills with the sled.

"Get in," he said. "The army mob is still loose in the streets somewhere. If they get wind that you're back, they'll try to cut us off."

"They tried to stop us at the airport already," Rehan said, while helping Mikandra into the forward-facing seat.

While Tarlen explained how he'd borrowed the sled off a highland cousin of his who was in town for winter, Mikandra sat down. The bench was hard and cold. Braedon came to sit next to her, Rehan and Taerzo opposite. Both with weary looks and their hands under their cloaks.

"I gather things are not well here?" Braedon said.

Tarlen flicked the reins and the sled started moving with great snorting and tossing of heads of the tiyuk as a display of power against the animals from the other sled. Like the drivers and passengers, the animals obviously came from different herds.

Tarlen had to shout into the wind to be heard. "They only put out the fire at the Ilendar house yesterday. It's burnt to the ground. It's a crying shame. They've lived in that spot for hundreds of years. All that heritage is lost. Gone."

"Is the house safe?" Rehan asked. "Mother and Gillay?"

"For now. It's become hard to get supplies. We've had to clear and reopen the north gate to get the sleds out to the stores via the fields rather than through the city."

"Access to the airport?"

"Secure, for now."

They crossed the central square. Few people braved the snow, huddled in their cloaks. Lights were on in Merchant Ranuddin's shop, but the rest of the building on the corner was dark. The brothers could now return there to work, but the group of people who stood outside the shop looked like some kind of sentry.

"Those guys have moved further uphill since I left," Rehan said.

Braedon nodded, his face grim.

"Can we still get to the office?"

Braedon shrugged. "Haven't tried. Been too busy surviving at home."

The sled turned the corner past the market hall.

Another group of men stood here, leaning against heaped-up

snow fashioned into a wall. In the middle was an opening big enough for the sled. Tracks in the snow showed that Tarlen had come this way. Sleds did not often go into the Endri quarter.

A man shouted. Two figures wearing heavy fur cloaks climbed onto the snow mound.

"It's them!" someone yelled.

Cheers went up. A few more young men climbed on the snow. One of them held a gun.

Taerzo waved to the men as the sled whooshed through the opening. They were mostly young, councillors' or merchants' sons, some Nikala and some Endri. They raised fists and crossbows.

"Has this been going on for long?" Mikandra asked.

"This mob, no," Braedon said. Rehan stared in to the distance. He clearly liked this development as little as she did. "They came out in support of the Ilendar family, but it was too late for them. Look."

There was the Ilendar house, or what was left of it. Most noble houses were built from a stone shell surrounding an interior structure made from plates of pressed straw and cement. While they sheltered against the cold, they were also flammable.

Blackened walls were all that remained of the house, silhouetted against the quickly darkening sky. Wisps of smoke still rose from the ruins.

Slogans had been scrawled on the walls. *Miran first* and *Rich people out*. The gates into the yard had been ripped off their hinges. Scores of sooty footsteps led in and out of the yard, some accompanied by drag marks. A half-burnt chair stood as sad sentinel in the middle of the yard, the seat covered in a thin layer of snow.

Mikandra shivered and remembered the times that she'd skipped through the gate and entered the house's huge kitchen. Remembered the smell of cooking. Remembered Aithno Ilendar seated at the table with his reader.

All gone.

Looters had gone through the possessions the family had been forced to leave behind.

In the next street, they ran into another barricade of rocks and bins and half-burned furniture stacked across the road.

Tarlen stopped the sled and for a moment all was silent. He rose and peered into the misty dusk.

Taerzo said, "Whoa, this didn't used to be here when we left."

"They're friendly," Tarlen said. "At least they were when I came this way." There was tension in his voice.

A few furred shapes detached from the mist and came towards the sled.

To the right were the stately houses with walled yards of the Endri quarter. Her own house was there somewhere, but it seemed Mother and Liseyo didn't live there anymore.

Four men came out from behind the barricade. They were all Endri, three administrators' sons from the Takumar and Azthunar families. One was Thaeron Tussamar's younger brother, a gangly man younger than Mikandra. He held a gun, pointed at the ground in relaxed fashion.

Mikandra stiffened. Did he know that his brother was in the lockup at Guild headquarters for attempting to shoot her?

"These are not allies," she whispered to Braedon.

His face was tense. On the opposite bench, Rehan sat with his jaw clenched and both hands under his cloak. A predator ready to spring.

Taerzo got off the sled. He spoke to the men, and there was some shoulder clapping and shaking of hands, accompanied by sideways looks at the sled. Not entirely happy. Their cheer was an act.

Taerzo climbed back into the sled.

"Go, quickly!" he whispered under his breath. "Before they change their minds."

The driver flicked the reins and the animals pulled uphill, grumbling and snorting.

Mikandra felt the suspicious gazes of the four men on her as the sled passed. Tarlen spurred the animals on and they ran, snorting and blowing steam. The snow had become heavier.

The sled whooshed through alleys with slogan-riddled walls and overflowing rubbish bins on both sides. One or two maramarang flapped away, disturbed in their scavenging of frozen food scraps.

A few turns later, the sled pulled up at the Andrahar house.

Normally, servants would have cleared the snow, but it had blown in the corners against the walls.

The gates, which she had never seen closed, were shut. Taerzo jumped from the sled and pushed aside a heap of snow so that he could open the gate. It creaked.

When Mikandra climbed from the sled and slung her bag over her shoulder, the front door of the house opened, and a child yelled, "There he is!"

Two small figures ran into the yard.

"Daddy, Daddy!"

Taerzo ran to meet them. He swept both boys in his arms and swung them around.

A couple of people had come to the porch. Mikandra recognised Isandra, Gillay and Calliandra and a middle-aged woman wearing an apron who had to be the family's cook.

Calliandra now came down the stairs and met Taerzo and the boys in the yard in a big group hug.

"I'm surprised to see you here," he said.

"The house isn't in a safe area." She lowered her voice. "Your mother sent Tarlen to collect us this morning. I think she has finally realised that the boys may be all she's going to see in the way of heirs for a long time."

"I have some news for you on that front. Let's go inside. It's freezing."

Mikandra followed the couple onto the veranda, feeling a bit lost and awkward.

Gillay smiled at her, and the cook bowed, but Isandra's eyes were searching and penetrating. She was slightly shorter than Mikandra, with a sharp face and the same long nose as Rehan. Her hair hung, very proper, loose over her shoulders. It was whiter than the snow in the yard.

"Well, it's you again."

Taerzo protested. "Mother, she is the only reason—"

"Quiet, son." She kept meeting Mikandra's eyes. An icy breeze blasted through the yard. It blew her cloak aside, but the biting cold didn't seem to bother her. "It looks like you are hard to get rid of. That must mean you're part of the family, much as I despise that traitor of a father of yours. He may have replaced his sister, but he isn't half, not a quarter as deserving of the position of High Councillor as she is. Pity she was too weak to stay."

"Mother, stop it—"

"It's all right," Mikandra said. Her father, High Councillor? "Tell me whatever you think of my father, but don't judge me by his actions. If I agreed with him, would I stand here?"

Isandra snorted. "If you agreed with him, you'd probably be on the barricades with the other louts. They're stupid, the lot of them, and Miran will pay the price for that stupidity." She turned around abruptly. "There's dinner on the table."

Mikandra followed Braedon inside. Taerzo still had his arm around Calliandra.

Rehan grinned, the first smile she'd seen from him since coming to Miran. "Just so that you know, being hard to get rid of is Mother's way of making a compliment."

"She's even worse than you."

He grinned. "I didn't get it from a stranger, then."

I NSIDE THE HOUSE, it was ridiculously warm.

Mikandra shed the cloak in the hall. Gillay took it from her and looked at the collar. Her eyes widened. "Where did you get this?"

"Braedon gave it to me."

"This was Master Jihan's. I thought all his clothes were still in the bedroom."

"I'm sorry, I didn't know. I didn't mean to—"

Braedon said, "I gave it to her, Gillay. It was either that or nothing."

Gillay clearly didn't like it. Jihan Andrahar had been a legendary figure, and there were some, including in this family, who had never accepted that the crash that claimed his life—into the eastern highlands—had been an accident. With a family this old, you couldn't go far without running into intrigue and suspicion. The house was filled with history and every item had meaning.

Soon, the hall was a chaos of shoes and wet puddles and two mounds of fur that were the boys' cloaks.

Isandra told her grandsons off for not hanging up their cloaks. "If you want to be like your father—and heaven knows who'd ever want to be like him—you better start cleaning up after yourselves."

The boys came back, wearing only socks, looking demure, and hung up their cloaks.

"And greet your new honorary auntie, Mikandra."

They bowed politely, eyes wide and their faces in such an acted display of meekness that Mikandra felt like laughing.

The boys were identical in everything, and introduced themselves as Miruhan and Iztho. The latter name surprised her, but then she remembered that Calliandra's father had also been Iztho.

Mikandra had to hunt for slippers that fitted her, because Calliandra was using the ones that she had used last time when she was at the house.

Dinner had been set not in the dining room but at the large table in the living room, where Mikandra had spent the night checking books.

All those books were now gone, and the table had been moved further to the middle so that there was plenty of room for chairs on all sides. The family's fine tableware stood neatly arranged at each seat. There was a bowl of fresh bread in the middle and twelve plates on the table. Mikandra counted only eight people.

Braedon said, "Mother, we've gone to Kedras for a couple of days, and you are already trying to use up all our stores. What are we going to eat for the rest of winter? How are we going to get enough fire bricks to keep us warm?"

"We will see," Isandra said. "I'm sure that if it is necessary, we will find a solution. I want us to have one more old-fashioned dinner, like we used to have."

"We haven't eaten here for years."

"Since your father died, in fact," she said. "Those were times of happiness. Once more, let us be happy."

"How can we be happy? The streets outside are a battle zone."

"Tonight, we will pretend not to notice."

"But all the best tableware . . . What's going on, Mother?"

"Tonight, I'm doing something I should have done a long time ago—"

A door opened and shut elsewhere in the house. There was the sound of voices from the hall.

"Ah. There they are."

Three people came into the hall and rummaged in the shoe rack to find slippers. The first, to Mikandra's huge surprise, was Eydrina Lasko, red-cheeked from the cold. The other two were an adult and a child, wrapped in their cloaks. Someone said, "Mikandra?" The voice was a child's, timid and familiar.

Mikandra's heart jumped.

Was that. . . ?

She went into the hall past Gillay and Taerzo who still stood at the door.

"Mother, Liseyo!"

Mikandra crossed the hall in a few steps into both their arms. She buried her face in Mother's dress. "You're all right! I was so worried."

Tears ran down Mother's cheeks. "I thought I'd never see you again. Look at you." She held Mikandra by the shoulder with one hand while wiping her cheeks with the back of her other hand. "Wearing the uniform already. And you look so healthy. Your face has colour."

Mikandra held her arm next to Liseyo's. Her skin had become noticeably darker in Barresh.

"I heard that Father is in the High council. What happened? You left the house?"

Mother's face twitched. "He blamed me for what you did. For days and days, he'd rant at me at the dinner table while Liseyo was watching. He blamed me for having useless daughters. He blamed me for your refusal to marry Geonan Takumar. It was all because I wasn't any good." She took in a deep breath, nostrils flaring. She had lost weight and the wrinkles on her face had grown. And now that the first shock of meeting them was gone, Mikandra noticed other things, like the mouldy smell of Mother's clothes.

She continued in a low voice. "It was worse at night. One day, Liseyo walked into the bathroom and she saw where he'd . . . hit me. And then she said she would stand up for me like you had done for her. I was afraid and I told her not to, because he would hit her, too. And then . . ." Her lip trembled. "One day it was really bad. He always hurt me where people couldn't tell . . . if you understand what I mean."

Her eyes were intense.

Mikandra couldn't bite her lip hard enough to stop the tears. "I'm so sorry."

"Don't be. It's because of you that I had the courage to get up when he was asleep and leave the house."

"Didn't he come after you?"

"Yes, but I told my sister everything and her husband protected me. Their house is not very big and they have his mother living with them. We've moved into a place of our own now."

But they clearly had no money for heating or new clothes. "How do you survive?"

"I mend clothes for a couple of families. People from the theatre have given us money." She didn't meet Mikandra's eyes. All her life she would have been taught that accepting charity was shameful.

"You should have told me."

"I couldn't. Rosep said you'd gone to Kedras."

"You only needed to have asked at the office. They would have contacted me."

Poor, poor Mother. Always timid, trying not to upset people, living in the shadow of Father. Leaving the house must have been a huge step for her.

"Enough with the sad stories now," Isandra said. "Sit down everyone."

Everyone chose seats at the table. Mikandra sat next to Liseyo, whose eyes seemed bigger than her face. Isandra made a big fuss over Taerzo and Calliandra who had to sit closest to the hearth, and next to each other.

Isandra remained standing at the head of the table.

"Tonight, we celebrate happiness. I wanted this to be a special occasion, and that is why I've invited Eydrina. Taerzo, Calliandra." She held out both hands. "It's time that we right the mistakes of the past. I should have given you the big wedding with the parade and the ceremony at the Foundation monument.

Unfortunately, we can't do that today, so we may need to save that for another day. Today, however, you will be married before Mirani law." She went to a cabinet against the back wall, took something out and came back to the table with a familiar box. The wedding armbands.

Taerzo was still staring at his mother. "Why this? Why now?"

"Shhh." Calliandra touched his arm. He gave her a bewildered look, and she smiled at him, clearly in on the plan.

Then he gaped at his sons. The twins, on Calliandra's other side, sat very quiet. Not their usual behaviour at all. One of them gave his father an innocent smile.

Taerzo laughed, but the tone of his voice betrayed that he was deeply moved. "You plan my life in my absence, huh? Don't you want a big party?"

Isandra said, "At the moment, neither our fellow Endri nor our city deserves a party at our expense—if you would come forward to speak the vows please, Eydrina."

Eydrina took the box off the table. She must have left the room to change, because she now wore a gold and red embroidered marriage celebrant's robe. Mikandra remembered that her former tutor also did weddings.

The ceremony was very simple. Taerzo and Calliandra stood before the hearth, holding hands. Eydrina made a speech of love in the past and future. She looked ethereal and goddesslike in that gown, with her bushy hair falling down her back. She took the armbands out of the box and opened them both. Taerzo and Calliandra each put their left arm on the cushion on the table and Eydrina fitted the armbands, first around Calliandra's wrist and then Taerzo's. The locks shut with a definitive snap. Taerzo and Calliandra faced each other. Eydrina unclipped the chain from the armbands. No, there were two chains—that was unusual.

Then she asked the boys to stand up, which they did, putting on their best well-behaved faces.

"Miruhan, Iztho. I'm going to ask you a big thing today for boys your age. As oldest sons, you must look out for your family. You must look out for your parents when they get older. You must also promise to look after each other, and any brothers or sisters you may still get. Do you promise that?"

Both boys nodded vigorously.

Ah, Mikandra thought she understood.

The secret of why they held the ceremony now rather than when all the trouble was over, clearly rested with the sentence *any brothers or sisters you may still get.* Calliandra was pregnant.

While Eydrina fastened the chains around the boys' necks, Mikandra glanced at Rehan. At the head of the table, he sat furthest from her. His eyes met hers, and he kept looking at her until she had to turn away from his intense expression.

Gillay and the cook brought in steaming dishes of soup, and bread, and beans in cream sauce, and perfectly cooked fish.

"Mother really *is* trying to run down our stores," Taerzo said while lifting the lid on a tray.

"I told you so," said Braedon. "It's not like our pantry is full and good food is easy to get. And if the fighting continues—"

Isandra slammed her hand on the table. "Stop it, sons. I want to hear no further word about it. We have *one* evening of good food, and then we can go back to what is necessary to survive the low-winter. Gillay, sit down."

The housekeeper's eyes widened. "At the table with you?"

"Didn't you hear me?"

"But . . . mistress . . ." Gillay's cheeks had gone red.

"You have been part of Taerzo's life since he was born. We appointed you when it turned out that I was pregnant long after Braedon had gone to school. You stood by me while my peers made fun of me. You, and a much younger Eydrina were with me that long night when he was born. As you may remember, it was not an easy birth. Sit down. You're part of our family."

Gillay did as she was told, after taking off her apron. She still looked very uncomfortable.

They started eating. Mikandra had finished her soup in no time. It was rich, creamy and just the right blend of delicate spices.

People from elsewhere would make fun of Mirani food, because in the hands of an unskilled cook, it was awful. A good cook, however, could turn it into a highly refined meal.

Liseyo had also finished her plate and had started on a second one.

Isandra was looking at her. "Eat up, eat up. You are much too thin. You need some meat on those bones."

"Thank you so much for this," Mother said. "I don't even know where to begin. Winter has not been kind to us."

"You have your daughter to thank. You can stay with us as long as your daughter is part of our business and as long as you need."

"Thank you so much." Mother's voice trembled.

"I think Mother likes having girls around," Braedon said. "I think she's trying to pay us back for having to live in a house with five men."

Isandra said, "Together, girls are stronger. If we stand together as a family, we will be stronger. The world outside this house is no longer a friendly place."

They ate and drank. It got late. Mikandra almost cried when she heard that wonderful sound, Liseyo's laughter, ring through the room when playing a game of dice with the twins.

Whenever she looked in his direction, she kept meeting Rehan's eyes across the table, as if he spent all night looking at her. And whenever she looked his way—which she could not stop doing—her cheeks glowed.

She hoped no one noticed.

34

ONE BY ONE, the people started to go to their rooms to sleep. Braedon said he was tired, Taerzo and Calliandra took the boys upstairs and did not come back.

When Isandra commented on that, Braedon said, "Give them some privacy on their wedding night."

Gillay went to show Mother and Liseyo where they would sleep. "I have you three in the upstairs guest room. Two of you will have to share the big bed in there."

They looked tired, and Liseyo's red cheeks were a telltale sign that this was the first time in a long while that they had been warm.

"I'll come up soon," Mikandra said.

They left the room and then she was left in the chairs by the fire with only Rehan and Isandra.

"You did well, Mother," Rehan said.

"Hmph. They'd been together so long that neither of them was ever going to marry anyone else."

"I worry about the future. There's going to be so much trouble this winter."

"You will just have to lead the family through it."

"You don't think Iztho will be back at all?"

"Not for a while. He always wanted to play music. He said so at every opportunity, but no one took him seriously. He told me he's found someplace where he can start again and where his name means nothing."

"Does he know about his son?"

"He does, but I think it was as much a surprise to him as everyone."

"Are you planning to contact the lady?"

"Eventually, but I'll wait until the anger is less raw and the lady has forgiven him."

"I think she already may have," Mikandra said, and they both looked at her. "I met the lady. Her husband is . . . strange. That's all I can say about him. Creeps me out. I don't know why she's with him. There must be a reason other than love. They like each other well enough, but I think she still loves Iztho."

"He snapped. We allowed him to drift away and he snapped," Rehan said.

"Don't keep blaming yourself," Mikandra said.

"We are to blame, all of us."

Isandra said, "Jihan should never have torn into him so much when he came across Iztho performing in the Trader bar. There was no reason for it, and Iztho hasn't been the same since. He turned inward. He stopped singing for us. I love his voice. Maybe he is a better singer than Trader. I'm sure he'll do well. When he comes back, we'll welcome him."

"Much needs to change," Rehan said. "We need to look after each other better. I love you, Mother. I know I was always closer to Father than you, but that doesn't mean I don't love you."

Isandra laughed, her eyes scrunched up with wrinkles. "I see the female company has made you soft already, my son." She sighed and pushed herself up from her chair. "Well, I'm tired, and everyone else is upstairs, so I think I'll join them and go to bed. Behave yourself." She winked and crossed the room to the door in the far wall.

What the hell was that about?

Mikandra met Rehan's eyes. He shook his head. "Mother worries me, sometimes. Come, I'll show you the room where your mother and sister are."

He slipped the cloak on his shoulders and went before her

through the cold hall and up the stairs. It was very cold and dark here, and Mikandra had to step carefully.

By the feeble glow of an oil light, she could make out a square hallway with four ornate wooden doors, all of them closed.

Rehan pointed at the door in the far right corner. "You sleep here. Gillay will have taken your things inside. The large bed is in the middle of the room. The smaller one is against the side wall to your right."

He hesitated and shrugged. "Well then, good night. My room is this one." The door at the top of the stairs.

After an awkward silence, she said, "Thank you."

"No, I should thank you for what you did today. There are no words for how much." He hesitated. "If I ever appear to be pushing you and am never satisfied, it is because I believe in you. I'm only nice and polite to the people I don't care about."

She laughed. "That's the oddest compliment I've ever had."

"I mean it."

He did, she could hear that in the very tone of his voice. He was so intense, her laughter seemed inappropriate. And people were trying to sleep behind those doors and she might wake them up.

There was an awkward silence.

"All right then, I'll go to sleep." She didn't know what else to say. She turned to the door, half-expecting—

"Mikandra."

She turned around again.

"The best things in life are the things we fight for, because the passion comes from within."

She nodded. She could relate to that. "You're very philosophical today. I'm not used to that. What happened to all the swear words?"

"You are the best thing that's happened to us for a long time. The best thing that's happened to me. I'm going to fight for you."

"What's that supposed to mean?"

"It means . . ." He came even closer to her, reached out and touched her cheek. His hand trembled. "It means I'm sorry for being stupid. If you think I'm a dick, I've probably deserved it. I'd very much like to prove that I'm not." His eyes were incredibly intense, the same expression they had carried during most of dinner. And she wanted to keep looking at him, but it was embarrassing, because she didn't want to go down the same path she'd been with Lihan. She *thought* he cared for her and it turned out that he didn't.

But here was his hand touching the soft skin on the side of her neck. His thumb caressed the line of her jaw. It was a pleasant sensation.

He continued in a low voice, "The truth is, I don't know what to say and that never happens to me. I always know how to bullshit myself out of some situation. Except now. I don't want to talk bullshit. This means too much to me. I'd like to be closer to you."

She said, flippantly, "You'll just have to marry me then." She laughed.

But he was staring at her. "You said . . ."

She was going to say *I was joking* but she wasn't. She'd had the thought before, about successful Trading couples.

"Are you serious?"

"I guess I could be, if you wanted me to."

He smiled as much as one can smile without actually smiling. His voice sang. "Well, lady, then you must do this properly. Here —" He slipped his cloak off his shoulders and handed it to her. It was warm and heavy in her hands. Now what?

"Come on, you play my role. If you're serious. If you're a kind of woman who wants to feel the heat and live as close to the fire as possible. If you think you can put up with a dick like me."

"You're not a dick." She spoke softly. "You like putting on a hard face with your rigid discipline and swear words. You terrify people who don't see through that façade. You care about hard work, you care about family, even though you'll swear at them. But your language is bluff. You care about doing the right thing. But underneath it, you are a deeply emotional man. In the letters you wrote, I saw someone intelligent, caring, engaging, someone . . ." her voice caught. ". . . someone desperately in need of love and a place of the deepest trust. I can only imagine what you must feel like when other people's lives encroach on your thoughts, knowing about your aunt and the way she's treated. I can only imagine the fear that you have inside and you cannot voice to anyone. The fear that you will go mad." She felt for the collar of the cloak. "The man who swears at employees and who turns off when emotional things are discussed is not the man I've seen. I don't want to live and work with *that* man." She raised the cloak. Her hands trembled. "But the man who pokes me when I'm lazy, who challenges me, who tells me his fears and happiness, and who is not afraid to cry in my presence, that is a man I want."

She had to reach up to put the cloak on his shoulders. While she reached over him, he grabbed both her arms, pulled her into the warmth under his cloak. When Lihan had kissed her, she'd been shocked, but now she knew what would happen. When his lips met hers, she was ready and kissed him back. He groaned softly, running his hands over her back. Shivers of delight ran through her. This was good. This was meant to be.

She lost herself in his warmth and thinking about nothing else except kissing and touching.

A door opened and closed in the hallway. A child giggled.

Rehan withdrew. "Damn Taerzo's boys," he said, kissing her softly on the nose. His breath was heavy. "Little rascals."

"Never mind them." She ran her lips along the line of his jaw and found his lips again. This was very addictive. She could get used to this.

The door opened again, and someone came into the hall with a light. "Miruhan, how many times do I have to tell you to—oh!"

Taerzo.

Rehan let her go.

"I'm sorry, I didn't know . . ." Taerzo grinned and then laughed.

"Well, yeah . . . Um. We were . . . busy." Rehan's cheeks had gone bright red. That was incredibly cute.

"Sorry. I didn't mean to interrupt." Both boys stood behind him, trying to catch a glimpse of the hallway. "This is . . . unexpected. Is this official?"

"For us, it is. We'll get around to telling everybody eventually. For now we might want to keep it quiet."

"Well," Taerzo said. "As long as you stand here, my sons are not going to sleep. They're just going to be giggling their heads off, so you can either go to bed in your allocated rooms, or in the same room. It's all equal to me."

He turned around, and shut the door behind him, plunging the hall into darkness. Taerzo's voice drifted through the door. Calliandra replied, laughing.

"Taerzo is a clown," Rehan said.

"But I like him."

"Yeah. Our family needs a clown." Rehan kissed her on the top of her forehead. "But he's right. We better go to sleep. There's a lot of things that need to be done tomorrow." He hesitated. "Unless you are happy to keep me company." She could hear the hope in his voice.

"Isn't a young and pretty bride meant to be a virgin?"

A small surprised silence. He frowned. "What? Are you kidding? Did Lihan never . . ."

"Nope. He kissed me, once." And never spoke to her afterwards. Why had she wasted all this time waiting for him?

He laughed. "Oh, I love the arsehole right now." Then his face turned serious. "I leave it up to you. It won't change my feelings either way. I guess I can be patient, if I have to."

Mikandra hesitated. She could say yes and sleep in someone's arms on this tense and horrible night. Feel safe for the first time since leaving Miran.

Still, she had to face the hard questions first. She did not want to be left hanging again. "What about the family succession? I carry the infertility curse."

"Fuck that. I'd say between themselves, my brothers have that part sorted out. I don't need children. I need a companion. You know, we just saw Ydana Ezmi and your aunt get together. They've been lovers for—what? Thirty years?"

"She met him when they were at the academy."

"I don't want to end up like that. It was the saddest thing I've seen for a long time. Here were these two old people . . ." His voice sounded unsteady. "And I could see myself in her. Because

Mother had been talking about getting married and she'd been scouting out some candidates. They were all limp, faceless, weak girls."

She slowly reached out for him, felt the tenseness of his muscles under his shirt. She pulled him closer until their lips met. His heart thudded against his ribcage.

After a short kiss, he broke free. "I take that as a yes? It's lot warmer in the room than it is out here."

She glanced at the door behind him. "Is this your room?"

"You're welcome, lady." His voice vibrated with happiness.

She opened the door.

The room was warm with the glow of fire. The bed stood in the far corner, covered with a fur blanket. There was a desk next to the door, with various items of gadgetry dumped on the surface. Two readers, a timer and a few other things of which she had no idea what they did. A carpet was soft underfoot. Mikandra stopped a few paces into the room while Rehan shut the door behind her. He came from behind, took his cloak off his shoulders and hung it over the chair at the desk.

"Welcome to my domain, which has never seen a visit by a woman who was not either in my family or employed by my family."

"Never?"

"Never. I've had a good number of lady friends, but none serious enough to bring here. But now everything has changed. I have you."

He took her in his arms and kissed her softly. Then he drew back and looked into her eyes. She was shocked to see that a tear ran over his cheek. He wiped it off.

"Look at me, I'm on my knees, reduced to a trembling wreck. This is my promise to you. I will train you, teach you to fly and I will rent you a private unit at the Guild headquarters, and I will spend any night there that I don't have to be anywhere else. Then, on the day you're handed your medallion, I will call you into the Guild bar and propose formally to you for the eyes of the Guild and anyone I care about. I will never leave your side. You will never be alone. We will work together and be the greatest Trading couple there ever was."

"Sounds good to me." Her voice sounded oddly high. All of a sudden, she fought with emotion as well. All her life she'd been told not to expect a marriage of mutual respect because of her infertility. Tears blurred her vision.

Rehan laughed. "Look at us."

She said, "You are the best thing that has happened to me."

He undid the buttons of his shirt and then hers. While he kissed her, his hand trailed over the naked skin on her belly. It gave her delightful shivers. She pushed his shirt off his shoulders. It rustled to the floor down his back. His pale skin glowed in the low light, with the family crest tattoo clear on his shoulder. When she touched him, the skin broke into goosebumps.

"You are one crazy woman," he whispered. "I want you so much. I've wanted you ever since you came to us that night. You could have gone home, but you didn't. You insisted in helping us. You will make it, and we will be the greatest Trading couple there ever was—come you're shivering."

He picked her up and set her down on the bed. He pulled up the covers and she slipped between the sheets in the smell of mountain air. Clean, soft, comfortable. He crept in next to her and folded her in his arms. His lips found hers.

For a long time, they kissed luxuriously, with all the time in the world. There was no hurry, there was no fear that parents would find out. They explored each other's bodies in increasingly hungry ways. He teased her, tickled her, kissed her in places no one had ever touched, until she begged him to go that one place where no one had been before.

He did.

He made love with the passion of a man who'd waited for years while his brother was fooling around delaying to get married. Of someone who watched his younger brother flout all the rules while trying to uphold those rules in the name of tradition. With the passion of someone who'd turned all his anger into ambition and found his life empty of love. Of a man terrified of being left alone, and terrified of being found to be emotional. And he was emotional. Passionate, not particularly gentle, and intensely vulnerable in the way he opened up for her. She saw a face that was secret from the rest of the world. A face etched with an intense desire to be loved and to find satisfaction. And considerate enough to give her the same.

When it was done, he lay with his head on her chest. She stroked his hair. He sniffed and wiped his eyes, but left a wet track over his cheek.

"Not afraid to show my emotions, huh?"

"You will do fine." She held him close, their hearts beating close to each other.

He said, his voice hoarse, "When my father died, I thought my world ended. Iztho is very close to Mother, and I adored Father. He was my inspiration, my life, my source of energy. He was why I wanted to be a Trader and how I wanted to be a Trader. When I got the news of his death, my life stopped. At the funeral, I was convinced that my heart would stop beating and I would die. I wanted to die so badly."

Mikandra only vaguely remembered the funeral, but she did remember how people, even years after the event, had spoken of Rehan, then barely an adolescent, giving the main speech. Unemotional, they said. He cannot feel anything. Too distant. How wrong had they been.

"When the accident happened . . . I went into a deep hole for many years. I couldn't relate to Mother, or anyone else. I thought I'd never love again. I was wrong. I knew it the moment you started arguing that you wanted to stay and help us. I poked you to see how you reacted. I knew for certain when you worked with us through the night. I don't want a matron who brings me food and asks me what I want to drink. I want a Trader who argues back and tells me that I'm an idiot when I deserve it. What you did today just blew me away. You are the best thing that has happened to me—no, don't say anything to belittle it."

So she said nothing. He stroked her gently and she was starting to feel very sleepy.

The fire was going out. He got out of bed—stark naked—to move the screen in front of the fire, and came back. After another long and deep kiss, she settled herself in the warm hollow against his body, and fell asleep.

35

"REHAN!"

There was a loud banging on the door.

"Rehan, are you awake?"

"The fuck I am, now." The heavy, comfortable warmth disappeared from Mikandra's back and the bed covers lifted, letting in icy air.

"Rehan, come, quickly!"

The door opened, and Braedon came in, carrying a light. He stopped in the middle of the room. Looked at Mikandra, who had pulled up the covers to hide the fact that she was completely naked.

"Oh." His mouth fell open. "I'm sorry."

Rehan stood on one leg, trying to wriggle his other leg into his trousers. He was also completely naked.

"Oh," Braedon said again, looking confused more than anything. "I didn't realise . . ."

"What's going on? What the fuck is the time?" Rehan pulled up his trousers, fished his shirt from the floor and shoved his feet into his boots.

He followed Braedon into the hall.

Taerzo and Calliandra were at the top of the stairs, the ghostly light from the single oil light on the wall lighting their faces. Calliandra was wide-eyed, her face pale. The twins hung onto her cloak.

Rehan shut the door behind him, plunging the room once more into darkness.

The sound of shouts drifted from outside.

Mikandra leaned out of the bed to light the lamp. She picked up the shirt she'd discarded on the floor last night. Put it on. Found her trousers. Put those on, too, although she felt more like having a bath. Her legs were sticky and itchy with dried slime. There were streaks of blood on the sheet, too. No doubt about what had happened there last night. She had bled like a good virgin.

She briefly drifted off into happiness. Marriage was something that had always seemed a threat to her. She was worthless as a true marriage prospect, only to be good as a plaything. The fact that it need not be like that came as revelation. A very happy revelation.

But the bubble of happiness burst with the urgent sound of voices outside. She grabbed her cloak off the chair and went into the hallway. Her ankle protested with each step. It felt stiff and painful.

Rehan just came out of one of the other rooms, strapping his gun bracket to his upper arm. He kissed her on her forehead, a fleeting feeling of comfort in this harsh awakening.

"What's going on?" she asked.

"Have a look," Rehan jerked his head at the door of one of the other rooms, which stood open. Then he looked somewhere over her shoulder. "Oh, I think you'd best get changed, too."

Mikandra turned. Mother and Liseyo stood at the door of the guest room in their night gowns. Mother's eyes were wide. Her voice was soft and frightened. "The mobs have broken through the perimeter."

"Afraid so," Rehan said.

"The guards must stop them."

"I fear some of the guards have joined them. We are Miran's enemy. I'll see if we can stop them coming into the yard." His eyes met Mikandra's. "Our first priority is our safety. Gather everyone downstairs in the hall. Get Mother and Gillay out of bed. Wait for us down there."

"Be careful," she whispered.

He touched her cheek. "Hey, I've been through tougher scrapes. Go." He winked. "Love you."

Mikandra went into the guest room where Mother and Liseyo were getting changed. Her bag stood there, untouched, on the single bed against the wall.

"Did you even go to sleep?" Mother asked her. "The bed is untouched."

"Um . . ." *How about we discuss that later?* Hadn't she seen Rehan kiss her?

There was a loud bang outside and an orange glow flared up.

Mikandra pushed the curtain aside.

A large group of people, showing up as dark shapes with some holding torches, had gathered outside the locked gate. One or two men rattled the bars.

"Someone should go and talk to them," Mother said at her shoulder.

"You can't talk to these people. We're an enemy of the kind of nation they want Miran to be."

"Did you do anything to cause this?"

"Discover the truth. Nemedor Satarin is a criminal. Come, hurry up. We need to go downstairs."

"I can't find my socks," Liseyo cried.

Mother went to the large bed where she and Liseyo had slept and dropped to her knees.

The shouts outside intensified. A group of men surged against the gate. One figure stood on the shoulders of others and managed to get a leg over the fence.

Someone shouted from the window in the next room—it sounded like Braedon. "Keep out! I'm warning you!"

Someone in the mob responded by throwing a burning torch over the wall. It fell midway between the gate and the house and lay in the snow in its own little puddle of firelight.

"Hurry up, Liseyo." Mikandra was shivering. The memory of Thaeron shooting at her was too fresh in her mind. There was no way they could defend the house if the gate broke.

Finally, Liseyo had found all her things.

"Quick, go downstairs."

Mother left the room first. They went past the open door to the next room—Braedon's, Mikandra thought. Two of the brothers showed as silhouettes against the glow of fire. Mikandra couldn't tell who they were. She hesitated. She didn't want to leave Rehan here. If this mob set fire to the house, the upstairs bedroom was a stupid place to be. But Mother and Liseyo were already halfway down, and she'd promised Rehan that she'd get Isandra out of bed.

Just as she was about to go down the stairs, there was a loud crash outside.

"They've pushed open the gate," Braedon yelled.

Heavy footsteps strode across the room. "Open the window." That was Rehan.

Someone slid the window open.

"Stop right there or I'll shoot!" Rehan shouted.

Voices cheered in the courtyard.

Mikandra ran the few steps back up the stairs to the door of the room. At the moment she looked in, a blinding flash went off.

"That was a warning," Rehan said, while lowering the weapon. Then he said in a low voice, "I wish I wasn't such a bad shot. I couldn't hit anything if my life depended on it."

"You better start improving your aim, brother," Taerzo said. "Because right now, your life does depend on it."

There was a clinking sound on the roof below the window and an orange glow came in.

Rehan yelled, "Fuck, they're throwing oil!"

Taerzo grabbed the washbasin off the table next to the bed and threw its contents out the window. It was no use. The fire was leaking down the entire side of the roof, setting the gutter alight.

"Everyone, get out, now," Rehan yelled. He met Mikandra's eyes. "What are you still doing here? Come on, get Mother."

She ran down the stairs.

Calliandra was waiting in the hall, shielding the boys under her cloak. On the ground floor, the smell of smoke was already starting to penetrate the hallway. As they walked past the kitchen door, a crash sounded above them and a piece of burning wood fell through the ceiling. One of the boys screamed.

Shouts of the attackers rose over the roar of the fire.

"Go with them, out the kitchen door," she shouted to Mother and Liseyo.

Mikandra ran into the living room, where the remains of last night's dinner had been cleared after she and Rehan left last night and a lifetime ago.

Through the living room.

There were further crashes on the roof above. *Rehan.*

"Isandra!" She banged on the door and opened it.

An eerie orange glow outside the window lit the room. There had been no fire in the hearth overnight. All the firebricks still stood neatly stacked in the corner.

"Isandra? Wake up." She walked into the room, but clearly, no one was there. The bed was untouched. Smoke was already leaking in from the ceiling.

What was going on? She'd seen Isandra go into the room last night.

She went back to the door. "Gillay!"

There was a huge crash and part of the back of Isandra's room fell in. Burning debris crashed into the room and took down half the ceiling. Mikandra ran into the living room, with debris falling down beside her. Past the glass cabinet that held the—

Wait.

With all her strength, she shoved against the cabinet's side. Her ankle protested with a sharp pain. The cabinet toppled and fell sideways with a clatter. The glass sides disintegrated, spilling its precious contents over the floor. Hundreds of years of Mirani history scattered over the floor.

Mikandra shoved shards of glass aside, and picked up the one thing in this house that had more value than anything else. The Foundation stone felt cold in her hands. She slipped the chain over her neck and hung the stone under her shirt.

The roar of fire in the house was deafening. The fire was not in this room yet, but the top floor of the house had to be well alight. Smoke poured from gaps between the ceiling and the walls. Breathing was starting to get difficult.

Out the living room, into the hall, where she found her boots. Where was everyone?

At the top of the stairs, she could only see an inferno.

"Rehan!"

He had to be outside, he had to be. She couldn't bear the alternative.

There was no answer in the roaring of the flames. Another beam fell through the ceiling near the front door with a crash of plaster and dust.

Mikandra raised the collar of her shirt over her mouth. She found the kitchen, managed to slide the bolts back and open the door.

She ran out onto the porch. A couple of dark figures stood at the far end of the veranda, not familiar ones. Male voices yelled, with Nikala accents. She clambered over the railing and let herself drop onto a pile of snow in the yard below. Ouch. Pain shot up her foot.

Someone yelled, "Here's one of them!"

Mikandra ran through the yard as fast as her ankle allowed. It was a hobble more than a run. She reached the back of the house and found the back gate, which led into a servants' alley, which was a lot wider than the usual passages between houses. There, she found a couple of people huddled under cloaks.

A woman's voice called, "Mikandra!"

"Mother."

She ran to Mikandra, and buried her head in her cloak, crying. Mikandra coughed from the smoke. Past her mother, she saw Braedon and Taerzo, Calliandra and the boys. Her heart jumped.

"Where is Rehan?"

"Still looking for Mother and Gillay," Braedon said.

No. No one could possibly still be in the house alive. The glow from the flames lit the entire neighbourhood. "I checked. Your mother wasn't in her room. The bed was untouched." She hadn't seen Gillay either. "Where is Rehan? Where is he?" She couldn't help it, her voice cracked. The alley blurred before her eyes. "Rehan!"

Mother put an arm around Mikandra's shoulders. "Shhh. He's a big boy. He can look after himself."

"Where is he? We were happy. We're going to be married. Finally, I was happy with my life. Why do bad things always happen when I'm happy? Why? Rehan!"

She huddled against Mother. On the other side of the wall, the fire popped and crackled. The glow of it hit the neighbours' house. There were people behind the windows, pale faces.

Male voices shouted on the other side of the wall. There was laughter and cheering.

The back gate yawned open. Orange glow from the fire cast a bright rectangle of light on the snow, but no one came through.

36

B RAEDON PUT a hand on Mikandra's shoulder. His eyes glittered. She hugged him, tears streaming down her face, thinking of how tender Rehan had been to her last night.

No, Rehan. How much more misfortune could the family stand?

A male voice yelled behind the wall.

Both Mikandra and Braedon whirled to look at the gate. A shadow of a running man grew on the snowy ground. Braedon raised his gun.

Taerzo did the same, yelling at Calliandra to duck.

Mother and Liseyo sheltered behind a rubbish bin. Calliandra pressed the boys against the wall and sheltered them with her cloak.

The person reached the gate, came through.

It was—

"Rehan!"

Braedon lowered the gun. Taerzo cheered, but at the same time, a flash erupted from somewhere within the yard. As if in slow motion, it hit Rehan square in the back. Blue light danced over his back and shoulders. He stopped running and fell face first into the snow.

There was a moment of silence, as if the world had stopped.

Mikandra screamed. Braedon ran to his brother's side and crouched in the snow. Mikandra helped him roll Rehan to his side. His eyes were closed, his face slack.

Mikandra met Braedon's eyes. They said, *too late.*

Mikandra couldn't move. All around her was silence. She could only hear her own ragged breathing, and the sound of her own heartbeat.

And Rehan's voice *When I got the news of my father's death, I thought I would die.*

No. No, no, no.

She fell to her knees, somehow found his hand. She pushed the sleeve up, pressed her fingers into the soft flesh of his wrist. Under the tips of her fingers, a vein pulsed.

Mikandra shouted, "Braedon, he's alive!"

But Braedon stood to the side of the door, peering into the glare and holding his gun. People were shouting in the yard, the attackers closing in.

"Rehan, can you hear me?" Mikandra shouted over the noise.

Rehan's mouth opened. His eyes were narrow slits. The irises *moved* under the eyelids.

He threw up. Coughed, and threw up more. Coughed, spitting slime onto the snow. But he was now breathing ragged breaths.

A volley of shots went overhead.

Taerzo was firing into the yard, but it was hard to see what was happening because of the mist and smoke and snow.

Taerzo screamed, "Can I have some help? I can't hold them back any longer!"

Braedon jumped up and reached for his gun. Discharges flashed in the darkness.

Mikandra stroked Rehan's hand. There was no way he could run. There was no way *she* could run with her busted ankle. They would have to defend this position and hope someone would help them. All the well-heeled Endri neighbours hid in their houses. There were lights on in upstairs bedrooms, and people standing in front of windows. In a flash, she thought, *Jocassa would never abandon anyone like this.*

"They're trying to climb the wall!" Taerzo shouted and then, "Fuck it, I'm out of charge."

Mikandra felt under Rehan's cloak for his gun, snapped it out of the arm bracket. Rehan raised a weak hand, probably to try and stop her.

"I'm all right," she said. "I used to go hunting with my father. Used to be a decent shot."

But hunting was with crossbows, and while she'd used guns, this particular one was unfamiliar. It was a lot heavier than the ones she'd used, too. Yet, she knew the drill. Turn it on, charge up—the light flashed—safety off. Liseyo watched with wide eyes, her face pale in the glow of the fire.

By the same light, Mikandra spotted the silhouette of a man climbing onto the wall. She was going to hand Taerzo the weapon, but there was no time. In one movement, she jumped to her feet, raised the gun and discharged. The charge went over the heads of Calliandra, the twins, Mother and Liseyo. It hit the top of the wall in a huge flash that blinded her. Did she hit anyone? She couldn't see for the steam of vaporised snow.

The men had stopped climbing the wall, she thought.

A roaring noise made the ground shake. A gust of wind blew through the alley.

Someone in the dark yelled, "What th' blazes is that?"

Another rough voice replied, "Oh man, let's get th' fuck out of here."

Two men ran past the open door.

There was another roar somewhere up in the mist. That sounded very much like an engine, like downward jets, to be precise.

"Th . . . there." It was Rehan's voice. His hand pointed, weakly, into the sky.

Beams of lights came on, piercing through the mist and smoke.

A huge black shape was coming down. An aircraft. Downward jets threw up a cloud of snow. Next, floodlights went on.

Mikandra stared up into the light. Wind tore at her hair.

"That's my aircraft," Braedon shouted, also looking up. His mouth hung open.

Slowly, and with the jets at full blast, the craft came down into the street. The door was open and someone stood in the entrance, someone chubby, hanging onto the side while reaching a hand out. "Come in, quickly!" The voice was female.

Taerzo cursed. "What the fuck—Gillay!" Then he laughed. "Come, get in. Calliandra, get the boys in!" He had to shout over the roaring of the jets. Powdery snow blew through the alley in great clouds.

While Calliandra and Gillay heaved the boys inside, Braedon and Taerzo lifted Rehan. Mikandra supported his head. He was shivering. His eyes were closed.

Liseyo climbed in, and Mother. Taerzo jumped in and together, they heaved Rehan onto the floor. Taerzo grabbed Mikandra's arm and pulled her up.

He shouted, "We're all in. Go!"

The engines roared before the door was shut, and snow whirled into the opening.

Mikandra dropped into the seat closest to the door. The engines roared, pressing her into the seat. Whoever was flying this thing wasn't very experienced.

Taerzo flung the door shut. "The fuck, Gillay."

"Young man, I still do not approve of that kind of language." This was another female voice, belonging to the pilot, someone in Mirani Trader uniform. Mikandra thought it was Aunt Amandra, but Taerzo said, "Mother?"

The pilot turned her head and indeed Taerzo was right.

"I didn't know you could fly."

"Your father believed that all the family should learn. At the time, I never thought I would need it."

"You've saved us all."

"We're not safe yet. The Exchange doesn't agree with us being here."

"Did you get a takeoff permit?"

"No time. They're protesting about that." She flicked on the radio-com. An emotionless voice said, "Unauthorised takeoff. Repeat, you do not have the permission to leave."

A beam of light cut across the snow-filled view of mist out the front window.

"They're already getting a fix on us," Taerzo said.

She turned the noise off. "We better be quick then."

"They'll shoot."

"Not as long as we're over the city."

Because the craft was using the downward jets, Isandra had to give the engines a lot of power, but the turbulence from them distorted the downward viewscreen. Down there, people probably scrambled to put other craft into the air in an attempt to force them down. Those craft would need to be defrosted first. For once, winter was in their favour. Mikandra also realised that this was why Isandra and Gillay had not been in bed: they'd been preparing the craft.

Isandra said, "Help me. Tell me which way to go."

A row of lights on the control panel flashed.

"That's a weapon's probe." Braedon slipped in the seat next to her. "I'll take the controls, if you want. It's going to get rough. Do you have permission to leave from the Exchange?"

"No." Isandra shifted aside. She seemed glad that he took over.

Braedon turned off the jets, and the craft became more quiet and more stable. However, turning off the jets meant that he had to speed up and tighten the circling pattern. The craft banked sharply. It was uncomfortable and disorienting.

"Where can we go if we have no Exchange slot?" Taerzo asked. "They'll follow us wherever in the country we go. As soon as we leave the airspace above the city, they'll shoot us down. We're trapped."

Mikandra said, "If you point the receiver to the west, do you think you can pick up Barresh?"

Braedon gave Mikandra a strange look.

She continued, "They've had a new core, and their signal is very strong."

"Most of it would be directed out of the atmosphere to the beginning of the anpar line. I can try." He fiddled with the settings. Listened, pressing the earpiece to his ear. "The signal is very weak, but I can pick it up here."

"It would be stronger at height, no? Away from the curve of the planet."

He frowned again. "Yes, it would. Definitely."

"So, instead of west, we go up, where no one dares shoot at us for fear that we'll crash into the city. We pick up Barresh and ask for a simple one-way transfer. It's not offworld, so there are no permits required."

Taerzo laughed. "Rehan, do you hear that? That girl of yours is a fucking genius."

"Mind your language," Isandra said.

"Rehan doesn't think it's serious unless it contains swear words."

"You're . . . a clown," Rehan said.

Calliandra and Mother had heaved him onto the bed. His eyes were half-open and unfocused and his skin was clammy.

Mikandra managed to get up from her seat and clamber past the twins and Liseyo over the sloping floor. She sat next to him on the bed. "Let me have a look at you."

He didn't protest. Calliandra passed her a med-kit.

She pulled the cloak away—it had a large burnt patch at the back and smelled of burnt hair. She undid the buttons and peeled Rehan's tunic open. The skin underneath was red, but not blistered. The blisters were all on his shoulder where the skin was angry and red and weeping clear fluid. She sprayed disinfectant on the skin she had caressed only last night. "That looks painful."

"It is," he said.

Taerzo said, "You took a direct hit. By rights, you should have been dead, brother."

"That proves my suspicions," Isandra said. "That is exactly why in the old days they used to behead those who were mad, never shoot them; the fire doesn't kill them."

Mikandra bandaged up Rehan's wound as best as she could with the emergency kit. Calliandra found a blanket and Mikandra mixed up some painkiller in a flask of stale water.

Braedon said from the pilot's seat, "Make sure he's strapped in. We're not clear. We've got someone on our tail." He was watching the rear viewscreens.

"Want any help?" Taerzo said. He took the co-pilot seat anyway.

The engines roared. The craft bumped and still circled higher and higher.

Taerzo put on the earpiece and fiddled with the comms panel.

"What are you doing?" Braedon asked.

"It's illegal to ignore communication, so I'm going to amuse them." He pressed some buttons.

"Helloo, who is that?" He put on a small voice.

He listened.

"No."

He listened again. "No. Just my brother and me."

Then he pressed another button and the voice of the Exchange operator came through the loudspeakers. "You mean, are there no adults on board at all? Who is flying the craft?"

"My brother. I told you."

The twins sat strapped in their seats, looking at each other with wide eyes.

"Your brother can fly?" the operator said.

"Yes."

"Aren't you a bit young for that?"

"Daddy taught us. He said it was a secret and not to tell anyone."

Miruhan started giggling and Iztho said, "Shhh, you don't want them to hear us!" So his brother covered his mouth with his hand but continued giggling.

The operator went on. "You are still climbing. Do you know how to land the craft?"

"Oh yeah, Daddy showed us. You got to press the blue button first and turn the lever up—"

Braedon was biting his lip. His shoulders shook with laughter.

"You do not touch the blue button, do you hear me?"

"But Daddy said—"

"No, take it from me, do not touch the blue button."

Another voice blasted into the cabin, in Coldi. "Unidentified craft, receiving. Please supply ID and destination."

Braedon balled his fist and pumped the air.

"Barresh?" Mikandra asked.

He nodded. "The problem is how to contact them without the Miran Exchange finding out what we're trying to do."

"Send them the coded ID," Isandra said. "It's old-fashioned, but still works."

Braedon did, without speaking.

The Mirani operator said, "I hear a voice in the cabin. Can you give me to the adult there?"

Taerzo said, "That was a man on the radio. I don't know what he said. I couldn't understand it."

A small silence. The Exchange would now be looking for another craft that may be in the area.

"Did this other voice ask you to say who you were?"

"Maybe. I couldn't hear. Do you think I should tell him?"

"Please, if your brother knows how to bring the aircraft down, tell him to do it now."

"But we're not there yet. We're going to see Jolan Izthunar. Because Daddy won't take us there."

"You can't. You'll have to use the Exchange."

"I know. We got the permit."

A long silence. Braedon was almost dying of laughter. His face was red and he fought to keep his mouth shut.

Then something scrolled over the screen in front of him.

His face turned serous. "Uh-oh. I think they've sent an interception craft to pick us up."

"Time to stop clowning. Did you get a reply about the ID?"

Braedon shook his head. "They're probably scrambling over themselves to locate the ancient decoder."

"No time to wait. Get them direct."

Braedon switched the channel and gave Barresh their calling number. He spoke Coldi very well.

The voice replied, "You request transfer *to Barresh?*"

"Yes."

"I'm afraid I don't understand. You are in Barresh."

"No, we're not. We're picking you up from Miran and we need urgent transfer. We'll explain when we get there—"

Something started beeping in the cabin and a male Mirani voice blasted through the cabin.

". . . Order to return to the airport immediately—"

The Coldi voice replied to Braedon, but Mikandra couldn't hear it well enough to understand.

The Mirani operator went on, ". . . return immediately, or you will be subject of military action."

"Anyone in range?" Taerzo asked.

Braedon turned on the radar screen and Taerzo studied it.

The operator repeated, "I request that you return to the airport immediately. Please file your intentions now, or be subject to military action."

Braedon spoke in Coldi, and then drummed his fingers on the panel. "Hurry up, hurry up."

The screen lit up.

Braedon punched. The white light started flashing.

Taerzo said, pointing at the radar, "There they are! Evade, brother."

"I can't. Barresh are trying to get a fix on us."

The red light flashed.

Three . . . two . . . one . . .

A white flash engulfed the craft.

37

I T WAS THE FASTEST trip anyone had ever taken from Miran to Barresh. No one used the Exchange for this distance, ever. The transfer probably broke a couple of proximity rules as well. For example, it was highly likely that the city of Miran shook in its foundations with the thunderclap of that transfer. Anpar transfers should be done *outside* the atmosphere for a reason.

They came down to Barresh just before sunset, in glorious sunshine reflected on large thunderclouds building over the escarpment.

Humidity hung like a mist over the surface of the marsh, softening the outlines of the two islands in the silver mass of water.

The megon trees had come out in full bloom while Mikandra had been away, coating the dark green stands in a layer of flaming orange.

"It's pretty," Calliandra said.

Braedon pushed his earpiece aside where he had been speaking to the Exchange. "There will be a reception party to deal with our formal asylum request. They're already patched me through to the council. It's pretty incredible. We haven't even set foot on the ground and they're already talking about an office for a Guild chapter headquarters."

"There are a lot of vacant buildings in town," Mikandra said.

When the craft landed, the sunlight cast long shadows over the cracked pavement that seemed so familiar to Mikandra.

"Not a lot of activity here," Braedon said.

Taerzo huffed. "There are no maintenance sheds?"

"They will be built," Mikandra said.

"No Traders?"

"There are three Traders here. That's a lot."

Braedon said, "I don't see—wait. You're talking about us, right?"

Mikandra grinned.

"Hey," Taerzo said. "Who in this dump owns a Gazion?"

"You'll probably meet him shortly," Mikandra said.

"Is this the legendary Daya Ezmi? I once spent an entire trip to Hedron chasing after him."

"He is the one inviting us. This is his town. We belong to the same people."

Mikandra went to wake Rehan, who seemed groggy, complained about a sore shoulder and a headache, but seemed otherwise fine.

Braedon opened the door. The air was warm and gentle, even though the twins said it was hot.

Taerzo and his family left the craft first.

Mikandra helped Rehan down the ramp.

Braedon stood at the door, enabling the craft's security at the panel next to the door. He looked up. "Looks like we have company."

As Mikandra had expected, both Daya and Anmi had come. What surprised her was that they were alone, with the little boy holding Anmi's hand. No black-guards, no council people. They walked slowly, because the boy's legs were short and lifting his feet over the cracks in the pavement seemed to be an effort.

Mikandra said to Rehan, "You know Foundation, when the Endri and Nikala came together and signed the treaty to build the city of Miran together, a treaty that probably everyone in town thought was rubbish and would not survive the test of time? This is like that. People hundreds of years in the future will write this moment in the history books and teach their children that the course of the city of Barresh changed when the Andrahar Traders came to town."

Taerzo gave her a sideways look. "You know you frighten me, sometimes?"

"That's what we're for," Isandra said, behind Mikandra. "Women see the bigger picture, where the men only see the immediate future."

Daya and Anmi stopped a short distance from the craft with the low sun on their faces. A breeze ruffled Daya's curls. Looking at the two of them from a distance, it struck Mikandra how their build was similar to the Endri. Anmi picked up the boy and held him on her arm, from where he stared at the strange party with curious eyes.

For a while, no one said anything. Anmi's gaze went from Taerzo to Braedon to Rehan. "You're all so much like your brother."

"Is that my grandson?" Isandra asked.

Anmi held out her arm and spoke softly to the boy. He turned around and hid his face in his mother's shirt, balling his little fists against her chest.

"Now don't be shy." Isandra touched her grandson's cheek.

He turned his head and looked at her from the corner of his eyes.

"See? I'm not scary." Her face had a tender look which Mikandra hadn't seen from her before. "Does he understand Mirani?"

"He's still a bit young to understand anything much, but I'm happy if you want to teach him."

Daya said, "Let's first stick to the important things. You'll be tired and want to change. I have secured a house for you. It is owned by one of our local merchants and is the best I can do at such short notice. My cook is there preparing a meal for you. The council's Account keeper is ready to see you to give you access to your accounts. If any of you are in need of any medical attention, we can look after that."

∾

The house was in the street that ran from the markets along the edge of the marshland. The front of it faced the quiet, tree-lined street and the back looked west. It was also the most luxurious house Mikandra had seen in Barresh, not that this was saying much. It had a huge hall with a coloured glass dome and a sparkling pond directly underneath. The twins had their shoes off in no time and were splashing in the water, declaring this *the best place ever.*

The paint and floors were a bit tired, the furniture was very basic, but adequate, and there was room for temporary offices. The back of the house had a huge living room, also with bath pool, which was empty, but Taerzo already declared that he'd fix the tiles and fill it up. The back of the house was right on the edge of the city, overlooking the marshlands.

Bedrooms were all upstairs and some of them, including the room Rehan chose, overlooked that marshland as well.

Rehan slid open the sliding door to a balcony that ran the length of the back of the house. He hadn't said much, and still looked unsteady on his feet. Mikandra went to stand next to him. A warm wind smelled of rain and thunder rumbled in the distance. "What are you thinking?"

"I'm ashamed that I never knew all this existed and lived so close to it. Have you seen how many building projects we passed on the way here?"

"Heh, I lived here for a while, remember?"

"You did right in getting us to come here. This place is a dump, but a dump with a lot of opportunities. Look at this house. It probably hasn't been used for years. It needs a lot of maintenance, but just look at this view. And think of it: I would say that if we cut that shrubbery, we could even extend the yard and keep our aircraft here, right in our back yard. Where else can you do that?"

She smiled and he kissed her softly.

"Do you think you'd want to go back to Miran?"

"Not for a while," he said. "Not while that idiot runs the council. Besides, if even most of our Trader colleagues don't support us, what is there for us?"

"Well, we have this." Mikandra dug under the tunic and pulled out the chain with the Foundation stone.

His eyes widened. "I thought it was lost in the fire."

"No, I thought it was too important to let it fall into the hands of the army. We have the stone and we have the oldest son of the oldest son. Think of what we could do with those things, if the time was right." Walk into the council at a crucial voting time, and send them all home.

Rehan's face split into a wide smile and then he started laughing. "You are priceless."

"I'd like to see that law changed to include the oldest daughter in a family, but for the time being, we'll abuse this particular law."

"When we have enough support to make real changes in Miran."

"Yes, we can wait." The change required in Miran would be slow, potentially violent and costly.

They spent the next days getting the business up and running. As Isandra said, the most important part was to start working again.

The application for a Barresh Trading office was rushed through the Trader Assembly.

Mikandra found out how much Taerzo was attached to fashion when they discussed uniforms. They eventually settled on a wide tunic and trousers like the locals wore, and made sea green and turquoise their colours. Rehan went the full hog and had his hair braided and cut in local fashion, with the stepwise lengths and beaded braids. The Guild granted the new Barresh chapter two other licences for the city and they selected a young Barresh merchant by the name of Tedris Havaru to take one of the places in the academy. It was harder to find a Pengali to take the other place, but they finally chose a female cousin of Bakimay's.

They rented an office above the shop in Market Street whose owner had been rude to Mikandra, although he conveniently seemed to have forgotten. Every day, she walked past the large guesthouse, wondering if Jocassa would still be there.

Taerzo set up desks and painted the walls. Braedon installed all their communication systems. There was an aircraft maintenance shed to be built and administration to be done, and aircraft to be maintained, and a new aircraft to be bought, although Taerzo was so busy with the office setup that Rehan used his for the time being.

"We need people," Braedon said two days before Mikandra was to leave to Kedras. "There are hardly any locals who speak Mirani well enough to maintain our administration, and we could use some runners. Not to speak of an engineer."

"I don't know about the engineer, but I think I know of others you could train," Mikandra said.

So the next day, they went to the guesthouse. Rehan was rather dubious, looking at its moss-covered façade. "You said these men are ex-army?"

"Just ignore the accent and let me do the talking. There are three men I owe deeply."

It was the end of the day, and the courtyard was filling up with people.

When Mikandra came in, a silence rippled over the crowd, which included a lot of the regulars, scruffy, poorly dressed, but familiar.

Someone said, "Youz are in th' wrong place, lady."

Several men laughed.

But then there was another voice from somewhere at the back. "Youz kidding? That's our Eydrina."

Rehan frowned at her. "Eydrina?"

"I could hardly tell them my real name, could I?"

"You sure get points for originality."

"Shut up, and let me talk to them."

She walked through the courtyard to the familiar table next to the fountain. Jocassa sat at his usual spot, and Dalit and Thasep were with him.

He looked up at her with open mouth.

"Wow, youz look different," Jocassa said.

Dalit nodded at her; he'd seen her in uniform.

Mikandra said, "When I came here, and fled from my parents, and was robbed, you helped me out. I wanted to pay you back, but you would not accept my money even when I had some. I saw in your eyes that you really wanted to be given a chance to improve your lives." She spoke loud enough that everyone in the courtyard could hear.

"The man who has come with me in his smart-looking uniform is the man who will one day be my husband, Rehan Andrahar. You may already have heard that the Andrahar Traders of Miran have relocated to Barresh. You may not care. We're hiring people, preferably those who can speak Mirani, preferably those who can write. But, if you can't, we will teach you."

The courtyard erupted in talk. Jocassa pointed at Dalit. "Youz be wanting him. He can write," he said. "He's really smart." Even now, he thought of others first.

"Jocassa, you idiot. I want you both."

"Me?" Jocassa's eyes were wide.

"You and Dalit and we can probably find something to do for Thasep. You're going to start dressing and speaking properly, and you'll learn to read Mirani, keihu and Coldi. I said I'd pay you back, and this is how."

Jocassa opened his mouth, but said nothing and closed it again. And then he did the same thing again. For the first time since Mikandra had met him, it seemed he had nothing to say.

"I'll miss you a lot," Rehan said when they sat at the upstairs balcony overlooking the sunset. "You are the most lovely and generous person I've come across. I think you totally made those ex-soldiers' day."

"They saved my life. When all my money and ID were stolen, they all pitched in and gave me some. They wanted no payment when I got a job. Their generosity is something we could learn from. I've seen too many of these people end up in the hospital stuck in hopeless cycles of abuse and drunkenness. They drink themselves to death and cannot see another path because life in

Miran encourages them to wait for handouts. It's spelled out in the Mirani Foundation that it is our task to look after them. That's rubbish. These people can look after themselves well enough, but what Miran seems to have forgotten is that the key to better lives is something useful to do and education. That, and not handouts, is what we can give them."

"Damn, I love you, and I'll miss you."

"I know. You've only said that about a thousand times today."

"Because it's true. I am already dreaming of the day that we can go out into the corners of the settled space together."

"Me, too, especially if you end up buying that Gazion."

He laughed, closed her in his arms and kissed her once more, and he had done that about a thousand times that day, too.

The last rays of sunlight vanished from the room. Rehan sighed. "We better go to that farewell dinner now."

Holding hands, they went downstairs into the happy talk of the family.

Thank you for reading Trader's Honour. If you go to the very end of this book, you can read the start of Soldier's Duty, book 3 of the Return of the Aghyrians series.

Buy Soldier's Duty direct from the author, with delivery via Bookfunnel.

FROM SOLDIER'S DUTY

CHAPTER 1, BOOK 3 OF RETURN OF THE AGHYRIANS

IZRAMITH OPENED her eyes, flicked back the blankets, rolled off her mattress onto her hands and knees. For a few dazed moments, she sat on the floor, staring into the utter darkness where her hands would be if she could see them.

Something was very, very wrong.

Through the roaring of blood in her ears, she couldn't hear the sound of weapons fire or explosions. There was no shouting, no one was swearing and rummaging for clothes and gear in the tent. She wasn't, in fact, in a tent, and there was no supervisor yelling orders. No group of fighters scrambling to get ready and armed for battle.

The soft stuff under her hands and knees was not sand, but the carpet in her bedroom. This was not a military base. She was at home, not in the warzone, and that the noise that had woken her up was not the general base alarm.

That damn child was crying again.

She leaned back, rubbing her face with her hands. The roots of her hair were damp with sweat.

A cold draft tracked over the floor, making her shiver in her night clothes. The hub at the door glared some impossible time in the middle of the night shift.

She jumped to her feet and was at the door in two steps, where she found her home clothes hanging on hooks on the wall. Her fingers brushed the tough fabric of her basic service uniform. She pulled her home pants and shirt from underneath, almost dislodging her gun from its hanger. It scraped against the wall, dangling to and fro.

The piercing cry of a baby grew louder when she opened the door.

"Thimayu!" Mother yelled from elsewhere in the apartment. "Go and feed that child or you pay off the neighbours' goodwill from your own account."

For two days in a row, that nasty Merani had filed a complaint about noise with the corridor caretaker, and twice Izramith had gone into the man's cramped office to deal with it. Pay up or we'll put in a challenge to the Good Neighbours regulation. Some neighbours were just insufferable, even when they knew what had happened, or maybe even *because* they knew what had happened, as Thimayu insisted.

Lights flicked on automatically when Izramith walked into the hall, their intensity low at first, so as not to be hard on her eyes. Before the light grew too bright, she crossed to the small room where the cot stood jammed in between the spare bed and the cupboard. The light above the cot gave an eerie blue glow that seemed impossibly bright.

The baby had kicked off his blankets and wriggled until he lay exposed and upside down in his cot with his feet where his head was supposed to be. In the time that Izramith had been awake, his cries had gone from loud to hysterical with great gulps of breath in between. With each cry, his mouth opened wide and his lips drew back over toothless gums. His little hands trembled. Poor thing.

Izramith prised her fingers between the mattress and the soft and sweaty body and lifted him, being careful to support the head. He was so helpless and fragile, a mere bag of loosely connected bones that felt like they would fall apart if handled too roughly. She held him awkwardly against her body, where he buried his face in her shirt, seeking something that he wasn't going to find. At least he stopped screaming.

The door to her sister's bedroom remained closed. Mother was nowhere to be seen, though obviously awake. Izramith hadn't seen either of them when coming off her shift last night, when the apartment had been quiet enough to look abandoned.

She went into the kitchen, cradling the baby in her arm as she had learned from watching the nurse teach her sister. He was still digging around in her shirt and getting frustrated, making protesting noises. For someone so young and so soft, his little hands were strong enough to pinch the skin.

Using only one hand, she found a bottle in the pantry, grabbed it between her knees and twisted the top to break the seal. A couple of drops of formula splattered on the floor. The baby started screaming again.

She flung the bottle in the heater, waited until it beeped, took it out and sat down with the bundle of screaming, shivering baby. The teat went into the mouth.

Silence.

The boy drank with great gulps, holding the bottle in both his hands. The milk behind the glass went down visibly.

While he drank, Izramith studied his fine-featured face. The skin below his eyes was wet from tears. How long had he been crying? She wiped the wetness away with the tips of her fingers, which felt coarse enough to damage his newborn skin. Poor, poor thing. If only she'd heard him earlier.

She folded her free arm around him and stroked his little head, ruffling the unruly mop of black hair that stood straight up from his head. It was so soft. He was so perfect against her rough, muscle-corded and scarred skin. New unblemished life in contrast with someone who made a living killing people.

He was her little nephew, the first of the next generation.

His birth two nights ago, in her sister's bedroom, had changed everything. Izramith couldn't get that horrible moment out of her mind. Thimayu sat, naked, on the birthing chair. Mother stood behind her, holding her shoulders, backlit by the light on the wall. The nurse crouched on the floor. The final moments of what had been—the nurse said—a pretty normal birth. But the emergence of the child and her sister's cries of relief were followed by a moment of silence. Stunned, horrible silence that said *there is something wrong*.

And into that silence, the nurse said, "He's *zhadya*-born."

Thimayu opened her eyes wide. "No," she shouted. "No, that can't be."

"Unfortunately, he is. Look at him." She held up the baby, thin, the skin pale, with his umbilical cord still attached.

"No. I don't want that. I don't want him. He's not mine."

Mother said, in a calming voice, "Thimayu, it's all right."

She whirled around. "No, it's not all right. I negotiated that this child would be mine, not Endar's. I don't want to look after some freak. I can't. I can't, do you hear me?"

Her sister's hysterical screams still rang in Izramith's ears. She had not wanted to hold the child, not then and not the next day when she calmed down. Since his birth, she had fed him only a couple of times, and then complained that he creeped her out.

But this little boy in Izramith's arms was helpless. He was now getting to the last dregs of his milk while his eyelids drooped and his hand kept falling off the bottle only to jerk back up when his eyes opened wide. He looked at her when he did this, as if he felt embarrassed by being caught asleep. It was so unbelievably cute.

Zhadya-born.

He looked healthy, if unusually thin. He would walk and talk long before any of his peers did, and grow into an extremely smart, precocious boy who outsmarted all the kids of his age. He would read and write at an unusually young age. He would know all his lessons backwards. Then, having grown bored with reading and writing, he would start playing mind games, manipulating teachers and elders with cold calculation.

He would become less coherent and withdrawn. Sometimes angry, usually brooding. Often scary, manipulative or downright malicious. He would lie to see what he could get away with, and he would set people up against each other. He would be nice or mean, often in the same sentence, continuously testing the boundaries of acceptance of the people around him. He would say one thing and do the opposite, and would never hold to his promise.

Everything in the house was fuel for fires, and fires would be his obsession. He would overheat his food until it burned, set his clothes on fire and watch the flames creep up his arms. Whenever they lost him, he would be found staring at the underground lava rivers. He would pluck mycelioids from the rocks and throw them in to see how they burned. Or undress himself and burn his clothes. Or he would climb down the rocks until the soles of his feet blistered with the heat. He might even push people into the lava and do nothing as they screamed and died. He would stick in his hands and peel the burnt skin off his victims.

Then he would be arrested by the guards and spend the rest of his life locked up, together with his twisted and crazy peers.

All that would be the future of this helpless creature in her arms. His eyelids drooped and his hands were slipping again. She took the bottle from him and set it on the bench.

His eyes jerked open and focused on Izramith's. His lips pursed and his face screwed up with a furrowed brow as if the very action was an effort.

People said newborn babies didn't see and didn't think, but she knew that wasn't true. Not for this boy. Two days old, and he knew everything. He watched her. He knew his mother didn't want him. He knew his grandmother wanted him out of the house. His mother and grandmother were afraid of him. He knew he only had his aunt to keep him out of the Respite Illness Centre, where people who were too ill to be in the community lived their lives in misery.

Izramith stared at his little face. As guard, she had seen the ugly side of the *zhadya*-born, she had seen the murders they had committed, the family members they had terrorised, locked in cupboards and fed rubbish. She had seen the scars one boy had cut into his sister's skin *because she annoys me.* She had spoken to bosses whose employees had played games of betrayal. She knew all that, but still couldn't believe that this helpless creature would do any of those things.

"Come, let's put you back in bed." She was on the early shift tomorrow, had been for the last few days, and these nightly escapades didn't help her level of alertness on the job. Nor would they increase her supervisor's satisfaction with her, and to be honest, after the warzone of Indrahui, coming back to a dull guard job had been hard enough.

The door to Thimayu's room opened when she walked back to the nursery.

Izramith didn't stop and didn't look at her sister, who stood in the doorway like a ghostly wraith in her nightclothes. She ignored the urge to start yelling and ignored the flick of her sister's head and the crossed arms over her chest and everything that screamed *Dare to criticise me.*

Izramith went into the nursery and put the sleeping baby in the cot. Her hands trembled and the skin on the back of her neck pricked with her sister's gaze.

The baby stirred only a bit when the warm arm at his back became a cold bed. His little hand flopped relaxed on the mattress with a soft thud.

Izramith pulled the messed-up blanket off the bed, draped it over him and tucked the ends in. She left the room after having planted a kiss on his head. The hair was so soft.

Thimayu still stood in the doorway, glaring.

Their eyes met. Izramith's anger flared. "Don't look at me like that, sister. I just fed *your* baby."

Thimayu said nothing. She looked pale, with hollow eyes and her belly still too big and floppy from carrying the child. Had she even slept since he was born?

Izramith reached her bedroom door. With her hand on the handle, she said, "You are allowed to say, *Thank you, sister.* That would be the least I expect."

No reply.

Another flash of anger welled in her.

Fuck it, fuck her stupid dysfunctional family who couldn't even agree on being civil to each other. Was this why she'd made the effort to come back?

She slid the door aside, went into the room and slid the door shut again with more force than necessary. It crashed into the frame with a thunk. The walls rattled and the door bounced straight back open.

Izramith whirled around. Stupid piece of furniture.

Thimayu was still glaring.

"I didn't ask you to feed him and look after him." Her voice was prim.

"Then what were you going to do? Let him cry, like you did last time? Get complaints from the neighbours? That bitch Merani has probably told everyone in the corridor how you've gone to pieces and aren't fit to be a mother."

"I'm not a mother." Thimayu turned on her heel and slammed the door behind her. Not as hard as Izramith had slammed it. The door stayed shut.

Izramith glared at the door. Her sister would probably stay there for most of the day, and ignore everything to do with the child. Mother might take pity on him, but she wasn't much better.

Izramith was on duty and couldn't look after him.

And the fuck, her sister was going to take some responsibility.

In a few steps, she had crossed the hallway. She grabbed the door handle to her sister's room and pushed. The door moved a fraction but wouldn't open. Thimayu was trying to keep it closed from the inside.

"Open the fucking door so I can look you in the face."

"Mind your own business!" Thimayu's shrill voice came through the door.

Izramith gave the door a huge heave. Something broke and slipped. The door opened. Thimayu screamed and retreated, holding up her hands. The nail on her left index finger had ripped off and blood streamed down her hand, dripping onto the floor.

"Now look what you've done."

"I don't fucking care. I don't know what's wrong with you. Since when are your nails more important than your son? I've had enough of your stupid obsession with clothes and other selfish things. You are going to promise me to take responsibility. You are not going to cause any more complaints from the neighbours, because I'm not going back to that office and pay another fee. And if that means Merani will turn up at the door to beat the shit out of you, that will be your problem." Merani *would* do that, too, being an ex-guard. And Thimayu with all her style and pretty clothes would be no match.

"Mind your own business. You can't tell me what to do."

"Yes, I can, because you're pathetic, hopeless and weak. I have spent a year in war, crawling in sand and mud, in the cold, to keep people safe. People who are poor but grateful. You have everything you'd want and you can't see it for self-pity. You'd let a baby suffer. You'd embarrass Mother. You can hardly look after yourself—"

"Shut up, shut up, shut up!" Thimayu covered her face with her hands, smearing blood on the front of her nightgown. "Go back to the war if you're going to be such a prick about it. Go and be a hero. I didn't ask you to come back to mother over me."

"You need to stop this. There is a child who needs a mother—"

"I don't want him! Leave me alone. Get out of my room." Thimayu crossed the space between them, and shoved Izramith in the chest.

Izramith grabbed her sister's upper arms and pushed her back until she hit the wall with a thud that made the walls rattle. Mother shouted something in the next room, probably about annoying the neighbours.

Panting, Izramith glared into her sister's eyes. They were not as richly gold-flecked as those of most Coldi, and their defiant gaze evoked a deep emotion in her. It wasn't hatred or jealousy, but a feeling that she had tried to suppress most of her life: the urge to fight.

From as young as she could remember, Thimayu had been Mother's favourite, because she was older, and smarter, and always did what Mother wanted her to do. And now it all fell apart and what did she do? Complain and hide in her room and shirk her responsibilities like an entitled brat.

Thimayu tried to push Izramith away, but only succeeded in smearing both of them with blood. Izramith held her sister's arms in a strong grip. She said in Thimayu's face, "You thought you could beat me, big sister? Don't you know that no one beats a Hedron guard in a fight?"

"Has it come to fighting now? Didn't we finish with that

when we were little?" She spat out the words. "I'm not afraid of you."

"What's this childish behaviour?" A voice sounded behind Izramith's back.

Mother. She stood in the doorway to her bedroom, her arms crossed over her chest. Her hair, now mostly grey than black, stood from her head like a fuzzy halo.

"She's bullying me," Thimayu said.

"Izramith, can you be more considerate with your sister? She's supposed to be resting, not being pushed against a wall."

Izramith let go of her sister's arms. She said in a low voice, "Of course you're not afraid of me while Mother is watching, coward."

Thimayu smirked and Izramith made a threatening gesture to her.

She knew what Mother would say. Fighting was not done. It was ugly and primitive. Fighting was how the Coldi people on Asto settled who belonged in which position in their *associations*. But they didn't do associations at Hedron. They were much more civilised than that.

Stuff like that. She had heard it so many times before.

Izramith met her mother's eyes, barely containing the anger. "Whether we fight or not, Thimayu is going to take responsibility for *her* child."

Thimayu said, "I've sorted it. I told you I want him to be looked after at the Respite Illness Centre. That's where he's going."

"What? He's only two days old. He hasn't even *done* anything."

Thimayu snorted. "For now. Don't be stupid. You know what it means to be *zhadya*-born. You know all the trouble he'll get into. You'll know he'll never have a normal life. You know that if he's allowed to bond with us he's likely to try to kill us. I can't look after him. You can't look after him. You're hardly ever here anyway. We can't expect Mother to look after him, either. I don't want any of us to become attached to him and then for him to betray us in some horrible way, or worse."

Izramith protested weakly. "He's a baby." But he would do all those things. Her argument was slipping and she knew it.

She turned around and went to the room's door. The anger still burned inside her, but she had become used to that feeling. Thimayu did everything to *avoid* a fight, and fighting might resolve the issue of who had the right to speak, but it would not help the boy. In fact, she wasn't sure anything could help him.

She wanted to pick him up and run out with him. She wanted to take him somewhere safe. But that wasn't going to solve the problem. A young boy had faulty genes. And he was going to grow up in a terrible place, and, with time, become a terrible, manipulative person. And there was not a thing she could do to stop it.

"When?" she asked, feeling weak.

"He'll be gone by morning."

∾

Soldier's Duty is available on all ebook retailers.

ABOUT THE AUTHOR

Patty Jansen lives in Sydney, Australia, where she spends most of her time writing Science Fiction and Fantasy.

Her career started in earnest when her story *This Peaceful State of War* placed first in the second quarter of the Writers of the Future contest and was published in their 27th anthology. She has also sold fiction to genre magazines such as Analog Science Fiction and Fact, Redstone SF and Aurealis, before making the move to independent publishing.

Patty has written over fifty novels in both Science Fiction and Fantasy, including the *Icefire Trilogy* and the *Ambassador* series.

pattyjansen.com

BOOKS BY PATTY JANSEN

MORE INFORMATION:
PATTYJANSEN.COM

For a complete list of books, scan the image below with your phone.

www.ingramcontent.com/pod-product-compliance
Lightning Source LLC
Chambersburg PA
CBHW032031120726
47901CB00001BA/138